To Stand With Angels

Rian sat with him for the few minutes it took him to drift off, all the while her mind worrying over the man in the guestroom below. She had the irksome feeling that her past was not going to let her be. Her guilty conscience tried to shove all the terrible memories from seven years before back into her mind. But she fought against them. She was certain that while her past actions may come to light once the marshal regained consciousness, it was not for that exact reason he had ventured across their homestead. The reason went far deeper. She didn't understand how she could know such a thing, but she was certain of it. She would stake her life on it.

"All us Keenes get that feeling, Rian." Her brother's words rang so clear in her memory that he stood beside her once again. *"It's that small, nagging premonition that most people get before a bad rainstorm. It pulls at the back of your mind telling you in your gut that your life is about to take a drastic turn. Don't ignore it, Rian. Those feelings are always right, so listen to them. They will save your life one day."*

She stood looking down at Kendall sleeping peacefully.

His tiny, boyish snoring broke her distant stare several minutes later. Rian shook her head as she kissed Kendall again and smoothed his blankets. *I'm tired and I need a hot bath.* She sighed. *But I doubt I'll get much sleep tonight.*

She blew out the lamp and headed back downstairs to finish the chore of cleaning the kitchen. Looking ahead to the task of watching over their injured and unwanted guest, she didn't know whether she should pray he would make it through the night or that he died in his sleep. But it didn't matter. She already knew he would live to see tomorrow. The fluttering pit in her stomach told her that a storm was brewing and, like Jackson, Moriana Keene knew better than to ignore her gut instincts.

An Eternal Press Production

Eternal Press
A division of Damnation Books, LLC
P.O. Box 3931
Santa Rosa, CA 95402-9998

To order additional copies of this book, contact:
www.eternalpress.biz

Edited by Lea Schizas
Copyedited by Lea Schizas
Layout and Book Production by Ally Robertson

eBook ISBN: 978-1-61572-093-4
Print ISBN: 978-1-61572-094-1
First eBook Edition * May 2010
First Print Edition * May 2010

Production by Eternal Press, A division of Damnation Books, LLC
Printed in The United States of America.

Coming soon by Caitlynn J. Gabriel

* * * *

At the Devil's Right Hand

Acknowledgements

I would like to thank my family and friends, without whose encouragement and prodding, this book may never have been completed. Special thanks to A. Shamaya, for his helpful insight and crit. Also, thank you to all my friends at Writing Forums.com, (Esp. SamW, Dreamworx, Strotha, BoredM, BrendanM, Eleuxia, KangtheMad, Tom, Candrah, Sieg007, & Ungood)

Dedication

To my husband, my Love.
To my children, the joy of my life.
To my God, the Light that leads me through Shadow.

To Stand With Angels

Caitlynn J. Gabriel

Prologue

The air was still. Damp. Heavy. Through the thin linen of her nightgown, gravel dug into her back and shoulder blades. Needles of terror pricked her heart. At first, she could not open her eyes. She didn't have to. She already knew where she was lying. This was not the first time she had been here.

Afraid to look, but unable to stop herself, she gazed up into the dimness of a bloodstained twilight and shuddered. Everything was exactly the same as before. She sat up, her fingers numbly scraping over rough bits of rock and dirt. A thick, sluggish breeze dried her sweat-drenched gown to her body and raised gooseflesh on her skin. She could feel him. He was here.

An empty street stretched without end in both directions. On each side, ramshackle buildings towered into the putrid maroon sky. The creak and clap of shutters turned their dark windows into blinking, vacant eyes that stared down at her. Watching to see what she would do this time.

She felt his approach before she saw him. Heard his voice above the painful pounding of her heartbeat.

"Moriana." It was a whisper.

Her eyes darted up the street to the place where he stood. A scream buried its talons in her throat, constricting itself into a wheeze which escaped between her clenched teeth. "No!" she moaned. "You cannot take me yet! I'm not ready! I'm not ready!"

The outline of a man loomed against the shadows,

blacker than the darkness around him. But he wasn't a man. He wasn't human. His deep laughter was soft as he started toward her. "My dear, you are mistaken. I have not come for you tonight." Red eyes glowed from a featureless, black face. White fangs glittered beneath the burning eyes. "It's not over yet. You'll come to me all in good time."

He walked to where she sat in the dust, her heart bulging in her throat, her fingers digging into the ground. She felt his cold, clawed hands close over her shoulders and drag her upward.

"I'm not finished with you, Moriana. Your sin has not come due just yet. I just want to taste your fear tonight. The blood on your hands is sweet in my mouth."

She wanted to scream but could not find the strength. As her eyes rolled back in her head, she saw a black horse at the edge of town. Its rider did not move. He sat watching. Just as he always had. In vague panic, she wondered again who the rider was as the black demon sunk its teeth into her neck…

Rian Keene sat up, her heart clanging in her chest as she fought to pull air into her lungs. The dream. It was always the same dream. The same nightmare. The dusty street, the deserted town, the horrible color of the sky, the demon…and him. The rider. He was always there.

How many nights had she gone to that same hellish town? How many nights had the red-eyed demon visited her? How many times had she felt his sharp fangs on her throat? How many nights had she awoken in her own bed still feeling the strength of his grasp and the heat of his breath on her neck? Rian did not try to stop the tears.

"How much longer will these nightmares go on? I can't take another night of that horrid demon's face!" she whispered to the stillness of her bedroom as tears burned down her cheeks. "I can't! I can't!" She drew her knees up to her chest and pressed her mouth against a knee, muffling the sound of her sob.

Finally, still frightened and exhausted from crying, she threw back her sheets and stood on weak legs. The moonbeams coming through the window pane painted a black grid across her nightgown as she walked to her desk and lit the lantern. She had to write. To exorcise the terror in her heart by banishing it to a prison of paper and ink. To stay awake. Sleep meant finding herself in that deserted town where Evil claimed its habitation. She would not do it again tonight. With shaking hands, she took out her journal, opened it to the next blank page, and frantically scribbled.

The Wyoming Territory
From the Diary of Moriana Keene: June 30, 1878

My Dearest Diary;

Another day has come and gone in this desolate, barren territory. Tonight I longed for sleep, and yet, when I finally lied down to slumber, I awoke in the town again. The nightmare that has plagued me for the past several months is growing ever worse. I fear, at times, that my sanity may very well be compromised if I do not seek some way to remedy the terrible demon that haunts my sleeping thoughts.

He is always with me. His face is as vivid to my eyes as the letters I am now writing on this page. Oh, that devil smiles so evilly! He lies in wait for the moment I lay my head upon my pillow and close my eyes in slumber. My conscience thrives on reminding me of what I once did. They are so very real, these dreams of mine. Alas! If only Jackson were here with me…if only there were some other living soul to talk to, I might find some relief from the terror that stalks my sleep and lurks, shadowed, in my daily thoughts.

Lately, I cannot say which is worse because, aside from the nightmares, a foreign sensation is plaguing me. There is a new fear growing inside my heart. I can feel the change approaching. I cannot shake the certainty that my past is about to revisit me. Perhaps it is only my guilty conscience, but I cannot rid myself of this knowledge or its tenuous hold over me. The thought of it frightens me more than the thought of standing naked and alone in the utter blackness of night whilst a lion stalks me.

I am very afraid, but I must remain strong and chipper for Kendall's sake. Bless his heart! A six-year-old ought not to have experienced such things as he has. He is such a blessed presence in my life and I thank the Good Lord for him everyday. I beg Him to protect us. For, though I could never stand in place of his birth mother, Kendall would have no one should anything happen to me.

When the darkening shadows draw long over the fields, I find my thoughts turning to the memories of my own mother and father. God rest their souls. The tears I shed are for what is lost, and for what is long forgotten. I dearly miss my childhood and the home of my youth. I find that this is the curse of a black past; you must leave those and that which you love the most behind to flee it. The heaviness of my heart brings tears again to my eyes…See? I have spattered the page.

May God have mercy on me for the sin I have committed. I have begged Him to guard my slumber from the demon that stalks it. But, I fear it will not be so…

Chapter One

When Rian saw the lone rider crest the hill and begin his slow descent down the grassy slope toward the ranch house, she knew that her greatest fear was about to be realized. Seven long years spent hoping that no one would find her vanished as Fate revealed its hand. For one fleeting moment, dark panic captured her senses. As she watched the rider's approach, the fear that ensnared her heart gave way to resignation. She had been expecting someone to come.

The uninvited caller was still at least a quarter of a mile away. A late afternoon shadow marked his progress across golden grasses bowed gently in the mid-summer breeze.

Rian stifled the sudden shiver that rattled up her spine. In a country where it was as far to the nearest neighbor as Satan was from the golden gates of Heaven, any woman alone feared the appearance of an unknown man, no matter how benign the stranger might appear. Rian's fear went even deeper. A stranger was worry enough, but she feared the appearance of someone she knew…or someone who knew her.

"Look! Look!" Her nephew, Kendall, pointed a dirty little finger in the direction of the horse and rider now coming at a lazy trot across the field. His luminous green eyes were wide with wonder and his mouth hung open in a slack manner that at any other time would have been comical. An unknowing observer would have thought that the small boy was seeing another human for the first time in his life. "Who do ya think *that* is?" he asked.

"I don't know," she answered. She tried to still the shaking in her hands as she laid her broom against the porch railing. Shielding her eyes from the glare of the low-hanging sun, she squinted to bring the rider into focus. Her brow creased into a frown. There was something wrong with their unwanted guest. *From the way he's sitting his mount, I'd wager he's either injured or ailing.*

His body was angled at a dangerous slump and he limply jostled from side to side in rhythm with the horse's even pace. As the horse drew nearer, probably catching the scent of water and other horses, it picked up speed and began trotting toward the barn. She felt certain she would see the rider tumble from his saddle at any moment.

"He looks funny." Kendall cocked his head at an inquisitive angle. "What's wrong with 'im, Rian?" He clutched a wooden toy horse to his chest. His grubby hand still hung mid-air but the index finger drooped as, with bewildered interest, he watched the stranger bob back and forth atop his mount.

"Kendall, go get the rifle," she ordered. Her voice was a restrained calm that did not betray the growing fear she felt constricting her throat. Better off safe than sorry, she reasoned ruefully.

She wiped her hands on her apron and tried to steady her nerves. Only once in seven years had anyone ever crossed their homestead unannounced. That single visitor had come through with evil intent, but her brother, Jackson, had been alive to protect them. Now that it was just Kendall and herself, Rian worried daily about just such an instance as this. She hoped the rider was sick or wounded, and not drunk, like the man who had come to the homestead last spring. *What if he's feigning injury or illness to garner a sympathetic, unsuspecting victim?* She set her jaw with determination. *Well he won't find one here. We're ready for him.*

"Here's your gun," said Kendall. To her relief, he had returned quickly. He handed the Winchester to her, along with a handful of ammunition. His eyes never left the oncoming stranger.

"Go inside, Kendall. Now," Rian ordered as she loaded a

round into the rifle's chamber. "Do not come out unless I tell you to do so, do you understand me?"

"Yes, ma'am." His obedient reply did not mask the disappointed expression that clouded his face.

By now, the large bay had closed most of the distance between itself and the ranch house, its hooves kicking up thin tufts of dust. She lifted the rifle to her shoulder and stepped cautiously off the front porch toward the visitor. "Halt!" she shouted. Her voice sounded miles away and far too weak. "Halt or I'll shoot!"

The rider ignored her completely and, as his horse drew nearer, she noticed that his head was resting on his chest. It whipped backward at an odd angle and then flopped forward again as the horse came to a stop in the barnyard. The man was no doubt unconscious, but she couldn't understand how he'd managed to stay atop his mount if he was. Her eyes dropped to his hands, resting slack in front of him, and she had her answer. Thick ropes bound his wrists to the saddle horn. Slowly, she lowered the gun.

"Who are you, Mister?" This time her voice was a high-pitched yell. She hoped to jar him awake, but again he failed to acknowledge her. Warily, she took deliberate steps to the man's tall gelding, her rifle still in hand.

The dark horse nickered and stamped an impatient hoof that was encrusted with dried mud and grass. The animal had come quite a distance without much food or water from the look of it.

Placing her hand on the animal's sweat-lathered wither, Rian moved to the side of the horse and looked up at its rider. Her heart thudded sporadically as she assessed him. The stranger's body was covered in horrific wounds. She felt her stomach turn and threaten to send up what was left of her lunch.

A thick, black mop of hair hung over the man's eyes so she couldn't see much of his face. The part of his face that she could see was cut and his exposed eye was bruised. Then she spotted the knife stuck in his left shoulder and her stomach revolted again. His shirt was filthy and torn beyond repair. Through the shredded cloth, she could see blackish purple bruises on his chest and ribs. Sock-clad feet hung beside the stirrups, lifeless extensions of his limp legs. She frowned and wondered briefly why his boots were missing.

His clear need of aid spurred her to action. Whoever he was, whatever he had or hadn't done, the man before her was most definitely *not* pretending to be hurt. Racing back to the porch to put down the rifle, Rian caught a glimpse of her nephew cautiously peeking around the front door. "Go heat some water, Kendall! That man needs our help…now!" she called over her shoulder as she ran back to the horse.

Moving quickly to unbind the ropes from the man's wrists, she managed to get them loose enough to wriggle his hands free. But once he was no longer tied to his horse, he lurched forward and nearly tumbled from the side opposite her. She reached up and grabbed his arm in an effort to steady him. When he suddenly fell toward her, Rian gasped. He slid from the saddle to her shoulder and she stumbled to the ground under his sturdy weight. Stunned for a moment, she sat in the dust trying to pry her legs free from beneath him. She succeeded only after pushing him until he incoherently rolled off them of his own accord.

Standing, Rian wiped the dust from her sweaty face and tried to pull him up. She almost had him on his feet. But then he slumped and went to one knee. His eyes fluttered wildly as if he were trying to wake himself from a dream. She shuddered, wondering how she would manage to get him to the house without help.

He mumbled, unintelligible words, and raised himself into a full-standing position before attempting a blind swaggering step in the direction of the barn. Rian caught his arm and braced her shoulder to his chest just as he was about to go down again.

"Can you hear me, Mister?" she asked. Her breath came in short gasps as she tried to keep him upright. "If you can, try to walk with me to the house, will you?"

The man made no motion to acknowledge her, but his feet moved in stiff, cumbersome steps as she coaxed him in the direction of the porch. An eternity of exhausting minutes elapsed as they made lagging headway across the yard.

When they finally reached the steps, she lowered him to the first stair and slumped down next to him. She tried to catch her breath and decide what to do with him once she got him inside.

Wondering if Kendall had started heating the water yet and trying to remember where she had put the cotton and the linen for binding wounds, she stood and began the task of heaving the giant man up the porch stairs one laborious step at a time. She half-dragged, half-pushed the injured stranger to the front door and, by some gracious miracle, managed to get him to the bed in the guestroom just off the kitchen. She groaned with loud relief as his weight plunged to the feather bed face-first. The blade in his shoulder reflected the light of the sun coming through the bedroom window; a glint of cold steel, hideous and bloodstained.

"Do you have hot water yet, Kendall?" she called into the kitchen. "And bring me the brandy, too," she added, without waiting for the boy's response. After pulling scissors, needle and thread, cotton, and linen cloth from various dresser drawers, she quickly cut the tattered remnants of the man's shirt from his body.

Rian swallowed the thick layer of nausea that coated her throat when her eyes came to rest again on the blade embedded in his shoulder. Resisting the urge to retch and run from the room, she put a wad of cotton on the wound and pressed down hard, pulling the knife out at the same time. The blade wasn't imbedded as deep as it had first appeared, but the cut would still need stitches. The other slashes across his back were not as deep. This knowledge gave her vague relief. At least those wouldn't need a needle and a steady hand.

Kendall brought the brandy, and then he hurried to retrieve a bucket of steaming, hot water. She smiled at him wanly when he returned. "Thanks, honey. You're a big help, you know?"

Kendall squinted up at her and returned her smile with bashful pleasure. But his smile was replaced with a wide-eyed stare when he saw the battered stranger. "Gosh, he's hurt pretty bad, huh?" His eyes surveyed the bloodied back and sides of the man lying face-down on the bed.

Rian turned him away rapidly and ushered him out the bedroom door. "You need to leave this part to me, Kendall."

Kendall frowned. But, the expression changed. "Wait a minute…" he said, snapping his fingers, his eyes bright. "I forgot the mister's horse! I'll go water him and feed him…may I, Rian?"

She nodded, surprised she hadn't thought of it herself. "Go ahead. If I need you, I'll call." She turned back to the dirty, beaten man lying on her mother's handmade patchwork quilt. She frowned, realizing that she hadn't thought to remove her treasured blanket before laying the man on the bed. Blood from his shoulder dripped a crimson splotch over a patch of baby blue cloth. Sighing, she pushed it from her mind. There was nothing she could do about it now that the damage was done. A more pressing task faced her. She needed to see what she could do for the bruised and battered stranger.

Rian washed his back gently, wincing at the gashes. She had seen this type of injury once before. He had been bullwhipped. The wounds would heal, but scars would be left behind as gnarled, life-long reminders of the beating.

She cleaned every single cut, no matter how small, and swabbed them with alcohol. He moaned, startling her. Thankful that he was still unconscious, she soaked the needle with the brandy and then held it over the lighted lamp to disinfect it. As she began stitching the stab wound shut, his whole body tensed. The muscles of his back flexed and bulged as the needle pierced the tender flesh. She felt her own stomach roll and clench as she sewed the slippery, severed skin. When finished, she wrapped linen over the wound and around his chest several times, which was no small feat considering his size and that he was unconscious. Rolling the stranger face-up on the bed, she again momentarily regretted the damage to her beloved quilt. She was almost certain the bloodstains would never wash out.

It was hard, but again she forced the quilt from her mind and proceeded to tend to the wounds on the front of the stranger's body. Washing his face, she noticed that despite a badly swollen right eye and another wicked laceration running down his cheek, he was an attractive man. And, with the blood and dirt rinsed from his face and chest, he didn't look to be in as bad as shape as he had first appeared. His upper body was heavily bruised in several places, but the bruising did not hide the mass of chiseled muscle that knotted its way across his chest and abdomen.

Rian placed a hand on his forehead, smoothing a downy shock of black hair from his brow. She drew her eyebrows together in concern. He had a temperature. Sweat beaded on his chest and stood out on his upper lip and unshaven jaw. A fever was the worst danger of sustaining deep puncture wounds, it almost always signaled infection. She had seen the effects of just such a fever with her own brother, Jackson, before he died. The notion of a complete stranger spending his last hours in her home atop this bed brought another sickening pit to her stomach. This was the same bed she had sat by in diligent vigil while her brother had languished and succumbed to death just over a year before.

She quickly poured some brandy into a cup and shook the bleak images of Jackson's death from her mind. Lifting the man's head, she tilted it back a bit and dribbled a few teaspoons into his parted lips. The stranger coughed and gagged. His eyes fluttered open a few times in a delirious panic. She murmured soothing words, doubting he heard a one, and then tucked him snuggly under the now-ruined quilt. She hurried to the linen cupboard to bring more heavy blankets. The only hope she had to beat his fever was to first help the fever fight off the infection in his injuries. That required more heat.

Wrapping the thick wool blankets around his body, she settled him in as comfortably as possible before she went to get some cool water to give him to drink and fresh cloths to swab his face and use as compresses. Kendall came in from taking care of the stranger's horse as she was pumping the water in the washroom off the kitchen.

"Is the mister gonna be alright?" he asked, his eyes alive with childish interest. "Is he gonna make it?"

"I don't know, honey," she answered as she walked back

into the kitchen and reached for a stack of clean cloths. "If he makes it through the night and tomorrow, I think he may have a chance."

"Look what fell out of his saddle bag." Kendall pulled a shiny silver object from his pocket and handed it to her.

Rian's eyes grew wide when she realized what Kendall had found. The U.S. Marshal's badge glinted as she turned it over in her hand abruptly. "*United States Marshal: Wyoming Territory*" was inscribed on the front. The name, "*Jared Dawson*" was etched on the back.

Stricken, she stood staring at the metal star for a second. The badge felt hot and accusing in her hand. *What if, somehow, the marshal knows who I am? Suppose he knows what I have done?* She dropped the badge to the kitchen table as if it had burned her.

"He's a *marshal*!" Kendall didn't seem to notice her frightened reaction. "A real live marshal! I bet he's killed plenty of cattle rustlers and bank robbers! Gosh, he must've crossed some pretty tough guys to get hurt that bad," he rambled with boyish excitement.

"Kendall Keene," she said, turning to her nephew abruptly. "You'll not speak like that. Marshals uphold the law. They do not go about killing men, even bad men, unless they are forced to. Besides, the marshal's dealings are none of our concern. He is hurt and we are obligated to do everything we can to help him. I'll not hear you say another word about shooting or killing. Is that clear?"

Kendall nodded and his green eyes lost some of their excited sparkle.

"Good. Now take that bucket of cool water to the guestroom, please. We have to make sure he gets plenty to drink."

Kendall humbly moved to obey her, but another thought caused his eyes to brighten once again. "Can I help you take care of 'im? I want to be able to tell him I helped out when he comes to. The marshal might tell me some stories about marshallin' if he thought I helped him get better."

Rian nodded her head and a small smile turned up the corners of her mouth. "If you want to help me, you are welcome to, sweetie. But I don't expect there is very much either of us can do now, besides watch over him and keep his wounds clean. Go on and take the water in, please. I am going to start boiling some broth and then I'll be right in. You keep an eye on the marshal while I get the broth going, all right?"

"Sure, I'll keep an eye on 'im." Kendall nodded. "I'll call ya if he wakes up."

Rian pulled a pot from the shelf and dug the beef stock out of the pantry, the whole while her mind was reeling. He was a marshal! A hundred questions tumbled through her head. *Why has the marshal been beaten and stabbed? Who did this to him? What if the men who did this to him are following him? What if they find him here?*

Then another thought occurred to her. It was far more frightening than the concerns of whom had hurt the marshal and if they were still following him. What if he had been tracking *her* when he had been waylaid and beaten? She struggled to remember if there was anyone that she knew who could have possibly told the marshal where she was. It seemed unlikely because she had seen so few people since coming to the Wyoming Territory, but still… Her eyebrows furrowed in worry as she picked the badge up from the kitchen table and put it into her apron pocket.

She set the broth to simmer and headed for the guestroom. The marshal was tossing and turning when she walked through the door.

"He hasn't woke up yet," Kendall said matter-of-factly. "I thought he did once, but I was wrong. He was only talkin' in his sleep." The little boy shook his head and sighed as the marshal muttered something unintelligible. "Just keeps right on talkin' in his sleep."

Rian placed a hand on the stranger's forehead. Sweat beaded on his brow and ran in streams down his temples and cheeks. He groaned and inaudibly mumbled something about a storm brewing as he tried to sit up. She gently forced him to lie back down.

"The horse is tired," he insisted. His mouth formed a few other disjointed words, but Rian couldn't make out most of them. She lifted his head and forced him to drink a dipper of cool water. His eyes remained closed and he swallowed easily this time. She ran a finger over his dry, cracked lips to close them.

Wringing out a cloth dipped in cold water she swabbed it over his face and then placed it on his forehead. Then she and Kendall stood staring down at the large man lying in their home beset by fevered unconsciousness.

After a long, restless silence, she went out to the kitchen to check on the broth. As she stirred it, she glanced out the kitchen window and was shocked to see the long shadows cast across the yard. It was already sundown and Kendall still hadn't had his dinner.

Feeling guilty that she'd forgotten to feed him, Rian began making a quick meal. Mixing batter, she poured cakes into a skillet and chopped up boiled potatoes. Her mind fretting over what danger the injured marshal's presence would bring to her home and her nephew, she suddenly felt very alone. Why did the wounded man have to make it all the way to the Keene homestead? Surely there must have been at least one ranch between their home and wherever he had come from that he could have wandered onto. A ranch filled with men who had plenty of ability to protect their womenfolk.

Jackson would have known what to do about the marshal. She smiled sadly. Jackson would have done exactly what she had done. He would have helped the marshal.

Rian brushed a sweaty strand of hair from her face and reprimanded herself for being so selfish. *The fear of danger should never interfere when it comes to helping fellow mankind in need. Even if the marshal is here looking for me,* which she prayerfully doubted, *I still cannot let myself leave him to suffer and die.*

And, there was also the chance that whoever had done this to him had not cared what happened to him. Maybe they had even presumed him dead and not bothered to follow him at all. Yes, she thought, trying to bolster her courage, perhaps we are in no real danger.

"What's for dinner?" Kendall asked, while reaching for a

fresh pancake. His tummy grumbled loud enough to be heard across the kitchen.

Rian took the pancake from his hand and pointed in the direction of the washroom. "You are not eating a thing until your filthy hands are clean. And then you set the table, young man. Just because we have an injured guest in the next room doesn't mean we are going to change the way we do things around here."

She couldn't resist the smile that tugged at her lips when he blinked up at her before answering meekly, "Yes, Ma'am."

Rian watched her nephew disappear into the washroom just off the kitchen. She stopped, listening for the sound of water running from the pump. Satisfied that Kendall was scrubbing, she called, "And don't forget the soap, Kendall Keene!"

Rian piled the potatoes into the skillet after the pancakes were done frying. Then she began setting the table since Kendall hadn't finished cleaning up yet. The smell of food wafted through the house, giving her some sense of normalcy in the midst of a strange and disturbing day.

Dinner was quiet. The marshal slept without a sound in the guestroom under the blood-stained quilt that she had never even dared to use, for fear of ruining it.

As the shadows faded into purple twilight, Rian busied herself with cleaning the dinner dishes and bathing Kendall.

"You wash behind those ears, honey," she called into the washroom as she dried the last of the dinner dishes and put them away in the dish cupboard. "I want you to be the shiniest clean boy in the whole territory."

"Aw, Rian," Kendall grumbled. "Baths are for sissies. When I grow up I am never takin' baths."

Rian laughed, unable to stop herself, and walked through the washroom door. "Well, as long as you live in this house, you'll take baths. When you grow up, you can decide to smell like a pig stuck in a dirty swamp and drive every person inside a country mile away. It will be entirely your choice then. But you won't be a dirty, smelly boy here. No sir." She handed him a towel. "Now you get yourself dried and ready for bed," she instructed as she ruffled his wet hair playfully.

A groan came from the next room, causing her to hurry to the marshal's bedside. His eyes were wide open. She shivered at the sheer vacancy in his expression. Dark blue eyes, beautiful but for the bloody, swollen lid of the right eye, stared back at her and then snapped shut again.

Rian placed her palm to the side of his face. It was hot. Horribly hot.

"Don't do it, Jared." The man mumbled. "I swear you'll regret it…" his voice trailed off.

She got a fresh cool cloth to replace the one on his forehead. He thrashed, knocking the compress from his brow. It hit the floor with a soggy slap.

"You crossed Briggs…Not that horse, damn it…Wait. I'll go and get her…" he ranted disjointedly.

Rian held the compress in place, hoping he would calm down.

Suddenly, he reached up and grabbed her wrist, his eyes open and unseeing. A smile touched his mouth in crocked fashion. "Wait, darlin'…." he murmured, pulling her down to him. "Kiss me, I…want…" His eyes closed again.

Her heart pounding, she pulled free. Her face flushed.

A huge hand reached out and gripped her arm. His eyes remained shut but his voice was full of desperation. "Don't go… I need you."

"Rian?" Kendall stood in the doorway, his voice barely more than a whisper.

Rian turned to her nephew. His eyes were the size of two tea saucers. Fear had turned his peachy cheeks a sickly ashen color. "What'd he do that for?" he whispered. His lower lip quivered the slightest bit.

Rian pulled her hand from the man's grasp and smoothed back her hair uncomfortably, "He's sick, Kendall. He's just sick. He doesn't know what he's doing…that's all."

She walked to her nephew's side and reached down to squeeze his hand. He was still wrapped in a towel and his hair was standing in wild, wet spikes all over his head.

"Come on. Let's go get you dressed for bed," she said.

"We'll leave the marshal to sleep for awhile. See," she pointed to where the man lay unconscious and silent again, "he's just sleeping now, honey." She rubbed Kendall's back to reassure him.

Kendall's eyes stared blankly at the form of the inert man. It dawned on Rian how much like his father's death this must seem to him. If she had spent the evening thinking of her brother's death, certainly Kendall would have entertained the same thoughts. Feeling ashamed at her insensitivity, she picked the small boy up and hugged him. "Come on, let's get you to bed. You have been such a big boy today. I bet you're tired," she whispered as she carried him to his bedroom on the second floor.

Kendall snuggled against her neck, his arms draped over her shoulders. "Is he gonna die, Rian?" he asked against her hair.

"I don't know, baby. He may." She could not bring herself to lie to him. "I'm sure he's a very strong man, and that is important if you're sick. He may be strong enough to fight the infection off." To her relief, her answer seemed to placate Kendall.

She dressed him in a fresh nightshirt and tucked him into his bed. "Sleep well, love," she whispered, kissing his soft cheek and brushing the damp hair from his forehead. "I'll see you in the morning, all right?"

Kendall nodded, his eyes weighted with sleep. He turned to his side and rolled the covers around him. "Sure. See ya in the mornin'."

Rian sat with him for the few minutes it took him to drift off, all the while her mind worrying over the man in the guestroom below. She had the irksome feeling that her past was not going to let her be. Her guilty conscience tried to shove all the terrible memories from seven years before back into her mind. But she fought against them. She was certain that while her past actions may come to light once the marshal regained consciousness, it was not for that exact reason he had ventured across their homestead. The reason went far deeper. She didn't understand how she could know such a thing, but she was certain of it. She would stake her life on it.

"All us Keenes get that feeling, Rian." Her brother's words rang so clear in her memory that he stood beside her once again. *"It's that small, nagging premonition that most people get before a bad rainstorm. It pulls at the back of your mind telling you in your gut that your life is about to take a drastic turn. Don't ignore it, Rian. Those feelings are always right, so listen to them. They will save your life one day."*

She stood looking down at Kendall sleeping peacefully.

His tiny, boyish snoring broke her distant stare several minutes later. Rian shook her head as she kissed Kendall again and smoothed his blankets. *I'm tired and I need a hot bath.* She sighed. *But I doubt I'll get much sleep tonight.*

She blew out the lamp and headed back downstairs to finish the chore of cleaning the kitchen. Looking ahead to the task of watching over their injured and unwanted guest, she didn't know whether she should pray he would make it through the night or that he died in his sleep. But it didn't matter. She already knew he would live to see tomorrow. The fluttering pit in her stomach told her that a storm was brewing and, like Jackson, Moriana Keene knew better than to ignore her gut instincts.

Chapter Two

Soft light and deep shadows swam together creating a blur of puzzling fascination. As consciousness came in ever stronger waves, his enchantment was replaced with the awareness of excruciating pain that ran the entire length of his body. His head hurt worse than it had ever hurt in his life. He ran a hand across his face and winced as he touched his swollen right eye. There was a cut on his cheek that hurt almost as badly as the ache in his eye. Something cool and soft covered his forehead. It felt soggy and heavy against his brow.

His vision remained untrained and watery for a few moments. Blinking and rubbing his good eye, he tried to bring his surroundings into focus. Slowly he moved his head, wordlessly cursing the pain that burned over every inch of his body. Looking around the side of the room his vision would allow him to see, he didn't recognize anything. His mind felt cloaked in a velvety fog. His tongue clung to the roof of his mouth, thick and dry. *How did I get here?*

An oak dresser stood across from the bed, the low-burning lamp setting on top of it cast a warm glow over the walls and curtains. He blinked again. The dimly lit room made it hard to make out shapes but he was certain he saw a woman sitting there at the foot of the bed. She was sleeping, her head resting on the high back of a chair. The lamplight created a halo of white light around her.

Her face… he thought despite the mind-numbing pain. He had never seen anyone so beautiful. Her eyes were closed as if in prayer. Her lips were parted as each breath came soft and even. She was peacefully still, her hands folded in her lap. Thick, dark brown hair fell over her shoulders and down the front of her glowing white gown. *I know her…I've seen her somewhere before. But where?*

He suddenly felt the ludicrous urge to touch her to see if she was real and not a distorted figment of his fevered mind. Trying to sit up, he felt agony paralyze him. It ripped the breath from his body and forced him to lie down with a ragged moan. The room clouded out of focus again and a dark, whirling haze filled his mind. *I'll wake her and ask for her name,* he promised himself. *I just need to rest for a moment. Just for a moment…*

****

For three grueling days and nights the man in their guestroom lay in the throes of fever and delirium. Rian worked with tireless fervor, cooling his face, changing his bandages, and holding his head to force water, brandy, and broth down his throat. The sweltering fever radiated from his body, washing her with its heat whenever she was close enough to feel his ragged breath on her face.

At times he slept quietly, his breathing even and deep. At others he yelled and moaned indiscernible ramblings and threats. He never reached out to grab her again, although he did speak to a woman in a few of his many delirious outbursts. He never uttered her name but, whoever she was, the man lying there sick and febrile, shared a very personal connection with her. The words he used, the sensuality with which he spoke, and the tenderness that came over his beaten face, even in delirium, told her that he was *very* well acquainted with this woman. And, even though Rian could endure his vulgar cursing and shouting, his explicit language and gentle tone when he spoke to the woman caused her to blush and flee the room

She gave him brandy and a little laudanum to calm him through his louder moments of irrational yelling and tossing. That remedy seemed to work best during the day when the warm wash of sunlight spread its summer blanket through the window and across the bloodstained quilt. At night, when the world was dark, silent, and even a little foreboding, and he tended to suffer from stronger nightmares and hysterical raging, the laudanum and brandy did very little to sedate him.

Rian sat with him day and night. She only left his side to cook or bring fresh water, cloths, bandages, and brandy. She had to leave him to chop the wood or tend to Kendall's needs, but, to her pride and gratitude, Kendall did most of the easier chores.

Finally, at some point during the wee hours of morning on the fourth day, his fever broke. She had drifted off into a doze and was jarred awake by his coughing. Lifting his head to give him a bit of cool water, she noticed that his forehead felt cool. She studied his face. He wore an expression of true sleep and not fitful unconsciousness. She sighed, relief flooding her. At least he would not die here while she and Kendall looked on helplessly, forced to reminisce the death of their beloved Jackson.

He was sleeping now, deep and peaceful, but Rian knew that when he awoke he would probably still feel a great deal of pain. She remembered the home remedy her mother had always administered in just such instances as these. White willow bark powder mixed with whiskey or brandy every two or three hours would help to dull the pain in his injuries and ease the throbbing in his head.

"How is he today?' Kendall asked as he came in with a basket of eggs. He had asked the same question with grave concern every morning since the marshal had arrived.

"It's good news this morning, love. The marshal's fever has broken. I think he's going to pull through," she answered.

The relief that came over Kendall's face mirrored the relief in her heart, though he knew nothing of the fear she had there too. "I can't wait 'til he wakes up," he said. "I bet he's the nicest marshal in the whole territory!"

Rian smiled in spite of her unease. "I bet he's the *only* marshal in the whole territory," she replied. "Why don't you go out and milk the cow while I get him some medicine and breakfast? Maybe if he feels up to it, you can visit with him later. I'm sure he'd be happy to know you've tended to his horse these past few days."

"All right," Kendall agreed in a very grown-up voice. "I'll get right to the milkin'. You just let me know if you need help. I'll be right out in the barn."

"All right," she answered. "You go on and feed the chickens. Then bring in the milk. Your breakfast will be ready when you come in from working, sir."

Kendall grinned at her before pulling his hat off the peg by the door and smacking it on his head with a very mature air.

Rian watched him go with a smile of affection. He's such a good boy, she thought as she opened the medicine cabinet and took out the flask of willow powder. She poured a shot of brandy into a tin cup and mixed a teaspoon of the powder into it. The medicine would probably have harsh effects on his stomach, especially since he had not eaten anything solid in over three days. Before she could give him the concoction she would have to wake him and try to feed him something.

Stirring the beef broth she had set aside to simmer that morning, she added some cooked cornmeal to it until it created a thick cereal mash. It wouldn't be the tastiest meal, but it would help him regain his strength. Besides, after at least three days of not eating, his stomach might not take to solid food very well and she didn't relish the idea of cleaning up vomit this morning.

Looking out the kitchen window as she waited for the cereal to heat a bit more, Rian smiled as she watched Kendall feeding the chickens in the barnyard. Her affection for him warmed her heart. She decided to make him fried chicken, his favorite meal, to reward him for being so brave and helpful.

She shuddered to think what she would do if something were to ever happen to him. He had been her dearest friend and closest companion since Jackson's death. The two of them had kept the ranch going all on their own. She loved him as much as she would love a child of her own. Maybe even more.

As she put the cereal and coffee onto a tray, Rian worried about what would happen to Kendall if the marshal were here for her. The thought of him being put into an orphanage or left to fend for himself brought a nauseating wave of terror. She fought it and told herself that everything was going to be fine, but as she carried the breakfast tray to the guestroom, she wondered if it really would.

Just take a breath and smile. He's not going to recognize you. Nobody knows you're here, she reminded herself as she entered the guest room and stopped dead in her tracks. She gasped.

The marshal had awakened and attempting to get out of bed. An agonized groan reached her ears. Sweat beaded and rolled off his chest as he tried to support himself, a hand on the bedpost. Unsteady, he began to sway.

"Don't do that!" she commanded. Scurrying to set the tray on the bedside table, she abruptly placed her hands on his shoulders and tried to push him into bed as gently as possible.

Startled at her sudden appearance and worn from the exertion of trying to drag his body from the bed, he didn't fight her. "Who're you?" he asked when he was lying down once again.

His voice weak and his face drained of all color. She assessed him. His eye was less swollen this morning.

"You have had a very bad accident, sir," she replied, not directly answering his question. "I wasn't sure you were going to make it until just this morning when your fever broke. I've brought you breakfast and medicine. You should eat something, and then you need to rest."

He stared at her, taking her in from head to toe. There was a hint of recognition in his expression that she did not like. It made her uneasy. She studied him as he warily glanced around the room. "Never knew a black eye to keep me from getting out of bed. Where are my clothes?"

Rian did not like the gruff, demanding timbre of his voice. "You've not just a black eye, sir," she returned. Suddenly, her patience became fragile, her nerves inexplicably taut. "You've been bullwhipped and stabbed in the back. Don't you remember?" She watched as confusion contorted his gaunt face.

"Whipped? Stabbed?" he echoed. "What're you talking about? Where am I?"

"I had hoped *you* would know what's happened to you," she answered, "You are at our homestead over thirty miles north-east of Laramie, Marshal. How you managed to make it this far into the wilderness without dying is beyond my comprehension." The man regarded her as though the words she spoke were in a foreign tongue and completely useless to him.

"Marshal?" he asked. "Thirty miles?"

"Here." She produced his badge from her apron pocket. "This is yours. You *are* Marshal Jared Dawson, correct?" she pressed when the look of uncertainty and disbelief washed over his face.

"No…" he answered slowly, taking the badge from her out-stretched hand. "I'm not Jared Dawson. Name's Bradyn Preston." He ran a hand over his face. "I can't remember much…I remember having a drink at the Silver Lady…" his face tensed. She wondered if a memory surfaced that he did not particularly want to share. "That's it. There's nothing after that…" He narrowed his eyes as if trying to recollect anything of what had happened to him. "Nothing…" he murmured. The last was more to himself than to her.

"You aren't a marshal?" Fear clutched its slimy fingers around her throat. But then relief came. He wasn't the marshal after all. At least, at the *very* least, he wasn't here looking for her. Then relief gave way to another concern. *If he's not a marshal, then who is he?* A new fear lodged in her heart.

"Nope."

His dismissive tone set her teeth on edge. "Then how did you get that badge?" she demanded, surprised to feel anger spark to life. It had not been squelched by her sudden apprehension after all.

"I told you I don't remember anything." He struggled to sit up again.

"Your injuries are going to need time to heal, Mr. Preston," she insisted. "You risk doing further damage if you don't allow your body to mend properly." Her heart raced as the moment of bravado slipped away and the terrifying realization that he was not a marshal settled in her mind with tremendous weight. *How did he come by that badge? Suppose he's done something illegal? What if he's* killed *the marshal?* She shuddered to think of the implications.

"Time to heal? I don't have time. I have to leave. Now. There's…" He paused. Rian stared down at him, a mixture of anger and fear building inside her. "I need to get up," he insisted.

The gruffness of his tone was like sandpaper to her rigid nerves. "You can't!" she protested in a voice high-pitched and unrecognized by her own ears. Her concern was born more out of fear *of* him than *for* him. "I'm sure whoever did this to you is nowhere near here. Please," she begged, "lie down. You are really in no shape to be up and about."

Ignoring her, he sat up. His face contorted with pain, he winced and swung his legs to the side of the bed. Irritated, Rian watched as he braced himself against the bedpost again. As he hauled himself to his feet, she immediately reached out to steady him. The instant he straightened his back and stood upright, he began to weave and had to lean on her shoulder for support.

"Please lie down!" she begged. Panting under his crushing weight, she came perilously close to collapsing. "If you pass out, I will never get you back into bed," she gasped.

Bradyn Preston smiled, to her consternation, and groaned. "I appreciate the offer, Miss, but I 'm not up to it just yet…maybe when I feel better."

Rian flushed with embarrassment and anger. "Don't be absurd. I was offering no such thing," she snapped.

He closed his eyes and she thought that he was about to faint. He looked dizzy and pale. His head drooped for a moment before he opened his eyes again. Suddenly, his weight was too much for her. "Please, Mr. Preston. Please lie back down," she gasped as her knees began to buckle.

"Now!" she commanded.

The man had no choice but to obey her. His body slumped to the bed with a ponderous thud. Falling to his back, he groaned again. Rian sighed with frustration when he passed out.

Whatever was she to do now? Her back ached with exhaustion. Her fear of him and her present situation were instantly combined with irritation and indignation. The man was an ungrateful, vulgar beast! If she only had the strength to pack him out to his horse and re-tie him to the saddle and send him on his way, she would have. Whoever this Mr. Preston was, for whatever reason he had stumbled in on her life, she decided then and there she did not like him. Not one bit.

"What happened?" Kendall shouted as he ran through the kitchen and into the bedroom. He came to a stop beside her and, his toy horse in hand, stood staring down at his new-found hero. "Did he wake up? I thought I heard ya talkin' to him."

"He was awake, but he tried to get up and it was too much for him," Rian answered in exasperation. "I told him to stay put," she grated under her breath.

"The marshal *is* gonna be okay!" Kendall shouted. He made a loud whoop and swung his fist in an arch over his head in victorious fashion. "He's gonna make it! I'm so darned happy!"

Rian bit her lip, deciding not to tell him that the man was not a marshal. Instead, she offered her best smile. "Looks that way, honey," she agreed. "If he'll stay off his feet and in bed, (*and doesn't open his stupid mouth again so I have to shoot him,*) he may have a shot at pulling through."

She looked at her nephew, disturbed by the admiration in his eyes as he watched the man sleep. "Kendall, run outside and feed the horses. I have to get some food and medicine into our guest." She bit her tongue before she could add; "Not that he deserves it."

"Okay!" Kendall rushed from the room skipping with joy.

Rian momentarily envied his light-hearted innocence.

She felt exhausted as she gingerly lifted Bradyn's legs back into bed and pulled the sheets over him once again.

She dipped a fresh cotton cloth in the pail of cold water and began daubing the sweat from his face and chest. No doubt the wounds on his back were stinging something fierce from all the sweat running into them. She couldn't help but smile a little. *Serves him right.*

* * * *

Bradyn started to come around. The little boy's shouts had roused him momentarily but the cold water woke him right up. Opening his eyes, he watched her. She was so busy wiping his chest that she failed to see he was awake.

She had amber eyes. Wide-set and lined with thick black lashes, they glowed as streaks of sunlight came through the window and refracted from their fiery depths. They reminded him of the deep color of canyon walls reflecting a sunset.

How do you like that? I managed to stumble across a pretty woman even though I was knocked out. Bradyn winced as she wiped a laceration on his abdomen.

Her lips were pursed in concentration. Creamy, golden skin covered flawless cheekbones and a slender neck. Her hair was twisted into a thick, dark brown knot at the back of her head, save for a few frazzled strands that hung in wavy curls around her forehead and neck. He smiled, imagining that they had come free during her frantic efforts to get him back into bed.

"What's your name?" he asked. His words came out low and raspy. *My throat feels as dry as the desert in July. Damn, I'm dying of thirst.*

She jerked and her eyes grew wide. Then her startled expression disappeared behind a mask of indifference. "Rian Keene," she replied, giving him a cool appraisal. "I didn't know you were awake," she mumbled as she went back washing his chest.

"Rian," he murmured thoughtfully as he watched her. She shifted uncomfortably under his gaze and kept her head low as she focused on cleaning his chest wounds. He supposed that his earlier comment had frightened her. He wished he'd kept his mouth shut. It wasn't very smart to offend the person who'd saved his life. From the look of her, she undoubtedly had a man about who would be more than happy to shoot him for insulting her.

He watched her pour some alcohol onto a wad of cotton. She dabbed at the cut on his cheek, her face void of emotion. Bradyn gritted his teeth together as the alcohol stung the wound.

The hair on his face itched. "Feels like I could use a shave," he said, trying to get her to make eye contact.

"You were delirious," she said. "The way you kicked and shouted, I wasn't about to try and shave you. The Lord knows you don't need another cut to add to your current repertoire."

"Delirious?" Bradyn looked around the room. He brought his eyes back to rest on her face. "Tell me, how long have I been here?"

Placing the cotton and the alcohol on the table, she wiped her hands on her apron. "Nearly four days."

"Four days…I've been unconscious that long?"

"Yes. Well, longer I'm sure. You were unconscious when your horse brought you in." She commenced to assist him into a reclining position and fluff his pillows.

His quiet groan was the only hint he gave to the pain that movement evoked. But on the inside, he was screaming. Bradyn couldn't remember the last time he'd been in this much hurt. He took a deep breath and settled back against the soft pillows.

"So you've been looking after me then," he said as he ran a finger slowly along the cut on his cheek. "I'm obliged to you."

Rian stirred the cereal that had cooled down since she had first brought it into the room. "Think nothing of it," she said. Her tone was indifferent. She scooped some cereal into the spoon and gestured to him, "I think you should eat this. Then I'll give you some medicine that will take the edge off your pain."

"I'm thirsty," Bradyn remarked as he took the bowl from her. "Might I trouble you for some water?"

Rian nodded and filled the dipper from the bucket. He guzzled the water greedily. It tasted wonderful. Cold dribbles of it ran down his chin and his chest. He drank three dippers full before he started eating his breakfast.

"You here alone?" he asked amid unhurried bites.

Rian frowned at him. Her unease at his question was obvious. "Of course not. My nephew lives here with me."

"Your nephew? How old is he?" Bradyn stopped eating and cast a side-long glance in her direction. "He's not that scrawny little kid that was in here before, is he?" He took a slow sip of the coffee.

"You certainly are very nosy," she deflected. "I don't see how that is any of your business, Mr. Preston."

He stifled a grin as she took a seat on the bedside chair and folded her hands in her lap as primly as any school marm. "You're absolutely right," he said as he lifted another spoonful of cornmeal to his mouth. "I would just assume that a woman of your fine appearance would have the good sense not to live in the middle of the wilderness alone. And, if you don't mind my saying so, having a kid ain't much better than being alone. In fact, it's probably quite a lot worse."

"My safety is clearly the least of your worries in my opinion, sir," she retorted. Bradyn admired the fire that leapt into her eyes. "I would be concerned with the preservation of my own neck if I were you. You seem to have some pretty vicious enemies, Mr. Preston. Perhaps justly so. Besides, any man who is foolish enough to endanger his own well-being by involving himself in brawling and Lord-knows-what-else, has no business questioning the choices of another," she finished sternly.

"What makes you think I am concerned with your safety?" he asked. He flexed the muscles in his jaw as he assessed her. "What if I just want to know how easy it would be to take advantage of you?"

He expected his words to frighten the living day right out of her, so when she laughed out loud, it startled him. "No offense, Mr. Preston, but I don't think you are in any condition to take advantage of anyone."

"And when I am well enough to try?" He knew he should've put a clamp on his tongue, but, the urge to ruffle her feathers was appealing and irresistible. She was so darn beautiful.

"I met you with a rifle the day you first came here." She sat up tall in her chair, her eyes flashing with amber challenge. "If you hadn't been hurt, I would have shot you square on the spot."

Bradyn raised his eyebrow. "Is that so?" he asked, resisting a smile.

"Damn right," she replied. "And if you don't be quiet and finish your breakfast, I'm liable to shoot you still."

He couldn't stop the chuckle that rumbled deep within his chest. "You've got a sharp tongue behind your pretty mouth, that's for sure. Tell me, how did such a lovely woman come to live in this God-forsaken country thirty miles from the nearest town anyway?"

Garnering a chuckle and a compliment from him seemed to give her a small sense of ease. However, her voice was full of sarcasm as she asked, "Would you prefer to hear the long or the short version of the particular story, Mr. Preston?"

"The long. I've got time it seems," he replied with enthusiasm.

Rian narrowed her eyes when he offered a dazzling smile. He wondered if his superfluous facial hair and injuries made him look repulsive to her.

"The short it is," she answered. There was a faint glimmer of mirth in her eyes. "My brother moved out here with his wife nearly seven years ago and I came along for the ride. Does that answer your question?"

Bradyn blew out a sigh of forced resignation. "Guess it does. Or at least, it has to for now."

Rian stood up. She looked anxious to leave the room. "Good, now that the only conversation we'll need to make is out of the way, and since you've finished your breakfast, you should drink this medicine. It will help with the pain and swelling." She handed him the tin cup and watched him swallow it in one gulp.

"That's awful!" He coughed while choking down the nasty mixture. "What is it?"

"Willow bark powder and brandy. It's a pain reliever," she explained, gathering the bowl, spoon, and cup and placing them back on the tray.

"Let me get this straight. You nearly choked me to death on some silly powder to help me feel *better*?" he asked.

He noticed the smile that tugged at her mouth when he gave her a dubious expression. "Medicine is not intended to taste good, Mr. Preston. That's why they call it medicine and not candy." There was a touch of pride in her eyes and a condescending, motherly tone in her voice.

"Well, thanks just the same, honey, but I'd rather not have that marvelous little treat again. Just give me a straight shot of whiskey next time," he snorted.

She rolled her eyes in a manner suggesting that she supposed his kind would always prefer straight whiskey, and made no comment. As he watched her pick up the tray and leave the room, Bradyn decided she was going to take some careful handling. She wasn't the type of woman who cottoned to his methods of teasing, that much was clear. Rian Keene was a skittish one, not the usual sort of woman he would be interested in, and yet Bradyn found himself looking forward to the next time she set foot in the room. I'll watch my big mouth next time, he vowed.

Chapter Three

A lone rider sat his horse atop a rocky crevice half a mile from a quaint ranch, watching. He'd seen only a woman and a boy so far. Not a man in sight. It was foolhardy to assume that the woman and kid lived there alone, but he could only hope. That would make his job easy. Very easy indeed. Through his spyglass he studied the homestead intently.

Smoke spiraled lazily from the chimney of a two story house that glowed brilliant white against the setting sun. The boy walked out of the barn with a bucket of milk. He tripped suddenly and splattered its contents along the path on his way to the house. The kid is only five or six years old, the rider guessed. *No problem there.*

The dark haired woman rushed out to meet him. The rider chuckled wickedly as she appeared to scold the boy for spilling the milk everywhere. She looked to be a handsome woman, finely crafted and assembled, though from this distance her facial features weren't very clear. The rider licked his lips. She would be no problem either. In fact, she promised to be great fun. He rubbed his groin in anticipation.

As for Preston, the double-crossin', gunslingin' bastard was nowhere to be seen. Probably inside licking his wounds and eating out of the pretty lady's hand. Liam Briggs had been shocked out of a year's growth when he'd learned that Preston had survived the beating and stabbing he'd ordered. So he'd tied the son of a bitch to a horse and set it loose on the prairie. He had sent two of his hired guns, Cheyenne Joe and Wes Stebbens, to follow Preston and finish him. That was if he didn't die from his injuries first. But when Preston's mount had happened on the ranch, Joe had sent Wes back to tell Briggs where Preston was. After Wes left, Joe had settled in to watch and see what happened. If Preston survived, Joe would kill him. Preston wasn't going anywhere except straight to Hell.

Now as he sat waiting, he could almost *taste* the scent of blood waiting to be shed. The instinctive, driving need to torture and kill filled his soul with dark excitement. He wouldn't wait much longer. Not a minute past tomorrow. Preston had been here nearly four days. Joe had waited long enough to be fairly certain the bastard had pulled through, and now he was gonna kill him. He wanted Preston to know who and what had hit him when he emptied a bullet into his sorry head. *Then I'm going to take care of the boy and the woman. It's been a long time since ol' Joe has heard a woman scream. Too long.* He licked his lips slowly. Savory expectancy worked his blood into a heated lather. She was gonna scream loud and long. He would see to that.

* * * *

Bradyn had slept most of the day. Without the fever and delirium to impede his rest, he'd awoken feeling quite a bit better than he had when he'd first come to that morning. His back still burned with a fury, but he'd been able to sit up without much difficulty when Rian had come in to change his bandages and feed him dinner.

She spent as little time near Bradyn as possible, a tactic which he found both humorous and irritating at once. She was wary of him. He had a feeling that while he'd been delirious she had spent every waking hour at his side. Maybe he had dreamt it, but he could have sworn he'd woke up once and seen her sitting at the foot of the bed. Now she would only pop her head in the door if he called her, or flit in to give him something to eat or drink, and then disappear quickly thereafter. She seemed intent on having as little conversation as possible, but he vowed he would chip through her icy exterior. He just needed a little time…

* * * *

The fourth evening came on with little incident. With Kendall bathed and tucked in for the night, Rian sat on the front porch steps distractedly watching the fireflies flickering through the waving bows of the willow tree, her mind mulling over the current situation in which she found herself. Mr. Preston still needed at least a few days of bed rest before he would be strong enough to hazard riding out.

Rian disliked the man. She felt a trenchant discomfort when she was near him. The way his eyes watched her every move when she was in his presence bothered her. He barely spoke a word to her. He just sat there, staring. And she wasn't a glorious judge of the human character, but she had the distinct hunch that he knew more about the origin of his injuries than he let on. She caught the brooding looks on his face when he was deep in thought. Those dark expressions bothered her more than his gruff manner and meddlesome questions put together.

Kendall was a problem too. He wanted to talk to the "marshal" and Rian still hadn't decided how to tell him the man in the other room was no lawman. Now unsure of who Bradyn Preston was or what he'd gotten himself mixed up in, she was afraid to let Kendall anywhere near him. She had shooed him away, saying that their guest needed rest, but she knew that would only work for so long. Sooner or later, she would have to tell him. Kendall had built a fantastic image of the "marshal" in his mind and she knew that when the little boy found out that the man in the guestroom was about as much a marshal as pig's hide was silk, he would be disappointed. However, as difficult as it would be for her to break the news to him, Rian knew it should be sooner than later. She wanted Bradyn Preston out of her home.

Rising to go inside, she looked up at the sky. The moon, just over half full, cast its pallid light over the earth below. Inexplicably, her spine tingled as she stood gazing up at it. A familiar tremor took her stomach. She was experiencing that feeling again, the one she had been getting more and more frequently over the past four days. Something dark and ominous was on the horizon. She knew it was approaching. Just as she had somehow known that someone was going to come to the homestead right before Bradyn Preston had showed up.

Then a strange sixth sense, the notion that someone or something was watching her, crept over her. The night air seemed to suddenly grow cooler. She rubbed her arms and looked in the direction of the barn. Nothing. The chicken coop, the corrals, and the outhouse, but still she couldn't see anything suspicious. Rian shook herself. She was tired. She hadn't slept in her own bed in almost four days. Her nerves were frayed and her mind exhausted. That explained the feeling better than anything. There was no one there. It was just her imagination.

Climbing the porch steps as slowly as an old, decrepit woman, she yawned. It had been a long week and her bed was waiting upstairs. She just needed to check in on Bradyn Preston before she headed up to a comfortable, feather-down cushioned sleep.

He was sitting at the kitchen table when she walked through the door. In his hand he held her Winchester rifle. Rian stopped short, fear lodging in her throat.

"What are you doing?" she asked.

Bradyn smiled. "Scare ya?" He was naked from the waist up, wearing only his filthy torn jeans.

Rian stood motionless. Her eyes felt as though at any moment they would burst from their sockets and go rolling across the floor. Fear, as dry as sawdust, filled her mouth. "What are you doing?" she repeated. Her voice was a seething, nearly inaudible whisper.

"I'm taking precautions," he answered as he began popping ammunition into the rifle's chamber. "I hope you don't mind. I found your cartridges in the pantry."

"Precautions?" she echoed, ignoring for the moment that he'd had the audacity to rummage through her cupboards. "What kind of precautions?"

"Someone may be following me." Bradyn's eyes never left her face as he loaded another round. "You may be a wonderful shot, but I don't know that, and I'll be damned if I leave our safety in the hands of a woman."

"Our safety? *Our* safety?!" Certain her yelling would wake Kendall, but too angry to care, she crossed the room and, coming to a stop in front of Bradyn, she shook her finger in his face. "Our safety has nothing to do with it! You are looking out for your own filthy carcass. Don't try to play the chivalrous knight with me."

Bradyn's only reaction was a cold smile. "It may come as a shock to you, Miss Keene, but I am not entirely the dirty rotten bastard you seem to think I am," he said dryly.

Rian snorted, stomped to a cupboard and, pulling a revolver from its top shelf, spun around to face him. Bradyn, who had finished loading the gun, sat watching her with curiosity, the rifle resting across his thighs. *This again. If he thinks he can unnerve me with his stupid staring routine, he is dead wrong! I am going to get some answers out of him. And I am going to get them right now!*

Bradyn watched her as she leveled the revolver at him in defiance.

"Suppose I just shoot you this instant and finish it?" she spat. "Save whoever is after you the trouble. What do you think about that?"

Bradyn leaned back in the chair and folded his arms across his chest. Complete nonchalance masked his features. "Go ahead," he answered.

Rian blinked. She had not been expecting that particular response. "On second thought, why don't you tell me why anyone would have a reason to be following you?" she said. "*Then* I'll decide whether or not I should shoot you."

He looked her up and down for a moment. She saw the smile that tugged at the corner of his mouth when she put her hand on her hip.

"Do you want the long story or the short one?" he asked.

A sneer crossed his face, causing her irritation to multiply. His voice was an all too perfect imitation of her tone earlier.

"You just tell me the truth," she snapped. "And I prefer the short version. The one with the least amount of bullshit."

Bradyn cocked an eyebrow and she caught the grudging admiration that passed over his face. "I got mixed up with some less-than-law-abiding citizens in Laramie. Does that answer your question?" he asked. Rian expected to see a smirk hidden in his expression, but his eyes were cold and serious. There was no humor to be found in them.

She bit her lip and chose to ignore his second sarcastic imitation of their earlier conversation. "No," she answered. Slamming her fist down on the table, she kept the gun pointed at him. "I want to know how you got that marshal's badge. I want to know why you were beaten, stabbed, tied to your horse, and turned loose in the wilderness to die. I want to know what you mean, exactly, when you say you got mixed up with 'less-than-law-abiding citizens.'" She took a breath and as an after thought added, "And I want to know why you aren't in bed. You aren't well enough to be up yet."

Bradyn studied her face solemnly for a few moments. It appeared he was trying to decide how to answer her questions, or if he should answer her at all. He leaned forward and rested his arms on his knees. A thick lock of black hair fell over his forehead, lending a dark, roguish quality to his appearance.

Blowing out a heavy sigh, he started, "I guess I owe it to you…what with you saving my life and all."

Rian nodded once. "It's the least you could do," she said.

"Laramie's a nice quiet town at face value, but underneath it's a rough place. Practically run by Liam Briggs and his little brother, Cameron. They own the sheriff, his deputies, hell they own half the people in town. And they own most of the businesses there, too. The Briggs' are not above breaking the law, you might say, but they are above paying for it when they do."

"Get to the point. How are you connected to them?" she pressed, using an impatient tone to mask her genuine curiosity. *I'll be darned if I give him the satisfaction of knowing I find him interesting.*

"I got mixed up with Briggs's woman, Contessa Lang.

She runs the Silver Lady Saloon. I'd only been in town a few weeks when I started seeing her. I was there on business. Tessa told me that she may be able to help me find someone that I was looking for. She never breathed a word about being Liam's woman until he came back from Denver last week. Guess you can figure out the rest."

Rian nodded slowly. His story jibed. This Contessa must have been the woman he'd spoken to in his delirium. "That explains the beating and all, but what about the badge? How'd you come by that?"

Bradyn looked torn. It was obvious he didn't want to tell her about that, but she could see that he was struggling; trying to decide what to say. "I found it," he said at length. "My guess is the Marshal got himself killed one way or another, but I wouldn't know."

"You just *happened* to find the badge lying around? Where? In the middle of the street or something?" She wasn't going to buy it. The expression on his face told her he was withholding something.

"No, I found it lying around Tessa's dressing room," he returned evenly. Again, she noted the smirk that tugged at the corner of his mouth when she frowned at his smart remark.

"And you have no idea how it got there?" she asked.

Rian knew her disbelief was as obvious as a splatter of mud on a white washed fence. She folded her arms across her chest and cocked a hip. The gun, forgotten for the time-being, poked out of the crook of her elbow.

"None. I figure that Briggs had something to do with it, but as you can see, I didn't have much time to investigate. I was too busy getting my fool ass beaten and shipped out of town." Bradyn gave her a slanted look as he appraised her.

His explanation eased her suspicions somewhat. She exhaled and put the revolver down on the table. When she locked eyes with Bradyn once again, she wondered if it was relief she saw in his expression.

Running her finger along the barrel of the gun thoughtfully, she asked, "So you think maybe Briggs suspects you know something and may try to have you killed, is that it?"

"Sounds about right. It's what I would do if I were him," he replied with an easy smile.

Rian was again immediately irritated. How could he possibly smile at such a horrid thought? She ran a hand over her forehead, feeling both tired and puzzled. "What business?" she asked, her mind mulling over his explanation.

"Pardon me?" He gave her a confused look.

"You said you were in Laramie on business. Those were your exact words."

"It turned out to be nothing. I was looking for someone," he answered quietly.

"Did you find who you were looking for?" She saw the uneasiness that crossed his face.

"No, no he wasn't there anymore." Bradyn looked away.

It took Rian off guard a bit when his usual steady, unsettling gaze was suddenly broken. "I see," she said simply. She pulled a chair out from the table, sat down heavily, and rested her chin on one hand.

The two of them sat in silence for several minutes. Somehow the news that he may have been followed hadn't worried her when Bradyn had first said it. She'd been too scared and angry at him then. Now that the adrenaline of their confrontation began to wear off, she remembered the feeling she'd experienced on the porch earlier. She shivered, wondering if there was, indeed, someone watching the house tonight.

"Rian?" Kendall's sleepy voice made her jump. He stood at the foot of the stairs rubbing his eyes and yawning.

"Kendall, honey." Rian rushed over and picked him up. "You're supposed to be in bed. Let's get you back upstairs." She spun and started up the steps, hoping to get him to his room before he fully woke up.

"Marshal!" Too late, Kendall's excited shout brought her to a halt. "Marshal, you're up!"

Kendall wriggled free and bolted across the kitchen to stand in front of Bradyn. Once there, he suddenly became shy. She walked up behind him, put a protective hand on his shoulder, and glared down at Bradyn. "Kendall, this man is not a marshal." She kept her voice soft and sweet, for Kendall's sake. "His name is Mr. Bradyn Preston."

"Is that true, mister? You ain't really a marshal?" the little boy asked.

Caught between her fierce glare and the little boy's disappointment, Bradyn shifted uncomfortably. His dark blue eyes registered uneasy confusion. Rian figured he had no idea why his being a marshal would be so damn important to a little boy.

"No, kid. I reckon I'm not the marshal," he answered truthfully.

"Gosh, what happened to you, mister? You were awful hurt, you know. Me 'n Rian doctored you up. Well, she did mostly, but I helped. I been takin' care of your horse, too." Kendall shifted his weight and balanced on one foot. His disappointment was quickly replaced with boyish curiosity.

"I'm very obliged to you, kid. Thank you."

Bradyn's eyes searched her face, gauging her reaction. He looked lost, uncertain of what to say or do next. Rian supposed he'd spent precious little time around children. As he shifted stiffly in his seat, she almost pitied him.

"Come on, Kendall," she said. "Time for bed."

She felt his eyes on them as they left the room. Kendall glanced back over his shoulder at Bradyn, and when he turned back, she saw the smile on his face. Apparently their guest still had one admirer in the house. She shook her head.

She struggled to keep her aggravation masked as she pulled back Kendall's blankets and helped him into bed.

"I like Mr. Bradyn, Rian," Kendall said as she straightened his sheets and re-tucked him in.

"Don't be silly, sweetie," she said defensively. "You don't even know the man. We have no idea who he is or what he's done."

"He's not bad. I know he's not," Kendall asserted. "He doesn't have the mean eyes. 'Member, like that other man." He shuddered and she knew he was referring to the man that had come to rob them last spring. The man who had killed Jackson.

"Let's not think about that now." She kissed his cheek and smoothed his hair fondly. "You need your rest if you want to grow up big and strong."

Kendall yawned noisily. "'Night, Rian," he whispered, his eyes already closing in sleep.

"Goodnight, baby," she whispered back, smoothing his blankets and kissing him again before leaving the room.

* * * *

Bradyn stood up as soon as Rian and the kid were out of sight. His back was a mass of dull, burning pain, which, in retrospect, was a great improvement over the white-hot agony he'd felt earlier that morning. He put the Winchester back on its rack above the pantry door. At least if they needed it, it would be loaded. He shook his head, wondering why a woman alone in the middle of nowhere with a kid didn't have enough sense to keep her rifle fully loaded in case of emergency.

He was in the washroom, pumping water into the heavy porcelain basin, when she came back down the stairs.

"You really should be in bed, Mr. Preston," she said with a frown.

"You really are a bossy little thing," Bradyn answered as he moved aside, allowing her to take over the pump. He watched her thoughtfully for a moment as she filled the basin. "What happened? To your brother and his wife, I mean."

Rian's back was to him but he saw the painful expression that came over her face in the mirror's reflection. She was quiet for a long time. Bradyn thought she had decided to ignore his question when she finally answered in a low voice. "My brother's wife, Sadie, took ill and died a few months after we came to the Territory. Kendall was just a little baby." She stepped aside to let him wash. "Jackson was killed by a drunken man who came to rob us last spring."

"I'm sorry to hear that. It must be tough on you, keeping this place going and raising that boy all by yourself." Bradyn splashed water over his face and relished the cool freshness.

Rian handed him a bar of soap. "We manage," she replied.

"Do you have a razor?"

His question seemed to pull her out of deep thought. She blinked and looked up at him. "In the cabinet, behind the mirror." She pointed. "Everything you need to shave should be there."

"Thanks." Bradyn watched her in the mirror as he lathered his face. "Tomorrow, I think I'll have a bath." He nodded to the giant cast-iron tub standing in the corner.

Rian blushed faintly but said nothing. She handed him a towel. "I think I will go mix you another brandy and willow powder. It will help you sleep," she contended when he gave her a look of disgust.

Bradyn shook his head, but didn't say a word. He watched her leave the room through the mirror. She fascinated him. She was bold and protective, but vulnerable in a way completely exclusive to her gender. Bradyn liked her. He liked her very much. He only hoped that his presence didn't put her or the kid in harm's way.

* * * *

Rian hummed a jaunty little piece of "Dixie" as she prepared the brandy. She heated the liquor with milk and honey this time, hoping the sweetness would detract from the powder's acidic flavor. Forgetting, for the instant, she was not alone in the house, she sang the last half of the second verse in a voice that was slightly off-key;

"...But when he put his arm around 'er,
He smelled as fierce as a forty-pounder,
Look away! Look away! Look away! Dixie Land."

She didn't hear Bradyn come into the kitchen until he cleared his throat.

"Haven't heard that song in awhile," he said casually. "Not since the War, in fact."

Rian shut her eyes, irritated that he had such a pension for startling her. "Yes, my mother used to sing it to me when I was a little girl."

"What part of Dixie do you hail from?"

"New Orleans," she answered.

Her back was still to him as she concentrated on stirring the milk. How she wished he would not ask questions about her past. Even if the questions were only intended to stir up conversation.

"Ah, yes. New Orleans. The home of river boat gamblers, Southern Baptists, and voodoo witch doctors." Rian heard the smile in his words. "I fell in love with a woman in New Orleans once. Her name was Tucson Maude. I was all of sixteen with a little money to burn and a pocketful of foolish dreams. She saw me coming a mile away. Took me to her place, took me, and then took me for every penny I had." He grew quiet for a moment. "Was a shame, too, I really needed those five dollars."

His comment brought an unwilling chuckle. She shook her head. "You seem to have a strange fascination for wild women who intend you no good, Mr. Preston. I should say you got your just desserts that time." She tried to subdue the hint of laughter in her voice.

"Well, now, I don't know," he replied with mock sobriety. "Can't say as I've been with a lot of wild women. I prefer to prey on lonely women. The sort who live alone on homesteads in the middle of nowhere."

Rian shook her head again. The man was exasperating. "Of course," she drawled sarcastically. "Next you'll be telling me you—," she turned and stopped mid-sentence.

Bradyn looked like a completely different person. With his face shaved he was the picture of masculine beauty. The black eye and jagged cut somehow enhanced his appearance in a way she couldn't understand. Leaning there, a slender hip against the table, his muscular arms folded over his bare chest, he met her gaze with a fixed stare of his own.

He seemed to find her tongue-tied reaction humorous. As if the heat that rose on her neck and stung her cheeks was all the indication he needed to read the thoughts that were tumbling through her head.

"Something wrong?" he asked good-naturedly. "You didn't quite finish that last sentence."

"What?" she asked, embarrassed and appalled at herself for letting such a trivial matter cause her to fumble and stumble over a simple conversation. "I don't remember," she muttered. Her face was burning as she turned back to the stove.

"Are your parents still in Orleans?" Bradyn asked.

For once she was relieved that he'd shifted the topic of conversation to her past. Rian shook her head. "My father died during the War. My mother passed on a year after Jackson and I came out West."

"How old are you?"

Another exasperating, intrusive question. "I'm twenty-four," she answered defensively.

"And you've never been married?" His tone was curious.

"Not that it is any of your business, but as a matter of fact, I was married. Once." She turned to face him, carefully concealing her emotions. "That was a long time ago, before I came to the Wyoming Territory."

"What happened to him?" Bradyn pressed.

Rian flinched at his question and turned back to stir the heating mixture. She hated to think about her past life. She had suppressed it for so long. Now the emotions and the pain came flooding back, returning her to that terrible, heart-rending time as if it'd all just happened yesterday. Thankful he could not see her face, she squeezed her eyes shut, remembering. It was all so very vague now…there were whole sections of time that escaped her recollection, but the darkness of her past still remained. A black shadow that haunted her.

Bradyn stood silent. Waiting for her answer.

She remained silent, too. The milk and brandy had finished warming. She added the willow powder to the sweet, creamy mixture. As she poured it into a cup, she felt the sudden, ridiculous urge to tell him everything, at least everything she remembered, about that horrible time nearly seven years in her past. No one, besides Jackson and Sadie, had ever known. Now that she was the only living soul left who remembered what had happened, it seemed a very heavy burden at times. She could forget about it for hours on end, but, when darkness came and she lay alone in her bed, the remembrance of it always came rushing back. Terror would grip her; fear that she would be found. She was afraid she would have to go back to face her past.

When she handed the drink to Bradyn, his eyes caught hers. She was surprised at the kindness she saw in their depths. Gone was the indifference and brooding cast. Those had been replaced with a gentle regard. You know you touched a sensitive subject, she wanted to say to him. *Don't stand there trying to look innocent. You know what you're doing and I can't say that it isn't working entirely. But it's not going to be that easy for you. I don't trust you yet.* And the desire to tell him faded from her mind.

"I'm sorry," he said, the tone of his voice kind. "My question was out of line."

Awful big of you to say, Rian thought. But she forced a very small smile and said nothing.

Bradyn drank the medicine quickly. She noticed that he stifled a grimace. The mixture still wasn't to his liking it would seem.

"I think I'll turn in," he said as he wiped a hand across his mouth.

Rian tried to conceal her relief. "I think I will, too. My room is the one at the left of the stairs. But, if you need anything just call me. I'm a light sleeper."

"Good night then," Bradyn replied, still studying her face.

"Good night, Mr. Preston."

Chapter Four

The next morning dawned hot and humid. The rising sun had only just breeched the horizon and already the air hung heavy and still. The heat of midday promised to be almost unbearable if the early morning temperatures were any indication. That was, of course, if the thick, intense atmosphere was not threatening a late-afternoon thunderstorm instead.

Rian rose early and made a hearty breakfast of eggs, biscuits, bacon, and fried potatoes. After feeding Kendall, washing the breakfast dishes, and tidying up the kitchen, she looked in on Bradyn. He was sleeping peacefully. His color appeared healthy and his injuries were even less swollen today. He would be able to take the stitches out of his shoulder in a few days. She was pleased with his speedy recovery. Very soon now he would be well and on his way. Sooner than she had expected just yesterday.

Rian felt a momentary, inexplicable sadness at the notion that Bradyn would be leaving. She shook her head, irritated at herself. *That's ridiculous. You didn't even know anything about the man. And what you do know about him is not at all a recommendation in his favor.*

He was abrasive and interfering. The way he made her feel obligated to answer his meddlesome questions vexed her. She disliked his silent, intense gaze that followed her whenever she was near. And, above all, she resented that his physical appearance had set her stomach to twirling like that of a silly chorus girl the night before.

Rian wasn't certain that those first stirrings of a deeper need were something she wanted. Frustrated that her mind was so consumed with Bradyn Preston, she decided she would put her hands to hard work. The past four days of constant nursing had consumed her mind with thoughts of the man who slept in their guestroom. Concentrating on something other than Bradyn was just what she needed today to redirect her mind and take it off the strange feelings she had been having lately.

The last four days the unattended garden had begun sprouting weeds in scores. The corn looked a little parched and the rows of beans had already ripened for a first picking. She set Kendall to fetching water to dowse the plants and she began hoeing the rows and pulling weeds.

The sun beat down with a scorching vengeance. She pulled off her shirt and sighed as a slight breeze cooled her through her chemise. Sweat rolled down her face, back, and sides. She was sticky from the heat and the dust stirred up by her hoeing clung to her skin in a thin, slimy coat. When Kendall brought her a cup full of water, she grasped it gratefully. "You're such an angel, Kendall." A trickle of water ran down the front of her chemise leaving a cool, muddy smudge.

Kendall squinted up at her, his face full of childish happiness, as she swallowed the water greedily.

"Will you run back inside and see if Mr. Preston is still sleeping, please?" Rian said, catching her breath after guzzling the entire cup of water. She wiped her mouth with the back of her hand. "If he's awake give him the plate I put in the oven. It's his breakfast!" she called out to him as he ran toward the house.

"Okay!" Kendall shouted over his shoulder, already halfway across the yard.

Rian watched him go and shook her head with loving disgust. *That boy would probably make friends with the Devil if he showed up with half a smile and a gunshot wound.*

Her mind turned to a less pondered fact. Sooner or later Kendall would need to have some form of human interaction himself. His immediate fondness for Bradyn bothered her. Kendall was so guileless and innocent when it came to other people. It was a trait that was at once endearing and disturbing.

By noon, Rian had weeded half the garden and she and Kendall had watered every plant. The dirt under her fingernails and the rough calluses on her hands gave her a sense of satisfaction. She was pulling the last weeds in the row of cabbages when a male voice behind her made her jump.

"Mornin', ma'am."

Rian dropped the hoe and spun around. Her eyes went wide.

The stranger was tall and lanky. Dirty blond hair hung around his face. His hat was tilted to the side in an awkward fashion. Baggy clothes that were faded and dusty hung off his slender frame. He stood easy, his right hand on his gun, his left holding a cigarette to his lips. The ripe odor of sweat and alcohol mingled with the cigarette smoke permeated the air around him.

He smiled. It was a menacing smile, full of dark thoughts and insinuations. Buried under thick brows, his eyes glittered with pure evil. She had seen that look before. He intended her harm.

"What do you want?" she asked, slowly backing toward the house. Her heart pounded. It was a roaring waterfall in her ears. Immediately, instinctively, she knew. The man was here for Bradyn.

She prayed Kendall would see the stranger and not come out of the house. She prayed he would go warn Bradyn. She prayed that by some mercy, Bradyn would have the physical strength to get out of bed and get to the gun before the malevolent man in front of her found him first.

"You got a injured man in there, Missy?" he asked. His smile grew wider as he watched her backing away. His teeth were caked with grime and stained with tobacco. "A man that goes by the name of 'Preston', by chance?" he pressed.

Rian stalled, her throat constricting into a dry, shrunken tube, "I, uh, I haven't seen anyone out this way in quite awhile," she lied. *Damn!* Her voice betrayed her. A weak, pathetic croak.

"Ha ahaha!" the man hooted. He took his slouchy hat from his head and slapped it across his knee as if she had just said the funniest thing he'd ever heard. She stood dumbfounded, torn between running for the house and standing her ground.

Suddenly, from nowhere, his hand shot out and grabbed her neck. He pulled her in a fluid, vice-like grip. "I ain't stupid. I know he's here, Missy." His hot, rancid breath clogged her nose and turned her stomach. "And I'm gonna kill 'im." He pushed his gun into her face. "Now you gonna take me to him, or do I have to break yer pretty little neck?"

Frightened nearly out of her mind, Rian nodded mechanically. She tried to slow her thoughts, to figure out how to alert Kendall and Bradyn. The man half-carried her to the steps, his arms around her waist and breasts. She tried in vain to think, her fingers clawing at his wrists as she fought to escape his grasp. But the only thought that riddled her mind was... *Oh, he stinks! He smells awful, he smells awful...Oh, God we're all going to die and he smells awful, he smells awful...*

"Rian, Mister Bra--," Kendall's sentence was broken abruptly as he came out onto the porch and saw the stranger holding her.

Rian closed her eyes in heartsick frustration. She had no choice, if she didn't make a move, if she did nothing, he would reach out and grab Kendall, too. There would be no hope of the boy getting a gun or alerting Bradyn. Mustering every ounce of courage in her body, she threw her head back with as much force as she could. It smashed into her assailant's face with a sickening smack that made her see stars. The man groaned and stumbled backward.

His hold on her momentarily loosened and Rian scrambled free. "Get the rifle!" she screeched, as a hand shot out to grab her hair and jerk her head roughly backward. Her neck snapped with blinding pain. Her eyes burned with tears as the man brutally pulled her back against him.

"If you move, I'll shoot yer mama, kid." The hammer on his gun clicked into place and she felt the cool barrel dig into her cheek.

Kendall stood paralyzed, his face white, his fingers twitching frantically. Rian moaned as her captor reached out and, his gun still firmly in hand, grabbed Kendall by the shirt.

"Git inside, both of you," he ordered in a low voice. "If either of ya try to yell out, I'll kill ya."

Once inside, the man pushed her to the floor and shoved Kendall into the open pantry. She looked helplessly at Kendall's terrified face, now streaming with silent tears, as the man slammed the door shut on him. The petrified expression of horror in his eyes was all the incentive she needed.

Rian lunged to her feet and ran at the man, shoving him as hard as she could; the action barely off-set his balance. He grabbed her arm, pulled it over her head, and forced her up against the wall. She saw now that she'd managed to bloody his nose when she'd rammed her head into his face.

"Yer gonna pay for this, whore," he spat, pointing his gun barrel at his bleeding, battered nose.

He leaned in until his nose was almost touching hers. His words chilled her to the bone as his rancid breath washed her face. "I'm gonna kill the man you got in here and then I'm gonna take you apart one piece at a time. Slow and easy-like. You and I are gonna have us a right fun night, Missy. Maybe I'll even make your son watch awhile before I blow his head off."

He dragged her toward the guestroom, his eyes keen, his gun ready to fire. Rian screamed and kicked, hoping that it would rouse Bradyn, hoping against hope that the wounded man would get out of bed and into hiding at the very least.

The dirty man walked through the door, pulling her by the hair. She couldn't see past him. She couldn't tell if Bradyn had been awakened by the noise or if he was even in the room at all. Her lips moved in silent prayer.

"What the hell do *you* want, Joe?" She heard Bradyn ask. His voice was smooth and easy.

Her captor chuckled evilly. "You know the answer, Preston. Yer a dead man. Briggs's orders."

Oh, God, Oh, God! Rian prayed silently. *What do I do? What do I do?!*

The man's grasp loosened on her hair briefly and she bolted upright. Bradyn was sitting up in bed. His face was calm. Except for the sweat that stood out on his brow and chest, he looked as though the man standing before him had come for nothing more than a friendly brunch of crumpets and tea.

Rian watched in horrified silence as the filthy man who'd come to kill Bradyn leveled his gun at him. She screamed and frantically pummeled the man's lanky back with animal rage. Her protests were rewarded by a square elbow in the stomach. Pain and shock sent her to the floor in a crumpled mass, the wind knocked from her. The room tilted in and out of focus as she fought to hang onto consciousness.

She heard the hammer click as the stranger cocked his gun. There was an explosion of gunfire. Two deafening shots reported in quick succession, followed by a man's scream.

The scream cut through her dazed mind. She buried her face in her arm and moaned loudly. Hopeless alarm at their precarious condition shattered her mind. With Bradyn dead, she and Kendall were completely alone. Stark, painful fear consumed her and she couldn't stop the sob that escaped her mouth.

Then followed the unexpected. The assailant slumped to the floor with a resounding thud. She lifted her face and gaped at the man lying dead beside her. His eyes were wide with an eternal expression of stupid disbelief. Blood dripped from his parted lips and spread a tiny crimson pool on the floor.

Rian slowly pulled herself to her knees. Confused and dizzy, the room narrowed, closing in around her as she felt nausea grip her. The scent of blood and expended gun powder pushed her over the edge. She retched into her apron. Thankful there'd only been water on her stomach she pulled the apron from her waist, wadded it into a ball, and dropped it to the floor. Then, taking a slow deep breath, she tried to work up the courage to look at the bed; certain that Bradyn was lying there with a bullet hole in his head.

She felt a hand on her shoulder, and looked up. "Are you all right?" Bradyn's voice, kind and concerned, brought a wondrous rush of relief. He was alive!

Dumbfounded, she nodded woodenly. "How did you…he had a gun! How did *you* shoot *him*?"

"I took your six-gun from the cabinet last night. I had a hunch Briggs or his men would try something like this." Bradyn pointed to the bed. "I'm afraid I ruined your quilt though."

Rising with a wobble, Bradyn grasping her elbow to steady her, Rian gazed down at the quilt her mother's hands had lovingly crafted. A singed black hole marked the spot where Bradyn's bullet had exited a yellow patch of cloth. A few forlorn feathers floated in the air and more littered the blanket. Blood and bullets. She shook her head, her mother's quilt had born the brunt of this whole mess since the first day Bradyn Preston had come to their home. Strangely, she felt no anger, just sad, exhausted indifference. They were alive, that was all that mattered at the moment.

"Kendall!" She rushed to the pantry and yanked the door open.

The little boy sat cowering in the corner beneath the shelves of raspberry and chokecherry preserves. Giant green eyes, full of petrified horror, stared up at them. His face was a sickly grey, his lips blue, and he'd wet himself. She pulled him to her, pressing his face to her neck and whispering softly, "Oh, baby, baby, baby…there, there. It's over, Mr. Preston got him. He's gone. It's over, baby. Shh, shh, now."

Kendall cried uncontrollably for a while, his small body wracked with heaving sobs. She sat on the floor in the middle of the pantry holding and rocking him; whispering quiet, soothing words that only the little boy could hear.

As his crying died down, Rian looked at Bradyn. He rested his body against the kitchen table. His eyes flashed and the stiff set of his jaw made her want to shiver. He was angry.

"Are you sure you're not hurt?" he asked her. His fierce expression softened as he assessed her.

Rian nodded, rubbing Kendall's back gently. "I'm fine,"

she whispered. Kendall's breath fanned her neck, slow and even now.

"If he hadn't knocked you to the floor, I never would have shot him. While you were standing behind him, I wouldn't have taken the chance that the bullet would have passed through him and into you," he explained. "But, by God, I want to kill him again for hitting you."

Bradyn's hand formed a fist, and Rian wondered if perhaps he would go back into the guestroom and shoot the man again, just for good measure. She drew a long breath. "It's over now," she said. "That's all that matters."

Bradyn walked to the pantry door and leaned against the frame. They exchanged a silent stare as she sat rocking Kendall.

She looked down at the little boy wrapped in her arms. Tears of relief stung her eyes. She held him for a few minutes longer, even after he had fallen asleep. She was torn. They owed Bradyn their lives, and yet in light of what had just taken place, she now, more than ever, wanted him to go. She was afraid. The next time, perhaps they would not escape so easily. Perhaps, they would not escape at all.

She was surprised when Bradyn knelt beside her and put a hand on her shoulder.

"He's asleep," he whispered. Without warning, he deftly reached around her and pulled Kendall up into his arms. "Let me carry him up to his bed. You can go wash. I'll take care of Joe's body."

Startled, Rian looked up at him. Part of her resented him touching her nephew with such easy authority, but another part appreciated the gesture of help. She had done everything for the two of them for so long. Alone. She felt a funny knot in her stomach. She nodded at Bradyn, feeling appreciation instead of irritation. An effortless pleasantness washed over her for one brief moment. The pleasure didn't last however. It quickly was replaced with her earlier fears. As Bradyn started up the stairs and she went to the washroom, her thoughts were laden with uncertainty.

Rian washed her face and arms, trying to rid herself of the stench of the man who'd put his hands on her. His scent still clung to her nostrils and her earlier nausea returned. As she dried herself, she studied her reflection in the mirror. A bruise stood out in purple fury against the tender flesh of her neck. She ran her hand over it and frowned. Better a bruise than a bullet, she thought. *And a bullet would have been getting off easy.* She shuddered remembering the horrible man's dark promise to her after he'd thrown Kendall into the pantry.

Turning to hang the towel beside the basin, she looked into the mirror fleetingly. She gasped in horror as she realized she was only wearing a chemise. How had she completely forgotten until now that she'd removed her shirt earlier? When she turned to the side, her heart sank. The low back and thins straps of the undershirt covered very little of her shoulders. *My scars. I'm sure he must have seen them.*

Rian quickly pulled a dry towel from the cabinet and wrapped it around her shoulders like a shawl. She rushed up to her room to get a fresh shirt, begging the heavens that he would not ask another of his blunt, uncomfortable questions.

Bradyn was coming back down the stairs as she hurried past, her face white and withdrawn. He knew it was no sense of modesty that had caused her to don the towel and hurry to her room. She was trying to hide what he'd already seen. And from the look in her eyes, she knew he'd seen the scars, too.

He'd seen the marks long before Cheyenne Joe came to the house. The window in his bedroom was some distance from the garden, but Bradyn had been watching her when she'd taken off her shirt. She'd had her back to the house. The sun had burned down on her golden skin, illuminating the jagged web of white that covered her shoulders and upper back.

He wanted to know how she had gotten them, but decided that it was none of his business. His big mouth had already alienated her enough. Bradyn made a pact with himself that he wasn't going to ask her as he walked into the guestroom to take care of the dead man.

Cheyenne Joe's blood had seeped into the wood floor. He

shook his head in disgust. That was going to leave a stain. Surveying the room, he pulled the crumpled quilt from the bed and began wrapping the dead man in it. The quilt was ruined. It would make a nice burial shroud. *Seems fitting to wrap the bastard in the quilt that hid my gun. Should've thought twice about trying to kill me, Joe.*

He rolled Cheyenne Joe onto his back. That was when he noticed Joe's feet. He was wearing Bradyn's boots. The ones that Briggs had been so kind to remove before setting Bradyn's horse free to roam the hills and valleys of the Wyoming Territory. "I'll just take those back, you bastard," he mumbled as he pulled one from Joe's foot and grunted in disgust at the odor. "You were one filthy son of a whore, Joe," Bradyn swore under his breath as he proceeded to take the other.

Rian was in the kitchen, busy over the stove, when Bradyn walked into the room grunting under the weight he'd slung over his shoulder.

Seeing her expression, Bradyn knew immediately he'd done something wrong. Her eyes went wide with shock, her lips parted in a silent "oh!", and her hand went to her throat.

"What is it?" he asked, his breath coming in short bursts under the cumbersome load on his shoulder.

She didn't answer him immediately. Instead, her face remained frozen in wordless disbelief. Bradyn shifted his burden and cursed inwardly. She needed to spit it out. He wasn't exactly in top shape and if he didn't get the body outside soon, she'd be dragging it out herself, and then hauling him back to bed to boot.

Rian extended a shaking forefinger. "It's the quilt. You can't...it's special. I don't want that filthy man in it." Moisture welled in her eyes.

Of course. The quilt. Irritated at his own stupidity, Bradyn said, "I'm sorry, I'll get him outside and then I'll bring it right back, okay?" When she nodded and turned back to the stove, he stifled a groan, braced himself, and walked out the front door.

You just never know what sentiment a woman will attach to something that a man would never think twice about. Take the quilt. To his thinking it was a utilitarian necessity. Made for covering and warming the body during sleep, or used as a soft sanctuary for lovers while passion's fire burned. When it got old or ruined, you threw it away and got a new one.

For Rian, the quilt obviously held an endearing value. *And why not? Some women sew and stockpile quilts the way some men do horses or guns or cattle.* Remembering his own mother, Bradyn thought about the forty-eleven different patterns she'd sewn into quilts herself when he was a young boy. Maybe a quilt left behind to a beloved daughter held the same importance to the opposite gender as a ranch left to an only son. Women weren't often allowed to feel the grandeur of receiving a piece of land or the honor of inheriting a great wealth. Perhaps to compensate they attached themselves to objects that men would never bother to worry over. Maybe it was their gender's own quiet legacy, passed from generation to generation as a silent testament to the love and hard-work of a woman who'd gone on before. Hell, it makes perfect sense, Bradyn decided.

A distant crackle of thunder sounded across an expansion of dark clouds that had begun boiling across the hills. Bradyn looked up at the fast-blackening sky. A wind worked itself into a jagged fury, blowing cool air across his sweat-dowsed body. He breathed a sigh of pleasure. *A good, hard rain would be very welcome right now,* he thought, as he found a shovel in the garden and lugged the body down the hill toward the creek bank.

He had gotten about half the hole dug when Rian came to join him. She was carrying a shovel and a bucket of water. Bradyn watched in mesmerized fascination as she approached. Her hair whipped loosely around her shoulders. Her dress billowed about her legs. She moved with agile grace; her face lifted with quiet dignity. Bradyn thought, for the second time, that she looked vaguely familiar and a strange sense of déjà vu tickled at the back of his mind.

After wordlessly offering him a cool drink of water, she began digging. Bradyn watched her for a moment before he put the dipper back into the water bucket. She surely is something, he thought as he again put his own shovel to the soil. The picture of her working in the garden came back to him and the sensation of familiarity grew stronger. *It's not just the way she looks.* He glanced at her out of the corner of his eye. *There's more to it than that. But, I'll be damned if I know exactly what it is.*

They dug in silence, side by side, sharing a same-paced rhythm. The only sounds heard were the scraping of shovels on earth and rock, accompanied by the intermittent growling of thunder.

Bradyn studied her out of the corner of his eye periodically. She made no sound as she matched him shovel-full for shovel-full. Her face was closed to any apparent emotion. He had no way of guessing what was going through her head.

After several eternal minutes of arduous digging, the hole was deep enough. The mound of dirt amassed next to the make-shift grave filled his nostrils with the pungent odor of fresh, dark earth. A smattering of rain began; light and refreshing. Bradyn lifted his head to the sky, blinking back water as the rain pattered down in an even sprinkle.

"Let's get him in this hole and buried before the rain gets too heavy and this grave turns into a lake!" he shouted over an ear-splitting clap of thunder.

Bradyn caught her nod as he pulled the quilt from the dead man's body. He folded it with practiced ease and handed it to her. Reverence for the blood-stained, gun-shot, and now wet and muddy blanket to which she held such attachment touched him for a moment as Rian took it.

As he unceremoniously rolled the body into the excavated ground, she looked on with the quilt clutched to her chest. He wiped the sweat from his forehead and reached for the shovel as the body landed face-up with a dull thump.

Out of the corner of his eye, Bradyn saw her shudder as she stood looking down into the grave. Cheyenne Joe's eyes stared lifelessly up at them. He started piling dirt back into the hole, his back aching. Her sudden movement caught his attention. The quilt was tossed on a nearby stump. Then she picked up her shovel and threw a giant scoop of dirt on Cheyenne Joe's head.

He observed her action with masked humor and curiosity, but said nothing. While she worked feverishly to cover the man's head, he shoveled dirt back into the hole with maddening speed. Rain, mingled with acid sweat, rolled down his naked back. His scabbed-over abrasions began to sting. Ignoring the pain, he forced himself to work faster.

Rian dug faster as well. Soon, Cheyenne Joe was nothing more than a patch of freshly turned soil. In a few short weeks, the grave would be nearly invisible. Bradyn caught her eye and gave her an affirmative nod which she returned. A job well done.

He sank down on the ground with a loud moan. His back ached, his head hurt, and just now, he could think of no better reward for his toils than a hot bath and long, uninterrupted sleep. He rested his head against a forearm and closed his eyes wearily.

"Are you alright?" Rian sounded guilty. She knelt beside him and touched his muddy shoulder timidly. "Mr. Preston? You must be exhausted. Are you in pain?"

Bradyn leaned his head back and focused his gaze on her. Dirt and sweat streaked her lovely face. Her warm eyes glinted with concern as she appraised him. The tenderness in her expression made his stomach jump. Perhaps she cared a bit after all.

"What is it?" she asked. The color rose in her cheeks as he continued to look at her. She shifted uneasily under his gaze.

Bradyn decided he had mastered the art of making her uncomfortable to perfection, but he didn't answer. He couldn't answer. Very aware of her closeness, of her small, dirty hand resting on his shoulder, he was suddenly, inexplicably tongue-tied. He felt an odd sense of pride in her. It was almost fanciful and completely ludicrous. She wasn't his, he barely knew her, and yet in the short time he since he had met her, she had earned his admiration. Rian Keene was an amazing woman, and he doubted she had the slightest clue that she was.

Realizing he was staring, Bradyn cleared his throat and looked away. "Should we say a, uh, prayer or something for him?"

Rian's laughter caught him off-guard. What could she possibly find humorous at a time like this?

"What's so funny?" he asked.

When he raised an eyebrow out of curiosity, she assured him quickly, "Oh, I'm not laughing at you. I just for the life of me can't think of a fitting prayer to say over a man like that." She sobered and appeared to think on it a moment. Dusting her hands, she said, "I think I know what should be said."

Standing and turning toward the grave, she bowed her head. Bradyn followed suit and rose to stand beside her, interested as to what she had in mind by way of a eulogy. Lord knew there was precious little to be said for Cheyenne Joe or the state of his soul.

"Thank you, Lord, for the bountiful mercies that thou hast bestowed on us today. Thank you for saving our lives and letting Mr. Preston blow the guts out of Mr. Cheyenne Joe, the bastard who tried to kill us. If he tries to get into Heaven, please send him straight to Hell and we will be eternally grateful." She paused briefly, opened one eye, and then quickly shut it again. "Oh, yes, and Lord, if it be thy will, it would be nice if no more of Mr. Preston's friends came to visit. Another dead man on my conscience is more than I've got the stomach for. Amen."

Bradyn felt his mouth drop open as he watched her pray. It wasn't any prayer he'd ever heard his mama lay at the good Lord's feet, but Rian's face was as serious as Moses passing the Ten Commandments down to the children of Israel. He knew she intended no humor with her words, but he found them hilarious just the same. He had to cough to suppress his laughter.

A rattling boom of thunder reverberated through a sky now as black as the inside of a dog's belly. Lightning sizzled across the horizon, blazing a purple-white glow behind the thick, rain-laden clouds. With no warning, the wind picked up its howling tirade, and the rain followed suit. In moments, they were both sopping wet.

Wrapping a muddy arm around her shoulders, Bradyn pulled her to his side. "Let's get out of this rain before we catch our death or get struck by lightning. I'm not too excited to find out if God took your prayer with good humor or not."

Rian bit her lip, as if she had been about to say something and then decided against it. Instead, she only nodded and leaned against him the slightest bit as they started walking back to the house.

* * * *

When they got back, drenched to the bone and muddy up to their eyes, Rian went up to check on Kendall and get into a dry change of clothing. Her nephew was still sleeping, his thumb tucked securely in his mouth. She brushed his hair back from his forehead and sighed. She hoped he would sleep clear through the night without any nightmares. Pulling the blankets up over him, she frowned. He was still in the clothing he'd had on earlier. She sighed again and gently pulled off his pants and shirt. As she tucked him under the blanket, the faint sound of running water reached her ears. That sound was unmistakable; the large cast-iron bathtub was being filled.

She shook her head. I guess he's going to make good on his promise to take a bath, she thought dryly. *He needs one for sure…could use one myself.*

Rian found Bradyn's muddy, torn jeans draped over the back of a chair in the kitchen when she came back downstairs. She pulled at one of the pant-legs and studied it. There was a trunk full of Jackson's old clothing in the guest room. Maybe one of the pairs of pants would fit Bradyn. At second glance, she decided that Jackson's pants would probably be a little big in the waist and a little too short in the length. But, at least Bradyn wouldn't be wearing this filthy, shredded, sorry-excuse-for-a-pair-of-pants anymore.

Rian rummaged through the large closet until she found what she was looking for. She dragged the trunk out and started digging through it for the closest fit she could find. While I'm at it, I'll get him a shirt, too, she thought, and some bvd's. The thought of Bradyn wearing Jackson's long underwear brought a feverish blush to her cheeks. It wasn't a picture she wanted to envision…really.

She smiled, remembering the look of disbelief that had come over Bradyn's face when she'd prayed over Cheyenne Joe's grave. *At least he's not the only one capable of making someone feel uncomfortable.* She grinned. *I'll wager he's never prayed a word one in his life…let alone heard a prayer like* that *before.* The thought was satisfying.

Rian selected a red-checkered shirt and the longest pair of trousers she could find. As an afterthought, she grabbed a belt. *He'll probably need one,* she decided as she pushed the trunk back into the closet and exited the bedroom.

She gently knocked on the washroom door, thankful that Bradyn had been courteous enough to close it most of the way. Momentarily, she hoped that he would have had the sense to pull the curtain around the tub as well.

"Come in."

"Did you pull the curtain?" she asked hesitantly.

The sound of water sloshing in the tub was followed by the rasping of the curtain hooks sliding across the wooden pole.

"Did now," he called. "Come on in. I'm decent."

Rian stifled a smile and opened the door. She walked over and laid the clothes on the chair next to the bathtub. "I brought you a change of clothes," she told him. "They're some of Jackson's old things. They may not fit perfectly, but at least you'll have something clean to wear."

"I'm much obliged to you," Bradyn replied. The sound of scrubbing reached her ears. "This is quite the contraption you got here."

"I beg your pardon?" she asked.

"This bathtub. I've never seen anything quite like it before," he answered. "It drains out of the bottom. I had a tough time filling it, before I noticed the plug. I like that the hand pump is mounted right on it, too. Makes it nice to not have to fill this thing with a bucket."

Rian nodded, even though he couldn't see her. "Yes. My brother put it together. It was his very own idea. Back in New Orleans, he owned a bank so he and Sadie were used to a little higher standard of living. When we built the house, he designed a way to make the plumbing a little more…how do you say it? Modern? He didn't like the idea of dragging that heavy thing outside to dump it after every bath, and he couldn't cotton to the idea of all of us using the same bathwater, so he built the drain to run through the wall and out into the side yard. It *is* pretty handy. But it sure makes one heck of a puddle."

She heard Bradyn chuckle. "Yeah. I was gonna say that this place is pretty fancy for a homestead. Most homesteaders just slap up a one-room log cabin and call it good. In fact, most of them would call it "modern" to put down a plank floor. I've been in a few where the dirt has been swept 'til it's as hard as granite and shines like marble." He chuckled again.

"You think *that's* something," she said, feeling the need to sing her brother's praises. "You should see the way he rigged it so we can have hot water for baths."

"How's that?" Bradyn asked, and she smiled at the curiosity in his tone.

"Did you notice the huge iron barrel on top of the woodstove over there?"

"As a matter of fact, I did. Was gonna ask you what the purpose of it is."

"Well, if you fill it and light a fire in the stove, the water heats right up. The tap on the side at the bottom runs through that length of pipe at the foot of the tub." She laughed. "So we only have to carry the water to the tank. Gravity does the rest. Ingenious, right?"

"Pretty fancy," Bradyn said and let out a whistle. "Pretty fancy. I think this homestead is the Territory's best kept secret."

Rian sobered. *I hope so*. "I'll leave you to finish up. There are towels in the cupboard above this chair here."

"Thank you." All of a sudden he sounded very tired.

"Are you feeling poorly?" she asked.

"I'm fine," he answered. "The cool water feels good."

Rian nodded silently and left the room, closing the door with a soft click behind her.

A few minutes later, she was re-heating the coffee and humming to herself when Bradyn came out of the washroom. This time she heard him before he could clear his throat and startle her. She turned around as he came through the door. A giggle bubbled up from her chest and escaped her lips before she could stop it. She put a hand over her mouth to stop the flow of laughter, but it was no use. Bradyn looked so funny.

Jackson's shirt fit him relatively well across the shoulders, but that was where the good fit stopped. The sleeves were too short and the rest of the shirt was at least a size too small. Bradyn had barely been able to get it buttoned. The pants were even more atrocious. He had strapped the belt around his waist, which made the denim pucker and balloon out over his slender hips. The ill-fitting trousers only got worse as they cascaded down his legs and came to an abrupt stop almost two inches above his ankles.

"I feel silly," Bradyn grumbled. Her laughter must have been infectious because he returned her grin with a crooked one of his own. "I look like a hay-seed farmer. And I don't much like the idea of wearing a dead man's clothes. Especially when they don't fit. Do you think that maybe you could just wash my pants for me?"

His reference to a "hay-seed farmer" made her giggle again. He surely does look like one, she thought merrily. She scurried across the kitchen and pulled his dirty jeans off the kitchen chair. "I'll get these cleaned up for you," she said after taking a deep breath to contain her laughter. "Sadie always left a few inches of excess on Jackson's clothes whenever she took up the sleeves and pants. She used to tell me, 'You never know when that extra fabric will come in handy.' I always thought it was funny when she said that, but now I guess Sadie is proven right. I'm sure we can get those let out to make a more suitable fit."

Bradyn nodded and started pulling off the shirt. "Thanks," he said as he slung it over the back of another chair and sat down. "That coffee sure smells good. Mind if I have myself a cup?"

"Of course not." She pulled a tin mug down from a shelf and proceeded to fill it. "Are you hungry?" she asked when she set the steaming cup down in front of him.

"If you'd have asked me that question fifteen minutes ago, I'd have said no. Bed sounds awful good right now. But the smell of that coffee is making my stomach do somersaults. I could sure use a bite to go with it." Bradyn eyed her cautiously. "How're you faring?"

His question caught her off guard and her defenses fell into place. Her smile faded like a violet under the hot July sun. "I'm alright," she answered stiffly and turned away. She preferred it when he was the focal point of the conversation.

Bradyn took a slow sip of the coffee and stared out the window as she went to pump water to wash the jeans. She was expecting him to say something like; "I noticed those huge scars on your back today. Where did you get them?" She prayed to God he would not ask her the question that was written across his face.

When she returned with the bucket of water, Bradyn watched her. As she pulled the washboard down from a peg and poured the water and soap into a large wooden tub, she brushed an unruly lock of hair out of her eyes only to have it fall back into place again. She stifled a sigh. It was a lost cause anyway since half of her hair hung around her face and shoulders. She supposed she must look a fright, but she was much too nervous under Bradyn's fixed gaze to give it a second thought.

Rian dropped his jeans into the sudsy water to soak, and then set about making a meal of sorts for him. The breakfast she had set aside for him earlier was cold now, but she managed to salvage the slice of ham and the potatoes. She put the meat on the stove to warm, along with the potatoes, and cut two thick slabs of bread. Soon, the ham began to spit and sizzle in the skillet.

Rian felt his eyes on her back, but she couldn't bring herself to turn around and face him. She knew he was going to ask. His question hung tense in the air. *Of all days for me to take off my shirt, it just had to be today. The day a crazy gunslinger decides to pay us a visit.* As she put the meat and potatoes onto a plate, and took a deliberate slow-pace in buttering the bread, she worked to construct an impenetrable poker face. She would not let him see any emotion, no matter how small, when she took him his dinner.

The stony gaze in her eyes was impeccably contrived when she placed the plate of food in front of him. Bradyn offered a smile. "Smells delicious," he said. She supposed he was hoping to set her at ease and remove the cast-iron set in her jaw.

Rian relaxed a little and nodded her head. "I hope you like it," she replied, handing him a fork.

Bradyn stabbed the ham and laid it between the two pieces of bread. He took a bite of the make-shift sandwich. "Tastes good. Do you know how long it's been since I had a solid bite of food?" He took another huge bite.

Rian watched him set to eating. Satisfied that the meal was agreeable, she walked over and started scrubbing the jeans in the washtub. The water splashed and sloshed as she pushed and pulled the faded cloth over the scrub board. She wrung the pants out and proceeded to repeat the process all over again. The interruption of Bradyn's voice set her teeth on edge.

"You say your father was in the War?" The question came in-between ravenous chewing.

Rian wanted to tell him it was impolite to talk with one's mouth full, but she supposed it would be a tremendous waste of time. Bradyn Preston would do exactly as he wanted. Of that much she was absolutely certain. So instead, she said, "Yes. He was killed in the First Battle of Bull Run." She looked up at him.

"Did he wear the grey or the blue?" Bradyn asked as he wiped his hands on the edge of the table cloth. The sandwich and potatoes were nothing more than a few crumbs littering the spotted blue tin plate now.

"My Poppa called the War the 'just another squabble

over tea'," she answered as she took up scrubbing the pants again.

Bradyn raised his eyebrows. "Another squabble over tea?" he asked. "That's the first time I've ever heard the War Between the States called that."

Rian nodded and kept right on washing. "My Poppa was a funny sort of man. He never owned a slave. Never a one, mind you. He didn't even think it was right or just to hold a man in servitude. But when it came to that war..." She looked at Bradyn. He gave her a questioning look, as if asking her why she hadn't finished the sentence. The truth was she didn't know how to finish it. She had never known how.

"I remember the day we heard that the South had declared succession from the Union. It was on my birthday. February 4, 1861. I had just turned seven years-old. My mother threw me a little tea party...all my friends were there. We were all dressed in our Sunday finest. I was young. Too young to understand the gravity of the situation, much less why my father would be going away to war." Rian sighed with sad memory. "I asked my Poppa, 'Why must people have wars? Why must they fight and kill each other?' And do you know what he said to me?"

"What?"

"He told me that for him it always boiled down to tea. He said that some bigger men than him had once fought a terrible king because of some miserable tea. 'They dumped it all in the bay one night,' he told me. I asked him why. He told me that it was because, when it came right down to it, they would rather be without their tea than lose their freedom. 'So you see, Moriana,' he said, 'this War is just another squabble over tea.' I was too little to understand it then, but the day I watched him ride away to war, I remember thinking, 'My Poppa's wearing that pretty gray uniform because he wants his freedom more than he wants his tea.'"

Rian turned to Bradyn and gave him a weak smile. "My mother never talked about the war. When we received word that he'd been killed a few months later, she shut it up inside and never breathed a word about it after. I think, in her heart, she had known he wouldn't make it back. When he left, I heard her call it a 'fool's errand'. And I think she was right." She turned back to scrubbing.

They were both quiet. The only sound that filled the room was the continual slapping and sloshing of the jeans as Rian washed them. She felt Bradyn's eyes on her when she wrung them out one final time and hung them on a peg next to the washroom door to dry.

After adding some wood to the cook stove she went to get another bucket of water. It hadn't been so bad telling Bradyn about her father. As long as the conversation steered clear of her scars and the reason she had come to the Territory, she didn't mind answering a single question he asked. But the problem was that her past was all connected. After all, it was *her* past. If he got started asking a lot of questions, inevitably the questions would start hitting closer and closer to home. She couldn't have that. Not yet anyway.

When she came back into the kitchen with the second bucket of water, Bradyn yawned loudly. "I think I'm going to lie down for a while," he said.

Rian felt relief. "Yes, I would expect that you are very tired. I'll heat some more whiskey and willow bark powder," she said.

"No!" Bradyn put up a hand and softened his voice with a smile. "No, that's not necessary. A shot of whiskey will do me. I'm just tired…the pain isn't too bad right now. If I start hurtin', I'll let you know."

Rian was too happy to hear that he wouldn't be hovering around the kitchen anymore to insist that he take the medicine. "All right," she said. "Just call me if you need anything." She poured a shot of brandy into his empty coffee mug.

Bradyn swallowed the brandy and put his cup in the dish tub. "Thanks. I'll probably see ya later."

"Sleep well," she replied. Over his shoulder, she caught a glimpse of the quilt lying forgotten on the bench next to the front door. *I'm going to wash that. Might was well, since I'm doing laundry anyway. Then I am going to have a hot bath.*

Wondering if they should be expecting another unwelcome caller today, her eyes darted to the Winchester hanging over the pantry door. *I'll take the gun with me this time…just in case.*

* * * *

Bradyn pulled back the sheets and wearily sank into bed, Rian's story fresh on his mind. He felt for her. *Sounds like she's lost just about everybody that meant anything to her. We have that in common. Maybe one day I'll tell her that. Maybe I'll let her know that I understand the hurt of losing the ones you love, too.*

Bradyn guessed that losing her father in the War was just the tip of the iceberg. It gave him a new perspective of Rian Keene. He decided that she wore a thick shell around her emotions to keep him, or anyone else, from getting to know the woman that lived inside because she was afraid of losing again. The desire to get below her marble veneer enticed him. He wanted to know Rian more than he'd ever wanted to know a woman in his life.

Listening to her, busy about the kitchen, Bradyn imagined her differently. The picture of a young gypsy girl running through a flowered glade captured his mind. It was both fantasy and memory. Though Bradyn, for the life of him, couldn't say how that should be so. *It's that trick sense of déjà vu again.*

He thought it might take him awhile to drift right off to sleep. His mind was so captured with the circumstances of the day and the gnawing feeling that somehow he knew Rian from somewhere. But, the gentle sounds of her working in the next room lulled him. He rolled onto his side and stared out the window that faced the west. The rain still drizzled down. His eyes grew heavy with sleep. Soon his thoughts were full of grassy meadows that smelled faintly of daffodils. A beautiful gypsy girl danced there. Her laughter mixed with the laughter of a man and carried to him through the trees.

Now, why the hell am I remembering Rian as a gypsy? The thought was vague as sleep pulled him into its warm cradle.

And who is laughing with her?

Chapter Five

Hazy smoke and the gaiety of laughter filled the Silver Lady Saloon. A group of rowdy cowboys stood at the bar whooping it up raucously after a long week on the range. Though barely audible over the din of gambling men, clattering glasses, tinkling coins, rattling dice, and noisy women, the piano clinked away, lending itself to the crescendo of infernal racket.

Contessa Lang sat on the bar, twisting an unruly strand of curly blond hair around her index finger nonchalantly. *Liam is in a piss-poor mood tonight*, she thought with sour frustration. He had been in the same dismal dumps for nearly a week, ever since he'd come back from Denver, but tonight his mood was worse. Tessa wasn't used to being ignored and Liam had barely spoken a word to her all day. He was angry at her. He had been ever since he'd found out about her fling with Bradyn Preston.

Tessa had not denied it. She hadn't seen the point. Sure she'd cheated on him. But Bradyn Preston had been a beautiful man. What girl in her right mind wouldn't have jumped at the chance to be romanced by the good-looking stranger? And it isn't as if Liam hadn't indulged in a few of his own romantic wanderings here and there, Tessa reasoned waspishly.

Take his Denver trips for instance. Tessa had known all along that he was seeing some chorus girl from St. Louis every time he went to Denver on "business." Besides, she had never promised her heart to Liam Briggs. Tessa Lang was just a pretty girl out to have a little fun. And when a pretty, adventurous girl owned a saloon, fun came walking through the door most every night of the week and at least twice on Saturday.

"That bastard is a loose canon!" Tessa heard Liam's tyrannical shouting from his usual table in the back of the saloon. She watched with irritated humor as he slapped the table's top. Liam was yelling at his brother, Cameron. "I want to know what's taking him so long. I want to know if he's killed Preston or if I need to send a son of a bitch with a backbone and some guts out to finish 'im off."

Tessa rolled her eyes. It was the same tired rant Liam had been riding for over five days now. Tessa smiled impishly. Served him right. Liam Briggs thought he was practically God in Laramie. It was about time something didn't go according to plan for him.

"Tessa!" Liam's impatient, resonant voice bellowed across the room, turning heads as it carried to her over the noisy saloon.

Sliding off the bar with the slinky grace of a cat, Tessa grab a tumbler of whiskey and sauntered through a group of cowboys standing around drinking and laughing. As she passed through their midst, they all exchanged appreciative glances. Everybody knew she was Briggs's girl, but that didn't stop them from looking. No sir. And every once in a while, some wayfaring stranger or dumb, love-struck jackass decided to tempt fate and take her for a ride. Heaven help the poor man who enjoyed a whirlwind romance in Tessa Lang's arms. He wouldn't live to brag about it -- that much was certain. Liam Briggs was a very jealous man.

"What is it, Liam?" she crooned in her sweetest, most accommodating voice. She bridled the irritated smirk that played at the corners of her mouth when she noted that he sized her up from head to toe. She'd worn his favorite tonight. The red crushed-velvet dress she'd ordered all the way from New York City. It exploited all of her curves in just the right way. She knew no amount of anger could keep him from noticing how stunning she was.

Tessa saw Liam's desire ignite when his eyes came to rest

on her face. He patted a thigh, and Tessa sat down. Kissing her cheek, he whispered a dirty promise into her ear and Tessa's soft, sultry laugh made him smile.

Tessa handed him the drink she'd brought from the bar. "Here, baby," she whispered. "You look like you could use this."

Liam's steel grey eyes, as cold as ice and as deceivingly beautiful as the Devil when he tempted Eve, caught a lurid sparkle. He was an attractive man, tall and well-muscled. His ruddy coloring and vibrant red hair were in keeping with his arrogant personality and short-fuse temper. Liam reminded Tessa of a Hereford bull. What with his sizeable physique and pension for snorting and trampling his adversaries into the ground, he was a dead-ringer twin to the big red beasts.

"What about Wes Stebbens?" Cameron was asking.

"No, I don't want Wes to go out there. He hasn't got the nerve to handle Preston, that's why Cheyenne Joe sent him back in the first place. For shit's sake, Cameron, I swear you couldn't get a slow, little, old lady killed with a cattle stampede!" Liam's tone was abrasive and condescending. He talked to his younger brother as if he were five instead of twenty-seven.

Taking a sip of the whiskey, he absentmindedly ran a hand down Tessa's back. She recognized the look in his eyes. Liam was "cogitating," his big-city business word for "thinking of a good, solid plan of action."

"I need someone new," he said at length. "Someone who doesn't know much about Preston or give a damn why I want him dead. A guy who's mentally sharp and dead-eye accurate with a gun, preferably at long range," he muttered under his breath. His hand brushed her hip and ran along her slender thigh.

"Baby, do you have to discuss this now?" Tessa protested. "Why don't you just enjoy a drink or two with the boys and forget about this whole silly business, hmmm?" She rubbed his hand, now resting on her knee, provocatively.

When she pursed her lips into a sultry pout, Liam jerked

his hand free and pushed her from his lap. "Shut your mouth, Tessa," he spat. "What's the matter? Don't you like hearing how I plan to kill the pretty bastard you bedded behind my back?"

As he slurred the last few words, Tessa wished she hadn't brought him the drink. Liam was already quite inebriated and now he was fast approaching the state of sheer belligerence. Instead of telling him exactly what she thought of his ridiculous jealousy and excessive drinking, Tessa rolled her eyes and decided to play the spineless, shrinking violet for a few minutes longer to humor him.

"I really don't care who you plan on knocking off, baby. I just thought you might like to have some fun tonight." She touched his cheek and veiled the sudden repulsion that crept over her. "Doesn't that sound good, Liam?" She leaned down and kissed his ear while running a finger over his lips. "You still want me don't you, baby?" she whispered softly.

With her smile, she hinted sweet, fleshy promises. Liam closed his eyes for a second. She knew he wanted her. When he opened them again, she saw the anger. He wasn't going to let her beauty help him forget. Tessa realized that this time, she wouldn't be allowed to gain his forgiveness with a night of passion.

"Not tonight, Tessa," he growled as he shoved past her and headed to the bar for another shot of bourbon.

Tessa watched him go in disgust. How dare he insult and humiliate her in front of her entire saloon? The lofty, self-righteous, pharisaical swine! To add insult to injury, he dared to play the part of the wounded lover. Him, of all people! How many times had she borne up under his indiscretions and adulteries? How many times had she played the adoring, kowtowing, *forgiving* one? How many times had she been the brunt of his condescending, patronizing rebukes and insults?

Not any longer, Tessa decided. *If you want to play it that way, fine, Liam. We'll play it that way. You will regret the day you ever crossed me. I'll make sure of it.* She had resources at her own disposal. Resources Liam Briggs had absolutely no knowledge about, or, more aptly put, resources he had completely forgotten she possessed. Tessa ran her tongue over her upper lip and smoothed her gown down her thigh. She would show him.

She watched as Liam drank another shot in a single swallow and, pounding his glass down on the bar, stormed out of the saloon with his brother and a couple of his hired guns in tow. Her mouth formed a bitter smirk. Cold anger seeped into her soul. *What is that saying? Something to the effect of Hell's fury being nothing compared to a woman who'd been double-crossed and double-dealt…or is the proper word "scorned"?* She couldn't remember, but it didn't matter much anyway. Liam Briggs had mistreated her one too many times. Now he was gonna pay for it. And he was gonna pay in spades.

"Trouble in paradise?" A cool, deep voice behind her caused Tessa to turn.

Green eyes, the color of Russian emeralds, were watching her with scintillating interest. Contessa Lang had seen and entertained many, many men in her lifetime. Some had been very rich and attractive, but few had ever struck her as indisputably magnificent. And, in a word, this man was exactly that: magnificent. Several inches taller than Liam, he was broad-shouldered and muscularly slender. His wavy blond hair was glossy under the saloon lamps.

The clothing he wore was expensive and polished. Very few men in the Territory dressed with such sophistication. Tessa decided that he was clearly from Boston or New York. Or possibly from somewhere further south like Savannah or Charleston, where gentility and fashion were as much a part of a man as a gun and holster were in the Wyoming Territory. His dress and carriage spoke to his gentlemen's status. The look he was giving her at the moment told Tessa, with blinding clarity, that he was indeed also a man.

Attraction aside, Tessa was in no mood to deal with another man tonight. Paying customer or not. She had too much on her mind. Too much she needed to think through.

"Can I help you, sir?" she asked. She knew that the edges of her smile were a dry and crumbling attempt at friendliness.

"Maybe you can. I was told that the gentleman who just walked away from your table is looking for a hired gun. Is that true?"

His virescent eyes searched hers with a vague hint of humor. He must have heard most of the exchange between her and Liam, Tessa supposed irritably. Nettled, her reply was unnecessarily short, "I wouldn't know. Why don't you go ask him?"

A perfectly arched eyebrow rose and the twinkle still remained in his eyes as he glanced around the saloon and then brought his gaze back to her. "Maybe you can tell me where to find him. He seems to have exited the establishment."

Tessa knew she was being excessively abrupt with the man and, attractive as he was, she regretted it. A little. Her response was less curt. "You might try Hodge's Cattleman Hotel. That's where Briggs hangs his hat when he's in Laramie." *Or, at least he has for the past nine nights. Ever since he quit hanging it on my bedpost.*

The tall, handsome stranger stood watching her for a moment or two. It appeared he couldn't quite decide whether he wanted to stay and chat or go in search of Liam. Finally, offering a dashing smile and a flourishing half-bow, he turned to leave.

"I am very much obliged. Perhaps, when I've finished my business with Mr. Briggs, I'll come back and buy you a drink, yes? It's so rare that I get the opportunity to enjoy the company of a woman as lovely as you."

His charming smile and flattering manner were contagious and Tessa was surprised to find she wanted him to buy her a drink after all. "Of course," she answered, returning his smile with one of her own. She didn't allow herself the time to think of a good excuse to say no. After all, why should she? She was a free agent. A grown woman capable of deciding with whom she wanted to spend her time. And besides, the man was gorgeous. Tessa's smiled widened in anticipation. "I shall look forward to it."

"*Au revoir* for now, then. I *will* be back."

His eyes, so utterly, brilliantly green, sparkled with

irresistible intrigue. Tessa thought they were the most mesmerizing set of eyes she had ever seen.

She watched him go with a funny little flutter in her stomach. The sudden intuition that this handsome stranger was going to play a very important part in her life passed briefly through her mind. She smiled. At any rate, he promised to be great fun. And maybe if the man was as good with a gun as he seemed to imply, Liam may have met his match. In spades…

* * * *

Liam's dark mood worsened when he got back to his room at the Cattleman Hotel. The baby blue wallpaper embellished with scrolling golden roses irritated the piss out of him. Every stick of fancy furniture, every scrap of expensive cloth, felt cheap and tawdry to him. It was not because he hadn't rented the most lavish suite in the place, but because when it came right down to it, the room just wasn't right without Tessa.

Part of him, the drunken, sniveling man inside, wanted to run back to the Silver Lady, to take Tessa to the room that they had always shared, *their* room, and make passionate love to her. Forgive and forget. *"You're a fool to try to live without her,"* the cowardly, lonely voice accused.

But the other half of him, the part of him that felt the pride of a stubborn man, the part that was hurt and angry, said, *"No. Tessa crossed you. Don't you dare forget that."* Liam knew he wouldn't be happy until she was sobbing and contrite. He wanted to see her groveling at his feet begging for his forgiveness and for entrance back into his good graces. Begging him to take her back. Begging him to make love to her. Telling him she could never live without him.

Contessa Lang was the most sensually infuriating woman he had ever met in his life. Her offer to bed him resurfaced in his mind. *"You still want me don't you, baby?"*

Liam slammed his fist against an expensive oak dresser. He wanted her alright, but he wanted to *own* her; body and soul. The problem with Tessa was that she was just too stupid to know a good thing when she had it. He would have given her anything her heart desired. But she had spit on it, and on him, by frolicking around behind his back.

Pulling his tie from his neck, Liam walked to the side board and poured himself a shot of bourbon. The knock at his door interrupted his glass halfway to his lips. Gulping the drink in one swallow, he crossed the room and, cursing under his breath, flung open the door. He was fully expecting to find Cameron standing there with a customary look of stupidity on his face. He was surprised to find someone very different indeed. He shook his head in disbelief.

"Bodeen?" he asked, his voice an intoxicated slur.

"It's me, Briggs." Kyle Bodeen nodded. "Surprised?"

Kyle's vibrant green eyes glowed with the ever-present look of one who'd just heard something that was very humorous. Liam shook his head again, trying to clear his alcohol-shrouded mind. He rubbed a hand across his eyes. "Yeah, yeah, I'm surprised. I thought you got your ass killed in Texas."

Kyle laughed heartily. "Not quite. Got my ass *shot,* but I made it. Magnus Kendrick will think twice before he tries to shoot me in the back again."

"Magnus? Magnus is the one who tried to kill you?!" Liam stepped back and gestured Kyle through the door.

"*Tried* being the operative word," Kyle replied. He stepped into the room and Liam shut the door behind him. "But it's behind me now. Magnus Kendrick's killing days are long over. Seems he has a little trouble holding a gun these days."

"What?" Liam asked, blinking with confusion. He still hadn't wrapped his head around the fact that Kyle Bodeen wasn't dead.

"To hear it told Magnus seems to be missing his hands." Kyle said matter-of-factly.

His eyes sparkled with a new humor that was cold and ruthless. The expression made Liam feel an uneasy tremor run up his back. "Huh? Missing his hands…what're you talking about?" he asked.

Kyle must have found the confused expression on his face funny, because he broke into a fit of laughter. "You sure are stuck out here in the woods, aren't you, Briggs?" he hooted. "I thought surely you'd heard. When I found out it was Kendrick who'd shot me, I tracked him down first thing and when I found him, I cut off his hands. That was the last time the bastard will lay in wait to shoot a man in the back. I made sure of it."

"Damn!" Liam swore and twisted his face in disgust. "You are one mean son of a bitch, Bodeen. Can't say as I blame you, though. I'd have done the same if I had been in your shoes." Liam poured another drink and downed it. "Cut off his hands," he murmured under his breath. Then, remembering his unexpected guest, he said, "Have a seat, Bodeen. Drink?"

"No, thank you." Kyle sat down on a blue velvet divan and pulled a cigar from his breast pocket. "I could use a light though."

"Sure thing." Liam nodded as he fished a match out of his pocket. "So what brings you to the great city of Laramie?"

He wasn't certain, but Liam thought he detected a note of appraisal on Kyle's face. "Personal business," he replied pointedly. "I was in the Silver Lady Saloon and happened to hear that my old friend, Liam Briggs, was looking for a gunman to take care of some unpleasant business. Thought maybe you could use the best."

"Meaning you?" Liam nodded and narrowed his eyes for a moment. The new idea was fresh and welcome to his ears. Kyle was more than capable of taking care of Preston. He rubbed his chin thoughtfully. "Yeah, I could definitely use you for that little matter. Would mean a lot to me to get the job done right, for sure."

"You want to fill me in?" Kyle inhaled and rolled cigar smoke around in his mouth before exhaling a bluish-gray plume that swirled toward the ceiling.

"Guy named Preston. Maybe you've heard of him? Showed up here while I was in Denver a few weeks back. Unpleasant sort of character. The type that likes to dig up things better left buried, if you get my drift." Liam didn't much feel like bringing up the fact that the man had managed to bed his woman as well.

Kyle nodded slowly. "*Bradyn* Preston?" he asked. His face was devoid of emotion.

Liam widened his eyes in surprise. "That's the man. You know him then?"

"His half-brother is a marshal. I had a run-in with him in Cheyenne a year or so back. Jared Dawson turned that town into Sunday school and knitting bees. Made it right hard for the rowdy crowd to have any fun. He closed down half the saloons and cathouses in the place for illegal activities of one kind or another." Kyle took another drag off his cigar and another cloud of acridly sweet smoke filled the room.

Liam studied his tumbler as Kyle continued; "Now Preston was a bit of a different card than Dawson. He had a wild streak a country mile wide when he was younger. His older brother wasn't too fond of it. I heard that Dawson bailed Preston out of one hell of a big jam down in Denver a few years back. Preston owed him big so Dawson put him to work as a deputy marshal for awhile. But, Preston and his brother don't get along so well. Last I heard Preston was in California or Montana or someplace."

Kyle paused and looked at Briggs thoughtfully for a moment. "I'll say one thing for him," he added, "Preston is damn good with a gun. I actually had the pleasure of making his acquaintance, briefly, a few years ago. Back when he was still on the other side of the law, that is. Saw him kill a man in a square gunfight in Tulsa about two years before I met you. I'd say from his reputation he's made quite a list of enemies. I think more than a few men would be happy to see him *and* his marshal brother dead and pine-boxed. Can't say as I'm too fond of the notion of going up against either of them in a gun fight though. Heard a few weeks back that Dawson was here in Laramie, is that right?"

"Nope. I got rid of him about a month ago. The marshal was noising around, trying to put me up on murder charges of some kind. The bastard had a nice little hunting accident. Somebody mistook him for a mule deer and shot him with a

Winchester at four hundred yards." Liam noted with satisfaction that Kyle was clearly impressed.

"No fooling?' he asked. "You hire guns to kill all your enemies, do ya, Briggs?"

"Sure," Liam retorted. Pride swelled in his chest and he curled his lip in a sneer. "I'm too busy running my ranch and this town to bother with a little nuisance blood letting. That's what money is for, Bodeen."

"Interesting," Kyle replied, his face still unreadable.

There was another pause and another burst of hazy smoke curled from Kyle's lips.

"Well, I'm happy to handle this one for you, Briggs. But it's gonna cost you. I've seen Preston in action and he's fast."

It was Liam's turn to laugh. "Don't tell me you're going to be honorable and face him in a square gunfight?!"

"I don't shoot men in the back, Briggs. It's uninspiring and tasteless to me. Besides, I like the challenge. I'll face him head-on and it's gonna cost you five thousand dollars. Sound fair?" Kyle fixed his face with the steel expression of negotiation and watched him closely.

Liam had poured another drink and taken a sip midway through Kyle's sentence. Now he spit the bourbon out of his mouth and coughed fitfully. "Five thousand dollars! Are you out of your head? Preston's neck ain't worth five hundred dollars. Besides, I got at least two men who I know can handle a rifle at five hundred yards or better. Of course, they won't be facing Preston in a square gunfight, but he'll be just as dead and I'll be just as happy. And I won't spend five thousand dollars getting the job done either."

Kyle shrugged and the perpetual look of humor crept back into his eyes again.

"Have it your way, Briggs. When you're ready to let me take care of Preston for you, just let me know." He rose to leave and extended his palm in a friendly hand shake.

"Thanks all the same, Bodeen, but I think I have this one handled." Liam took Kyle's out-stretched hand and shook it once, stiffly.

Kyle shrugged again. "Well you might, and then again, you may lose a hell of a lot of men before you get the job done. Preston's no damn fool. He's survived living on both sides of the law for a long time. A man doesn't do that without having some guts and a whole lot of gray matter. Think about it, Briggs. Five thousand dollars for a job done right may save you a lot of trouble when it's all said and done." Kyle pulled his hat back on his head and left the room while Liam looked on in vexation.

* * * *

The night air was cool and the streets of Laramie were deserted as Kyle Bodeen exited the hotel and headed back up the plank sidewalk to the Silver Lady Saloon. Whistling a merry tune, he gazed up at the three-quarter moon hanging pale and desolate in the night sky.

Soon. Frenzied anticipation began to course through his veins. *Very soon now I'll take care of what I came here to finish. I know you're near, I can feel it. I can't see your aura yet, but I can almost taste it, you're so close. It's been a long time since we last saw each other. You might have thought you beat me then, but this time* I *am going to win."* His chuckle was humorless as he grinned up at the moon.

Seeing his old friend, Briggs, had been an invigorating experience. Kyle knew without a doubt, that Briggs would need him to finish Preston. *Briggs* just didn't know it yet. Or, perhaps better put, Kyle would need Briggs to help *him* finish Preston. Kyle's smile widened. Either way he could afford to wait. In the meantime, there was a beautiful vixen at the Silver Lady he wanted to get to know. If everything worked out alright, Laramie might prove to be the place Kyle Bodeen hung his hat for awhile.

* * * *

Liam watched Kyle Bodeen leave with a mixture of irritation, uneasiness, and bewilderment. He had no idea how the man had survived a bullet in the back after being shot by Magnus Kendrick. Kendrick's talent with a revolver was legendary, or at least it had been. It sounded as if the mighty Irishman had fired his last shot.

Liam rubbed his head and willed the cloudy fog of alcohol to lift long enough for him to think. The real problem, as he saw it, was that Kyle was right. Preston was a force to be reckoned with. Even Liam knew that Preston's skill with a six gun was impressive. Liam's best bet was to hire Kyle and get it over with. No one could beat Kyle in a gunfight. No one. After all, that was why Liam had hired Magnus Kendrick to shoot the bastard in the back in the first place.

He sighed and poured a shot of bourbon. It was a problem. There was no mistake about it. But he would figure it out. He just needed time to think, and another drink.

There was a knock on his door for the second time that night. True to form, Cameron stood in the hall, hat in hand, the permanent look of sheer stupid on his face. There was something else in his expression as well tonight. Nervousness. Cameron's eyes darted back and forth. It was the irritating trait that always came as the frontrunner to bad news.

"What the hell is it?" Liam roared. His voice carried down the hall and turned the heads of a couple headed to their room for the night.

Cameron cleared his throat, his hands working busily at the brim of his cowboy hat. "It's Cheyenne Joe. His horse came back to the livery tonight without him."

"What?!" Liam's bellow echoed back from the lobby below. "Where the hell is Joe?"

"Wes said the horse just turned up in its stall and Joe ain't no where to be found." Cameron's eyes came to rest on his brother's face, and he flinched slightly.

Enraged, Liam jerked the cowboy hat from his brother's hand and threw it to the floor. "Cut that shit out! It drives me crazy when you get all wall-eyed and sissy. You need to get some guts and backbone to you, Cameron."

Liam crossed the room at a fast pace and came back to stand in front of Cameron. "Damn, Joe!!" he growled. "I told him. You heard me tell him, right, Cameron?" He cast a narrow glance at his brother. "I told that stupid bastard to shoot Preston from a distance! Now the dumb son of a bitch is probably dead and has got Preston wise to the fact I was having him followed!" Liam's fist pummeled the wall sending a wicked crack along the rose-covered wallpaper, exposing some of the plaster and lathe beneath.

"Whatcha gonna do, Liam?" Cameron asked in a quiet voice. His expression betrayed fear, as if he was certain the simple question would send his brother over the edge.

Liam blew out a gush of air and put his hands on his hips as red-hot anger blended with the disorientated equilibrium of his alcohol. "Get Buddy Sanders and Tex Forrester. Tell those two dumb-shits to take two horses each. They are to ride out to Flat Top and find this homestead by tomorrow before noon. Wes knows where it is. Tell him to give 'em directions. If they push their mounts and don't stop for the Devil, they'll have plenty of time to locate Preston. I want them to wait for Preston to set foot outside the house, or start riding out, before they make a move. Tell them if they so much as wiggle a blade of grass in plain sight of Preston, he'll shoot 'em dead. And if he doesn't shoot 'em for it, I will."

Liam paced the room like a caged cougar, his mind whirring too fast for his drunken legs. "I don't want anybody trying to best the son of a bitch in a gun fight or getting a closer look before they finish him. I want him shot at five hundred yards or better. I don't want the piece of shit to know what hit him. I want that bastard dead, Cameron. Dead! And then I want to see his body. Got that?!"

Cameron nodded meekly.

"Good." Liam started for the bourbon decanter for the fifth time since coming into his room. "Let's finish this, little brother."

Liam watched Cameron leave the room. His drunken head was spinning with anger and unquenchable blood-lust. Then a smile of satisfaction tugged at his mouth. Maybe with Preston gone, he would know a little peace for once.

* * * *

Tessa was sitting on the bar, distractedly listening to a drunk cowboy's sad attempt at coherent conversation, when the handsome stranger returned. He caught her gaze from across the room and smiled. Tessa smiled back, relishing the flutter in her stomach and sudden quickening of her heartbeat. He was so deplorably handsome.

She eased off the bar as he came toward her. "I see you decided to come back after all. I thought maybe Liam had made you a better offer for the night." Tessa winked as he drew up next to her and took off his hat.

"Of course I came back," he answered. He lifted her hand to his mouth and kissed the tips of her fingers. "How could I resist?"

"Well now, how do you like that? A gentleman *and* a man of your word," Tessa quipped. "Will miracles never cease?" The teasing smile she directed at him took the edge off her sarcasm. She nodded at the bartender who promptly came to their end of the counter.

"Elijah, get this man whatever he wants," she instructed. Her eyes never left the handsome stranger's face. "The drinks are on me tonight."

"I'll have a Scotch. Double, if you please, bartender." He leaned in close to Tessa and looked into her eyes. "Beautiful and generous. Will miracles never cease?"

His crooked smile and intense stare made her stomach whirl. Tessa laughed. "You got a name, stranger?" she asked.

"Sure do, but just now it seems to have slipped my mind." He chuckled. "It's been so long since I heard a pretty woman laugh."

Tessa waved her hand dismissively as Elijah returned with a tumbler of Scotch. "Ah, come on now. None of that two-bit, range hand flattery. It doesn't become you. I'm certain that I am not the first attractive female you've seen in the Territory. And I know that you're far too intelligent to have forgotten your own name." She handed him his drink. "So?"

"Name's Bodeen. Kyle Bodeen." He took a long, slow sip of the Scotch. He studied her face over the rim of the crystal glass. "What's yours?"

"Contessa Lang," she replied. "But just plain Tessa to my friends and customers."

"Well, I don't know about that now. There doesn't seem to be anything plain about you, darlin'." Kyle assessed her from head to toe in a manner that would have made a lesser woman blush, but Tessa just smiled up at him. "Nothing plain at all."

"Thank you." She put a hand on her hip, touched her tongue to her upper lip, and raised an eyebrow. "So did you settle your business with Liam Briggs?"

Kyle's green eyes caught a steely glint before he smiled and the humorous sparkle came back to them. "In a manner of speaking," he answered. "But that would be between him and I, now wouldn't it?"

Tessa shrugged and did not let her curiosity or irritation show. "Anything you say," she answered, putting a cool touch to her voice. "If you'll excuse me for a moment, I need to see to my other patrons. Just let Elijah know if you need another drink."

Kyle grabbed her arm gently as she started to turn away. "Hold on a minute, I distinctly remember you agreeing to have a drink with me. Isn't that right? Now, I am not about to let you walk away without making good on *your* word."

His smile was irresistible. Tessa felt her insides turn to butter. She pushed her irritation away. She could find out what he and Liam had talked about later. Right now, she could think of nothing more enjoyable than an hour or two of drinks and flirtation. "Alright," she winked. "But you just better watch yourself. I've got a jealous fella."

Kyle raised an eyebrow. "A man that lets you wander around dressed like that, in a place like this, alone? He must be pretty jealous alright." He took another sip of his drink. "Or completely insane. I wouldn't let you a minute out of my sight if you were my woman. Who's your man? Liam Briggs?"

Tessa demurred. She wasn't going to let the conversation steer toward Liam unless *she* was the one getting some information. "So how long have you been in town, Kyle?"

"Just came in on the train this afternoon. Thought a change of scenery would be nice." The hard glitter came back into his emerald eyes for a brief moment.

"Where are you from?" Tessa asked, silently hoping that he would say Savannah or better yet, New York City.

"I come from all over. But most recently, Reno." He took another taste of the Scotch. "How about you? I think it's fair to guess a girl that looks as good as you do isn't from around here." He raised his glass in a sweeping motion and glanced around the room briefly before offering his most dashing smile.

"I'm from all over too, you might say," Tessa returned evenly. "But I've lived in Laramie for nearly three years. My longest stay anywhere to date."

"I'll drink to that." Kyle started to take another sip and then paused. "Where's your drink?" he asked when he noticed she wasn't sharing the toast.

Tessa winked. "Hey, Elijah! Get me a shot of Scotch! And bring another round for the gentleman. Heck, just bring us the bottle!"

Every head at the bar turned when Tessa called to the bartender. There was a lull in conversation as most of the cowboys took notice that Tessa was buying a drink for someone who was not Liam Briggs. Tessa Lang had a strict policy about buying drinks for customers; she didn't. Tessa laughed inside. *Oh, Liam is going to be so mad when he hears about this!*

When Elijah brought her the drinks, his face was a cool expression of concealed worry, though he didn't say a word. However, the silent question in his eyes, *"What the hell are you doing?"* was loud and clear as he slid her drink across the bar and put the bottle of Scotch down next to it. Tessa ignored his tight-mouthed stare and grabbed the tumbler.

"Thank you, Elijah," she said dismissively as she lifted her glass to Kyle. "Now what were we drinking to again?"

"New beginnings," Kyle answered. His tumbler clinked against hers. "Let's drink to new beginnings."

Tessa nodded. "That's the best toast I've heard all day," she said and downed the shot in a single swallow. "So where are you planning to stay while you enjoy the scenic city of Laramie?"

"I have a place in mind." Kyle's eyes grew full of smoldering insinuation and Tessa felt tingles run from the top of her head to the tip of her toes.

"Sounds mysterious. You mind telling me where this 'place' is?" She couldn't help but envision running her fingers through his hair as they lay wrapped in crimson sheets. The mental picture made her legs weak and her breath come in a short, quick burst. Tessa grabbed the bottle of Scotch, poured another shot, and drank it. This man was going to be too easy. And Liam was going to be so angry. Tessa didn't know which was more exciting; making Liam sick with jealousy, or the thought of sharing her bed with Kyle Bodeen.

Just then a group of ten or twelve cowboys exploded through the door. They were fresh off the range and in search of a grand time. The noise in the saloon tripled in that instant.

"Is there somewhere quiet we can go to continue this conversation?" Kyle asked over the roar of the hectic saloon.

Tessa's slow, enticing smile worked its way across her mouth. She leaned up against him, her eyes full of wild, erotic promise. Her lips brushed across his ear with complete seduction.

"I thought you would never ask," she whispered. "Follow me."

Edgy anticipation grew inside her as she grabbed the bottle of Scotch and pulled him in the direction of the stairs.

Chapter Six

It had been three days since they had buried Cheyenne Joe and, at times, Rian could almost forget the whole damnable, bloody incident had ever happened. Almost. Of course, there was the dark blood stain left on the guestroom floor, Bradyn's presence, and Kendall's ever-present need to talk about the whole mess. Still, she had managed to push the recollection from her mind at least three or four times a day. The blood stain had been dealt with easily enough. She had pulled the woven rug from under the kitchen table and put it over the gruesome memento. Bradyn and Kendall were not as easily ignored.

Rian had barely exchanged ten words with Bradyn since the evening after they'd laid Cheyenne Joe's carcass to rest in a muddy grave. Fortunately, he had slept for the better part of the past two days. The time she was forced to spend around him was limited to the few minutes it took to clean his stitches or bring him food, which she found easier than enduring a tense meal with him seated at the kitchen table while Kendall went on and on about Bradyn's skill with a gun.

Several times already she'd had to tell Kendall to refrain from speaking about "Bradyn's shoot-out with the outlaw", as he'd decided to dub the incident. At first, Kendall had protested, but after awhile, he grew tired of being hushed and settled into a quiet reflective mood. It troubled her to look over at him and see the far away, dreamy expression on his face, but she didn't mind the silence. In fact, it suited her just fine.

She was having an emotional struggle. While she was grateful that Bradyn had saved their lives from a horrible fate, she knew that if it had not been for his presence in their home in the first place, she and Kendall would not have needed rescue.

Rian also had the solid suspicion that this Briggs fellow had a bigger reason for wanting Bradyn dead. Or a bigger reason than Bradyn let on, anyway. There had to be more to it than the explanation he had given her the night before Cheyenne Joe had shown up at her door. She didn't think a mere romance between Bradyn and Briggs' woman, Contessa Lang, was enough of a reason for the man to pursue Bradyn so relentlessly. Especially after the sound beating Briggs had already given him.

She wanted to understand what had happened to incite someone to chase Bradyn with a hired gunman. She'd almost asked Bradyn once. But then, she'd thought better of it. If she wanted information from him, he'd most certainly want information in return. And, even though he'd asked no more perturbing meddlesome questions, at least not aloud, he had asked them often enough with his eyes.

* * * *

The rain was coming down in a dreary drizzle on the eighth morning of Bradyn's stay in their home. He had apparently decided that he no longer needed to rest, and had settled himself at the kitchen table for breakfast after making himself a pot of coffee. Rian had been stiffly polite and Kendall, ecstatic. Breakfast had been mercifully quiet, though not without its awkwardness.

After all of her regular chores were finished, Rian decided it was about time she altered some of Jackson's clothes to fit Bradyn. Or at least sewed him a shirt. It was the kind thing to do since his only clothing was the clean, but torn, jeans he'd shown up in. The memory of Bradyn in Jackson's clothes brought an unwilling smile to her lips. They hadn't fit him worth a lick.

Rian announced her plans to fit Bradyn over a late lunch later that day. "I think I'm going to start sewing a few things for you to wear," she told him as she spooned mashed potatoes onto Kendall's plate.

Bradyn raised an eyebrow, as if he saw reason why going about shirtless and in his own torn drawers would be unacceptable, but he simply replied, "Thank you."

"You're gonna make him some new clothes?" Kendall asked around a mouth full of bread.

"Yes, Kendall," she said. "Please do not speak with food in your mouth."

Kendall swallowed and took a gulp of milk before asking, "We don't have much cloth left for sewing clothes, do we? What're you gonna use to make him clothes?"

Out of the corner of her eye, Rian caught the curious look Bradyn passed her. "I'm going to alter a few of your father's shirts for him, honey," she answered. "I think that we can afford to share with Mr. Preston, don't you? We can't allow him to leave with nothing on his back, can we?"

Kendall frowned and rubbed his forehead with the back of his hand. "You're leavin', Mr. Bradyn?" he asked, his eyes reflecting disappointment. "Can't you stay a little longer?"

"Mr. Preston is welcome to stay on for awhile, but sooner or later, he will have to be on his way, honey. You cannot expect him to give up his life and stay here forever. Isn't that right, Mr. Preston?" She turned to look at Bradyn, a stiff smile cramping the corners of her mouth.

Bradyn cleared his throat, about to answer, only to be interrupted by Kendall.

"Why don't you like Mr. Bradyn?" he asked her.

Rian coughed nervously. "I like Mr. Bra--, I mean, Mr. Preston, Kendall. I just know that he isn't going to want to stay around here indefinitely. We have to be realistic about these things, sweetie."

"But he saved us from the bad man!" Kendall protested. "What if more bad men come and he's not here to save us?" The little boy turned to Bradyn. "Why don't you stay with us for awhile, just in case?" he entreated, his eyes wide and pleading.

"Well, I don't know," Bradyn put down his fork and rested his elbows on the table. "I'm not sure your aunt wants me around here. I'll only stay if she asks me to." He caught her eye and winked.

"You'd let him stay, wouldn't ya, Rian?" Kendall begged. "I know you don't like him, but I really want him to stay with us."

"Kendall," Rian said uncomfortably, "I like Mr. Preston. He's a fine person, I am sure. Now please go feed the chickens," she said before either of them could interject to add their own thoughts. "And see about gathering up those eggs. You neglected to do that this morning."

"But—"

"Kendall!" she scolded, instantly regretting the harsh tone of her voice. "I asked you to do something, young man. Now you go feed those chickens before the rain gets any heavier. We'll discuss this matter later, is that understood?"

Kendall nodded and scurried out the door without a sound.

"Harsh."

Bradyn's voice set her teeth on edge as she watched Kendall through the kitchen window. She could hear the laughter in his tone, even though he must have thought better of letting it escape his lips.

She rose from her chair and glared at him. "What's that supposed to mean, exactly?"

"You make a very bad liar, Miss Keene," he replied, standing up too.

"I would not pride myself on being a liar, either good or bad, Mr. Preston," she snapped, folding her arms across her chest. "Perhaps being able to deceive someone is a trait you admire, but I think that defrauding and misleading people speaks to a flawed nature."

"And yet you just told your nephew that you like me. A lie, and quite an obvious one, since we all know you don't like me one damn bit. How do you justify lying to the kid?" His question, along with his raised eyebrows, was seemingly offered in good natured humor.

Rian didn't take it that way. Feeling quite cornered, she

bit her lip and didn't answer. She owed him no explanation. Irritated, and a little embarrassed that she'd trapped herself in her own argument, she started past Bradyn on her way to find the measuring tape and chalk. But he caught her by the arm.

"Rian," he said quietly. "It doesn't take a smart man to see what's going on. You're hiding from something out here. Something pretty big from the feel of it."

She pulled her arm free and looked down. "Mr. Preston, please—,"

Bradyn put up a hand. "It's all right. Your past is none of my business and I'm not asking you to explain it to me. But I did happen to notice this morning that you're low on coffee and pretty much every other staple in your pantry. That boy is in need of some new clothes and just now he mentioned that you're nearly out of cloth. Tell me something, how have you survived out here for this long?"

Rian closed her eyes for a moment. "Jackson used to make a trip into Laramie once a year for supplies. When he was killed last spring, I didn't know how we'd manage. I've rationed everything as best I could, but..." It was one of her greater, yet less dwelt on, fears. She had no idea what they were going to do once everything ran out. "I guess I just figured we would have to learn to do without a few things," she murmured.

"Tell you what," he said. "Make up a list of everything you need and when I leave, I'll send back your supplies."

"No!" she exclaimed sharply. "You can't send anyone to this house. It's bad enough that you know where we are!"

"Look, Rian," he said. "I have an old friend over in Cheyenne. He ain't much to look at, but I can trust him with my life. He'll bring you everything you need and he won't tell a living soul about you or Kendall or this place. You have my word."

She blinked, suddenly unsure of how she should feel about Bradyn Preston. "I don't understand, you're offering to help us? Why?"

Bradyn sighed. "You saved my life. I owe you. Besides, you're the only one who offered safe hiding to me when I needed it. I feel like I should return the favor."

Rian pondered that for awhile. She wondered if he had an ulterior motive, or if it was just true kindness that had inspired his offer to help. "Thank you," she said at length.

He studied her for a moment; his piercing blue eyes seemed to read her thoughts. "Sure," he replied, heading for the door.

"Where are you going?" Rian asked.

"I need some fresh air," he answered. "I'm gonna see about helping Kendall with those eggs."

She watched him go, perplexed. It seemed that every time she had decided exactly what she thought of that man, he did or said something that completely threw her intuition off. Shaking her head, she went into the guestroom to find her measuring tape and chalk.

After nearly fifteen minutes spent searching drawers and cupboards all over the house, she finally found what she was looking for in her oak hope chest upstairs. Returning to the kitchen, she noted that Kendall and Bradyn still had not come back inside. Out of the corner of her eye, she caught movement through the kitchen window.

The earlier drizzle of moisture had now become a torrential downpour. Bradyn was carrying an armful of chopped wood to the porch. Water soaked his hair and seeped down his arms and chest.

Kendall was skipping along beside him with the basket of eggs swinging from his arm. The boy's clothes and blond hair were completely drenched. He was speaking with animation, his free hand gesticulating wildly. On his face, he wore a happy, lighthearted expression.

Rian's eyes went to Bradyn and narrowed as she watched his handsome face break into a smile. Then he laughed at something Kendall said. The merry resonance of his laughter carried into the house. She shook her head.

Kendall was becoming more than just a bit of a problem. He was completely consumed with his adoration of their guest. He had no idea about Bradyn's past or why evil men were chasing him. He only knew that their lives had been in danger and that Bradyn had saved them; something that even his own father had not been able to do. *He's only six, well nearly seven, but he's still too young to understand the danger* that *man has invited into our lives.* She felt a strange pit in her stomach. The truth was, Bradyn made her feel oddly safe as well.

"Where do you want me to put this wood?' Bradyn asked as they entered. His eyes swept her face with the same unsettling interest that she had become accustomed to seeing in his expression.

"Just set it in the wood box, in the washroom," she said, taking the basket of eggs from Kendall. "I'll take care of these while you two dry off." She frowned. "You're dripping water all over the floor."

Rian set the basket of eggs in the pantry and went to get some towels. Bradyn smiled at her when she handed one to him. "Thanks," he said.

Her cheeks felt warm as she offered him a small smile in return. "You're welcome."

Going back into the kitchen, she dried Kendall's shoulders and hair in a precursory manner. "Run upstairs and change into some dry clothing," she said. "Then use this towel to dry your hair better. When you're finished, you may play in your room while I measure Mr. Preston, all right?"

"Yes, Rian."

The disappointment in Kendall's expression was unmistakable. Rian supposed he wanted to stay and hover around Bradyn some more. As she watched him climb the stairs, she couldn't help but feel a little guilty. For all of his irritating and intimidating habits, Bradyn had been very kind to her nephew.

She caught Bradyn's smile as he, too, watched Kendall leave. When he turned to look at her, the towel in his outstretched hand, a flutter rippled through her stomach.

Hastily, she took the towel back to the washroom. "You're being ridiculous, Rian," she murmured to herself as she hung the wet towel on a peg. "He's just a man, like every other man. Stop being silly."

"Pardon me?"

Rian jumped and spun around. He was standing right behind her, his arms folded and a crocked smile on his lips.

"You must quit doing that!" she said, putting a hand on her chest. "I hate it when people sneak up behind me."

Bradyn chuckled. "Where you talking to yourself?" he asked, his eyes twinkling.

She shook her head. "No," she answered.

He gave her a funny look. "So are you about ready to get this measuring business over with?" he asked.

She nodded. "Let's work in here," she said as she walked out into the kitchen, "that way I'll have plenty of room."

Rian pulled a stool from the corner, set it in the middle of the room, and climbed on top of it. "Come stand right over here," she instructed. "I'll measure your neck first, and then work my way down."

Bradyn did as she asked. As she wrapped the tape gently around his neck, her face was level with his. Level and very close. She felt heat tingle in her cheeks as he watched her. She muttered the measurement and tried to avoid looking him in the eyes.

"Do I scare you?"

His abrupt question caused her to blink and look at him with dazed perplexity. In his expression, she again saw the vague recognition.

"What?" she asked. Her breath caught in her chest as she looked him square in the face. "Whatever would give you that impression?" Flustered, she fumbled as she pulled the tape from around his neck and backed too hurriedly off the stool. Her foot caught in the hem of her skirt and she tripped.

Bradyn grabbed her by the elbow just as she began to topple. He pulled her back up onto the stool with an arm around her waist. Frowning he replied, "You really are a very bad liar, Rian."

"I don't know what you are talking about, Mr. Preston," she said rapidly. She tried to step off the stool correctly this time, but he grasped her firmly by the waist and held her in place.

"Let me go," she ordered.

"There it is again," he said. "Right there in your eyes. Fear. Now why are you afraid of me?"

Rian lowered her head and worked her fingers under his knuckles, trying to break his hold on her. A hand, strong and firm, lifted her chin and forced her to look at him. She was again momentarily bewildered by his handsome face. The lid of his eye was no longer bruised. The cut that had run in a jagged line down his cheek appeared to be a mere scratch now.

She stared at his mouth and willed herself not to look into the eyes that glittered like two sapphires. She was afraid alright. The flutter in her stomach, the ridiculous arrhythmic beating of her heart, the sweat she felt tickling the small of her back; they *all* signaled fear. Fear of the worst kind.

"Look at me," he said quietly.

His voice was strangely warm. Rian reluctantly lifted her eyes to meet his and in that instant the fluttering in her stomach became a churning, whirling tornado. She had no doubt that she would have fallen right off the stool if it wasn't for his hands on her waist.

Piercing, no *electrifying*, blue eyes held hers. It was not precisely a look of passion that he gave her, but it was a look of concern, kindness, and… And what?

Rian didn't honestly know. But if she hadn't known better, she would have let herself think there was tenderness in those eyes. She might have even let herself believe there was affection in his expression, if she hadn't known that the two of them had been unaware of the other's existence not much more than a week before…and if she hadn't known that he probably had a woman waiting for him in Laramie. Of course she realized that it was unlikely for a man to fall in love in eight days, especially since he'd been unconscious four of them, but she could swear before God and men that she saw desire in those penetrating cobalt depths. She was on the verge of trembling, but she stopped herself.

There was a truth in his eyes that she could not deny. Somehow, someway, she knew that she had seen him before. He was so familiar. She couldn't shake the feeling. An image of something that only existed in her subconscious was almost captured in her mind, but then it escaped her. She shook her head. Perhaps it was only déjà vu, but then maybe she really had seen Bradyn Preston somewhere before.

"Tell me," he whispered. His gaze was firm and unyielding.

"Tell you what," she whispered back, her galloping heart blocking both her throat and her ability to breathe. *Where have I seen him before? Where?*

"Tell me why you are afraid of me?"

"I'm not." Her voice shook and she was unable to look away from his eyes now that she had stared into their fiery azure depths. They captivated her. She was enslaved by the blue eyes of a near-stranger. *"He's like a snake…Don't cobras hypnotize their victims with their stare? The Serpent spoke and Eve was lead astray by his beauty…"* she thought with random revelation.

"Then tell me what you *are* afraid of." Bradyn's voice was kind and firm.

Rian did look away then, her mind pensive with conflicting emotion. Even the thought of answering that simple question was staggering in its immensity. It was ludicrous. How could she possibly explain to a man she knew practically nothing about, that everyday for the past seven years she had feared being alone? How could she tell him that this singular fear was enough to make her feel weak, dizzy, and claustrophobic? How could she tell him that if it weren't for Kendall's presence she would have probably taken her own life by now?

And then there was the contrast, and it was more appalling and confounding to her still. How could she possibly elaborate on her ever-present terror of both companionship and intimacy? Would he even be able to begin to understand why she wrestled with two opposing emotions: the need to give and feel love and the absolute gut-wrenching fear of love itself?

Rian saw no point in drawing his attention to the fact that she was no stranger to the pure happiness love could bring to her life. She had, after all, experienced it before, if only for a brief time. Besides, to endeavor to explain the inner workings of her own heart and emotions would only force her to explain her past to him. She wasn't ready to open herself that much to Bradyn Preston. Because, finally, when it came right down to it, she *was* afraid of him. No, more correctly put, she was *terrified* of him. She was frightened that if he didn't go away very soon, she would want him to stay. And, if he stayed, that he would prove to her that love was synonymous with agonizing pain, and that being alone would never equal the desolate and vast emptiness of love unreturned. She had survived it once before, and she had sworn to God she would never go through it again.

"I'm not afraid of you," she repeated, her voice quiet. "I am afraid of what your presence in our home could mean for Kendall and me." She searched his eyes carefully. *Not a lie. Not the whole truth, but definitely not a lie.*

Bradyn's hands loosened on her waist. "You are afraid of the men that may come after me, is that it?"

Rian looked down and nodded. "Yes, that. And…" She blew out a breath, lifting her eyes to his once again. "I'm afraid that perhaps you haven't told me the entire story. Not that I need to know *everything,*" she added hastily. "I just think that there may be more to this Briggs fellow's agenda than getting rid of a man who slept with his girl. I think that maybe you're afraid to tell me the exact circumstances because they paint you in a less than law-abiding fashion." *Excellent work, Rian. Do you really think he is too dull to realize that you just practically accused him of being a criminal?*

"I understand," he said.

She raised her eyebrows and pursed her lips thoughtfully. "And that's all?" His sudden, simplistic silence irritated her.

Bradyn's expression became hard and unreadable. "What do you want me to tell you?"

"I want to know why you're here. If you're not hiding from the law and you haven't murdered or robbed someone, why do you stay here? I want to know why this man, Briggs, wants you dead so badly. If you can't tell me that, then I think you should saddle your horse and get out." She was surprised at the anger she heard in her own voice.

Bradyn grabbed her wrist and pulled her closer toward him. "I'll tell you. I'll tell you everything, but first you need to know that if I tell you the whole story, I'm putting your life in danger. And Kendall's, too. If you can live with that on your conscience, then I'll tell you anything you want to know."

Rian swallowed hard. She could live with her life being put into a perilous situation. Kendall's safety was another matter. She wanted to know. With all her being she wanted to know. She wanted to understand Bradyn Preston. But endanger Kendall? Subject him to the horrors like those he'd almost met the day Cheyenne Joe came? Then realization struck home.

She nodded. "I want to hear it," she replied, filling her voice with brave challenge. "I doubt knowing what happened to you could put us in any more danger than we are in now. And as far as being harmed or killed for knowing the truth, well, you didn't hear what Cheyenne Joe told me he was going to do to us after he'd killed you. We didn't even know then why you are a hunted man, Mr. Preston." She nodded her head, more sure of this than she had been of most anything in her entire life. "Tell me. I want to know."

Chapter Seven

The rain had slowed to a gentle sprinkle. Its dancing droplets created a symphony of rhapsodic pitters and patters on the roof. The fragrant scent of the summer shower, mingled with the aroma of freshly brewed coffee drifted throughout the kitchen.

Bradyn watched Rian as she studied him from across the table. He hardly knew where to begin. He had never shared much of his life story with anyone before, let alone a woman he'd only known for a few days. It wasn't that he didn't want to tell her. In fact, sitting across from Rian he realized that the real problem was that he did want to tell her. And that was the damnable truth. A nervous energy ran the length of his spine.

Trying to decide what to say and where to start, he couldn't help but notice again, wistfully, how beautiful Rian Keene was. She sat with her hands folded on the table, and an expression of ingenuous curiosity lighted her fiery eyes as they searched his face with quiet fascination. Her guileless countenance promised that she would give no judgment until she'd given proper hearing and thought to a matter. It was an honesty that he appreciated.

He could almost envision spending his life with her. Almost imagine how wonderful it might be to have such a brave and intelligent woman by his side. He knew, with uncanny certainty, how perfect it would feel to kiss her, hold her, and make love to her. But he steeled his mind against such thoughts. Besides, when Rian knew all that there was to know about him, her love would most likely be as unattainable as wingless flight over the ocean. Even conquering the loftiest mountain's height would seem a small hurdle by comparison. Such frivolous fantasies were best left tucked away to be painted by his imagination at a later time.

The silence grew heavy as he tried to put his life story into words. The rain drizzled to a stop. Yellow rays of sunlight began fading in and out as the gray storm clouds began to relinquish their dark reign in the skies above, if only for the moment.

As Rian sat studying him, her fingers playing with the handle of the white china mug, he ran a hand through his hair with ragged nervousness. "All right. Here it is," he started. "Just remember, you asked to hear this."

Rian nodded, her amber eyes soft, and Bradyn momentarily had second thoughts about telling her everything.

"Liam Briggs does want me dead because I bedded his woman, but you're right, there is a whole lot more to it than that. Briggs has got a shady…hell, a downright *wicked* past. A past, that I am sorry to say, involves me." He paused to look at her. Her face was still and expectant.

"I have a half-brother, well *had* a half-brother," he clarified. "Ah, damn it!" he said under his breath as he rubbed his face. "I've never told anyone all of this before," he admitted, wrinkling his brow in frustration. "It pretty much involves my whole life, so I can't start in the middle, I reckon."

"I would suppose not," Rian replied. "Take your time."

She put one of her hands on the hand he rested on the table. Her eyes held his with soothing assurance and Bradyn mustered the words to continue. "I guess the best place to start is with my mama. She was…" He was interrupted as movement caught his eye outside the kitchen window. Squinting, he leaned forward, unsure if what he saw was real or just his imagination.

"What is it?" Rian asked, turning in the direction he was looking. "What do you see?"

He stood up and pointed a finger. "There, by that outcropping of rocks about a half mile away or so. Do you see it? Looks like smoke."

"I see something… it *could* be smoke." Rian looked up at him, her eyes wide. "You don't think—"

"Briggs." Anger ignited inside him as he watched the thin gray ribbon of smoke for a moment. "That bastard!" he growled as he turned and headed out of the kitchen.

* * * *

Rian watched Bradyn leave the room, unsure what to expect him to do next. When he returned, he had her revolver in his hand and his eyes glittered with the fury of a storm-swept sea at midnight.

"What are you doing?" she asked, trying to suppress the spidery chill she felt creeping up her spine. She didn't really need him to tell her, she already knew the answer.

"I'm going to kill that bastard up there, who ever he is, before he comes down here. That's what."

His jaw flexed and his free hand formed a tight, white-knuckled fist. Rian didn't know whether to fear or admire a man who wanted to meet his enemies dead-on in such a foolhardy manner. "You can't go!" she said as she ran to his side. She tugged at his arm. "You'll be killed. You still haven't healed yet, and suppose there are two or three men this time? You won't have a chance! Please wait."

He looked down at her. The fierce expression on his face was withering.

Wait?" he asked angrily. "Wait for what? Wait for them to come to us? Wait to shoot them until they're here, where Kendall can see it? Or so he can see them shoot you? Wait to see if they come during the day or at night? They'll show up when we least expect it and it might not go down as easy as it did with Joe. They might kill us next time, and I am not going to wait around for that."

Bradyn pulled the Winchester down from its perch atop the pantry door. "Here." He handed the rifle to her. "You and Kendall stay in this house until I come back. If anyone but me comes up to the place, you just shoot 'em. No questions asked. Got it? Don't trust anyone. And, Rian?" His voice was hard as steel but coated with velvet smoothness.

She met his eyes across the room. "Yes?" she whispered. Her heart was galloping in her chest like a runaway horse.

"Shoot to kill."

Bradyn disappeared out the door. She watched with a sinking heart as he doubled back behind the barn and down toward the creek bank. *He may not make it back. Then who will protect us from the men that might come here?*

* * * *

Bradyn moved with animal-like stealth through the cottonwoods and aspens that lined the creek bed. If he kept to the trees and brush, he could circle around the back of the rocks and come out just behind the intruder. It was going to take some time to get there. He was navigating the long way around and he had to be cautious. Any ill-thought movement could alert their visitor to his presence. Bradyn would be a sitting duck at such a long range. He needed to be close to shoot. The revolver's accuracy would prove piss-poor at any great distance.

Sweat poured from his body as he crept slowly along the gurgling creek's edge. His ears were tuned as he listened for the first sounds of danger. He worried over Rian and the kid. If the man up on the bluff decided to approach the house while he was gone, he wouldn't have enough time to make it back to save her and Kendall. He hoped she would take his instructions seriously and shoot the bastard if he showed up.

About halfway to the outcropping, Bradyn paused. The thin wisp of smoke he had seen spiraling upward only minutes before was gone now. He wondered what might have happened if he would have missed that split instant when the smoke's scant ascent had drawn his attention. He wondered if there was no one there at all. *No. Rian saw the smoke too.* They had both known someone was up there. Besides, his gut told him that Briggs had sent another man and that he would find him crouching behind those rocks atop the bluff.

Sliding silently behind a lichen covered boulder, Bradyn called Rian's face to mind. He had barely begun to tell her his life story. The smoke, in retrospect, had provided a fortunate interruption. Perhaps it was a sign. He may have been about to make a stupid blunder, expecting her to understand his past and the long, trouble-riddled life he had lead. Expecting her to comprehend the stupid choices that had brought him here, of all the places on God's green earth.

Bradyn shook his head, a firm decision cementing in his mind. He was going to spare Rian Keene the dirty account of the past that stalked him like a tiger in the night. And, he was going to spare *himself* the inevitable look of pity mixed with abhorrence that she would most certainly give him when she knew the sordid details of his life. After he took care of the gunman that was lying in wait only a short distance away he was going to leave this place. He felt well enough to make the ride. Hell, he had for the last couple days. He'd find Briggs and settle their unfinished business. After that, he was going to head out of the Wyoming Territory. For good.

Then another thought interrupted his mental meanderings. What if the smoke was a trap? What if it had been deliberately released to draw him away from the house? Bradyn stopped and crouched on the muddy bank, his body shielded by a lilac bush. Should he go back? He paused, momentarily considering the options before him. If he got to the rocks and the gunman wasn't there, he would have to run half a mile back to the house. There wouldn't be enough time to get back there. He'd already drawn that conclusion earlier. If he turned back now, he could sit and wait for the gunman to make his move. Waiting was never a good idea. He shook his head. He had to go on. He prayed silently that Rian would be watchful. If the dirty bastard made it to the house, he was going to have to rely on her to shoot him. *She* was going to have to rely on herself to shoot him.

Bradyn moved on. He quickened his pace as much as he

dared. The sooner he got up to those rocks, the sooner he would know where the son of a whore was.

The creek bed jogged to the south. Bradyn was forced to leave the cover of the steep embankment and climb out into view of the outcropping. He waited until he came to a thick stand of aspens. Pulling himself up the muddy embankment, he swore under his breath as he lost his foothold momentarily and slid backward. Mud slicked his chest and belly. The second try gained him the grassy slope inside a thick foliage of trees and underbrush. He blew out a breath and moved forward. The outcropping was only a few hundred yards away now, but Bradyn hadn't seen any movement or sign of life yet.

The wind picked up and a new blanket of thunder clouds came rolling across the plain. Bradyn paused to catch his breath. His head had taken up a terrible throbbing. He looked up at the sky with weary anticipation. A good rain might play to his favor right now. A lot of thunder and lightning would make a hell of a lot better cover than just the trees, bushes, and grass that stood between him and the jagged stratum of rock hiding his pursuer.

The slope of the land took on a sharp incline as Bradyn reached the edge of the cottonwoods and aspens. From here, a good span of two hundred yards contained nothing but an open field; not a single tree or bush. His heart sank. He couldn't chance that distance in broad daylight, even under the cover of a storm. It was far too risky. He would have to wait for the shield of night to go on.

He crouched in a clump of choke cherry bushes and waited. Watching the rocks, he saw movement for the first time. A pair of horses lifted their heads briefly before returning to leisure grazing. Bradyn ground his hands into fists. His instinct had been right. There was somebody up here alright. At least two men from what he could see. He fretted again over the concern of a man getting to the house. One to watch, one to move in. He didn't like the feel of this. His whole body tensed. The waiting was going to be murder, but he had to do it. The place where he was hidden offered him one small comfort. It was to his advantage that he could view the whole of the bluff from where he sat. At least if one of them made a move toward the house now, he would see it.

The low rumbling growl of thunder sounded over-head. Rain began to pour out of the sky, drenching his body and making him wish Rian would have had time to get him fitted with a shirt. He sat still as stone, water rolling down his back, arms, and legs in bone-chilling streams. Watching and waiting. "You have to wait for darkness," he told himself, "Just wait for darkness..."

* * * *

Bradyn had been gone for nearly five hours. Rian paced the kitchen, holding the rifle to her chest and whispering a dozen rambling, disjointed prayers as she watched out the westward facing windows. As evening drew on, her pacing quickened. Her heart thundered in her chest in rhythm with the storm bellowing and growling in earnest outside.

Where are you, Bradyn? You've had plenty of time to get to the rocks by now…unless, unless… She shook herself. He was fine. She wasn't going to allow herself to contemplate otherwise. Perhaps Bradyn just hadn't found the man yet. She'd heard no gunshots. That was probably as a good indication as any that he was all right. Then again, with the rain battering down in buckets and the thunder roaring like the Devil had been set loose in Heaven, she could have easily missed the split-second sound of gunfire.

"Rian?" Kendall's small voice interrupted her frantic stride from one end of the kitchen to the other. She spun, fearful that he had seen someone or something since she had instructed him to watch out the west facing window in the guestroom.

"What is it, Kendall?" she asked. Her voice was barely louder than a whisper.

"I need a drink of water," he said. The expression on his face, white and drawn, told her he expected a good scolding for abandoning his station.

"Go get one, baby," she ordered and quickly took her

place back at the window. When he returned, she patted his head. "It's almost dark, you go on up and rest in your room, Kendall. I'll stand guard for awhile, okay."

Kendall shook his head. "I wanna stay with you, Auntie Rian. I don't wanna go to my room." He put his small hand in hers. His green eyes were pleading and apprehensive.

Rian smiled at him. Her affection for the small boy soothed the frantic fear that raced through her. "All right, Kendall," she whispered and squeezed his hand tightly, "you can stay."

Together they sat watching the water run from the roof in torrents and erupt in muddy trenches as it plummeted to the ground below. With the thick blanket of black clouds overhead, darkness came earlier tonight. Soon, the failing grey light was enveloped in night. She could barely see to the barn through the rain and utter blackness. Only periodic sizzles of lightning illuminated the yard with blinding electric-white flashes. Silently, she lamented the handicap the weather imposed on them. If anyone rode up in the storm, she wouldn't be able to see them until they were nearly to the house. And that was if there was a timely flash of lightning. Otherwise, she might not be able to see them at all.

Kendall drifted off to sleep as Rian rocked him. She forced herself to remain seated for his sake, though she wanted nothing more than to jump from the rocking chair and take up her frenetic marching across the floor again. Where are you, Bradyn? she wondered for the hundredth time that night. *Where are you?*

* * * *

Black came the night; black, cold, and miserably wet. Bradyn remained crouched beneath the clump of choke cherry bushes where he had sat all afternoon. His legs no longer felt connected to his body. They had become two thick, frozen chunks of wood on which he gingerly balanced. He cursed under his breath as he rose slowly and felt the sensation of needle pricks in his extremities. Rubbing his thighs and calves to work the feeling back into them, he watched for any sign of life from behind the rocks. He needed to move in now. The time had come.

Crawling on hands and knees across the rain saturated earth, grass clinging in frigid, moist strands to his arms and chest, he edged ever closer to the outcropping that hid his assailants. Every breath was a prayer that a sudden flash of lightning or false step would not give away his presence or position. Ice-cold mud caked on his hands and oozed through the knees of his jeans. *Keep moving, keep moving, keep moving…* His mind, mechanical and repetitive, ordered him onward.

After long, eternal minutes of crawling, he reached the first stand of trees and underbrush. He rose to his feet and narrowed his eyes, bringing the landscape into focus through the dark and the rain. The stand of rocks was to his right. If he moved quietly and quickly, he would be in the trees behind it within a few minutes. He reached for the revolver he had placed in his pant's waist and drew it with fluid ease. Moving forward, he made barely a noise. The rainfall generously covered the faintest sounds of an occasional snapping twig or a swinging branch.

Bradyn was close now, directly behind the outcropping. He looked to the broad, flat place behind the rocks and froze in his tracks. He had been mistaken. There stood, not two, but *four* horses. Sudden panic gripped him. *Four men!* He could see two of them from where he stood. They were under a make-shift tent where a very small campfire washed their faces in orange glow. But where were the other two? His grip on the gun tightened. *Two to watch, two to move in.* He had to make his attack now. The other two men were no doubt using the cover of darkness and rain to make their way to the house.

He stole to the edge of the rocks. His heart hammered in his chest; a pulsating, deafening drummer's march. Judging from the posture of each man, they were both dozing. One man rested his head on his chest while the other was leaning back against the rock with his hat shadowing his eyes. *A lucky break in my favor. Most likely the only break I'll get all night.*

One of the men coughed and stirred for a moment as Bradyn glided to the fireside, his gun aimed at the cougher. He took a deep breath. It was now or never.

"Get up!" he bellowed at them.

Both men jumped and looked around in confusion. They had not expected Bradyn Preston. *That was your mistake, my friends.* Bradyn smiled with cold humor as he leveled the revolver squarely at the first man.

"Preston," he said with his hands lifted in truce-like fashion. "Come on now, we ain't meanin' you no harm."

"Shut up, Tex," Bradyn growled. "Just how dumb do you think I am? I know Briggs sent you to kill me, you stupid bastard. You should have thought twice about building a fire up here." Bradyn raised his gun, his thumb resting on the hammer. "Now you're gonna tell me where the other two are."

"The other two? Now what the hell are you talkin' about, Preston?" Confusion registered on Tex's face.

Bradyn caught the other gunman's movement out of the corner of his eye a moment too late. He shouted as gunfire exploded in the night.

* * * *

At some point during the stormy gale, while she sat rocking Kendall with soothing motion, Rian had drifted off. The sudden, staccato crack of gunfire echoing across the field jarred her awake. A harsh rush of realization flooded her awareness. She jumped from the rocker, nearly tumbling Kendall to the floor in her haste. Her face burned hot and her blood ran solid ice. What had happened? She wrung her hands frantically. Her voice warped with panicked distress, she pleaded, "Please let Bradyn be alright. Please, God. Please let him be alive."

Kendall rubbed his eyes and looked up at her, his peaceful, groggy expression changing when he saw his aunt's face. She recognized the terror in his eyes. He hadn't forgotten Cheyenne Joe. Kendall knew what she knew. If

Bradyn didn't come back to them, someone else most probably would.

Rian pulled the Winchester against her body. If that man up there had gotten Bradyn, she was the only one left to protect them. She was the only one who could stop someone from hurting Kendall or herself. The weight of her current situation threatened to crush the air from her lungs and wreak frenzied havoc on her mind. She gritted her teeth and her jaw popped audibly. *No! I am not going to panic. I am going to stand my ground and protect this home. And if some horrible man has killed Bradyn, I am going to kill him! God help me, I am!*

"No questions asked. Shoot to kill," she repeated aloud Bradyn's last words to her as he'd left the house. "Shoot to kill."

Kendall stood beside her, his face set as bravely as his six years would allow. His hand shook as he placed it on her hip. "We're gonna be okay, Auntie Rian," he affirmed with a weak nod. "We're gonna be okay. Mr. Bradyn'll come back. You'll see."

"I hope so, Kendall," she answered. His courage and certainty bolstered her weak valiance. "I hope so, baby."

The two of them stood at the window, watching through the rain, trying to catch a glimpse of movement. Her legs shook. Her throat constricted and clicked as she swallowed at the gelatinous lump of fear lodged there. She took a deep breath. The room tilted dangerously for a moment, then came back into proper balance. *I have to be brave. I have to. For Kendall, for Bradyn, but most of all, for me. Anytime now, anytime, someone is going to ride into this yard and…* She tensed as movement caught her eye. *What was that?*

Rian squinted. The rain made it difficult to see anything. There was something out there though. She could see movement out near the barn. From this distance, she couldn't make out much more than a dark blurry outline, but it was moving toward the house. Drawing closer. Her heart lurched to her throat, her fingers felt instantly paralyzed. *Someone is coming!*

"Kendall, there's someone out there. You stay in this

house. I'm going out onto the porch to see who it is. If anything happens to me, hide in the root cellar. No one will find you there, do you understand?" She put a hand on his shoulder. When he didn't respond, she shook him. "Kendall! Listen to me! You have to hide, do you hear?" His eyes were huge as he stared past her. She couldn't help but shudder. He looked as if he was in shock.

Rian half-turned to see how fast they were approaching. They were closer now, nearly in the yard. She could see two… no, three horses. Her heart skipped a beat. *Or are there four horses?*

"Kendall!" she screamed, kneeling to look her nephew in the eye. "Listen to me! They're coming, they're almost here. Tell me you'll hide in the root cellar, now!" She shook his shoulder hard, causing his teeth to clatter and his cheeks to jiggle.

Kendall nodded as if in trance but his eyes never left the window. "They're here," he whispered, his finger pointing in dream-like motion outside. "They're here, Auntie Rian."

Another tremor ran through her body as she turned to look out the window. A bolt of lightning split the sky and eerily illuminated two riders shrouded in dark billowing clothes. They sat just outside, motionless, while thunder boomed overhead. The darkness and rain obscured any further detail other than their position in the front yard. There were four horses. The third horse was without a rider.

As another jagged bolt of lightning pierced the sky, she saw that a body was draped over the fourth horse. A strangled scream escaped her lips. The body was shirtless, its bare limbs dangling lifelessly over either side of the animal. Rain ran over his back, down his neck, and dripped from wavy black hair. *Bradyn!*

An ear-splitting clap of thunder ricocheted through the heavens shaking the windows of the house with the fierceness of its reverberation. It was followed by a loud voice, "Hello in the house. Come on out! We got Preston!"

Rian stood frozen, her fear holding her in place. He was dead. Bradyn was dead! She wanted to run away, to fade away into the stormy night. She wanted to hide anywhere…but where? Where could she go? She was alone. Kendall was standing there beside her. His lips were blue and moving soundlessly. He had seen the body too. Her heart thundered on at reckless speed as another bolt of lightning tore the sky.

"Come out!" the voice shouted again. This time it was muffled by a jarring boom of thunder.

"Go," she whispered, her voice was hoarse and faint. She pushed at Kendall with rough urgency. "Go hide! Go hide!"

She lifted the rifle to her shoulder, a fierce anger gripping her, stark reality shaking her to the very core. Bradyn was dead. She had to protect them. She had to protect them! "Shoot to kill," she murmured in a dazed voice. "Shoot to kill. Shoot to kill."

Rian didn't pause to see if Kendall had gone into hiding. She didn't linger to tell him to be safe. She didn't stop for anything. The kitchen door flew open with a pounding smack. It was only after she had walked through it that she realized it had been opened by her own hand. A gust of rain-laden wind slapped her face as she took her stand on the front porch, the rifle pressed into her shoulder, her finger on the trigger. She was trembling but ready.

"Don't ask questions. Shoot to kill." Bradyn's words came to her again. Her finger tightened on the trigger as she leveled the gun at the first rider. A burst of light and sound roared through her and numbed her senses as she discharged a round. The rifle kicked back into her shoulder with a heavy jolt. The second rider bucked and slumped as the bullet drove into him, but he didn't fall to the ground.

"Don't shoot!" the first rider hollered. "Don't shoot! Rian! It's me!"

She lowered the gun and blinked against the water that ran down her forehead and into her eyes. She raised the rifle to her shoulder again. "Who are you?!" she screamed.

"It's me! Bradyn!" the masculine voice answered.

She watched as the first rider dismounted and ran toward the porch. Her eyes were surely deceiving her. She'd seen Bradyn's body draped over the back of the fourth horse. She was certain he was dead. But no, there he was;

alive and running through the rain to the house.

Bradyn gained the porch in three strides. She fell against him shaking uncontrollably. "You're alive?' she asked. Relieved disbelief brought her very near to tears. "But how? I saw you there." She pointed to the body still draped over the fourth horse. She turned back to look at him with a shaky hand over her mouth. "They didn't kill you?"

Bradyn smiled wearily. "Nope." he answered, looking past her toward the house. "What about you and Kendall? Did anyone show up here?'

Rian shook her head. "No. No one. Until now. What happened? I heard gunshots and then when I saw the riders..." She paused and touched his face, still unsure that it was indeed him standing there in front of her. He looked at her, his face still and unreadable. She frowned. "Who's that other man?" she asked of the second rider.

"That *was* Buddy Sanders. One of Briggs' men. The other unfortunate bastard is Tex Forrester." Bradyn paused and studied her for a moment as her hand settled on his neck.

"You were gone for so long. I was certain you were dead when I heard the shots," she admitted.

"I came to an open space this afternoon, one that was in plain sight of the rocks. I couldn't chance running across it and letting them know I was coming. So, I had to wait for dark." Bradyn paused again and gave her a curious look.

Suddenly aware that her fingers were still stroking his neck and that her body was pressed up against him, she cleared her throat and stepped away.

He rubbed his neck with the vaguest hint of a smile before continuing. "When I finally got up behind the rocks, I saw that there were four horses. About then I didn't know quite what to do. I had to shoot those two. But then that left me thinking that the other two would be here. Are you sure you haven't seen anyone?"

Rian nodded. Her body grew still as her violent shivering came to a stop. Bradyn put his arm around her and pulled her securely against his side again, a motion that was at once startling and of great comfort. "I thought we were going to die," she whispered. "My God, I have never been so afraid in my life."

"Sorry I frightened you, but I couldn't take the risk that someone was here waiting for me, ready to use you or Kendall as leverage the first chance they got. I had to try to draw them out of the house if I could. I tied Buddy's body to that horse and took Tex's outfit. He was about the same height and coloring as me or, at least a close enough match in a rainstorm. I figured if they thought I was Tex and that we'd gotten Bradyn, they'd come out peaceable enough. Kinda backfired though. I'm glad you were aiming at Buddy when you shot. That could have been me wearing my guts on the outside." Bradyn smiled. "I'll think twice before accusing you of being a lousy shot again."

Rian's knees nearly buckled as the realization that she might have killed him herself suddenly dawned on her. "Oh, my God, I'm sorry, Bradyn. I am so sorry. I should have asked you to identify yourself before I fired. I could have killed you!"

Bradyn's chuckle was muted by the low growling of thunder, but Rian felt it as she pressed against his chest.

"You did exactly as I told you. Don't be sorry, it was a good shot," he assured her.

Rian shuddered and refrained from telling him that she had, in all actuality, been aiming at him when she'd pulled the trigger. She drew herself away from him as the powerful adrenaline of the moment began to fade. Bradyn stared down at her. His eyes were clouded. She smiled faintly. "Come on inside. You look like you could use a drink and a warm blanket."

As Bradyn followed her into the house, Rian let out the deep breath that she'd been holding since she'd fired the rifle. She had never been so relieved to see anyone alive in her life.

Kendall came running up to them and hugged Bradyn about his knees. His merry laughter filled the kitchen. "You're alive! You're alive! I told ya, Rian. See, I *told* ya he was gonna come back!"

"You did tell me that, Kendall," she answered. Her relieved laughter blended with his. She patted Kendall's head but kept her eyes on Bradyn. "And we couldn't be happier, could we, baby?"

"I haven't been this happy since my birthday!" Kendall affirmed, his eyes snapping with unabashed joy. "Gosh, I never want you to leave, Mr. Bradyn."

"Thanks, kid," he replied rubbing Kendall's head. "I appreciate it." Rian caught a note of uneasiness below the smile that Bradyn gave her nephew. She wondered if he was worried about something else as she put coffee on to brew.

Still feeling weak and lightheaded from the emotional drain of the past few hours, she listened as Kendall excitedly rambled on about how he'd sat watch with her. "Rian was so brave to go out on the front porch," he was saying, "even when she didn't know it was you out there. Don't you think so, Mr. Bradyn?"

"You both did alright, kid," Bradyn replied. "I think you and your aunt are very brave indeed. I'd go to a gunfight beside the two of you any day."

Rian studied him as he talked with her nephew; his blue eyes sparkling in the light of the lantern. As Kendall continued to chatter, Bradyn looked up at her and winked. The warmth in his expression was smoldering, but the dark concern hiding just below the surface was still visible too. It made her uncertain. Even a little afraid.

She bit her lip, distracted by the notion that perhaps there was something he hadn't told her, until it finally dawned on her that he was wearing a shirt for the first time since he come to their house. The shirt fit very well. It was soaked through and in need of both washing and mending. Mud and blood stained the denim cloth.

Blood? She stopped short. The small blood-stained, gunpowder-blackened hole on the chest was no doubt where Bradyn had shot the man he called Tex. The blood that was spreading on the arm was most certainly Bradyn's. "What's happened to your arm?" she asked, her eyes wide with concern.

Confused, Bradyn looked down and pulled at his sleeve. "I guess I did get shot after all." He shrugged.

Rian pulled the brandy out of a cupboard. "Take off your

shirt and let me have a look at it."

"I'm fine," Bradyn said, the tone of his voice gruff and defensive.

"Let me see!" she insisted. "I swear you make a better target than any man I've ever met."

Bradyn made a noise that was a mixture of a growl and a sigh. "Is she always so bossy?" he asked Kendall. The boy nodded meekly and quickly glanced at her, obviously trying to catch her reaction to both the question and his answer.

Rian just shook her head and kept silent. She poured a drink and handed it to Bradyn as soon as he'd taken off his shirt. He took the whiskey as he sat down and commenced to watch her beneath a half-disgruntled expression.

Ignoring his pretense of irritation, she bent to examine his latest injury. It was a clean shot. The bullet had only grazed the outer flesh of his upper right arm. Bradyn winced as she poured some alcohol into the bloody wound.

"That's going to be sore in the morning," she said absently and with a hint of sarcasm. "I'll go get some bandaging for it. Don't move." She reached for a towel sitting on the counter. "Here, hold this firmly on it. It'll help stop the bleeding and keep the blood from making a mess on my floor."

Bradyn pressed the towel she handed to him against his arm. She gave him a smile to soften her bossy tone. He didn't reply, but a crooked grin played at the corners of his mouth just before she hurried to the guestroom with Kendall tripping along behind like a bouncy puppy.

"Does it hurt much?" she asked loudly over the scraping and squeaking of the drawers as she opened and shut them.

"Nope," he called back.

She shook her head. His arm was probably burning with the vengeance of hellfire, but he would be damned if he let her know it. Men were strange that way.

"You must have been born under a lucky star, or sign, or something, Mr. Preston," she replied.

"How's that?" Bradyn asked.

"Anyone else would have been dead long ago, I think," she said as she returned with cotton and linen. "Here we are.

I'll have that arm fixed up in no time. And to think you were nearly healed from your last run-in with this Briggs fellow and his men." She shook her head. "Well now you'll have another scar to add to your long list of survived injuries."

Bradyn watched her as she cut the cotton and wrapped the wound. Normally, she would have felt uneasy under his piercing stare, but tonight he seemed lost in his thoughts. As she wrapped the final layer of cotton gauze around his muscled arm, he cleared his throat uncomfortably.

"I need to get those bodies buried tonight," he said.

After a few seconds, his words finally found their way into her concentration. She frowned at up at him. "Tonight?" she echoed. "In this rain? With a bullet hole in your arm. You really are a brute for punishment, aren't you, Mr. Preston?"

"Tonight." He nodded as he stood and pulled the soiled shirt back on.

"But…" She noticed the look of resolve in his eyes and thought better of arguing with him. Instead, she blew out a gusty sigh. "Let me put Kendall down to sleep, and I will come help you."

"I can mange." His reply was curt as he turned and disappeared into the rainy night.

Rian watched him go as the strange feeling of unease grew stronger. "Kendall!" she called. "Go upstairs and get ready for bed. I'll be up in a moment to tuck you in."

When Kendall didn't answer her, she looked around for him. "Now where did he get to?" she muttered. "He was just with me in the guestroom."

She walked to the room in which she had last seen him and poked her head around the door. A smile touched her mouth. Kendall had lain down on the bed. His eyes were closed in peaceful sleep and on his face was a small smile of supreme contentment. She kissed his forehead and gently pulled the quilt over him. Her fingers brushed the bloodstained patch of cloth with a sad fondness.

Quietly closing the door, she went to fetch an overcoat out of the hall closet and a lantern from the washroom. Lighting the lantern, she stepped out into the storm to help

Bradyn bury the bodies of two more men who had met their deaths on the Keene homestead.

Chapter Eight

Perpetual rain, falling in a sheet of icy nails, hammered down from a sky as black as Bradyn's mood. He figured that even if the angel Gabriel had the mind to stop the storm, he probably couldn't have; so strong was its fury. The onyx heavens and chilly precipitation lent themselves to an eerie, fiendish atmosphere. An atmosphere that was conducive to the burial of the two men who had come to murder Bradyn, only to meet their Maker themselves in the end.

He was leading the wet horses carrying Tex and Buddy's bodies into the side-yard when Rian walked out onto the porch. He watched her run to the barn in the rain, feeling that same perplexing, gut-ache swell inside him. If only she were less than perfect. Maybe if she were not so honest and kind or so courageous and intelligent, it would be easier to tell her that he was leaving. Perhaps if she wasn't so damnably beautiful he wouldn't be having so much trouble trying to convince *himself* to leave this place.

When Rian returned, she was dragging two shovels with one hand and holding the lantern in the other. Bradyn didn't say a word to her. He just took the shovels and hoisted them over his shoulder. Soundlessly, she followed his lead as he headed, once again, for the creek bank. The two of them walked down the hill side by side. They made a grotesque parade, him leading the horses and Rian carrying the lantern. The flashes of lightning illuminated their faces with a peculiar, stark-white cast and distorted their shadows into long, black ghoulish aberrations that scurried along the ground beside them with lives of their own.

Neither spoke. He supposed she was reminiscing the last time they'd been to the creek together. It was a bleak memory of death. Her prayer had gone unanswered. They were burying again, not one man this time, but two. He wished he could have spared her this circumstance.

He found his mind in a place of agony. He hated the indecision that weakened his resolve. A part of him wanted to send Rian away, to tell her to leave him to bury the men in peace. To make her stop getting more involved in this ugliness than was necessary, from getting more involved than she already was. He wanted to tell her she was not obligated to help him in any way and that as soon as these two murderers were put in the ground he was riding out and she would never see him again.

The other part of his mind reprimanded him for being irritated at her silent gesture of help. Everything she had done, all actions of kindness or courage, had been forced upon her by no one other than him. She was no more a part of this entire debacle than the moon was a pebble, and yet she had become integrally embroiled in the whole mess out of pure fate. That part of him wanted nothing more than to let her be the one. The one he opened himself to, the one he told everything to, the one he could run to and lean on. That One.

And, finally, for the hundred-thousandth time, Bradyn Preston cursed his life. A life that had been twisted and warped with all the ridiculous choices he had made and immoral accomplishments he had achieved. He hated the day he had laid eyes on Liam Briggs. He vowed then and there on that muddy path destined for the creek bank and another tasteless burial, that he would not rest until Liam Briggs was dead. Dead and in Hell, paying for his many transgressions and iniquities. And if Briggs managed to kill him first, it would be good riddance. He was ready to pay for his own sins. To hell with living a half-life, shrouded by the past and the evil he had summoned on his soul.

* * * *

The creek was a raging, muddy river now. The rain storm threatened to run it over its already engorged banks. Cheyenne Joe's grave was nearly covered by its waters. Bradyn paused at the stump, handed Rian the shovels, and proceeded to tie the horses' reins to a nearby tree branch. When he was finished, he silently gestured for a shovel. She handed him one and then began digging a hole; ignoring the intense, wordless stare he gave her before setting to work himself.

The coat she had worn was proving to be no real protection against the wet and cold, and digging in the mud was an almost fruitless effort. The rain filled the hole as quickly as she could pull out a shovel full of mucky earth. It made it almost impossible to judge her progress. The thunder and lightning mixed and blended to produce a grim, grotesque scene. Two people digging under the watch of dead men. Death stalked the shadows, showing his face when the lightning pierced the sky and reflected from the sightless, glassy stares of the two dead bodies.

Rian shivered, as much from bleak horror as from the frigid moisture, and dug faster. She was immersed deep in her own thoughts. Relief and happiness that it was not Bradyn's body for which she was digging a hole in the earth made the task a bit easier. She watched him out of the corner of her eye. He dug with an inhuman fury, favoring his injured arm only a little. From her vantage point she couldn't be sure, but with each brilliant sizzle of lightning it looked as though the blood stain on his shirtsleeve was spreading. That nagging uneasiness she had felt earlier returned. Something about his demeanor was different. Tense and withdrawn, even maniacal in a way. She shivered again and turned her mind to the slow-growing hole at her feet.

Bradyn finished digging first. He pulled one of the rigid bodies from the buckskin and dumped it into the murky, water-filled grave. Shoveling the earth back over the dead man was a messy affair. The mud sloshed and splattered everywhere. It slid off the body in slimy, oozing streams as the rain washed it from the carcass almost as fast as he could shovel it on. She heard him swear under his breath a few times, but was unsure if he was cursing at the laggard process or the fiery spasms in his right arm. Eventually, the body was buried under a thick layer of miry sludge and Bradyn turned his attention to the hole that she had begun, her efforts only accomplishing a fair start.

He shook his head. Whether it was a motion of humor or disgust, she could not tell, so she decided to ignore him again and continue shoveling. Even after he began helping her, she worked hard to exhume the muddy earth.

With the two of them digging, the project progressed a little faster, though their headway was not measurable by much. It was late into the night by the time the second body had been covered and the two of them headed wearily up to the house. There had been no prayer over the graves this time, only an unspoken, somber word of "thank you" from Rian to the Good Lord for the safe return of Bradyn Preston.

* * * *

The warm glow of the house was a welcome sight. Soaked and muddy, Rian went upstairs to change into dry clothing. Bradyn stood at the door, trying to decide how he was going to tell her he was leaving. Now. Tonight. Maybe it would be better to just go. Without a goodbye. Without the horrible, uncomfortable explaining. Maybe it would be easier to just disappear into the howling storm outside.

Then it was too late. Rian reappeared at the foot of the stairs, her wet hair falling down her shoulders, a heavy quilt in her arms. Bradyn's breath stopped momentarily as her presence had its customary effect on him.

"Here, I brought this blanket down for you. You can clean up and I'll get your clothes washed." Rian paused and gave him a questioning glance when he didn't immediately acknowledge her. A frown etched its way across her countenance. "Is something bothering you? Why are you standing at the door like that?" she asked. He saw the dread wending its way across her face.

Bradyn took a deep breath and ran his fingers though his

wet hair. "I'm going to head out tonight."

"What?" Rian asked. "Why are you leaving tonight?" She clutched her throat, her face betraying her disappointment.

"You know why, Rian," was his quiet reply.

"I don't," she said, defiant hurt in her voice. "Maybe you should explain it to me."

Bradyn narrowed his eyes and stared down at her. Rian fidgeted under his unblinking gaze. She rubbed her collarbone and her eyes darted around the room before resting on his face again. "Why are you leaving tonight?" she repeated.

"Liam Briggs." His voice was brittle, like wood splintering under an axe. He directed his anger at her for he could not lash out at anyone else. "For God's sake, Rian. How long do you think we can sit in this house hoping to better each and every hired gun that bastard sends out here? I'm going into Laramie, tonight, to finish this."

The look he gave her and the tone of his voice made her recoil. She stared at him; speechless for a moment. Her silence didn't last long. "But, you're hurt! You were no match for Briggs when you were in good health!" she exclaimed.

He looked at her with bitter aggravation for a moment. "I was no match for a sneaky, low-down son of a whore who woke me from a sound sleep with a gun in my face. This time I am going to meet Briggs on my terms," he said.

"You can't just go. It's raining and your arm…" Her voice trailed off as his expression remained untouched. She walked toward him. "Kendall and I… *We* both think very well of you, Bradyn." She spoke his first name for the first time since his arrival. "Please don't go yet. Maybe Briggs will give up, maybe he'll send no more men." Her voice was barely a whisper, as if she knew that the words sounded foolish and unlikely.

However, her closeness affected him. The anger waned somewhat.

"You know that won't happen, Rian," he answered in a softer tone. He crossed his arms and stood looking down at her with curiosity. "Why?"

"Why?" Rian echoed as if she didn't understand the intent of his question.

"Why do you want me to stay? Your life was fine before I showed up here. The two of you were safe. You and the kid have witnessed nothing but murder and pain from the day I arrived."

She fidgeted under his stare before she swallowed and lifted her eyes to his. "Well…I suppose I just don't want to see you die for something as stupid as a lapse in judgment. Anger has a tendency to cloud a person's common sense."

Bradyn felt the warmth in her expression as a faint smile touched the corner of her mouth. In the dim lamplight of the kitchen her eyes caught an amber sparkle. Her next words held a hint of challenge.

"I think that you are a good person, Bradyn, regardless of what has happened between you and Briggs in the past. But I can't help but wonder what hold that man has over you. What have either of you done to make you want the other's blood on your hands so badly? I think you should tell me why three men have died trying to kill you. If you are going to ride away and leave us, you owe me the truth, Bradyn Preston. And I'd like the long version," she added, placing a hand on her hip.

He raised an eyebrow. Her words both irritated and comforted him at once. "To start with, Moriana Keene, I am no good man. If you knew what you were asking for, you'd turn tail and run right now. The truth, as you so aptly put it, is nothing a woman like you should have to hear. Ever."

"You were going to tell me earlier today, before those men showed up. Why not now?"

Her eyes explored his, and Bradyn began to feel vaguely ill. *Why the hell couldn't my horse have missed this house and kept right on walking into the wilderness like Liam Briggs intended?* For the tenth time in five minutes the thought crossed his mind.

The attraction and affection she worked in him was terrifying. It felt as if a rod of smoldering steel were being driven into the very center of his soul. His mind scrambled over this new and foreign ground until it came up against a rock of solid anger. He lodged against the fury for emotional safety. Grabbing her by the shoulders, he gritted his teeth. "If you want the truth, you'll have it. All of it. And after I've told you everything, you'll change your tune about me, Rian. You'll beg me to leave."

Her eyes grew wide. She blinked and stared up at him, apparently uncertain of how to react to his outburst of irritation. Bradyn saw the tremble in her lower lip and regretted touching her. Her next words confused him as the challenge in her eyes brightened and turned to set determination.

"You are not the only person in the world who has made wrong or terrible choices. Contrary to what you seem to think, you are not the first sinner to walk this earth, Bradyn Preston. Tell me everything and let me decide for myself how truly despicable you are."

"Fine," he answered. He still kept his hands on her shoulders, but his grip loosened. "Just remember that it was your idea and not mine."

Rian nodded, her gaze unmoving and patient.

Bradyn blew out a rush of air. "I guess I was telling you about my mama when I was interrupted this morning."

"Yes, you were," she said.

Bradyn lowered his eyes to the floor before he continued. "Yeah, my mama," he pondered heavily. "Now there was a woman to figure out. She was a dance hall girl in New Orleans when she met my father. He was a religious man, a circuit preacher they call 'em, and mama never really knew why she caught his eye. But she did."

He chuckled. "I have often thought it was because inside my father was as black as any man. But not mama. She thought the sun set on his head and the moon hung in the sky just for him. Whatever my father's reasons, he fell for mama hard. Oh, he set her straight. He took her to church and got her praying and packing around a Bible the size of Texas. Then he married her. My father was a widower, you see. He'd lost his wife almost five years before he met mama. She died giving birth to a baby boy, my half-brother, Jace."

He rubbed his thumb against Rian's shoulder

thoughtfully for a moment. She studied his face. Bradyn caught her gaze and decided she was wondering what any of this had to do with his current predicament.

"Wasn't much more than a year after my father married my mama that I came along. My father always did say that me and my brother were as opposite as night and day, or to put it in his words, 'as different as Lucifer and Michael the Arch-Angel.' Jace was nearly seven years older than me and he was pretty damn near the perfect son. Good, smart, always got the best marks in school and everybody loved him."

Despite his efforts to curb it, anger crept over him and sarcasm that gave his voice a brittle edge. "I, on the other hand, was a far cry from even good enough to get by. My father whipped me until he gave up and mama would just bawl and sometimes say things like, 'You're just a bad seed, baby.' or 'It's the curse I carry for being such an evil woman before I met your daddy, Bradyn.' When I was little, I felt awful about it, even tried to change once or twice, but it really did no good. I grew up brawling and cheating and getting into a thousand kinds of trouble. Mama said I was wilder than a mustang and meaner than a drunk with a ten-day drinkin' binge hangover.

"My father died when I was ten, then mama went back to dancing in the saloons and keeping company with strange men. She told me once; 'You can take the girl outta the saloon, but you'll never take the whore outta the girl, Bradyn.' Shames me to say it, but I ran away from home when I was fifteen. Haven't seen my mama since."

Bradyn's face twisted into a sneer as he ran his eyes over Rian's still face.

"You're a smart woman, Rian. I'll wager you can guess what happens to a fifteen-year-old runaway hellion. I got myself into one filthy mess after another. If it wasn't drinking and fighting, it was thieving and chasing women."

Rian offered a faint smile. He guessed she was recalling their conversation about Tucson Maude. He supposed it wasn't very hard for her to imagine the younger version of Bradyn Preston out looking for a good time and only finding trouble everywhere he went. It seemed little had changed in his life in all these years. He was still in trouble.

"I went from one riverboat casino to another, from saloon to whorehouse, gambling and carousing until my money would run out. Then, I'd go find a way to get my hands on more. When I was sixteen, I was caught trying to sell a stolen horse and damn near got killed for it. The judge who tried my case sent me away to the Confederate Army to help build railroads during the War. You'd think with all that pain and dying around me, and the fact that Death was a daily demon I had to face, it would have brought me up short and made me think. But not me. Once the war was over, I went back to my old habits."

Bradyn cleared his throat. "I wandered all over Mississippi and Louisiana. Then I tried my luck at gambling in St. Louis for awhile. Took up cheating at cards and wore out my welcome quicker than a whore in a ladies' church social. The sheriff and his deputies ran me out of town and told me if I ever set foot in St. Louis again, they'd shoot me on sight."

"So, I headed west, to Denver. Decided to see how many suckers I could take with my slick gambling tricks." He chuckled again, but this time there was no humor in it.

"Turns out, my brother, Jace, was the sheriff in Denver. Shocked the living hell out of me when he was the one to arrest me one night after I got caught cheating in a poker game with some of the city's upper class gents. Jace and his wife, Helena, tried to straighten me out and take me under their wing, but there's not much sense you can talk into a rowdy twenty-one-year-old hell bent on raising Cain."

He looked at Rian. Her sad expression was comforting, but he knew there was little she could do or say that would ease his turmoil.

"I made my brother's life miserable. In part, just out of pure spite and jealousy. Jace had always been the better of the two of us and he was reaping the rewards. What with a pretty little wife, a baby on the way, and being the sheriff of a town and all, he had it made. And I hated him for it." Bradyn paused and took a deep breath.

"That's when I met Liam Briggs. Briggs made cheating at the poker tables and petty theft look like a game of tag at a church picnic. He ran big rackets, like swindling land and robbing stagecoaches. He stole firearms from the Calvary supply trains and then sold them back at outrageous prices, the whole time the Calvary never even knowing it was him that was robbing them blind both ways to Sunday. He could get his hands on whatever he wanted, whenever he wanted. He lived the high life. He had everything Jace had and then some and that appealed to me. When he offered me a spot in his crew, I was more than happy to go along with him. Wasn't long before I was right in the middle of all his dealings. I was just like a dog set loose in a butcher's shop, so to speak."

Bradyn paused for a moment. Memories and black misery brought back the hurt. His distant gaze was broken when Rian asked, "What happened after you met Liam Briggs?"

"We spent a couple years traveling around; Liam, his three brothers, Lincoln, Cody, and Cameron, and me. We went from Kansas to Texas to Denver and back again, wreaking havoc wherever we went. We stole cattle in Oklahoma and sold them in New Mexico, robbed a bank or two in Kansas, Liam shot a man in the back in Dodge, then we swindled more than a few ranchers out of land in Texas with a brilliant railroad scheme that Liam put together. Liam nearly got himself killed in Houston, so we came back to Colorado to cool off for awhile."

"You were an outlaw, then? A robber and a murderer?" Rian asked.

He nodded. "I was involved in more messes than I care to remember."

Rian bit her lip. "What happened when you came back to Colorado?" she asked quietly.

"Once we got to Denver, Briggs decided he was gonna settle down and invest his "earnings" in a saloon and gambling joint. The saloon took off with a bang, but Jace got wind of our crooked gaming methods. We fixed everything, from the card decks and dice to the roulette tables. When

Briggs found out Jace was sniffing around, he tried to persuade him to back off. But when he tried to bribe him, Jace wouldn't take his money. Jace threatened to close Briggs down and see him hung if he didn't start running his business on the up and up. Let me tell you, Briggs doesn't threaten well. He got mad. Real mad."

Bradyn paused, as he allowed the memory of that terrible night to come back. For years, he had not let the pictures of what had happened enter his mind, but the nightmares of it had always afflicted his sleep. It had carved an abominable scar on his heart that he would be forced to carry forever. He pushed his breath between his teeth with a low hissing sound and forced himself to look Rian in the face again before continuing.

"I knew then and there that Briggs and Jace were gonna have a showdown. I knew it was going to end with only one of them standing. I should have warned Jace, I could have, but Briggs promised no one would get hurt. He said he was just gonna teach Jace a good lesson.

"Oh, God," he whispered, not wanting to continue, but helpless to stop. "We took her and the baby. Jace's wife, Helena, I mean. Cody and Lincoln broke into Jace's house and brought 'em to Liam. Briggs had always had a fancy for Jace's woman. Cameron and Briggs went to get Jace, while I stood watch over her and the baby. She begged me to let her go, she cried…" his voice broke.

Bradyn ground his jaw as he cleared his throat again. His hands tightened on Rian's shoulders as his heart clouded with a distant, dark misery. How he wished that he could change it all! How he wished that he could tell her the story with a different ending!

"I told her that Briggs wasn't gonna hurt 'em, he just wanted Jace to back off him and his saloon. Nothing was going to happen to her or the baby. I gave her my word." He closed his eyes and shook his head.

"But Briggs had different plans," he murmured. "He brought Jace to where he was keeping Helena and was gonna make him watch while he forced himself on her. That was more than I was willing to take. I would have rather been skinned alive and put in boiling water than let that happen. I never did cotton to men hurting women. Ever.

"I told Liam if he wanted to die, all's he had to do was lay a hand on Helena or the baby. Cody and Lincoln tried to shoot me, but I gunned them down. Cameron must've snuck behind me and clobbered me a good one because the next thing I remember was waking up on the floor. Jace was tied in a chair and beaten beyond recognition. Helena and the baby were dead."

Rian took in a sharp breath. "Oh, Bradyn!" she whispered. "That's the most awful thing I've ever heard." She put a hand over her mouth. "What did you do?" she asked in a small voice.

"Liam and Cameron had skipped town, of course, and Jace was in a bad way. I was arrested and put into jail for murder. I never argued the charges. I was more than deserving of death. There have been many days since that I wish I would have hung. I'll never make it right. Never. I could live like Saint Peter for a thousand years and never make it right. " Bradyn grew quiet. His eyes were sightless with memory and his heart full of remorse.

Rian watched him with a mixture of dismay and sympathy. He had expected that expression. It gave him physical pain to look into her eyes. "Then what happened?" she asked in a soft tone.

He looked away, unable to take her expression of gentle horror. He drew a slow breath. "Jace pulled through. He got me acquitted of the murders, though I couldn't for the life of me understand why he would want to. Jace had a capacity to forgive that I will never understand. He witnessed me kill Cody and Lincoln trying to save Helena and the baby. But, it doesn't matter. I still feel the guilt of his wife and baby's deaths in my gut and bones every day."

Bradyn closed his eyes for a moment. "Jace set me on the straight and narrow, you might say. He was given a job as marshal of the Wyoming Territory over in Cheyenne. I stuck with him for awhile, doing what I could to help him keep law and order. We set about trying to track down Briggs, but it was no good. Liam and Cameron had left the country." He paused and ran an absent hand over the wound on his arm.

"Eventually, I just couldn't take looking at Jace every day. I didn't like remembering the terrible pain and loss I'd brought to him. I left him for a couple years and went up to the Big Horns to hunt and trap. This spring, Jace sent me a letter. He'd heard that Briggs was in Laramie and he was going to find him and take him in for a trial and hanging. Even then I thought that Jace should have just found the bastard and shot him on the spot. He had a right to, after what Briggs had done. I decided to ride down to Cheyenne and see if Jace had found Briggs, but when I got there, I found out that Jace hadn't been back to Cheyenne in over a month. I followed him to Laramie, but he was nowhere to be found. That's when I got involved with Briggs's woman. You probably can figure out the rest of the story."

Rian nodded as if it all made sense. Then she frowned. "So who is the marshal whose badge you have? Jared Dawson. How does he figure into all of this?"

Bradyn shook his head. "Jared Dawson *was* my brother. 'Jace' was his kid nickname. "

Her brow furrowed in puzzlement. "And you are brothers with different last names? How is that possible if you have the same father?"

"I took my mother's maiden name when I left home. I guess I felt I was more like her with her wild, worldly ways than like my father with his squeaky clean living and bible-thumping reputation. In all honesty, I didn't want to soil a good man's name with my riotous living. It was a silly notion. Hasn't soothed my conscience one bit and I know my father's turning over in his grave." Bradyn shrugged and set his face in stone. He studied her, wondering when the scope of what he'd just told her would settle in her mind and she'd tell him to get out.

Rian watched him. She rubbed her cheek slowly as he watched the tears seep into the corners of her eyes. Then, she abruptly turned away. Bradyn saw the silence as her judgment. When she turned her back it was unbearable and all too expected. He had known it would come to this, but it made the experience of it no less difficult. He walked from the house and shut the door behind him with quiet force.

* * * *

Rian turned when the door slammed, confused that he would leave so suddenly. Wiping a stray tear from her cheek, she rushed out after him. "Bradyn, wait!" she shouted breathlessly. A clap of thunder nearly drowned out her voice. "Wait!" she cried again.

Bradyn quickened his stride when she called to him and appeared to ignore her footsteps behind him as she splashed through a puddle in her haste to catch him. "Bradyn!" She caught his arm and pulled at his sleeve. "Wait! Why are you angry?"

He turned, frowning with impatience. "I have to go."

Rian followed him. Tripping to keep up with his fast pace as cold mud sloshed over her bare feet, she wondered what she should say. What *could* she say? She understood his need to face Briggs. She understood how horrible his past was and how it must continually haunt him. *It must follow him everywhere he goes, like a harsh, merciless shadow. He probably feels like there is an accusing finger pointed at him every waking moment, cruelly reminding him of his horrible mistakes. I know that feeling myself. My God, do I know that feeling.* Another empathetic tear trailed down her cheek. She hurriedly brushed it away and followed him to the barn.

Bradyn threw open the barn door with more force than was necessary. Rian followed him to the first stall, trying to decide how to approach him. "Bradyn, please," she whispered as he tossed the saddle blanket onto his gelding. "Please don't go yet." Her voice wobbled as she fought like fury to hold back tears. "I don't want you to go."

Bradyn turned to look at her. His jaw was set with granite resolve. "Rian, this is not about you. This is not even about me *wanting* to leave. This is about a choice I made nearly seven years ago. A choice that cost lives. A choice that is *still* costing lives. I don't want to relive the night that I helped to get a good woman and an innocent baby killed. I don't want to see you tied to a chair, beaten and dead, or to see Kendall with bullets through his head and chest. You can't understand that. You never will be able to understand it because you've never lived it. You don't know what it's like to be directly responsible for the death of another human being, Rian. People like you will always sit in judgment…" He sighed and did not look at her face. "Hell, I guess you got a right," he said as he strode across the barn and pulled his saddle down from the wall.

Rian stopped dead in her tracks. She was stunned. "How can you possibly say that?" she asked, her anger slowly starting to grow. "What gives you the right to tell me how I should feel about your past? How would you know if I hold what you've done against you or not? You didn't even bother to ask me! You just assumed that I'd passed judgment and you decided to leave."

Bradyn came to a stop in front of her and dropped the saddle. He grabbed her arms and leveled his face with hers. "Look at me. I'm a murderer. A murderer! Am I the kind of person you want here? The kind of person you want around Kendall?" He let go and turned his back on her as he bent to pick up his saddle.

He might as well have punched her in the stomach. Pain and white-hot fury clouded her vision. The compassionate emotion was gone. In its place, came indignant rage. She grabbed Bradyn's arm and turned him to face her with more strength than she knew she possessed.

"You listen to me right now, Mr. Preston!" she shouted, her voice shaking. "You can have your lofty self-incrimination and wear your penitence on your sleeve like a badge, but you have no right to tell me that I could never fathom how dark your past has been. I know better than you can imagine the horrors you live with. I, too, know the guilt of taking a human life." She let go of his arm and stood glaring up at him. "So don't you *dare* presume to tell me what I don't understand. You don't know anything about what I have or have not done."

"What are you talking about?" Bradyn asked. His voice was filled with the abrasiveness of gravel on bare skin. His eyes were cobalt disbelief.

Realizing that her words had opened a floodgate of curiosity, she felt instant regret for speaking them. "Never mind!" she said and marched toward the door, her shoulders back and her spine erect. *Oh, Good Lord! What was I thinking?* Her fingers twitched as she clasped and unclasped her hands. *Now he's going to want to know. I should have let him go. I should have just let him go! Damn, my ridiculous pride and illogical, smitten heart!*

Bradyn ran after her and caught her by an arm. He spun her around to face him and Rian saw that his angry expression had been replaced by urgent curiosity. "What do you mean 'you know the guilt of taking a human life'?" he demanded. "Who did you kill?"

She glared up at him, her mouth a firm, thin line of obstinacy.

"Does this have to do with the scars I saw across your back?"

His eyes were softer now; his voice had lost its agitated edge. The hand on her arm pulled her toward him and she felt a strange happiness at the gentleness in his expression.

"Tell me who you killed, Rian," he insisted.

She fought against him for a moment. But it was impossible to resist as Bradyn pulled her toward him. She dug at his fingers, trying to loosen his grasp around her arm. It did no good. The need to understand, the need to know, was etched in his face. He wasn't about to let her go without an explanation. Her decision was cemented in her mind. *Fine. I'll tell you. Then we'll see who judges who. We'll see what 'Mr. Martyr' here does when he finds out about* me *and what I've done.*

Her eyes narrowed, the fire of her anger still burning in her checks. "All right, Bradyn, I'll tell you. I'm a damn fool, but I'll tell you everything. Then we'll see if *you* have the ability to withhold judgment." Her voice was cutting and cold. "The other night when you asked me if I was ever married, I almost told you then. I think it would have saved you a lot of worry. You wouldn't have had any trouble telling me about your past. You probably would have left yourself." She couldn't keep the harsh sarcasm out of her voice.

"What're you talking about?" he asked, looking a little dumbfounded.

Rian pulled free of his grasp as his blue eyes bored into hers. She searched his face, stalling for a moment. *Maybe I don't want to tell him…Maybe I should just tell him to go. Now. Before I make another stupid mistake. Perhaps I should keep the past buried where it belongs.*

Suddenly, she wanted to leave the hurt and the horror of that night almost seven years ago tucked forever away in her heart. She wished she had never even started this conversation.

"Rian," he sighed, "Your past, whatever it is you have done, may be terrible. But you are talking to someone who has no right to pronounce judgment. You already know that. You already know what I've done. Tell me what's happened to you, I want to understand. I want to know, Rian."

Bradyn's voice was so kind. His eyes were full of sapphire empathy. She knew then that irregardless of the outcome, irregardless of his reaction, she had to tell him. She had to. If he was the one she should love, it would be futile if it wasn't founded on the truth. It required not just his reckoning, but hers as well.

She walked to the horse stall and looked in at the partially saddled gelding. Bradyn came to stand beside her. Rian felt his eyes on her face, but she could not bring herself to look at him.

"It's strange how time can change your view of everything," she said quietly. Her eyes wandered over barn floor. She did not see the litter of hay or the rough-hewn timber walls, only distant memories.

"The immaturity of youth is blinded by the intoxicating glow of a world full of promise and no evil or ugliness," she said. "I was so oblivious to reality. Oblivious to how easy it is for one's life to change in moments and a bright future to be torn away. "

She paused and took a deep breath. "When I was fifteen, I fell in love with a young man. To me, he was perfect in everyway. Everyway. I loved him more than I loved my own life. Oh, he had his flaws." She knew her voice sounded bitter and cold. "He was a horrible gambler, for one. Little more than a drifter really. But, when you are fifteen and in love, none of that matters. We were both incredibly young and extremely foolish. We were certain we were meant to be together, so nothing could keep us apart.

"My mother and my brother tried to warn me, but I was completely irrational on the matter. They told me he was no good, no happiness could come of it. But I was young and stupid. I ran away with him to be married. We traveled abroad for awhile, well, only a few months, really, because soon we were out of money. My dashing young groom had gambled away every cent we had to our names. After I pleaded with him, we went crawling back to my mother. She disliked my husband, but, because she loved me, she had pity on us and took us in. My brother, Jackson, gave my husband a job at his bank. He mended his ways for awhile…in retrospect it was purely to stay close to my family's money. But the change wasn't to be permanent.

"My husband became a clerk in my brother's bank. It was a sheer mercy on Jackson's part, giving him a job the way he did. We moved into our own home a few months later and everything felt as though our marriage were a happy union…at least in my mind. But the euphoria didn't last. Not long after we'd moved in and gotten settled, my husband started gambling and drinking heavily again. His drinking grew progressively worse. Sometimes he would be so intoxicated he wouldn't even know who I was. He would ramble incoherently about seeing spirits and ghouls. Sometimes his face would change. I can't explain it, but sometimes it became black, almost evil. That's when he brooded and talked of seeing crazy things."

Rian ran her fingers over the rough beam of the stall, wishing she could crawl beneath the hay and never be seen again. "I remember there was one night in particular when he got horribly drunk. He grabbed me by the arm in the den and said, 'A man came to me today, Rian. He told me there's someone coming for you. He wanted me to kill one of the Devil's children. He told me to fulfill my destiny…but I don't know if I can do it. I don't know if I can…' His words scared me to death. I didn't know what he was talking about. He was drinking so much that I thought he was losing his mind. When morning came, and he was sober, he remembered none of it. But I did."

Humiliated pain sought to steal her voice, but she resisted it. "Not long after he started drinking hard and hallucinating, the beating started." Rian felt the familiar ache engulf her heart as if it were a memory from yesterday. It all felt so very near to her now. She stole a glance at Bradyn. In the dim light of the stable, she could make out the rigid line of his jaw. Momentarily, she wished she could touch his face again and feel his arms around her, like she had earlier tonight on the porch. She forced herself to go on.

"I thought… it wasn't so bad at first. A slap when he was drunk and dinner was a little late. Or sometimes he'd punch me if his whiskey glass wasn't refilled promptly." She shrugged. "I made excuses for him because, at first, it was not horribly unbearable. 'He is just struggling with his new job,' I reasoned to myself. Or, 'he is working so hard to provide for us.' I have lists of stupid excuses a mile long forever engraved in my mind. They all soothed me a bit. Even after he had bloodied my nose, left bruises on my back and stomach, and had broken my hand in two separate outbursts."

Rian turned and looked up at Bradyn again. His blue eyes were warm and kind. That expression was nearly her undoing. She had to close her eyes and swallow hard before speaking again. "When we'd been married for almost a year and a half, there came the bittersweet. I learned I was going to have a baby. I couldn't have been happier or more horrified at the same time. I felt almost as if I were coming to the surface after being under water for too long. Fear, true fear, entered my life for the very first time. Of course I'd been afraid of my husband for months, but having a child was different. I feared bringing a baby into the world more than I'd ever feared him. Ever."

Rian pleadingly searched Bradyn's face, willing him to understand what she had experienced. "How could I raise a child in the home of such a brutal man? But where could I go? I was so ashamed of the mess I'd gotten myself into! My family, while they hadn't ever truly liked my husband, believed that our life was fine. They didn't know about the mountains of empty whiskey bottles that filed through our house. They didn't know that he was drinking as many as three bottles a day. They didn't know he struck me repeatedly, leaving me bedridden for days at a time. I always thought up convenient excuses and down-right lies to avoid them whenever he left marks on my body."

Rian sighed. "It took me three months to get up the nerve to tell my husband that a baby was on the way. I thought that perhaps a son or daughter would give him something that I had never been able to. Maybe having a child would fill a void in his life and help him to stop drinking and gambling. Oh, how wrong I was!" Her voice trembled and her lips quivered, but she shed no tears.

"When I told him, he was happy. He was ecstatic…at first. He even quit drinking for awhile and his mood was better than it had been since we'd first married. Then one night, when I was almost eight months into the pregnancy, he came home from work later than usual. He'd been drinking and had lost an exorbitant amount of money in a poker game, money that I later learned he'd stolen from my brother. I was furious with him, but I was too afraid to voice it. In the end, it didn't matter that I kept my mouth shut, he threw me down the stairs anyway." She swallowed. "I wasn't hurt too badly, but I…I lost the baby."

Rian lowered her gaze to Bradyn's shoulder, unable to take the pity she saw in his eyes. Unable to take his sympathy because she knew that in a few moments, he might not feel much sympathy toward her at all.

"After he threw me down the stairs, he vanished. I don't remember how long I lay there bleeding and screaming. Jackson happened to come by and find me that night. I was practically unconscious and not too far from dying, I'm sure. He immediately sent for my mother, who was understandably terrified when she arrived. They tried to save the baby, but it was no good. I lied and told them that I had tripped and fallen down the stairs. I don't know why I didn't tell them the truth…looking back, I think it was because I wanted it to end the way it later did. But from that day on I hated my husband with every bone in my body and every breath I took. I hated him for killing my baby."

She looked up and studied Bradyn for a moment; biting her lip to stop the tears that stung her eyes. "You're probably wondering why I didn't leave the man right then. I've asked myself that same question a thousand times. The truth is I really didn't care anymore. I just felt…*dead* inside. Nothing that he did to me after that could have possibly hurt as much as losing my baby."

She frowned and rubbed her forehead. "This may sound a little strange to you, but I can't remember much of what happened after that night. I think that when I lost the baby, it made me a little sick in the head, because there are whole sections during that time that are just…*black* to me.

"I *do* remember when the inevitable happened. My mother saw a bruise on my face a few months later. My husband had beaten me in a drunken rage the night before…I can't really remember why. Finally, I was forced to tell her the truth. She was heart-broken and angry. I think a part of her felt guilt because she hadn't guessed it earlier. When Jackson found out what had happened, he swore he'd kill my husband. I can't lie; a part of me wanted him to. But I tried to reason with him. I didn't want my brother to go to the gallows for a foolish mistake I had made. I told Jackson that I would leave my husband if he would promise not to do anything rash.

"My husband came home unexpectedly the next day at noon and he was already intoxicated. He found me in our bedroom where I was packing my things. I expected him to be angry when I told him I was leaving, but I have never seen such savage, animal fury in any human in my life. He…" She paused and searched Bradyn's face, wondering if she could possibly continue. She wondered if she could endure to hear the words spill from her own lips. They were words that she had never before spoken aloud.

"He…he tied me to the banister and bullwhipped me.

That's where I got the scars," she said in a quiet tone. "I honestly don't remember much of that either. In fact, if he hadn't told me that he'd whipped me, I wouldn't even know that was what he'd done to this day. I just remember feeling awful pain and seeing a blinding purple light before I lost consciousness. He left me tied there for two days and wouldn't let my mother or brother see me. He threatened that he would hurt me if they ever came to our house again. He told me that I would never, ever get away from him and if I ever tried to leave him again, he'd kill me."

Rian noticed the flexing in Bradyn's jaw. She saw the raw anger snapping in his eyes. "I couldn't stay. I couldn't. I played the obedient wife long enough for him to believe I wasn't leaving and then one night as he slept, I shot him." Her voice cracked. "I shot him dead."

A tear, solitary and hot, trailed slowly down her cheek. She felt Bradyn brush it away with his finger.

"I remember standing there, looking down at his body thinking, 'I should feel remorse…I just murdered a man. I should be weeping…or at least feel some contrition. But, God help me, I can't. I can't bring myself to feel anything but *relief*.' I was free of him. I had been living so long in the iron cage he had built for me I had forgotten how it felt to be free. I had forgotten how it felt to be *alive*.

"That night I ran to my brother's house. When Jackson found out what I'd done, he and Sadie brought me here. They packed up Kendall, who was just a small baby, and every basic necessity. They gave up everything. Jackson's bank, their home, their families and social obligations, all of it, to protect me from the authorities. My mother had been making me the quilt, the one on the bed in the guestroom. She gave it to me the night we fled. It had been intended to be for the baby… It is the last memory I have of her face." Her voice broke and a stream of tears wetted her cheeks. "I spent the next year adding patches to it and remembering my mother's face that night."

Bradyn looked stunned. The grave mixture of irritation and shock on his face filled her heart with uncertainty as he seemed to weigh her story thoughtfully. After a few moments of silence, she started to turn away. Wondering if she had made the right choice telling him everything the way she had, she was startled when he caught her by the arm and turned her back around. One hand lifted her chin, while the other wrapped around her waist and gently drew her toward him.

"Bradyn, I—," She'd wanted to explain somehow. To tell him that if he couldn't understand, she didn't blame him, but the words were silenced as his lips closed over hers.

She wasn't sure why he did it. Maybe it was her tears, or that her story had made him feel sorry for her. It may have been due, in part, to the harrowing situations they'd managed to survive, one right after the other these past few days…or because of pure, impulsive desire. She hoped that perhaps it was the kindred longing of two lonely people; both trudging through life with past memories that threatened to crush them into the dust; both searching for the proof of love's reality.

Whatever the reason, she could not deny the fire his kiss worked in her soul or the sure and certain knowledge that, amidst all the turmoil of the past several days, she and Bradyn were destined for this…and much more. As he twined his fingers through her hair and pulled her against him, the hunger in his embrace brought her life into beautiful, spiraling perspective.

For an instant, she could remember how she knew him. She was with him in a flowered glade, the sun warm on their bodies as they rolled through soft grass. Their laughter echoed across the field as the perfume of gentle blossoms permeated the air around them. But then the picture faded and her mind was returned to the present as Bradyn pulled away and looked into her eyes.

He watched her, his arm around her waist as if he was afraid she would try to run away at the first chance.

Wide-eyed, she looked up at him. "You don't think I'm a heinous coward of a woman?" she asked. For all her will power, she couldn't stop the tears that seeped to the corners of her eyes. "I shot him in cold blood. While he slept. You don't think me evil?"

"Nope," he replied as he gently wiped the tears from her cheek with his free hand. "Although I'm not quite sure what 'heinous' means exactly."

A crooked smile wended over the corners of his mouth and Rian was suddenly very afraid. "Please don't leave, Bradyn," she whispered, her lips only inches from his. "Please."

"I won't leave tonight," he answered softly, as he kissed her cheek. "Not tonight."

He carried her to the house through the pouring rain. Rian laid her head against his chest and closed her eyes as the raindrops sprinkled her cheeks. The scent of him was intoxicating; the musk of masculinity. She supposed it was too good to be real, but she couldn't shake the excitement and anticipation that ran like fire through her blood. There was no stopping herself. She wanted him to love her so badly.

Once they were in her bedroom, Bradyn searched her eyes. He looked uncertain. "You don't have to do this, Rian," he whispered. "I won't make you if you don't want to."

Rian placed her hand on his cheek and studied his face for a moment. Her fingers played with a thick strand of ebony hair that had fallen across his forehead. Her entire body hummed with desire. She knew there was only one way to rid herself of the terrible, lonely pain inside. Slowly, she shook her head and ran her thumb along his upper lip. "I want you, Bradyn," she said. "Wild horses couldn't stop me from making love to you tonight."

He pulled her up against him and held her face between his hands. The electric blue of his eyes sent a shiver through her. "Then those wild horses had better damn well stay away," he whispered as his lips brushed over hers again.

Haloed light and living shadows blended, creating an exotic moving tapestry on the wall. The rain came down in sprinkling rhythm against the bedroom window. She felt her heart pounding in her ears as Bradyn laid his body over hers. Her breathing was shallow and quick; his was deep and ragged. The taste of delicious kisses and the friction of bare skin created a frenzied need in both of them.

The bittersweet pain of love too long unknown and ecstasy reborn flooded every inch of her awareness as Bradyn made gentle love to her. She trembled at the fierce passion in his eyes and wondered if she had found the true meaning of pure bliss. There had never been a time in her life when a man had held her with both reverent awe and burning lust in equal measure. The aching need in the center of her body grew until she could stand it no more. Tears of euphoric joy slipped noiselessly down her cheeks as the room slid dreamily out of focus. All she heard was the sound of the rain and Bradyn whispering her name against her neck over and over. "Rian."

She lay awake for a long time after he drifted off, her fingers lightly tracing the lace of kisses he'd left along her stomach. The heat of their love was still warm in her core. She feared to hope and yet hope grew. It blossomed from a tiny ember into a roaring flame as she lay listening to his soft breathing and feeling the weight of his arm across her hips. Bradyn was the one. He had to be. She loved him.

Chapter Nine

Cigar smoke, sweetly acrid and curling upward in swirling chiffon wisps, filled an ornate bedroom on the second floor of the Silver Lady Saloon. Contessa Lang sighed with lusty content. She lay among crimson silk sheets, the liquid cloth twisting around her pale body, her curls spilled over a velvet-covered pillow. She smiled with sanguine satisfaction at the man sitting on the edge of the bed smoking.

Kyle Bodeen had shared her bedroom for three nights now. Each new romantic tussle in the sheets had proven more exotic and uninhibited than the last. Her romance with Liam Briggs would never compare to the complete abandon she felt in Kyle's arms. Tessa's gaze wandered with slow hunger over his naked back; his muscles gleamed taut and golden in the dim lamplight. She ran a hand over his chest and felt her body awaken to sultry need again. She sighed once more, louder this time.

Kyle smiled down at her. His lips were crooked with unspoken, provocative insinuation. His green eyes glittered with dark desire.

"Again?" he asked. He put out his cigar in the crystal ash tray atop her expensive teak nightstand.

Tessa nodded and stretched up to pull his mouth down to hers. A smile spread across her lips as she gazed into his beautiful face. "Again," she affirmed in a soft, seductive tone. Kyle's lips closed over her neck and burned a nibbling, wet trail down her collarbone. Her breathless moan was interrupted by a resounding knock on the door.

"Tessa?" a voice shouted. Though muffled by heavy oak, its owner was unmistakable. "Tessa, open up!" Two more impatient bangs followed. Tessa looked up at Kyle with cross surprise.

"What's he doing here?" she hissed venomously. "He hasn't come to my room in almost two weeks!" She threw back the sheets and climbed limberly from the bed, irritated as all hell that Liam should choose, now of all times, to pay her a visit. She pulled a purple organza wrap from the damask-covered divan and hurriedly pulled it on. "Stay out of sight," she whispered coarsely to Kyle.

His easy, humorous smile was no assurance that he would obey her. Tessa frowned at him and left to open the door. Walking from the bedchamber into the sitting area, she felt uneasy anger fill her. She opened the door with an impatient jerk. She was ready to fight.

"Why aren't you downstairs?" Liam asked as he took her in from head to toe.

Tessa knew sheer cloth of her dressing robe left nothing to the imagination. When Liam licked his lips, she tried to push the image of her naked body, pressed against his as both of them writhed in a sea of vibrant red silk, out of her mind. "I didn't feel like working tonight," she answered casually. She rested an arm against the door jamb and forced an expression of indifference.

"What do you mean you didn't feel like working? You have a packed house down there!" Liam shouted. The noisy ruckus of piano and men's laugher in the background escalated as if to prove his emphatic assertion.

"I have a headache, Liam." Tessa replied, rubbing her eyes wearily and trying with all her strength to mask her annoyance at him. But, when he pushed past her and walked into her room, she felt instant rage. "What the hell do you think you're doing?" she demanded.

"Since when am I not invited into your room?" Liam returned. His voice was even and lethally calm.

"Since you got up on your high, self-righteous horse and tossed me to the side of the road like a dirty, well-used boot!" Tessa answered. She put her hands on her hips in defiance. "You are the one who left *me*, Liam, remember? You made your choice, now live with it. And get out!" she commanded, pointing at the door.

The scent of cigar smoke filtered through the room and Liam's eyes gleamed with suspicion. A chilling, evil smile crossed his mouth. "So, you're entertaining tonight, are you?" he asked.

"And what if I am?" Tessa retorted. "It's my prerogative to entertain whomever I wish, whenever I wish, Liam Briggs. I'm surprised that you seem to have forgotten my chosen vocation so easily since it seems that the neglect of my duties is what brought you to my room in the first place."

Liam's smile remained. His cold appraisal of her was startling and vengeful. "Who is it?" he snarled.

"Evening, Liam."

The pleasant, crisp voice drew Liam's gaze to the bedchamber door. Kyle was leaning against the doorjamb with nonchalant elegance. He was naked from the waist up and his cigar was tucked neatly between his lips. Liam's eyes narrowed when he noticed that Kyle's gun hung with lackadaisical ease around his slender hips.

Liam's face filled with blood-red rage. Fury like none Tessa had ever seen. "Bodeen, you dirty bastard, what're you doing here with my woman?"

"*Your* woman, Briggs?" Kyle asked. He took several slow, deliberate steps to the middle of the room with a smile of disbelief on his face. Taking a drag off his cigar, he placed a hand on his sidearm with indifferent smoothness. "I was under the impression that Miss Lang was a free agent. An adept and capable businesswoman whose livelihood entails entertaining gentlemen for a reasonable rate," he said evenly.

Tessa crossed her arms and rolled her eyes. *As if I have asked you to pay me one copper cent for your 'entertainment', Kyle.*

Liam's body shook with anger. Tessa knew his wrath was only put into check by the hand Kyle rested casually on his gun. His fury was almost inhuman as he headed for the door. "You want her?" Shoving past Kyle, who was now blocking his exit, he grabbed Tessa and flung her unceremoniously at Kyle's feet. "You can have the bitch!" he said. "Oh, but you'll pay. Mark my words. Both of you will pay! Especially you, Tessa. *Especially* you, whore!" he swore as he slammed the door behind him.

Tessa stood up and dropped wearily to a high-backed mahogany chair. She exhaled a long, drawn-out sigh. "Why did you have to come out of the bedroom?" she glared up at Kyle. "You just made everything worse, you know? If he would have thought I was up here alone, he wouldn't have been so angry."

Kyle chuckled. "Liam Briggs doesn't scare me."

Wide-eyed, Tessa gaped up at him. "Are you insane? Do you even know *who* Liam Briggs *is*?"

Kyle gave her a smile that was full of ruthless humor. "Why don't you fill me in, honey?" he asked coyly as he leaned down and hoisted her up against his body.

"Do you have any idea what he did to the last man he found in my bed?" she continued, ignoring his impish grin and the way he started nibbling her ear provocatively. "He had him beaten, stabbed, and bullwhipped. Then Liam tied him to a saddled horse and turned it loose to wander around the territory until he died." She pushed Kyle's face away from her ear. "Are you listening to me?" she demanded.

"Did he now?" Kyle whistled. "He sounds like a pretty tough guy. Wonder if he'll try to do that to me?" He frowned and rubbed his chin with mock sobriety. When Tessa shook her head at him, he shrugged. "Oh well, the cat's been done let out the bag, darlin'," he drawled. "Might as well enjoy the vixen my neck's been put on the line for." He pulled her playfully toward the bedroom. The whole while his hands busy pulling the thin, shimmering dressing gown from her body.

Tessa giggled. His persistence made it hard for her to want to detour him. "Listen to me, Kyle. I'm serious. Liam is bad news when he gets as angry as he is tonight. Please. I don't want anything awful to happen to you."

Kyle sobered. "You don't need to worry about me,

Tessa." He smiled and rubbed her back with reassurance. "I can take care of myself. Now come on, let's enjoy the night while it's still young." He sat down on the bed and patted his thigh in wordless invitation. The burning desire and mischievous humor on his face was irresistible. His adorable expression stroked the animal passions in her.

Tessa nodded and dropped onto his lap, her mouth closing over his with sensual force. "Let's," she said as he rolled her to the bed and began devouring her with kisses.

A cloud of smoke and listless gloom hung over the table at the far back of the Silver Lady. Liam sat there, his face solid stone, with a half-empty bottle of bourbon at his elbow.

Cameron twitched nervously. Whenever Liam got that vacant, glowering look in his eye, someone was about to buy a one-way ticket into a small pine box. A man could bank on it.

"That whore!" Liam cursed under his breath. He'd only come down from Tessa's room fifteen minutes ago and already he had swilled down four shots, one right after another. "That low-down, cheating whore!"

"You want that Wes and I should take care of 'em?" Cass Banks, the farcical excuse for the town's sheriff, asked with an unlit cigarette dangling from his lower lip.

Cameron stifled a smirk when Liam ignored the sheriff's remark. Instead, his brother's eyes stayed locked on the far wall and a sneer played across his mouth. Liam held his whiskey glass out and Cameron filled it promptly. He watched as his brother swallowed the bourbon and rocked in his chair with short, agitated motion.

"Can't. Not yet," he intoned. "Damn it!" he shouted. Cameron winced as Liam threw his glass to the floor where it shattered into a thousand tinkling shards. "If it weren't for that bastard, Bodeen, I'd have shot the wench myself tonight. But I can't afford to piss Bodeen off yet. I might need him to kill Preston…Has anyone heard back from Tex or Buddy?" When an uneasy look was passed around the table, Cameron locked eyes with his brother.

"What is it?" Liam demanded.

"We ain't heard nothin'," he answered quickly.

"Damn it," Liam cursed again. This time his voice was quiet and maniacal. "It's been almost two days. They should have been back by now."

Cameron lit a cigarette, the feeling of a rabbit cornered by a fox filling his gut. He hated it when Liam used that quiet voice of his. It was twice as frightening and three times as lethal as his loudest shouting.

"Want us to ride out an' find 'em?" Cass asked. His eagerness to win Liam's favor was glowing wildly in his eyes. Cameron glowered at him, irritated that the sheriff had taken up the role of Liam's advisor in his stead.

"No!" Liam barked. He ground his teeth together with audible frustration. Then he began rocking again. Cameron guessed that the cognitive wheels of his mind were whirling like a well-oiled machine.

"No…" he murmured, more to himself rather than to his companions. "I think that if Preston survives those two, he'll show up back here." There was a pause as he signaled for the bartender to bring him a fresh glass. "Umhmmm. That's it." He pressed his thumb to his lip repeatedly as he finished talking to himself.

There was a loud smack as Liam's hand came down on the table. Cameron noticed that everyone sat up a little straighter, their eyes became a little more attentive, and a collective swallow passed round the table. "Listen up. Preston might just be stupid enough to come back here and that'll work out nicely with the little arrangement I'm gonna set up with Bodeen."

"Bodeen?" Cameron's incredulous snort garnered an irritated look from his brother, though he chose to ignore it. "What the hell kind of deal are you making with him? I thought you wanted him dead!"

Liam smirked and nodded his head with condescending patience. "I do. I already told you that, Cameron. But I need Preston dead first. Bodeen's the only one fast enough to go up against him and win. He offered to do it for five grand. I think I'll take him up on that offer."

"Five thousand dollars?" Cameron whistled. "That's a lot

of scratch to cough up just to have Preston killed."

"Oh, Bodeen won't collect," Liam stated firmly. "I'll see to that."

"How?" Cameron asked in equal parts disbelief and curiosity.

"You leave that to me," Liam said. "I'll make sure Preston buys a bullet and then I'll take care of Bodeen." He smiled and rubbed his hands together. "I'll finish the bastard myself this time. Like I should have done back in Amarillo instead of handing the job off to Kendrick," he said as the bartender returned with a glass. Cameron quickly filled it with another shot of liquid courage.

* * * *

"Are you asleep?" His voice, deep, relaxed, and a thousand miles away, came to her.

"No," she answered dreamily. She snuggled up closer to him, pressing her body against his side. He rubbed her shoulder as he smoked his cigar. Tessa sighed. Her eyes were heavy with contented exhaustion. "I'm tired," she murmured as her fingers traced a line along his chest. "Are you?"

"A little." Kyle replied. He sounded preoccupied.

Tessa sat up on an elbow and looked at him. His expression was one of deep concentration. It was a look she hadn't ever seen on his face. With the constant look of humor gone, she saw that his green eyes took on a cold cast that was chilling and vicious in its way. She touched his cheek. "Is something bothering you, baby?" she asked hesitantly.

Turning to look at her, he winked and the sparkle returned to his eyes. "Not a thing. Just thinking is all."

"What about?"

"Briggs, I reckon." He shrugged casually.

"Are you worried about his promise to make you pay?" She pressed a hand to his shoulder in concern.

"Nope," he returned.

Tessa watched him flick ash into the crystal tray before

taking a deep drag on the cigar. "Then why are you thinking about Liam? If you're not worried, I mean."

Kyle twirled one of her golden curls over his index finger thoughtfully for a moment. "I was just figuring is all."

"Figuring what?" Tessa's voice was small. Frankly, she expected to be barked at for asking so many questions.

"Figuring on how I'm going to kill him," Kyle said.

The twinkle in his eyes let Tessa believe for a brief second that he was joking. The iron set of his jaw told her otherwise. Her eyes went wide with fear. "You're gonna kill him? Liam Briggs." The half smile of incredulity that pulled at the corner of her mouth melted under the frozen fury that flashed across his face. "Why?" she gulped.

"Let's just say he owes me."

"Owes you. What the hell is that supposed to mean?" she asked, disbelief warping her tone as she sat upright in the bed.

"I can't yet..." Kyle said to himself, apparently thinking aloud. "He'd going to need me for Preston. I'd bet my gold pocket watch on it. He's gonna come ask me to take care of Preston as sure as Judas got his thirty pieces of silver. Then we'll see...I may need him for awhile. But mark my words...I *am* going to finish that bastard when he is of no further use to me." He patted Tessa's arm reassuringly. "How would you like to visit Paris, or maybe Venice? I could show you the world. How does that strike you, honey?"

Confused and irritated at his lack of explanation, Tessa shook her head, "I don't know. It would help if I knew what the hell you were talking about. What do you mean Liam is going to need you to finish Preston? I thought Liam sent a man out to find Bradyn and shoot him already. And why the hell did you say Liam owes you? Did you know him before you came to Laramie?" Her eyes narrowed with suspicion.

Kyle just chuckled, but when he answered her his voice was razor sharp. "Let's just say we were business partners at one time. Had a good racket going down in Texas until the bastard got greedy and decided to hire some two-bit, second rate gunman to shoot me in the back."

"He didn't!" Tessa gasped. "What happened?"

"Other than me taking a plug, not much. But he's gonna pay. You can bet your pretty face, Tessa, he's gonna pay. In spades."

The anger that glittered in his eyes was almost inhuman. Tessa had never known a person whose expression could change from a teasing and attentive smile into a ruthless and calculating glare in one instant. Not like Kyle anyway. The harsh vacant expression on his face made Tessa shudder, it was almost as if he were somewhere else besides in the room with her. In that moment, she had no doubt that Kyle was going to make good on his word. Or at least die trying.

"So Liam is the reason you came to Laramie. You want revenge, is that it?" Her voice was small and childlike.

"Well, let's just say I came to Laramie for a few different reasons…and leave it at that. But I'll tell you this much; I am going to have my revenge, I promise you that. You can bet your soul on it."

Tessa shuddered again, but said nothing.

"Does that scare you, Tessa?" His voice was as smooth as her crimson silk sheets.

Tessa shook her head, a weak smile parting her lips, "No. I think Liam has it coming."

"That he does, my lovely," Kyle agreed, taking another puff of his cigar, "That he does."

Tessa was quiet for awhile as she thought about Kyle's words. "You know what I don't understand?" she asked finally.

"What's that?" He ran a finger down her spine as he took another drag of his cigar.

"If Liam wants Bradyn Preston dead so badly, why didn't he finish him when he had the chance? He had the opportunity when he beat the man within an inch of his life, so why didn't he just kill him and get it over with then?"

"It's simple," Kyle replied as he turned to look her in the face. "Briggs can't kill Preston and he knows it."

"Why not?" she asked.

The cold smile that crept over his mouth sent a strange tremor through her stomach. "Because," he answered. "I'm the only one that can."

* * * *

Liam paced his hotel room an hour later. Haunting pictures of Tessa frolicking in Kyle Bodeen's arms flashed and faded across his mind. It was unforgivable, damnably unforgivable. But he had a bigger problem at the moment. It was a problem that required delicate handling. Would he be able to convince Bodeen to face Preston? Would Bodeen accept his offer after their confrontation earlier tonight? Liam ground his teeth. Asking Kyle for help after seeing him in Tessa's room felt lower than a rattler's sliding belly. The notion was bitter and repulsive to him.

But it has to be done, he reminded himself. After all, this wasn't about Tessa and her loose, man-whoring ways anymore. This was about Liam saving his own hide. If Bodeen didn't get Preston, Preston would get Liam, and then it was not going to matter one drop of water to a river if Liam had Tessa or not. And when it came right down to it, he didn't care who ended up dead or in what order, just as long as he wasn't in the body count when the dust settled and the smoke cleared.

He had laid his plans. Now he just needed to get Bodeen's cooperation. That done, it was going to be an easy finish. Liam already knew how he was gonna handle Bodeen. He licked his lips maliciously. And Tessa would be the sweet icing on the proverbial cake. He was going to finish her after her two miscreant lovers were dead and there was no one left to save her sorry ass.

"And I'll drink to that." Liam toasted aloud to the empty hotel room as he took a long swig of bourbon. "Damn straight I will."

* * * *

When Liam knocked on Tessa's door it was nearly midnight. He expected a groggy, half-naked Tessa to open the door so when Kyle answered, fully dressed and looking wide awake, Liam was surprised. He found it irritating, and a little unsettling, that Kyle didn't appear startled in the least that he had come calling. In fact, Liam got the vague impression that Kyle had been waiting for him.

"Hello, Liam," Kyle said with a dark twinkle in his eyes. "What can I do for you?" His tone was light and taunting as he added, "Besides your woman, of course."

Liam bit his tongue against an eloquent stream of curses and forced a smile. "I was actually hoping your offer to finish off Preston for me was still open?" He ground his hand into a tight fist behind his back. His finger nails drew blood as they sunk into the flesh of his palm. He had to remain calm and cordial or else the whole plan would be worthless. Bodeen figured in. Liam couldn't get what he wanted without him.

Kyle appeared to think on it for a moment, setting his jaw with rigid calculation. "I guess I could still take care of that little matter for you. Only it's gonna cost you more."

"More?" Liam's voice wobbled as he tried like the Devil to hang on to his composure. "How much more?"

"It'll cost you ten thousand," Kyle answered smoothly. "Take it or leave it."

You bastard! You think you're going to soak me. Liam wanted to laugh right in Kyle's face. Instead, he forced a slow smile. "Sounds fair," he agreed. *What does it matter? Ten thousand dollars or one hundred thousand, you ain't going to collect it you dumb son of a whore.* The voice in his head laughed with demented amusement. *You ain't gonna collect.*

"You wouldn't be thinking of double-crossing me, would ya now, Briggs?" The pleasant smile on Kyle's face was nearly Liam's undoing.

"Now why would you think a thing like that, Kyle?" Liam asked, his voice almost defying his mental command for calm restraint.

"Just a funny feeling I get in my gut." Kyle leaned against the frame of the door. His fingers played with the wood molding as he appraised Liam in a shrewd manner. "Maybe, just to be sure, you better pay me half up front. The rest when the job's done. I don't want you getting any fancy ideas about skipping town before I collect my just due."

"Fine," Liam acquiesced. "I think I can manage that nicely. You'll have your money tomorrow. You have my word." He turned to go. "Ah, yes and one more thing."

"What's that, Briggs?" Kyle asked. His expression had turned hard and frozen as ice.

"When you face Preston, you have to leave Tessa with me. Call it an insurance policy. I don't want *you* skipping town with five thousand dollars before I get my money's worth. If you get my drift."

Kyle shrugged, his features masked by a nonchalant exterior. "Sounds fair. But what makes you think I'd give a damn about Tessa if I was gonna skip town?"

It was Liam's turn to smile. "Because, if you don't finish the job, I am going to cut a chunk of flesh off her body for every dollar you leave town with. I figure even you couldn't live with that on your conscience, Kyle."

"It seems we have a deal," Kyle replied. Liam did not like the pure anger he saw in his expression.

"I'll be along to fetch her tomorrow then. You'll get your money and I'll get Tessa. Got it?"

Kyle's glittering stare and the heavy door swinging shut with a dull thud were all the answer Liam received. But he didn't care, he had accomplished his goal. Turning to leave, he wore a brilliant smile of victory.

The stupid son of a whore agreed! Oh that was far too easy. Much easier than he had anticipated or dared to hope. He laughed to himself all the way back to the Cattleman's Hotel at how easily Kyle had fallen into his trap. He wondered, for the third time since Kyle had appeared in Laramie, if the slow-witted bastard had figured out that it had been him who'd hired Magnus Kendrick to shoot his sorry ass. He chuckled, pouring more bourbon into a crystal tumbler. Probably not. If Kyle knew, he'd have shot Liam by now. Still…

Liam slowly sipped his liquor, his mind playing the scene over and over. First, Preston and Bodeen would face off, and then, Liam was going to take out the last man standing. No one would ever know. It was the perfect plan. He looked at his reflection the mirror behind the side board. The wild excitement of one who'd gone stark-raving insane lighted his features as he chuckled with demented glee and rubbed his hands together.

Kyle Bodeen's days were numbered, and so were Bradyn Preston's. And neither of the stupid jackasses knew it. Yet. Just wait until tomorrow, or the next day at the latest. Then they'd figured it out. But, by then, it would be too late for both of them. And, after he'd had his revenge on Bodeen and Preston, Contessa Lang would get what was coming to her. Liam rubbed his hands together again and licked his lips in anticipation as hot fury ran though his veins. Oh the thought! He was going to give her what she had coming with utter pleasure.

* * * *

Kyle stood staring at the door for a moment after Briggs left. A smile worked its way across his mouth. Liam Briggs was a bigger fool than he'd estimated. Clearly, Liam still believed that Kyle had no idea that it had been his bright idea to hire Kendrick to waylay him. He chuckled and walked across the room. *You just keep thinking that, you stupid bastard.* He lit another cigar and took a seat on a velvet covered ottoman next to the window. *Just keep right on thinking that.*

He sat in darkness, his face illuminated periodically by the red light of his cigar when he took a drag. In the window's reflection, his eyes gleamed ebony and malevolent, the pretense of casual, light-hearted humor was gone.

Liam Briggs thought he had him all figured out. Too bad Briggs was such a stupid, pitiful idiot. A smile, cold and demonic, slowly crept across Kyle's mouth, twisting his face with wicked satisfaction. Liam Briggs had such a short time to live and the dumb, illegitimate son of harlot didn't even know it.

The clouds in the sky parted and an almost full moon, bloated and ghost-like, cast its pale beams through window and across Kyle's face. With fluttering wings a raven landed on the windowsill. Its coal-black body gleamed baleful in the moonlight. The bird stared at him with bloody, unblinking eyes and then, with cawing laughter, pecked at the window pane. Kyle's smile widened.

"Hello, old friend," he whispered as he opened the window. "I've been waiting for you."

Chapter Ten

Rian awoke with a start. Cold sweat was running down her back. She sat up and felt not the soft down of her bed, but the hard grit of gravel and dirt beneath her finger tips. She looked about in confusion. Then, with terror, she recognized her surroundings. She had been here many times before.

It was twilight. The sky was still an ugly, murky orange marbled with engorged, blackish-red clouds. She shuddered as she looked up the empty street. The buildings on either side stood dark and stared vacantly down at her with windows that were hollow, ominous eyes. Their shutters flapped sluggishly despite the fact that the air was eerily still and malignant. A chill ran down her spine as she turned to look along the other side of the street.

At the far end, just at the town's edge, was the outline of a man sitting on a horse as black as the Devil's heart. It was not the horse, but the man, injured and slumping atop the horse, that drew her attention. This time, she knew who it was.

She could not make out his face but the picture was all too familiar. A scream, silent and gagging, wedged in her throat. Rising with the horrid sluggishness of one trapped in a nightmare, Rian ran to the horse. Her footsteps clanged like the fall of a blacksmith's hammer on steel as they struck the ground. "Bradyn!" she cried in a voice barely more than a mocking whisper. "Bradyn!"

Limp and lifeless, he sat upon the horse whose eyes glowed with the raging fires of Hell's brimstone. His body was riddled with bullet holes, but only a thin trickle of blood ran from his chest. She screamed out to him again and this time he lifted his gaze to her. Rian felt her blood run cold as she looked at his face. He was missing an eye and his mouth was nothing more than a bloody, bashed-in hole. She saw that his hands had been sliced and bruised, then tied to the saddle horn in horrible reminiscence of the day she'd first seen him.

Fierce anger and numbing fear drove her to his side. Stumbling up to the horse, she worked frantically to untie him.

"I wouldn't touch him if I were you." A voice as deep as a river and as electrifying as a jagged streak of lightning filled the street. "I wouldn't touch him."

Rian turned slowly and felt the fury of a thousand hurricanes begin to churn through her blood. Two figures stood at the other end of the town. They were black against a dismal setting sun. Their dusters flapped lifelessly in the heavy, unmoving air. Why were there two men now? Who had the demon brought with him?

"Stay away from us!" She heard her voice, a foreign and distant shriek, echoing down the dead-calm street.

A rumbling chuckle drifted through the town. Quiet at first, it grew in volume until it was an eerie, ubiquitous thundering. Ravens gathered by the hundreds on the roof tops and along the streets, their cackling caws blending with the demonic laughter.

"Stay away from us!" she shouted again. Her eyes searched the town for someone, *anyone* who could help her.

One of the men began walking toward her, his body weaving hypnotically. He floated down the street as though his feet did not touch the ground. She worked furiously to untie Bradyn, but the knot only grew tighter with her efforts. "Bradyn!" she shrieked. "Bradyn, you have to get out of here! You have to! If you go into town, they'll kill you!"

"Who'll kill me?" Bradyn asked. His brutalized face twisted into a horrific, toothless smile. "No one is going to kill me, Rian," he assured her in a taunting voice.

"It's too late for him." The voice, menacing and barely

more than a whisper, touched her ears. She turned. He was standing right behind her now. Shrouded in the purest black, his eyes glowing red from beneath the brim of his hat, he stared at her with a wide grin upon his face.

Rian choked on her tongue as it rolled with thick, terrified indolence to the back of her mouth. She knew him, she knew his face. Long, bony fingers closed around her arms as he smiled evilly down at her. His teeth were sharp fangs, long and viciously canine. His eyes were a dastardly, malicious yellow now.

"I'm coming for you," he whispered as he licked his lips like a feral dog. "I'm going to kill your precious lover, and then I'm going to rip your heart out of your chest and eat it. I'm coming for you, Moriana."

"No!" Rian screeched as she felt his teeth sink into her neck with rabid hunger. She looked up at Bradyn sitting lifeless on the horse. His eyes were glassy with death. She hadn't been able to save him. "No!" she screamed again. "Oh, Bradyn, I'm sorry, I'm sorry…"

* * * *

Bradyn was awakened by her tossing. The moon's beam fell across the bed and illuminated her body in its gray wash of light. Her skin was slick with sweat. Her chest glimmered with it. Damp hair partially covered her face as she jerked wildly in her sleep. Wiping the unruly strands from her perspiring brow, Bradyn frowned at the tears that leaked from the corners of her tightly shut eyes. "Rian," he whispered. "Rian, wake up." He nudged her arm with gentle urgency.

Gasping, Rian bolted upright in bed, her eyes full of crazed fear. "Bradyn?" she choked. Her voice was little more than a hoarse breath pushed from between her teeth as she fell against him shaking.

"You were dreaming," he answered. His fingers traced a tender path along the line of her spine.

Rian nodded and shivered. Slowly, she sat back to stare at him. In the moonlight, her face was ashen and her lips were trembling.

"What is it?" he asked as he pulled her back into the cradle of his arms and rested his chin on the crown of her head.

"It was nothing," she replied. "Just a nightmare. Only a bad dream is all."

He rocked her small frame in his arms, hoping to sooth her. Her heartbeat fluttered against his chest and her breath came in quick gasps. He kissed the soft skin of her shoulder. "Tell me, Rian," he whispered against her ear. "Tell me what you were dreaming."

Rian stiffened and pulled away. She looked terrified. "I—I don't want you to go to Laramie tomorrow, Bradyn," she answered, clutching her throat. "I know...You're going to die if you do. I...I can feel it."

Moonlight glistened from a tear that caught in her lower lashes. She blinked. The tear glided down her face and hung in a sparkling diamond on her chin before plummeting to the sheet across her breasts. A second tear slipped from her other eye and Bradyn caught it with his index finger before it came to the same fate as the other.

"Rian," he soothed, pulling her back against him. "You know I have to. If I don't, Briggs will just keep on sending one gunman after another out here 'til he gets what he wants. I have to finish this. I'm tired of running from my past. I'm not going to do it anymore."

"What if you are killed?" she gasped as she pulled away and looked up at him again. Her eyes were wide with anxiety and perplexed irritation. "Why?! Why must you take your life into your own two hands?" She shook her head. "Briggs has gunmen to protect him! You could be easily outnumbered! Have you even considered that?"

"I won't be killed," he promised. "I'm going to finish the business I have with Briggs then I am coming back for you and Kendall."

Her eyes went wide with surprise. "Kendall and I? Why? I don't understand."

Bradyn smiled at her. "I've waited a lifetime to find you, Rian Keene," he whispered with fierce emotion. "I knew the first day I laid eyes on you that I wanted you, but I was afraid. Afraid that if I told you what I've done, you wouldn't be able to love me because my past would be too horrible for you to accept." He stroked her hair. "Now that you know what I've done, now that I know who you are, I'm not going to let a son of a bitch like Briggs, or anybody else, stop me from spending the rest of my life with you. I love you."

Her delight glistened in her eyes like tiny liquid jewels. Bradyn stroked another stray teardrop from her cheek. "Can you love me? Can you love me even a little?"

"I already do," she whispered. Her smile wobbled as she fell against him. "I already love you, Bradyn."

His mouth found hers. Her kisses whispered sweet, delicate promises to his soul. He was enveloped in amber passion when she pulled away for a moment and sat staring up at him.

"Is something wrong, darlin'?" he asked, suddenly uneasy. "Why are you staring at me like that?"

She ran a finger over his lips and then traced the line of his jaw. With a slow shake of her head, she answered, "It's probably nothing…it's just, well…" She studied him.

Bradyn raised an eyebrow and wrapped his fingers over her small hand. "Just what?" he asked. "Are you having second thoughts about letting your heart be taken by a tarnished soul like me?"

Rian smiled then. "No, no, it's nothing like that. It's just that sometimes—this may sound a little silly," she drew a deep breath, "sometimes I get the strange feeling I've seen you before. It's almost as if…as if we've been in this same *situation* before. Déjà vu, I think they call it…Silly right?" She shrugged a creamy shoulder and looked up at him sheepishly.

Bradyn was shocked. So he wasn't the only one that felt a strange sense of familiarity. Rian had felt it too. He nodded slowly, uncertain if he should tell her he'd been having the same feelings. There was so much riding on his visit to Laramie. He worried that she might make a bigger fuss of him going if she thought there was some kind of significance to the fact that they'd both had the exact same déjà vu. "I guess I know what you mean…I've had those feelings in the past myself."

"About me?" she pressed. "When you first saw me?"

Bradyn pulled her against him. "The first time I laid eyes on you, I was so taken with your beauty that I hardly think it's possible we've seen each other before. I'd surely remember you if we had," he deflected.

"Hmmm," Rian murmured against his chest, her fingers drawing circles over the small of his back. "You know, I'm mighty glad I haven't managed to shoot you yet," she drawled. "Contrary to my first opinion of you, you've turned out to be quite the flatterer."

Bradyn smiled when she giggled, relived that his answer had satisfied her and that she seemed to have forgotten about her nightmare. He lifted her chin. "Well if pretty words are all it takes to keep you by my side, then, honey, you ain't seen nothing yet," he replied as he brushed his lips over hers. "I'm gonna spend the rest of my life telling you how beautiful you are…in as many different ways as I can think of," he added, running his fingers over her soft thigh, "and words are only *one* way of telling you."

"And the others?" she asked, her eyes dancing merrily.

"Those, I'll have to show you," he whispered as he leaned down to kiss her mouth again.

Their lovemaking was slow and passionate. Bradyn reveled in the fire of her eyes as she smiled up at him. Gone was the sting of years spent in loveless loneliness and a heart buried deep within a hollow shell. To hold her was to know completion. Completion and utter satisfaction like none he had ever known before. She was the one. The one he would spend the rest of his days with. He had never been more certain of anything in his entire life.

They lay side by side. Neither one spoke. Their fingers and legs were entwined as the heat of their passion hung over and around them like a canopy of enchanting mist. Bradyn rolled to his back, putting a hand behind his head, the other pulling Rian's securely to his chest. He stared out at the night sky, pondering his own personal discovery until she yawned and he watched as her eyes closed heavy with sleep.

He lay awake listening to her gentle breathing and watching the rise and fall of her chest as she slept. He ran a finger along her face and, for a moment, wished he had known her long before now. Long before he'd ever met Liam Briggs. Perhaps she could have changed his life. But, then, perhaps he would've just ruined hers. Maybe he still would…

His thoughts turned to the dawn and the task that lay before him with morning's light. For the first time, he felt nervous. The bleak precognition of something fearful, yet distant and vague, permeated his mind. He had never been afraid to die, he was not afraid of death itself even now. But he was terrified of missing a lifetime loving the woman who lay sleeping beside him.

He would better Briggs. He swore it with every ounce of will in his being. He would get rid of him. Briggs was the only man left who was connected to the pain and hurt of his past. Bradyn was going to send Liam Briggs to a shallow grave and return, triumphant, to her. His Rian. And she would be waiting for him. Waiting to start the rest of her life with him. He smiled as his eyes closed with the pleasantness of beckoning sleep. Rian Preston, he thought dreamily, *My wife, Rian Preston.* And, rolling to his side, he pulled her against his body in a protective, loving embrace and fell asleep breathing in her scent.

* * * *

The first streaks of morning dawned cool with the crisp freshness of a land washed clean and revived to a brilliant green with the passing of the rainstorm. Rian stretched and yawned with lazy abandon. Her arm brushed across the pillow next to her own. The pillow that Bradyn had rested his beautiful head on last night. She frowned and turned on her side. Bradyn was not there.

Rian sat upright and panic wrapped its tiny talons around her stomach. He hadn't left yet…had he? Without saying goodbye? She quickly pulled her clothing on, the whole time terrified that she would rush out to the barn to find his horse and saddle gone. Afraid to find he'd left her life as suddenly as he had entered it, she ran down the stairs two at a time. Her heart was thundering along with uneven pace.

"Where are you off to in such a hurry?"

She stopped a few feet short of the front door, a wild, wide smile parting her lips and relief flooding her heart. She turned to see Bradyn sitting at the kitchen table, a mug of coffee in his hand, staring at her. The same familiar, crooked smile was on his face.

"I thought you'd left," she admitted sheepishly. "I thought you'd left without saying good-bye."

Bradyn patted his thigh. "Come here," he said.

As she walked across the kitchen floor, his eyes narrowed.

"Good morning, Rian." He pulled her into his lap when she stood in front of him. "You are a beautiful sight first thing in the morning," he whispered, running his fingers through her long, tousled hair.

His kiss sent teasing tingles down her spine. She loved the look of tenderness on his face, a look reserved only for her. His cobalt eyes glittered warm with gentle desire, telling her that he loved her as much now in the cool light of morning as he had last night in the softness of lamplight and passion's euphoric throes.

"Good morning, Bradyn," she whispered back.

"Did you really think I would leave without saying good-bye?" There was feigned hurt in his voice.

Rian shook her head. "I did. But I don't now." Her fingers played absently with the thick hair at the nape of his neck. She watched his face as he smiled. It was a sad, distant sort of smile.

"I have to go," he said at length. "Whether we like it or not, I still have to go to Laramie today."

Rian lowered her head and stared at her hands, which were clasped tightly in her lap. She would not argue with him, but the vision of the nightmare kept repeating itself in her memory. *What if he is going to face serious danger?* Don't be ridiculous, Rian, she scolded herself. *Of course he is riding out to face serious danger! The question is what can you do about it? How can you stop him from leaving?*

"Rian?" She jerked as he called her name and interrupted the horrible pictures of her dream as she recalled it once again.

"Yes?"

"I said if I'm not back by tomorrow night, pack up Kendall and head for Sheridan. I know a guy up there named Albert McCoy. He owns the hotel and café there in town. He'll take you in. Just tell him I sent you, okay?"

She shook her head. His words were ridiculous and confusing. "I'm not leaving," she insisted. "You can't ask me to leave without you. I won't!"

The look he gave her, smoldering and authoritative, angered her. "Rian, if something happens to me, and Briggs somehow manages to get the upper hand, he'll come here and take you. It's his way. He leaves no loose ends. Not even theoretical ones. You have to leave if I'm not back by tomorrow night. Swear to me that you'll leave." He shook her shoulders, forcing her to look him in the eye. "Swear it, Rian. Swear it on your love for me that you'll do as I say. I need to hear it. I need to know that you'll be safe."

She nodded as that same sick fear knotted and twisted in her middle. "I'll go," she answered in a voice that barely resembled a whisper. "I'll go, Bradyn. I swear."

He gave her a tender kiss as his relief, clear and unmistakable, spread across his face. "Thank you," he said.

They sat together silently for a few moments, each lost in their own thoughts. Finally, Bradyn rose, drawing her into his arms as he stood. "I guess it's about that time," he sighed. His face contorted with a tense expression. "The sooner I get this over with, the sooner I'll be back here to get you."

Rian nodded, the lump of loathsome fear in her throat making it impossible to speak. She didn't want to cry. She *couldn't* cry. But she'd be damned if a solitary tear didn't escape her eye and trickle down her cheek anyway. Wiping it away quickly, she took a deep breath to steady herself.

As if he saw the scared look in her eyes and the hastily wiped tear, Bradyn lifted her chin and gave her a reassuring expression. "I *am* coming back," he promised. "No one is going to stop me from coming back to you, Rian." His voice was raspy with emotion. "No one."

She, again, nodded weakly, trying to squelch the ominous fever she felt creeping over her. His kiss, while wonderfully enchanting and fiercely passionate, did nothing to assuage the horror that ran hot and dizzying through her blood.

She followed him to the barn. A hundred arguments, a thousand reasons for him to stay here with her, were bitter pills on her tongue for they were left unspoken. She watched with a deep sadness as he saddled his horse. His face was set resolutely in stone. It was the last time she would see him, her mind shouted at her with disquieting volume. The last time.

Rian watched as he belted her gun around his waist. The gun that had brought down three men in the last week. The gun that would mean the difference of life and death for him as he faced the man who'd destroyed his past and haunted him like a demon to this day. Exhaling a quiet breath from her lungs, she stepped to his side, her hand on his arm in one last pleading attempt to change his mind. She spoke no words, but stood gazing up at him with a look of utter entreaty. A firm shake of his head was her only answer.

Pulling her against him, he smiled down at her for one final time. "I love you, Rian," he whispered as his lips brushed over hers. "No matter what happens, remember I love you."

Tears of fear, mingled in equal parts with love and fury, fell down her cheeks as she watched him ride away. Every part of her being wanted to chase after him and beg him to come back, to plead with him to see the error of his thinking. The only thing that stopped her was the look he'd had in his eye just before he'd left. He had to go. It was his destiny. Whether she liked it or not, the key to his future, the key to his freedom, lay in Laramie. If he didn't take care of Briggs, he would be tormented by him for the rest of his life. Bradyn had to face his demons. His very life depended on it. And now, to the greatest degree, so did hers.

She paced the kitchen with frantic steps for nearly an hour before Kendall awoke. The whole time her mind racing and reeling in forty different directions at once. A part of her, locked-up, buried, and unopened for many years, felt a familiar churning fear. There was something going on. Something she couldn't pin-point. Something that was not right about this whole mess. But what? Why did she carry such a vague, nagging sensation in her stomach?

A little voice inside her warned; *"There is something big brewing over in Laramie tonight, Rian. Bradyn's riding toward a bigger fight than either of you realize."*

Rian shook herself and forced the voice out of her head. *It was the dream last night,* she reasoned. *My nightmare. It was so real…that is why I have this horrible fear inside me.* Her nightmare had been so vivid. She *knew* it was only a dream…so why couldn't she shake the utter terror it worked in her heart?

"It's because, Rian, last night wasn't the first time you've had that dream…" the little voice replied.

Rian shuddered because she knew the words were true. She *had* been having the same twisted nightmare all summer. In fact she'd been having forms of the dream ever since she'd come to the Territory, they'd just gotten worse and more vivid with time. *The only reason last night's dream was different was because I saw who was on the horse this time… It was Bradyn.* The realization stunned her. How long had she had that very same dream and never seen the face of the rider on the black horse?

"He's always been there, Rian," the little voice whispered. *"You knew that someone was coming long before Bradyn got here. You knew that your past couldn't stay away. The reckoning is coming, Rian. Are you ready for it? Are you ready to face your past?"*

The little voice frightened her out of her mind. She wanted to scream at the top off her lungs into the quiet kitchen; "Of course, I knew that my past wouldn't stay buried! I knew it was only a matter of time until someone found me. But I don't understand what my past has to do with Bradyn. He wasn't a part of what I did! And what the hell could my past possibly have to do with his showdown with Liam Briggs?!"

Rian poured a cup of tepid coffee. Her nerves were on the verge of explosion. She hadn't had a good night's sleep in days. To add to the strain, she was growing more frightened for Bradyn with every passing moment. And now, to make matters much worse, she was becoming so paranoid of a ridiculous nightmare that it was causing her to hear voices in her head. She rubbed her temples and tried to reason with herself. *It's only a silly nightmare. Bradyn will come back. He promised.*

"Is it only a silly nightmare?" Jackson's words back came to her from a long-forgotten night more than year before. He had come to her room after she had awakened him with her screaming. That had not been long after the horrid dream had started plaguing her sleep almost every night.

"Dreams are thoughts and memories that come to us at night when we can't repress them or push them away," he'd told her. *"Mark my words, there's a lot of truth in dreams, little sister. Never presume a dream or a gut instinct is silly, Rian. You know that. You've been having this same nightmare for a long time now. Long enough to tell me that there's something to this dream of yours. Remember what I told you when we first came to the Territory? Someday your instincts are going to save your life. You need to figure out what it is your heart is trying to tell you. Listen to your heart and your gut instincts. Do what you need to do…you're a lot stronger than you think you are, little sister."*

Rian shook herself again and pulled her mind back from memory. This nonsense in her head was ridiculous. Bradyn was going to be fine. He was. He had promised her, hadn't he?

"But…what if he isn't fine?" the little voice asked. *"What if he needs your help? What if he dies alone in Laramie because there is no one there to save him? You are not going to leave him to die…are you, Rian?"*

The idea, brilliant and utterly ridiculous, flashed across her mind. *She* could go to him. *She* could save him! Perhaps that was what her nightmare had been telling her to do! Yes, it made sense. She stopped.

Except… she reasoned.

"Except what?" the little voice replied.

What will I do with Kendall? A gunfight is no place for a woman, let alone a child…I won't do anything rash. I'll just think about it for awhile. That's it… I'll think about it." So she sat sipping her cold coffee and thinking about what she should do.

By the time Kendall awoke, she had made up her mind.

"Where's Mr. Bradyn?" the little boy asked after searching the house and the barn. His confusion and disappointment left two watery trails down his cheeks. "He's gone, Auntie Rian. Where did he go?"

"He's left for Laramie," she answered. Her eyes were fixed determinedly outside the kitchen window on the hills to the west. "Get dressed, Kendall, we're going after him."

Chapter Eleven

Rian and Kendall rode double. Sky and plain lost all distinction as the grass and sagebrush whirred past in a blur of grays, greens, browns, and yellows. She kept the sorrel mare paced at a steady gallop. The wind blew through her hair and rushed past her ears with invigorating coolness.

It was rough going and Rian fretted a thousand times before noon that she would get them lost in the vast wilderness that separated their homestead from Laramie. Fear that she would be too late to save Bradyn caused her to push their mount to breakneck speeds whenever they came to an open stretch of ground.

Kendall grasped her waist with silent strength as the large horse charged forward underneath them. Absently, she ran her hand over the butt of the Winchester that hung in the saddle holster. Feeling the smooth wood of the stock gave her a minimal sense of courage and assurance.

Her thoughts ran together in jumbled, repetitive snippets. She did not understand her sure and certain knowledge that if she did not make it to town in time, Bradyn would perish. But question that knowledge, she would not. Periodically, she worried for their safety. She worried that Bradyn would be furious when he discovered she had followed him into Laramie. And, she worried over what she was going to do to protect Kendall when the time came. Dark fear of the unknown assaulted her mind with disjointed regularity and caused her to spur the horse to faster speeds.

With urgent frequency, her reflections were captivated by

her nightmare. More and more, it seemed, with every passing mile she felt its cold presence filling her mind. It began to replace every other concern in her head. The nightmare nagged at her with frustrating, yet vaguely familiar, obscurity. There was something…something in the dream that she could almost remember. Something from her past that she had somehow forgotten. However, when its frightening images fully absorbed her mind, she could only remember the horrors of the dream itself and nothing of its significance to her past life.

With every passing hoof-beat, every fleeting glimpse of a new horizon, Rian felt her stomach tumble and flutter as if carried by the wings of a butterfly. The curious sensation that something or *someone* was beckoning her onward, a presence urging her to hurry, ran in spidery tendrils from the crown of her head to the tips of her toes. From deep inside, that same small voice commanded her to waste no time else all would surely be lost. The voice gained amplitude with every passing moment.

Then, a new terror, no longer just a basic human fear for life and safety, but of something wholly evil and largely unknown, filled her with sudden dread. Twice her vision blurred and went out of focus. Sky and hills, rocks, grass, and water were violently enveloped in a rainbow of iridescent colors. Startled and awestruck, she blinked to clear her vision. But the vibrant hues only became stronger, almost tactile. Then the mirages faded out of existence as quickly as they'd come.

Stranger still, the scars across her back began to tingle inexplicably until her back was fairly throbbing. The throbbing was not painful. Instead it was bizarrely frightening and exhilarating at once. She was unsure of what to attribute to these new sensations. She didn't know whether she should be frightened or mesmerized.

As the horse charged across the creek bed sending up a spray of translucent emerald mist, Rian felt a prickle of excitement race along her skin. *What is happening to me?!*

Kendall's grasp tightened around her waist as the mare surged forward up the steep embankment on the other side of the creek. She felt his fingers close over the handle of the knife she had strapped to her thigh before leaving the house.

It was the dagger her brother had given her for protection when they'd left New Orleans all those years ago. It had been his prize possession, given to him by their late father. Its hilt was made of pure silver and the handle was molded with the image of an angel. Somehow feeling the weight of it against her leg gave her more comfort than the rifle hanging from her saddle. She squeezed Kendall's hand affectionately.

The sun burned down with blazing fury. Rian knew sweat was trickling from her face and running down her back, but she felt only the heat of her scars as they tingled with radiating warmth. As their mount raced along the water's edge, she looked at the passing reflection with numb awe. The water was glass, perfectly clear and unmoving as the horse ran along its edge in thunderous passage. In the still water, the horse gleamed as white as the freshly fallen snow.

Rian shook her head and tried to clear the weird illusion from her sight. But the image of the horse remained. Forcing herself to look away, she blinked and tried to retrain her vision. A scream wedged in her throat.

The westward sky had gone a deep yellowish-orange, even though it was only late-afternoon. Everything blazed with a brilliance she had never witnessed before. The grass looked nearly blue, the trees and rocks glowed vibrant shades of purple, yellow and crimson. Fascination, not fright, gripped her. A magnetic force allayed her fears and awakened something primeval and fierce deep inside her. Minutes ran into hours as they flew across the countryside. The colors continually ebbed and flowed before her eyes in hypnotic waves.

"Rian! Rian, I have to stop. I need water," Kendall gasped against her back. His voice sounded weak, and miles away.

Rian roused herself and the world came back into its ordinary, mundane view. She felt like she had been floating above her body as the passing landscapes encompassed her in a ghostlike reality. The sensations that gripped her were so intense that she had nearly forgotten Kendall. She halted the horse and pulled the canteen from the saddle horn. "Here, baby. Drink up," she said. Her voice sounded faint and unreal to her.

Rian dismounted and let the horse rest a moment before allowing it to drink from the creek. As the mare lowered her head to the water, she rested her hand along its sweat-lathered neck. The image of woman and horse shone back in a rippling, wavy mirror. She gasped in spite of herself.

In the water's reflection, not only had the horse's image changed, but this time so had hers. Her hair had gone as black as the night and her eyes were two flashing amethysts. She looked away from the water and at her horse with frantic surprise, but saw only an ordinary rust-colored mare drinking peacefully. Rian pulled a thick strand of hair around her shoulder and studied it. She was relieved to see it was still her same shade of chocolate brown.

"Rian!" Kendall screeched, "Look!"

She turned, wondering if Kendall, too, had seen her hair change color or if it was merely a figment of her over-taxed imagination. But Kendall wasn't looking at her. His eyes were fixed on the skyline. The canteen hung forgotten, half-way to his mouth.

Rian turned in the direction he was pointing. She did not understand why, but she already knew exactly what she would see. A cloud, thick and black, loomed in the murky, orange westward sky several miles away. Small and boiling at first, it grew until it shadowed the sun from view. But it wasn't a cloud. She *knew* it wasn't a cloud.

As the cloud passed overhead with a sudden rush of ominous flapping, Rian breathed in a trance-like voice; "The ravens…He has called the ravens." It was of little consequence to her how or why she knew this. She just knew. Or, more precisely, *something* inside her knew. Death's ravens had been summoned and now he stood waiting to collect his due.

* * * *

The sky was a pale blue, cloudless and almost colorless under the scorching late-afternoon sun. Bradyn stopped his horse on a plateau that overlooked the valley. Dismounting, he stood beside his mount gazing down on the city of Laramie now barely five miles in the distance. A wind whipped upward from the plain. It cooled his body as it billowed through his duster. Steel determination and angry resolve set his face in granite. His heartbeat and the empty noise of air whistling through grass were the only sounds that reached his ears.

It wasn't much later than five o'clock, but the sky suddenly grew dark. The horizon began to glow with an orange haze. Laramie gleamed charcoal against a backdrop of heavens the color of sunset. But sundown wasn't due for at least four hours. Bradyn watched with sickened amazement as a black cloud began to form in the west. The cloud grew until it covered the sun from view. Then it began to churn and swell across the sky.

But, it was not a cloud at all. It looked like…birds. Bradyn squinted and raised a hand to shield his eyes. A nebula of flapping wings drifted across the prairie with maddening speed. Ravens. Malevolent cawing filled the air as they passed overhead and continued east. He watched with fearful curiosity as they flew over him, leaving the sky to the west the color of flame.

Bradyn felt a chill enter his bones. A fathomless understanding that the ravens were significant filled his awareness. The birds were a harbinger of a coming dark event. He had never witnessed anything so bizarrely evil in his life. What could it mean? Staring out over the vast horizon, now washed with the orange of fire, he pondered the uneasy feeling he had in his gut. He wondered if he had made the right decision in coming to Laramie to face Briggs.

Rian's words resurfaced in his memory, *"I don't want you to go to Laramie tomorrow, Bradyn. I know…you're going to die if you do. I feel it."*

Then, Bradyn's doubt was replaced by anger. He shook his head vehemently. "No!" he shouted aloud to the empty wind. "I am going to finish this. Come hellfire or floodwater, Liam Briggs is going to die tonight!"

The searching scream of an eagle drew his attention as it circled overhead in an ever widening pattern. Its bloodthirsty gaze swept the plain with keen vigilance. He watched with breathless fascination as the bird began its spiraling descent to the ground below. Its shrill warning lent no aid to the rabbit captured in its fatal, grasping talons.

Bradyn closed his eyes. He inhaled the wind and felt the strength of the plain rush under his feet and up through his body. It filled him with anticipation and power.

"Liam Briggs, I'm coming for you." His quiet whisper was swallowed up by the empty air swirling about him. Mounting the horse, savage determination raced though him. "Prepare to take your bourbon with the Devil tonight, old friend. I hear he serves it hot."

* * * *

Contessa Lang paced her room in frantic irritation and unfounded panic. *Where is Kyle?* She wondered for the thousandth time.

He had not been in her bed this morning when she awakened. She hadn't seen him all day. Now it was late afternoon, nearly four-thirty, and still he had not come back to her bedroom. Liam's threat blared at her with unsettling repetition. Tessa was convinced that Kyle had met some horrible fate and that she was next.

She had not bothered to dress yet. Her scarlet silk bathrobe flew about her ankles as she spun and retraced her steps back across the room. She had stayed in her bedroom all day. Afraid that if she left it Liam would see her and do something awful to her, she had become a prisoner in her own saloon. Liam had been so angry last night. Fear gripped her heart when she thought of what, exactly, he had planned as her promised retribution for taking Kyle Bodeen into her bed.

Her mind turned back to Kyle. *Where are you?* She ran a slender hand through her disheveled hair with absent nervousness. Something wasn't right. She had felt it all night.

Her sleep, normally deep and peaceful, had been filled with disjointed, macabre dreams. Dreams of demons with the faces of men. Dreams of blood spilled on the earth around a fire that spiraled upward in green flame and orange smoke. They had been nightmares filled with yellow-eyed cats eating the eyes of dead men and ravens gathering by the thousands to witness the dancing of shapeless shadows around the eerie fire.

Just remembering the nightmares caused her to shudder and wrap her robe about her body in an attempt to banish the chill that permeated her skin.

Tessa vaguely remembered Kyle waking her in the wee hours of morning. Her body had been drenched with sweat as she shivered in his embrace. He'd given her a shot of whiskey and soothed her back to sleep. He had promised there would be no more nightmares.

But the nightmares had been worse.

Tessa had dreamed that she was running through a dessert. The air was hot and tasted metallic. It was the flavor of freshly spent blood. She was fleeing from something huge and loathsome. It was a man, but at the same time it was not a man at all. The sky grew dark and she found herself lying on a dusty road. She moaned as the black being ravaged her body, the vast size of it crushing the air from her with cruel sensuality. She a tried to rouse herself, to end the nightmare, but it was no use. The dream had been as real as waking light. Teeth sunk into her neck as the form of a man took her repeatedly with fierce passion both exotically arousing and horribly frightening at once.

She had awoken with a start to dawn's cool light creeping across her pillow and a bed empty of Kyle. She had rushed to the mirror, fully expecting to see bloody, jagged teeth marks on her neck. But there had been nothing. The details of the nightmares had slowly faded from her mind, but the terror of it remained firmly etched in her heart.

Tessa walked to the window. She pulled back the lace curtains and stared down on Main Street for the hundredth time since waking that morning. Kyle was nowhere in sight.

In fact, there was not a living soul out on the street today. Her skin prickled with inexplicable gooseflesh. She stepped away from the window and let the curtains fall back into place. She shook herself. *You're just being ridiculous, Tessa,* she scolded. *Kyle is fine. He's probably downstairs right now, having a drink and playing a round of poker.*

She laughed aloud. The noise of her laughter rang back shrill and hollow to her ears.

The grandfather clock in her bedroom chimed four-thirty. Finally, Tessa could stand it no longer. Let Liam do what he would to her, she was not going to spend another nerve-wracking, agonizing moment in her room wondering if Kyle was alright. Rushing to the closet, Tessa pulled out a dress and began putting it on. She would prove it. She would prove to herself that Kyle was fine. She was going to go down into the saloon and find him. And when she did, she was going to buy him a drink out of the sheer joy that he was just fine.

Tessa ran a brush through her hair. She pulled out the tangles with long, haphazard strokes. The whole time she was twisting the golden lengths into a chignon her eyes kept darting back to her reflection in the mirror.

She looked different this morning. Dark circles shone from under her lashes and her eye color had changed. Her eyes looked more green than blue. Her lips were red even though she'd not applied her lipstick. Tessa ran a finger over them. They were fuller this morning, too. Stifling another shiver, she turned away. Her mind was playing childish tricks on her.

As she reached for the door knob, the door swung inward with slamming force and nearly hit her square in the face. Tessa reeled backward. Her breath was crushed from her body as she landed on the divan. She knocked it over as she toppled over the back of it and rolled to the floor in a heap of skirts. Dazed, she stared up at the intruder.

"Liam," she gasped. Terror pinched her voice into a small, mocking squeak.

He smiled and when he did, his grey eyes danced with vile intent. "Hello, Tessa," he whispered. He leaned down and pulled her up to eye-level. "Did I scare you, love?" His voice was cool, eerily calm. Only his eyes betrayed the fury burning within him.

Wide-eyed and breathless, Tessa tried to push him away. "Take your hands off me, Liam and get out of my room."

Liam's hysterical laughter scared her more than his angry shouting would have.

"What's so funny!?" she demanded. For all her terrified shock at his presence, her voice shook with indignant courage.

"Nothing you would understand, I'm afraid," he grinned. "I was just thinking of how easily your newest lover sold you out, Tessa." He tisked mockingly. "You really should think twice about some of these handsome Romeos who woo you. Your judgment of human character is sadly lacking, I'm afraid."

A new fear riveted her. "What are you talking about?" Her question sounded logical enough but her mind felt only the panicked threat of uncertainty.

"Oh, didn't Kyle tell you? He is going to take care of Bradyn Preston for me. I traded him ten thousand dollars for your pretty head and Preston's dead body. How does that grab you?" Liam grinned again. Gleaming white teeth glistened, reminding Tessa of her nightmare lover's bite.

"He did not," Tessa protested. But her confidence was shaken. What if Kyle had? That would explain his sudden disappearance. Tessa shook her head. He wouldn't have done that! Kyle needed her. She knew it in her soul. "I don't believe you!" she shouted. Her hysteria threatened to take her voice completely. "Get out, Liam. Get out now!"

The room tilted and the floor came up to meet her head after his fist connected with her mouth. Black fog filled her mind as she felt consciousness slipping away. Liam's face appeared over her. His smile was gone. "Damn it. I loved you, Tessa." His garbled voice came to her from the far reaches of encapsulating dark space. "Why did you have to go and make me kill you?"

* * * *

Kyle whistled a merry little tune as he exited the livery and headed up the street to the Silver Lady Saloon. He'd had a wonderful early morning ride. The sunrise over the eastern plains had revived him following a long night of sleeplessness and the brilliance of mid-morning had enticed him to ride long into the afternoon. Kyle decided to turn back toward town once the sun had reached its apex in the sky. By then, he had been nearly four hours outside of Laramie.

After Briggs had left him the night before, he'd sat staring out the window at the nearly-full moon until Tessa had called out in her sleep. She had been lathered with sweat, nightmares torturing her sleep with atrocious pictures. He knew exactly what she had been dreaming. The change was beginning to take her. He had given her opium in whiskey to calm her and ease her sleeping thoughts.

Kyle smiled, remembering the fire in her unseeing eyes as he'd made love to her for nearly two intoxicating, ethereal hours. When he had finally gained the summit of satisfaction, sleep was as distant to him as Hell's black mouth was from the golden gates of Heaven. So Kyle had climbed to the roof of the Silver Lady and sat crouching. He had closed his eyes and let his soul roam out across the plains to the east. His spirit was searching. Always searching. His being floated out over dark nothingness as he explored the nocturnal world. He was looking for the One. The One who had drawn him to Laramie.

The moon, nearly full and scalding white, revealed nothing to him for several hours. But then, hovering over the ground, he'd felt the tremors of an earthquake rumbling deep within the confines of mortal space. The tremors were born of passion. They radiated a faint red aura into the eastern night sky. Kyle had climbed down from the roof in the early hours of morning. His ability to see the radiating aura of passion had been enough to tell him that the time was drawing near. The One was nearby and would be coming soon. Tonight he would meet the person that he'd come to Laramie to find and destroy.

He smiled with dark excitement as he pushed through

the saloon doors and started up the stairs to Tessa's room. He was going to look in on her and let her know he had some business to take care of with Briggs. Then he was going to go collect his five thousand dollars and come back to make wild, exhausting love to her. He smiled with jagged anticipation. Things were shaping up to perfection. According to plan.

But a cold, extrasensory anger seeped through his veins as he walked through the door and noticed that the divan was overturned and the carpet was crumpled. "Tessa?" he called as he stepped from the sitting room into the bedchamber. The room was empty. Where had she gone? His eyes fell on the large clock in the corner. It was nearly five. He walked to the window and looked out over Laramie. Then his eyes lighted on the Cattleman's Hotel three buildings down across the street.

In an instant he knew. Liam Briggs. Kyle closed his eyes. His knuckles popped as his hands formed tight, bulging fists. When he opened his eyes, they were unseeing black marbles flecked with crimson. A tremor of fury ran through him creating the low grumble of thunder. It made the floors and walls shake with deafening force. The windows rattled, threatening to shatter from their frames in a violent spray of glass.

Then they came. The ravens came in flocks. They blotted out the sun and turned the skies to the color of fire in their wake. As the grandfather clock began to chime the hour, Kyle smiled. A black, loathsome grin parted his lips and revealed white, gleaming fangs. He was going to find Tessa and get her back. He needed her.

* * * *

Liam Briggs paced his room in the Cattlemen's Hotel. Tessa was tied to a chair and still unconscious. Her face was bloody and her lips were swollen where his fist had connected with her mouth. Her dress, torn by Liam's rough grasp, had fallen off a pale shoulder exposing violet bruises on her collarbone and chest. He had hit her repeatedly with blind fury after he'd knocked her to the floor senseless. He smiled down at her with evil anticipation. Killing her was going to be pure pleasure. But before he finished her, he was going to make certain Bodeen finished *his* little task. When both Preston and Bodeen were dead, Liam would make sure Tessa felt slow and agonizing torture before her end.

Liam frowned as he felt a tremor run through the room. Barely perceptible at first, it grew until it was rattling the walls and windows with enough force to make him grab a chair to stay on his feet. If he had been drinking, he would have thought very little of the sudden upset in balance. But he was dead sober. He looked around the room, unsure of what was going on. Then his eyes went wide with surprised terror as he glanced out his window. The sky was orange and full of smoke. It appeared that the whole city was on fire! He ran to the window and pulled the curtains back with an unsteady hand.

No. Not fire, not smoke. The air was full of… birds. Swirling like sooty haze and numbering in the thousands overhead. Liam squinted, perplexed. He had never seen so many ravens in his whole damn life. With a frigid, quivering hand, he dropped the curtains back into place. The sky…what was wrong with the sky? He looked at his pocket watch. It was only a few minutes after five. Why did the sky look orange, like it was already sundown?

Behind him, the door burst open with splintering force. Whirling, Liam pulled his gun from its holster. Kyle stood in the entrance of his room. His expression was blistering in its intensity. His voice, distorted with rage, sounded almost inhuman. "Where's Tessa?"

Unnerved, Liam attempted a controlled smile and pointed to the chair to which Tessa was bound. "She's there. Your five thousand is on the desk. As promised." He gestured to the opposite corner of the room, hoping the mention of money would assuage Kyle somewhat.

Ignoring him, Kyle stepped to Tessa's side. He appeared to remain composed when he saw the wounds on her face, neck, and chest. Kneeling, he touched her mouth. His fingers wiped the blood from her lips. "What have you done?" he whispered. The roar of barely restrained fury vibrated in his voice.

Liam's chuckle, treacherous and mirthless, filled the room. "You made the deal, Kyle. Tessa is mine until you finish Preston for me. I guess you should think twice about the bargains you strike, my friend." He held his gun steady. Kyle Bodeen was squarely in his aim.

Ever so slowly, Kyle turned and rose. Rage contorted his face. His eyes turned black as he flexed his jaw and studied Liam. His words, barely audible, confused Liam. "Not now," Liam heard him whisper. "Not now. We can't kill him now. We need him. We need the evil in his heart. Wait… Wait." Unfathomable seconds passed.

Then, Liam watched with paralyzed wonder as Kyle appeared to…*flicker*. He shook his head and blinked. Kyle looked transparent, like smoke; there, but *not* there. Suddenly, inexplicably, Kyle was one instant standing across the room, and then in the next, standing right in front of him. He took no steps. He merely materialized only inches from Liam's face.

Kyle's eyes glowed obsidian flecked with red as he lifted Liam from the floor and hurled him across the room with blinding ferocity. The crash of body against plaster and wood shook the walls. Fragments of debris exploded everywhere and a cloud of dust boiled outward.

Liam slumped to the floor as numb blackness settled over his consciousness.

* * * *

When Tessa woke up, she didn't know where she was. Everything around her was red. Her first thought was blood. Blood was everywhere. Her mouth was filled with the scarlet flavor of it, hot and acidic.

Then she knew. It was not blood, but silk. She was in her own bed. Kyle's face drifted in and out of focus for a moment. Confused, she tried to sit up, but Kyle's hand held her gently in place.

"Lie still for a moment," he whispered as he smoothed a

strand of hair from her forehead. "Just lie still."

"Kyle?" She touched his face, incredulous and perplexed. "What happened? Liam…he was here, he…" A tear slipped down her cheek and she heard it drop to the velvet pillow.

"Shhhh, Tessa," he soothed. His voice was soft and husky. "I took care of Briggs. I took care of him. You just lie still and rest for awhile."

Tessa touched her face feeling the place were Liam's fist had struck her mouth. Nothing. Hadn't he..? But he had. He *had* hit her. She remembered him striking her. She remembered the blinding pain and falling to the floor.

But there was no pain now. No bloodied lip or swollen jaw. Everything was hazy. Had she dreamt it? Was it all a dream, just as the nightmares she had suffered last night? Perhaps, it hadn't happened at all. Perhaps, she was just now waking up…

A tremor raced through her body. It was fire and ice. Something was wrong. Something was horribly wrong. Her head spun. Her stomach lurched sharply. She felt a presence inside her body. It was ravenous and lethal. She felt it was struggling; fighting. *It's almost as if something is…is… Is what?*

"Trying to come out." She heard the voice inside her head, but it wasn't her voice. It came from inside her, but it wasn't *her* voice.

"Kyle…what's happened?" she asked again as blind panic seized her heart. "What's happening to me? I feel strange…something…something is wrong with me."

Kyle's hand was under her head, tilting it back.

She stared up into emerald eyes as Kyle pressed a tumbler to her lips. She felt liquid, warm and scintillating, pour into her mouth and burn down her throat. The room began to blur in and out of focus again. Kyle's voice came to her from miles away, his words were strange, yet oddly they made perfect sense to her. "You are changing, my love. Soon you will be ready to serve your calling. Rest now… rest. When you wake, all will be revealed to you."

"Yes." She breathed, entranced as sleep came to her. "Yes, I'll rest, Kyle. I'll ..."

Chapter Twelve

Liam Briggs came to as twilight was setting on. He shook his head as blaring pain ran the gambit of his body. What the hell had happened? Trying to sit up, he winced as his hand scraped across splintered wood and fragments of plaster. He looked up at the wall. A hole the size of a buffalo gaped back at him. Liam rubbed his eyes and tried to remember…Kyle Bodeen. Kyle had done this. Looking around the room, he cursed when his eyes lighted on the chair to which Tessa had been bound. She was gone. Kyle had taken her of course. *And the money?* Liam looked at the desk…It was gone too.

"Damn it!" he swore aloud. Moving slowly, his head throbbing with the severity of a mallet pounding steel, he pulled himself to his feet.

Bourbon. He needed bourbon. A stiff drink and a moment to think. A moment to remember what had happened. The details were sketchy…he remembered the sky going dark with smoke. But…it had been the ravens, not smoke. He remembered Kyle coming through the door in search of Tessa. He remembered Kyle changing somehow.

No, that must have been an illusion. Though the way his hands were shaking gave him cause to wonder. He knew Kyle *had* thrown him across the room. The giant hole in the wall was sufficient proof that it had happened.

But did I really see what I thought I saw? Did Kyle somehow magically move himself across the room? Liam gauged the distance from the door to the window. Then he snorted and shook his head. *No. That didn't happen. That must have been something my mind conjured up while I was knocked-out.* He was convinced that there was no possible way a man could move nearly fifteen feet in the blink of an eye with out taking a single step.

Reaching the bar, he fumbled with the crystal stopper in the bourbon decanter. His hands were still shaking uncontrollably as he poured himself a shot. The tumbler full of liquor went down in one swallow and was quickly followed by another. The alcohol warmed his veins and steadied his nerves. Laughter began to gurgle from his chest. The idea that Kyle had transported himself across the room became absurd and almost comical to him. Of course he had imagined it.

Liam started to pour another drink and then stopped himself. "You need to think, Briggs," he murmured aloud. "Think about how you're gonna beat him. How are you gonna beat Kyle? He's got Tessa now, he's got all the cards…So how are you gonna beat him?"

Suddenly, he knew. It all became very clear to him. Then, his eyes fell on his revolver. It was lying on the floor below the window. Walking across the room to retrieve his gun, Liam stifled a groan. He rubbed a hand across his chest feeling excruciating pain in the left side of his ribcage. *I'd bet at least a rib or two got broken when I hit the wall. Damn that low-life, two-timing Kyle Bodeen!*

Anger surged through him. Fury at Kyle, fury at Tessa. It was a sweet and all-consuming fury. He relished the taste of it in his mouth. He was going to ride out to his ranch and round up every gun he had on the place. Then he was gonna come back and finish this once and for all.

* * * *

At first, the ride to his ranch was absolute torture. Every jolt and bump riddled his body with agonizing pain. With every new flare of burning torment, Liam felt his anger grow. Like a maggot burrowing into dead flesh, his fury dug deeper and festered. It drew momentum and strength from his physical pain. As he spurred his horse on, the brutal pang of his injuries subsided.

Soon he forgot the silly notion that Kyle had in some way transported himself across a room. All he could think about was how wonderful it would be to finish Kyle Bodeen. He imagined watching Kyle writhe in agony as he stripped the skin from his body with soulless pleasure.

He wanted to watch Tessa scream as he tore her heart from her chest and crushed it in his fist. He wanted to see her blood soaking his hand and dripping from his wrist. Black evil spread its oily fingers over his soul as he made his way across the seven miles that separated his ranch from Laramie. The flavor of death filled his mouth and churned sweetly in his stomach. He'd sold his soul many years ago and he'd done plenty for the Devil since. It was about time for the Devil to pay him back in kind.

Cresting the hill that overlooked his ranch, Liam gazed down at the work of his own hands. The land glowed red against a twilight horizon. The crimson wash of color was eerily fitting. The very soil he owned had been bought with human death and suffering. None of the purchase price had dripped from his body. All of it was the blood and torment of the innocent. The pride that usually ensnared his heart whenever he looked over the work of his blood-stained hands was lacking tonight. Instead he only felt the cold hand of vengeance squeezing his soul and guts. He spurred his horse into a gallop. His mount's thundering hoof beats were silenced by the white-hot fury that raced through his bones and filled his ears.

Liam fired his pistol into the air as he passed under the wooden archway that marked the entrance of the drive which led to the ranch house. Over ten cowhands tumbled from the bunkhouse, their surprise evident in their scurried scattering toward the barnyard. Liam Briggs never fired a round unless it was urgent. Five or six cowboys stood on the ranch house porch smoking. When they saw Briggs, they dropped their cigarettes and scuttled off the porch in the direction of the drive. Briggs was alone…and they all wondered why he had come out to the ranch at all. He hadn't been here in almost two weeks.

"Gather 'round, you men!" Briggs shouted, his voice carrying into the barn and throughout the house. "Move it! We got work to do! Where's Cameron?"

"He rode back into town this afternoon, Boss." Wes Stebbens answered from the fast-growing group of gun hands that were gathering in the yard.

Liam nodded. That may prove to work in his favor. Cameron would no doubt keep tabs on Kyle's whereabouts while Liam was here at the ranch collecting his men.

Better than twenty cowboys came to stand around Bryant's lathered mount. A few of them drifters, a few of them robbers, a few of them flat out murderers; all of them gunslingers. Liam smiled in spite of the harsh pain which shortened each breath that rattled from his ribcage.

"All of you strap on your side-arms and mount up. We're going back into Laramie tonight. We're gonna find Kyle Bodeen and kill 'im. Then we're gonna find Bradyn Preston and kill him too. We're gonna kill 'em all, boys. The streets of Laramie are gonna run red with their blood by dawn."

The shout that went up from his men was far more intoxicating to Liam than the strongest bourbon. A ripple of savage excitement passed through the ranks drawing evil smiles that shone ghastly in the twilight. Their reaction sent the blood pounding through his body and filled him with brutal energy. It had been a long time since Liam Briggs had summoned all of his men to blood shed. A very long time.

* * * *

Bradyn circled around Laramie and entered from the west, a tactic he had hoped would keep Briggs form discovering his presence. The city lay quiet under a bloody orange sky. A dead calm encompassed it deserted streets. An eerie fear tickled at Bradyn's ribs and ran the length of his back. A malevolent air filled the town. He knew all was not well.

He tethered his horse in the alley behind the mercantile and sat in the shadows watching the Silver Lady Saloon directly across the street. The saloon was lifeless. Too slow for a Saturday night, Bradyn noted. A stump-drunk cowboy walked out of the Silver Lady and disappeared down the street, his body weaving disjointedly as he meandered into the shadows of twilight. A hoot of laughter echoed through the night, but he saw no more people. *Where the hell is everyone?*

Bradyn tried to pull his thoughts into order. He needed a plan. Briggs would be in the saloon tonight, at some point, drinking. He was certain of it. What he wasn't certain of, was how to go about cornering Briggs alone. Only a complete fool would hazard trying to best Briggs in a gunfight if Briggs was surrounded by his own men. Bradyn needed to draw him out, to find a way to cull him from his herd. But how?

A trio of cowboys wandered past, black and baleful against the backdrop of golden light coming from the saloon. One of them turned and appeared to consider going inside, but thought better of it and followed his comrades up the street to the Cattlemen's Hotel instead. Bradyn settled deeper into the shadows, watching and waiting. Sooner or later, he was sure to see Briggs, but he had to be alert. His window of opportunity might come as a flash of lightning, here and gone in an instant.

Minutes slipped into hours as he sat watching. His eyelids grew heavy. Sleep came tapping on his shoulder and bidding him to rest. Twice he shook himself as blessed slumber nearly lulled him away from his vigil. And, as time wore on in an inactive blur, he momentarily succumbed…

…then, his eyes flew open.

Blackness. Everything around him was utterly dark. He heard a scattering of garbled sounds, the flapping of wings. But none of it could be seen. Bradyn felt a hand on his shoulder. He heard a voice whispering in his ear. Soft and beguiling, it was a presence reminding him of his past.

"Your heart is black, Bradyn Preston. So very black. You have shed innocent blood before, and you will shed it again. The ways of evil and cruelty are no stranger to you. Come with me, Bradyn, do my bidding and I will repay you well."

In the darkness, he looked down. His feet were on the brink of an enormous precipice, the world unfolded before him as a blanket. It glittered warm and welcoming. It taunted him, beckoned him, with every conceivable luxury and lurid vice.

"Do what I ask of you and all that you see will be yours, Bradyn Preston. I ask so little and yet I am willing to give you so much in return."

Rancid air filled his lungs. Fear gripped his very soul. But there was nothing but the blackness. Thick and heavy, it clung to him, threatening to squash the life from him. He could refuse, he wanted to refuse. But a spell, vile and hypnotic wended its way through his awareness. It was overpowering, crushing. He fell to his knees, his eyes streaming rivers of molten tears. "I can't!" he screamed as agony tore through him.

"Of course you can…" the voice soothed. "Of course you can. And you will," it snarled. "I have power to control the darkness and shadow. You are darkness, you are shadow. Your soul is mine!"

Then out of the blackness came a light. It was so brilliant that he could not look upon it at first. As his eyes grew accustomed to the brightness, he saw that a woman stood in the vortex of spiraling incandescence. She was dressed in white and in her hand she held a sword. Bradyn could not look upon her weapon because it was from her sword that the blinding light emanated. Her voice sounded across the blackness of the space between them. "Leave him, foul Demon. Do not touch that man. His heart and soul are the possessions of another."

Laughter boomed around him, shaking the precipice on which he stood. The roar of waves upon the sand filled the utter blackness as the voice spoke to the woman in jeering ridicule. "The possessions of another, you say? You must be mistaken. See…I have the one of whom you speak here. She was nothing to him. Look! She lies here, murdered by his hand."

Bradyn stared in horror as he saw the form of Rian. A mist of black swirled round her broken, bloodied body. A dark, scarlet slash ran the length of her torso.

"Look at your hands, my son," the mocking voice ordered. "Look at your hands." The taunting laughter that rocketed through the nothingness made Bradyn's heart thunder audibly in his chest.

"You lie!" he screamed into the dark, unable to bring himself to look at his hands. "I would not kill Rian. I love her!"

The sudden silence was more deafening than the horrid laughter had been. Then Bradyn heard the voice again. It was snarling and demonic. "Look at your hands, you fool. Look at them."

Bradyn held his hands in front of his face while the malevolent, mocking laughter began again. Blood…Where had all the blood come from? In his right hand he held a dagger, its silver hilt dripped crimson and deadly. Hurling the knife far away, he yelled out. "What have you done? Show yourself and tell me what you did to Rian!"

He heard only the emptiness of the dark. There was no one there. No one at all.

Then he heard a whisper. "Your heart is black. You've murdered again. There is no hope for you, Bradyn Preston. Your only future is blackness and utter pain…"

Bradyn jerked, his eyes flying open. The lights of the saloon glowed back at him through the darkness. He pushed a ragged breath between his teeth as he looked at his hands. Nothing. No blood. No dagger. He ran a hand through his hair, trying to calm the horrible beating of his heart.

But the dream had been real. So very real. Even in a waking state, Bradyn felt its presence. Corporeal, tangible. He could almost reach out and touch it. He could feel the precipice beneath his feet. He heard the sinister voice echoing through his head. What did it mean? Was it only an illusion constructed from fear and exhaustion, or was it something more?

His thoughts wandered over the events of the past few days. In retrospect, he saw a pattern. Everything was building…moving toward something. He knew it. He felt it in his blood and bones. The ravens, the darkened sky, the empty town, his dream. All of it meant something. But what did it mean? What could it possibly mean?

* * * *

Rian stopped her horse atop the same plateau on which Bradyn had stood only a few hours before. Kendall was sleeping in her arms. Her gaze traveled across the valley lighted by a dim red horizon. She had no idea what time it was, but she knew that sundown had come too early today. Far too early.

The lights of Laramie glittered in the distance. What would have been a welcoming, heart-warming sight for a wayfaring stranger only filled her heart with dark apprehension. A black aura had begun building a cocoon around the city. It was the presence of evil making itself known. She shuddered and shifted Kendall gently.

Bradyn was down there. He was there in the town. She could sense him. She could see his light. It was a tiny, shining speck of blue against the black.

The auras had come and gone all afternoon until she and Kendall had seen the ravens. After that, the colors had remained. As their journey had progressed, she had begun to feel excitement at the new phenomenon that had captivated her senses. A turbulent knowledge awakened within her. This was all happening for a reason and she knew she had some part to play in whatever dark horror was coming.

Wind and shadow encompassed her. A fierce tremor ran through her body as she sat looking out into the twilight sky. She ran her hand over the dagger strapped to her thigh, its cool hilt filling her with valiant anticipation. A fluid understanding pulsated deep inside her soul. It was ancient and powerful. She didn't know where the knowledge came from, but she knew a battle lay ahead. A battle of Life and Death. It was fast approaching, and she knew that there was so much more at stake than a few human lives. She didn't know if the man Bradyn had ridden into town to meet was there, but she felt a presence. An evil presence. She knew it was waiting for them to come.

Her dream from the night before, which now seemed eons in the past, resurfaced in her memory for the thousandth time that day. *There are two of them and they are waiting for you Bradyn.*

She ran a finger down the length of the dagger. "Please be careful. Please be safe. I love you," she whispered as she watched his aura twinkle in the darkness below. "I love you."

The mare blew out a breath and shifted its weight easily underneath them. Kendall slept on, his breathing deep and even. He was so unaware, so untouched by the world around him. Rian sat watching his face with silent awe. She was unwilling to wake him just yet. She didn't even want to move. A voice inside told her to wait. Tonight she would have to ride into the valley of shadow, but not right now. Her presence would be needed very soon, the voice told her, but not yet. Not yet.

Chapter Thirteen

Tessa awoke to the sound of her own heart beat. Slow and steady, yet somehow hollow and empty. She turned her head slowly, her gaze drifting to the window on the far side of her bed. The world was dark. The blackness of night was riddled with the deep reddish-purple of twilight. Had she slept all day? Blinking, she tried to sit up.

The velvet quilt felt heavy, a slab of marble feathers lying across her chest. The sudden urge to giggle loomed within her as she pushed with drunken clumsiness at the crimson sheets that enshrouded her body. Gaining a sitting position, she clutched at her stomach as a raw blade of nausea pierced it.

She stumbled to the door of the bedchamber with the steps of one who was fully intoxicated, the room sliding in and out of focus. Trying to remember what had happened to her to cause the upset stomach and drunken imbalance she searched the room for Kyle. His face was her last cognizant memory.

"Kyle?" she whispered. The floor tilted jaggedly to the right, she slipped and tumbled to her knees. "Kyle…where are you?" Her voice was a mere breath, inaudible and raspy.

"Tessa." She heard him call her name. Then he was at her side, pulling her from the floor. She was lost for a moment in the color green. His eyes, so beautiful, so cool, searched her face. "Are you alright?"

"I feel sick to my stomach…only a little. It seems to be wearing off a bit now." And, strangely, her nausea *did* seem to be fading. "Kyle, what's happened? I feel so…*different*. I—I don't remember anything. What happened after Liam hit me?"

His face clouded. The emerald of his eyes glowed luminous, vibrant and darker somehow. "Tessa, there is something I need to tell you. It is going to change you forever. You will be afraid at first. You will feel pain, but after…after you will only know bliss. You will have power and freedom. The world will lie at your feet and I will give you anything you desire."

She frowned, feeling her heart beat come to a stop. "Kyle, what are you talking about? I don't understand." The urge to giggle flooded her again as she felt the nausea return.

Kyle pulled her close to his body. Seductive electricity snapped in his eyes. "You are my chosen one, Tessa. The one I will spend eternity with." His lips were only inches from hers.

She felt smoldering heat radiating from his body. She shuddered as a cloud of uncertainty filled her senses. "Kyle," she begged, "Kyle, I don't understand. I don't understand."

"Let me show you," he whispered as his lips closed over hers.

Jaundiced green haze encapsulated her vision as she closed her eyes to his kiss. He inhaled sharply and paralyzing panic gripped her. She felt him draining her, absorbing the breath from her lungs, drawing the very essence of her soul into his mouth. At first she struggled, trying to escape his grasp. Fire licked her insides turning the blood in her veins to liquid flame. Excruciating agony engulfed her senses. It felt as if the flesh was being torn from her body. She would have screamed had she a breath in her and Kyle had not been covering her mouth with his ravenous kiss.

Ever so gently, he exhaled into her. The essence of Contessa Lang had been taken away to be replaced by something new. Ice crystals formed in her blood. Rough spikes of slow moving sludge seeped through her iron-clad veins. Her heart beat was no longer hers, but echoing in the space around them. The pain was gone. In its place came only cold, dark nothingness.

Tessa saw the shape of a man standing in front of her as Time slid to a slack halt and then began whirring past her with blinding speed. She was transported through mists of black. She felt the years fold back and melt into darkness as she was taken to a time and place centuries in the past.

She saw a young woman, beautiful and innocent, dancing among a stand of trees. The woman's laughter carried to a man standing at the edge of the forest. Tessa knew his face. It was Kyle. Tessa could feel the longing and lust the woman ignited in his body. Intoxicating and sweet, her laughter roused his senses. Tessa saw the look of determined lust on his face. Somehow, she knew he wanted the woman dancing through leaf-dappled, summer shadow. His expression told Tessa that he would have the beautiful gypsy girl.

But as Tessa watched, the mystic enchantment disappeared from his face. In its stead came anger. A man, old and feeble, was arguing with Kyle. He was the gypsy king and he would not give his daughter to the feudal lord as wife. She was already betrothed to another. The love of another held her heart.

Hot primeval fury riddled Kyle's visage. He was the feudal lord, the sovereign of all he surveyed and he would have her. *Droit de seigneur. Ius primæ noctis.* The right of the lord. The right of the first night. He would have her innocence if he could not have her heart. But the wedding night came and she was not brought to his manor.

As Tessa looked on, Kyle found the gypsy woman in the forest gathering wood among the trees. He took her. He forced his will upon her body. But after his passions were spent and his lust satiated, he felt only indifference and cold hatred toward her; this one whom he'd desired so fervently before. A dagger to her heart, a sudden slash of death as blood ran crimson and splattered upon white silk. He left her lying in the tent of her husband. Contrition and remorse were strangers to his soul.

Tessa saw them coming…the gypsies came and turned

his soldiers to stone with strong and ancient magic. They took him captive and carried him away to the forest. He was to pay in his flesh for the innocent blood he had shed. The blood of the gypsy girl.

She felt his torture. She felt his suffering as the fire crept higher. All was agonizing pain and intolerable heat. Flames lashed his body while his screams went unheeded by the undulating shadows that chanted his demise in the language of ancient gods. They gyrated hypnotically round a fire of white flame as his punishment lingered long into the night. His vehement cries of torment and the stench of burning flesh were witnessed only by those who had pronounced his fate. Tessa watched as the life faded from his body. His final breath was a drawn-out and strangled moan.

Then all was darkness. Blackness was all she could see. But there came a movement of air, the flapping of wings. She opened her eyes and beheld the stake to which his body was still chained. She felt Kyle's soul, hovering somewhere above the ground. She felt him…waiting.

Tessa watched as the ravens came. Sinister ravens flocking by the hundreds to the embers of dissolution. But, amidst the churning of the birds, something else grew. Blackened coils of sooty mist shifted and swirled upward taking human form. A man, garbed in flowing ebony and enshrouded in the blackness of shadow, walked among the ashes. His voice, aged and timeworn, carried deep authority when he spoke in the tongue of devils.

"Arise, my son, arise. From the ashes of curse I bring you forth. I have chosen you among men because your heart is exceedingly black and your sins are great. To you is given the spirit of Apollyon, the Angel of the Pit. You shall be called the Destroyer for you will arise anew in every generation to be a plague to the innocent and a snare to those who bare the mark of evil upon their souls. You will be given the power to delude the children of men for the many shapes of evil, both beautiful and vile, will be yours to wear as garments when you so wish. The creatures of the night will obey your will and the principalities of darkness will come when you beckon."

He lifted his arms and outstretched his hands to the heavens. In a loud voice, like the deep thunder of waves smashing against alabaster cliffs, the man shrouded in shadow uttered a warning. "Hearken to my words! You must be watchful and on your guard, for One will be brought forth in every generation, born to do battle with you and abolish you from the Earth. The two of you shall meet at the appointed time and one of you will destroy the other. My son, you must walk the world searching out your enemy with every new rebirth, for in one chosen generation the Final One will come. Born of the love of Shadow and Light, this One will have the power to break your line of rebirth and destroy you forever. You must find and destroy this One before true love seeks him out. For if you do, the world will be yours and you will live to walk among men forever. "

Then Tessa watched as the Man of Shadow breathed life into the charred body still bound by heavy chains. The air moved thick with green haze and emerald flame as the one she knew only as Kyle Bodeen stepped from the ashes a whole and beautiful man. She felt her soul shiver for there was something wrong with his face.

His eyes glowed red, serpentine and cold. The vengeance of death glittered in their depths. She watched him with mystified horror as he changed form. His face became elongated and reptilian while four horns twisted and grew from his head. Black, oily scales emerged first on his face and chest, then spread as liquid across the rest of his body. The hands of a man became the grasping, gnarled talons of a bird. His legs grew hairy, his feet turned to silver cloven hooves. Smoke poured from a mouth now full of ferocious fangs as he rose with a scream, raven-feathered dragon's wings carrying him up into the night air.

Then there was darkness again, a bloated cloud of mercurial smoke…Men of stone were being brought to life. Their bodies twisted and writhed into unspeakable creatures as they marched across the fields to destroy all those who had exacted the fiery retribution on their lord.

Screams went up in the night as flesh was rent from bone and limbs were torn asunder. Then Tessa saw the fire. Toxic green flames sent up boiling orange smoke. The heads of gyspies littered the ground while their bodies burned on an emerald pyre in the circle of a blazing encampment.

The ravens gathered by the hundreds. They swooped down to perch on severed heads and peck at the blood-soaked ground. Black cats swarmed in the firelight, feasting on the eyes and the ears of the dead as the Destroyer's laughter, malevolent and austere, echoed throughout the forest. Jubuliant, he watched the bodies of his judges burn and burn…his minions casting long, fiendish shadows as they danced round the Hell-flames.

Then images began to curl together. They blurred around her. Time and space reeled past Tessa with maddening speed.

Suddenly, all was still and Tessa was standing in a yard. Brown grass bent bleakly against a late autumn wind that churned blanched orange leaves in the air around her. The yard was familiar. The dull yellow two-story house and faded white picket fence reminded Tessa of a place she had once known. A place that felt as far away as a childhood dream. In a daze she looked at the house number. Four hundred, Oak Street. It was the house she had grown up in. The house of many horrors.

Tessa watched as the younger version of herself came trudging up the sidewalk. Her schoolbooks were slung over her shoulder, her flaxen braids trailing down her back in desolate neglect. Tessa shuddered remembering the dread that would creep over her everytime she came back to this house.

Everyday, the fear of the monster living inside would grasp her heart and twist it until she felt only hatred and anger toward the evil man posing as her father. The man who had beaten her from the moment she could remember. The man who had driven her mother to flee and never look back. The man who had ruined her adolescence and tortured her every waking breath, her every sleeping thought.

Tessa watched as the young girl entered the house. The flaking, decrepit door swung inward on its hinges and then squeaked in weary reproach as it swung closed again. She listened, hearing the same angry shouting that she had heard almost every day, all those years before. Quietly, she stole to the kitchen window and looked inside.

Fists of fury cast evil shadows on the wall as they pummeled the young girl's face and stomach. When she was lying nearly senseless on the kitchen floor, the shadow monster refilled his whiskey glass and stormed back to his dark lair. Tessa watched with tears in her eyes as the girl came to and crawled, sobbing, toward the back door.

Tessa knew she was going to flee to the woods at the back of the house. The place where she'd always run after he'd beaten her. Her heart ached for the girl, the younger version of herself, because she knew that this day would be different. Today she would not seek the shelter of the trees. She would not find solace in the bubbling brook as it rippled past. After today, she would have blood on her hands.

Pulling herself up-right, the girl frantically fumbled with the doorknob. Then her eyes fell on the butcherblock by the door. A blood-stained cleaver's blade gleamed up at her, tempting her to pick it up.

Tessa looked on in horror, empathy, and memory, as the young girl pulled the cleaver from the block of wood slowly, as if in a trance. The girl sat in the shadows of the hallway, waiting for her father to emerge from the study as he did every night. She waited for him to drink himself into a near stupor and then leave his demon lair to come to her bedroom.

Tessa shivered. She remembered cowering under her covers, waiting for him to appear in her doorway drunken and violent. He would always…but no, she would not allow herself to think of that now. He wouldn't touch her tonight, she reminded herself. Tonight he would cease to haunt her. Tonight would be the last night Tessa would see his face. And, after this night, he would never be able to hurt her again.

The study door opened many hours later. Her father's form cast a freakish silhouette against the dim light emanating from the room behind him. She jumped from the shadows, the cleaver glistening in the faint light of the study as it struck the chest of the black figure swaying drunkenly in the doorway. His scream was muted by the blood gurgling in his throat as the blade slashed the life from him. And for all the horror of it, Tessa remembered that she had felt only sickened joy and utter relief. Finally free of him, the young girl crumpled to the floor in a dead faint.

As she looked on, something took place that Tessa did not remember happening that night so long ago. A man, dressed in ebony clothing and a black tophat appeared behind the young girl. He lifted her into his arms to carry her away. Tessa followed him window by window as he made his way through the house, one room at a time until he came out of the front door.

Tessa slipped behind the tall oak tree and watched him from a distance, all the while wondering who he was and what he'd wanted with her. As he passed through the front gate, a strange thing happened. The air around him grew red and misty. He spoke words that were quiet and ghoulishly foreign as he touched his finger to the base of the young girl's throat. A crimson sphere of vapor glowed at the tip of his finger and then dissappeared into her skin, radiating for a moment before vanishing from sight. Confused, Tessa drew nearer, watching as the shadow man whispered to the younger version of herself.

"What have you done to me?" Tessa called out to him as he held her girlhood form. Her voice came back to her as if echoing along a dark tunnel. "What have you put into my neck?"

"It's your mark, my child." He kept his back turned to her as his answer filled the air around them. "One day you will know why I have placed my mark on you. You have been called to a higher purpose."

Stepping up behind him, Tessa was very afraid. "Why have you called me?" she whispered, gazing over his shoulder upon the young girl sleeping in his arms. "For what purpose?"

"You will know in time, my child. All in time." His voice was almost inaudible, a mere whispering breeze. A stirring of dark mists followed and the shadow man and the girl he held in his arms were no more.

Tessa stared blankly into space as four walls began to appear around her. At first she did not know where she was. Then she recognized the giant grandfather clock in the corner and she knew. They were the walls of her bedroom in the Silver Lady.

Kyle was standing over her, his eyes burned green and understanding. She knew that everything she had seen, he had seen too. The smile that spread over his face was no longer kind, but feral and lascivious. "So now you know my purpose, but do you know yours, Tessa? Do you know the reason you bare the mark upon your soul?"

Wide-eyed, she gazed up at him, the waking revelations still settling into her conscious mind. "No," she whispered, with confused wonderment. "No, I don't know my purpose, Kyle. Tell me, what is it?" She turned her head inquisitively. "What is it?"

"Do you know of the demon called Lilith?"

"Lilith?" The name was familiar somehow, as if it were a part of her. A part of her that was hidden and forgotten until now.

Kyle's smile was cold, "Lilith. The Woman of Red, the Temptress of men, the bride of demons. Many have said she was the first wife of Adam, the one who tried to tempt him to eat the forbidden fruit, but she was not. She was born in Woman the day Eve gave the fruit to Adam and caused him to know Good from Evil. The day mankind fell from Grace."

"Yes…" Tessa's expression grew faraway and thoughtful. A sudden understanding, strange but very real, filled her. "Yes…I am Lilith…aren't I?"

"You are the black spirit of Woman. The dark temptation that seduces men to come away from the path of Light. For thousands of years you have been a snare to evil men and a temptation and destruction to the innocent. They have called you by many names: Jezebel, Delilah, the Harlot of Babylon, the bride of Satan. You have lead many men astray, you have brought them to utter ruin. Now, your time has come again."

"My time has come. What shall I do?"

"My father who gave me life, over six hundred years ago, also brought you to life in Contessa Lang. He has called you forth and marked you upon a young girl in every generation since my birth. Together we have waged war on many who have dared fight against us and now our time to destroy has come once again. Do you understand, Tessa? The One is coming. I need you by my side to defeat our enemy. I feel the battle drawing nearer." Kyle inhaled, crimson embers glowing in his eyes.

"How do you know that a battle is near?" Her voice was warm, a seductive purr.

"I have searched for this One for many years. Everyday I have felt this fight drawing closer. Now, I can taste it in the air. I can feel the its presence. I sense a dark past is haunting this One, making it's aura different, weaker somehow." Kyle mused. "The only thing that can weaken them is true love... but very few of them ever find it. They have always been unbound to a human passion. Their sole purpose for existence is to destroy me. Perhaps this one is different, perhaps this one will be easier to slay." He smiled down at her, fangs glimmering white in the dim lamplight of the bedroom. "Will you help me destroy our enemy, Tessa?"

An evil smile, crooked and enticing crossed her mouth. "I will," she answered as she ran her tongue over her upper lip. "I am hungry…" A frown crossed her countenace. "There is someone here. I can sense a presence in this town. Do you feel it too, my love?"

Kyle smiled. "Yes, I have sensed it too. He has been here for sometime now. But, we have been waiting for him, have we not?" He walked to the window and looked out over the dark town below. "He is right outside now, watching the saloon from across the street. I see the blue of his soul. Come. Let us go to him, Tessa, my chosen one. When the battle is over, you may have his blood as your reward."

* * * *

The darkness of night had settled down over Laramie with malignant weight. Bradyn felt, more than saw, the evil that encapsulated the city. A pressence, tangible though unseen, was teeming in the air around him. He felt a churning in his soul. A force was coming to life inside him. It smoldered below the surface of his awareness, just out of the reach of his comprehension. His purpose hadn't yet revealed itself to him, but he knew that in time he would understand what it was. His path was marked, his destiny set in stone; he had only to wait for it to awaken itself inside him. "Liam Briggs will die tonight," he thought. And that single thought gave him the strength to wait a bit longer.

* * * *

Cameron Briggs cowered in the corner of the Silver Lady Saloon. A fear he couldn't understand nagged at him. Something was very wrong in Laramie tonight. He hadn't seen Liam since earlier that afternoon. Now his brother couldn't be found in his hotel room and he wasn't in the saloon. Buddy and Tex still hadn't come back yet. And, most disturbing of all, at close to five o'clock there had been an earthquake and the sky had gone dark as sundown. To make matters worse, and even stranger still, thousands of ravens had begun flying through the streets. Cameron didn't know what the hell was going on, but he knew that whatever was happening, it sure wasn't normal or right.

As he sat pondering the weird events of the past few hours, Cameron surveyed the saloon. Two cowboys sat at the bar drinking and there wasn't a saloon girl in sight. The place was dead for a Saturday night. Plumb dead. He shuddered involuntarily. Even in the middle of winter, the Silver Lady never had fewer than a dozen cowboys on a Saturday night. Never. The streets outside were quiet, dark, and empty. It was almost as if the whole town was privy to some horrible secret that he hadn't yet been let in on. He shuddered again, wishing that Liam would show up. For all his older brother's faults, right now the mean bastard would be a welcome sight. At least then Cameron wouldn't be sitting in an empty saloon alone wondering what the hell was going on in Laramie tonight.

His mind so vividly consumed with the strangeness of the day, Cameron almost didn't notice Kyle and Tessa come down the stairs and into the saloon. They were walking arm in arm, startling, vacant smiles on their faces. The unseeing glance Tessa cast Cameron before they stepped through the swinging doors scared the breath from his lungs and curdled the blood in his viens. A freezing shudder ran the length of his body as he swallowed the last of his whiskey with rattled haste.

Liam would want to know what those two had been up to when he got back. He nervously decided to keep tabs on them, certain his unease would surely pale in the light of Liam's anger should something happen and Cameron not know about it. He rose, rubbing his sweaty palms across his thighs. Walking to the window, he watched them as they crossed the street. Their feet did not seem to touch the ground and a green and crimson light exuded a faint trail behind them as they moved into the shadows and on up the street.

Afraid to look at them, but determined to keep track of them, Cameron watched as they dissappeared into the darkness. Then he cautiously stepped through the saloon doors to follow. Expecting to see them wandering up the street in the direction of the Hotel, he rubbed his eyes and looked around in confusion. Kyle and Tessa had dissappeared. The street was dark and desolate.

He crossed the deserted street and approached the mercantile from the far side with quiet steps, hoping against hope they were not lurking in the shadows waiting for him. Hoping his heart beat would not alert them to his pressence. It was pounding so loudly in his ears he was certain that half the town must be able to hear it. Then he heard their voices in the alley and came to a dead halt at the edge of the building.

Peeking around the corner, his eyes went wide and his mouth hung limply agape. He felt his legs go slack beneath him. The strength of his body rushed from him as a child's kite torn free and carried away by a feirce wind. Kyle and Tessa stood in the alley. Bradyn Preston was in between them looking at Tessa.

As Cameron watched, Kyle's form changed. He grew. Soon he was towering over Preston as Preston, unaware, backed toward him. In the darkness of the shadows, Cameron could not see Kyle's features, but he could see his shape. Huge, black, and looming. Cameron watched as horns grew from his skull and ebony feathered wings slithered gleeming satin behind him. Seeing that was enough for Cameron. Enough to send him running madly down the street in the direction of the Cattlemen's Hotel, laughter boiling from his lips as hysteria ripped through the threads of his reality.

* * * *

Bradyn had seen Contessa and a man come out of the saloon. He had recognized her, but in the dark, he couldn't tell who the man was. All he knew was that he wasn't Liam Briggs. As they crossed the street in the direction of the mercantile, he sank deeper into the shadows of the alley.

The two of them looked to be out for an evening stroll. He watched as they passed the alley entrance and walked slowly onward toward the Hotel. Something was definitely amuck with the whole scene. Besides the fact that Contessa was with another man and Briggs was nowhere to be seen, Bradyn was baffled, and a little curious, by the way the two of them were walking. It was slow and even. From his vantage point, it looked as though they were a few inches off the ground. Floating.

Bradyn blinked and rubbed his eyes. But when he looked again, they were gone.

"Good evening, Bradyn." He spun hearing her feminine voice directly behind him. Turning, Bradyn knew it was Tessa before he saw her face.

Startled and confused at her sudden appearance in the alley when he'd just witnessed them walking down the street only seconds before, he stepped backward. "Tessa? How did you know I was here?"

The glitter of gold in her eyes and the apple red of her

lips as they parted in a twisted smile made her look brutally sinister. "We've been waiting for you. Haven't we, darling?"

"That we have, my love. That we have." A voice, aged and resonant vibrated behind him.

Bradyn felt seering pain as a hand clamped down on his shoulder and another closed around his throat with superhuman strength. As he struggled to break the vice-like hold on his neck, Bradyn couldn't see the form grasping him from behind. But as his breath was constricted and his consciousness slipped away, his last fleeting thought was that the hand on his shoulder did not belong to a man. The thick talon-like fingers that peirced his skin were wholly evil and completely inhuman.

Chapter Fourteen

Rian sat motionless atop the plateau. A battery of illusive thoughts skittered through her mind. With equal parts apprehension and anticipation she regarded the shifting black clouds that spread their sooty tentacles over the city below. Laramie glistened obsidian in the bleak darkness. Its streets were lightless and without a sign of life. The full moon that hung just above the eastern horizon shone crimson and deadly from a starless sky.

A cool breeze picked up and as it touched her face and whispered through her hair, Rian felt a chill prickle across her skin. The evil waiting in the dark city was as real and tangible as the horse upon which she sat. A palpable, seething blackness that sought only to cause pain radiated from the poisonous mists that surrounded the town. She could feel it hunting, seeking out those it wanted to destroy.

Bradyn's aura glittered up to her, a faint, unmoving speck of blue. Being able to see it, to see *him*, gave Rian a small sense of comfort. As long as she could see the light of his soul, she knew he was still alive. She watched the city for movement, Kendall still sleeping contentedly in her arms, as the hours slipped slowly past.

She was on the verge of dozing when, with no warning, she saw Bradyn's aura flicker as two other auras, gleaming green and red, entwined and fused with it. Instinctively, Rian knew he was in danger. She saw the sparks of sapphire fear his aura cast upward and then his blue was gone, like a candle's flame suddenly snuffed out by a gentle gust of air.

She bolted in the saddle, unmindful of Kendall, as stark fear for Bradyn's safety gripped her soul.

Rian nudged the mare forward. Her only thought was that she must go to him. He needed her to help him. But the hand on her wrist and the gentle voice beside her stopped the beating of her heart and caused her mount to go perfectly still. In an instant she knew that this was why she had been waiting. She had been waiting for *him* to come. As if in a dream, she turned when he spoke her name.

"Moriana."

She watched in awe as he materialized out of the night. A blazing embodiment of equal parts illusion and reality, he hovered over the ground with translucent wings that whispered a trail of bright white light around him.

Mesmerized by his splendid light and sudden appearance, her only cognizant thought was; *I know his face. I have seen him before…somewhere.* The revelation frightened her. It caused her to tremble. *I must be losing my mind! He can't possibly be real…can he?* She could see very little of his face for it was so brilliantly light. But his eyes, a timeless azure, seemed to read her thoughts and bore straight into her heart.

His hand remained on her wrist as he spoke in a voice of calm authority. "I know you fear for the one you love, Moriana, but you cannot go to him yet. I have come to prepare you for what is coming. The time for battle is approaching, even now evil is drawing its followers to fight, but you must wait a little while longer. The One who is creating the blackness around the city is not of flesh and blood. He is an evil born of the Ages and he is not easily conquered. You know this, but you have forgotten it. Before you can face him, you must remember your past and the side for which you fight. You also must remember why you fight, or else all will surely be lost."

A feeling of vague memory, not entirely warm although strangely reassuring, began to trickle through her. A faint smile touched her mouth as she gazed at him, "I *do* know you…somehow. What is your name? Who sent you to me?"

"My name cannot be spoken in the tongues of mortals,

but I have walked among the human race since the Dawn of Time. Many have called me Michael the Archangel, but it is only the name given me by men. The day Lucifer marched his fallen angels against the Gates of Heaven I was called to be a Guardian and Defender against the powers of Evil. I have served the One who is Light from the day I was created. He is the One who has sent me to you tonight."

His words sent a shiver through her, though it was not born of terror. The dark fear that had been growing in her heart for the past two days seemed suddenly groundless and distant. She felt herself awakening to long-forgotten dreams. Her mind was assailed by tiny prisms of recollection that struggled to fall into place and resurface as whole pieces in her memory. She knew his words. She had heard them before.

"Darkness has raged against Light for many millennia. It came into the world the day The Morning Star fell from Grace and it has been a plague to mankind ever since. The fight between the two is largely unseen by the masses of humanity that progress from birth to the grave wholly unaware. Only a few chosen souls are ever called to do battle with it in physical form. Their blood has been spilled countless times through the centuries. The chosen that follow after have continued to fight, even if it cost them their lives. Many champions have perished taking a stand against the Devil's minions, but they are not forgotten. Those that have fought a brave battle have been given eternal life. It is a reward that will never perish. It is because of these champions that the human race lives on, safe from annihilation.

"The one you love has been called to this very task. He must stand against the Devil's Champion tonight. The Evil One will try to turn him, to use the blemishes of his past to seduce him, but Bradyn must stand. If the Evil One does succeed and fully turn him to his side, Bradyn will be unable to come back. Then the battle will be lost."

The angel cast his gaze to the malevolent city barely visible now in the thickening, black fog below. "There is hope yet in this time of darkness, for Bradyn has a great power. He does not know what it is, but he will soon learn it. This power can save his life and the lives of countless others. The Devil's Champion cannot destroy him as long as he holds onto his soul and does not exchange it to save his life. Look, even now, his soul-light remains."

Rian looked down at the city and saw Bradyn's aura. It was dim, only a weak shimmer, but it was visible once again. Mild relief touched her heart, but it was brief. Fear and doubt cast a jarring warning as she noticed that the red aura she had seen early was still with him. "What is his power? What can he use to fight against this one of whom you speak, my lord?"

"He has the possession of true love. Your love, Moriana. He will fight for it. He must if the evil is to be destroyed. The side of Light has always fought for love. In its purest form, love is the beginning of all things. No human soul has ever truly existed without it. Some have warped it into what it was never intended to be, others have distained and disregarded it, but Love lives on in those who follow after the way of Light and do not fall into the path of Shadow."

His gaze swept over the plain below them and Rian could feel the sadness in his expression. "But, there have been many who have not let the light of Love touch them. They are black souls, marked out by the Devil himself. He delights in using them to bring hurt and sorrow to the children of men. The demon who walks the world tonight was once such a man. He was a feudal lord in his day, a cruel tyrant to all who were in subjection to his rule. The misery of his fellow man did not move his heart to pity. Instead, he sneered at the pain and weakness of those less fortunate than himself."

"How did he come to be a demon?" Rian asked. Her voice was quiet as she watched the flickering auras of blue, green, and crimson in the city below. The red was still with Bradyn, but the green aura was some distance away now.

"Largely, it was through his evil heart and the folly of mortal men. Long ago, over six hundred years past, he walked the earth as all men do. He had great power and wealth. The world bowed at his feet. But, he was an evil man. Light could not touch his soul. A heart that was made of solid stone beat in his chest.

"Then one day, a band of gypsies passed through his lands. The gypsy king's young daughter, his only child, captured the attention of the wicked lord. It was said that he took one look at her face and it melted his icy heart. Love beckoned to him, but the wickedness that possessed him was much stronger than the quiet wooing of love. The feudal lord vowed that he would have the woman, but her father would not give her to him. She was pledged to be wed to another man.

"Rage took the young lord's heart. He would know no peace if he could not possess her. Like thousands before him, he measured his life only by physical gain, and not by the virtues of spiritual enlightenment. The love that so sweetly called to him was pushed aside because his eyes were blind to the true worth of life. Instead of learning to love and release this one he desired to the love of her own heart, he took her against her will, foolishly believing that he would satisfy his longing by force. In the end, he found that the desire that had once burned so feverishly within him had turned to ice because he'd taken that which was not his to take. Love that is stolen is dead and bitter. Only love that is given in return can grow and blossom. In his haste to satiate the lust of his wicked heart, he discovered that he could not find love, for he was incapable of loving. This revelation drove him to madness and in rage he murdered the beautiful gypsy girl. By taking her life, he sealed his eternal fate.

"The gypsies were outraged at the evil lord's deed. Foolishly, they forgot that vengeance should be left to He who is Light. They exacted a cruel punishment on the feudal lord by burning him alive. They did not know that by killing the man, they were, in fact, opening the door to a much greater evil. The side of Light is not alone in its reward of those who fight for it. The Devil came to the lord that night and raised him to life. He promised his servant that he would have life in every generation. He called his new champion after Apollyon the angel of the Pit whose name means "The Destroyer." The Devil gave him great powers over everything that was evil and carries the darkness of evil within it. For over six hundred years, the Destroyer has been set loose to walk among mankind."

The angel pointed toward the silent, black city. "He is there now, waiting to kill the one who will be sent to fight against him. He is stronger now. With every rebirth, his power grows."

"How can he be stopped?" Rian asked as a new fear crept over her. Her temples pounded as the blood hammered through them. "If his power is so great, how can he be conquered?"

"No darkness exists without light, Moriana." The angel replied, his vibrant blue gaze turning to her face for the first time since his appearance beside her. "For every evil force that is brought into existence, there is a defender of Light raised up to fight against it.

"You must listen closely to my words, Moriana, for it is your story tonight that you must first remember. When The Destroyer came into existence, the side of Light knew that he would wreak immeasurable havoc on the human race. To keep him from destroying the world of men, a spirit of Light was brought into being to fight him at the appointed time after every new rebirth." His hand grasped hers tightly. "This one is called the Avenger."

The name roused excitement in her, but it was paired with grave apprehension. Her worry for Bradyn's life was only growing with the angel's explanation. "This Avenger, what power is given to him to ensure he wins?" Rian asked.

"There is never a guarantee that the Avenger will win the battle, Moriana," he answered. His voice was kind but laced with solemn sadness. "The Destroyer grows stronger and wiser each time he regenerates. He will not triumph in the end, but the road to victory is a hard fought war. Some who fight lose their lives; others lay them down because they can see the path clearly and know it must be so. All things come to pass for a reason. You must understand that everything that comes to be, everything that takes place, is as it should be. A greater purpose binds all things with a single thread.

There are no accidents, no unforeseen events from the eternal aspect. It would only appear that way from a mortal viewpoint. Everything that has happened in your life has been destined, my child. Everything. The unborn child you carry now will someday have a role to play in the battle of Light and Darkness. Even your son, who sleeps in your arms, has a purpose in this fight."

Rian gasped, his former words capturing her attention before his latter ones. "How can you know such a thing, my lord? I cannot be with child. It is impossible," she breathed. Then she frowned. "And, you are mistaken about Kendall. He is my nephew, not my son."

She felt his smile, though the orb of light haloing his face hid it from her sight. "He is your son, Moriana. This fear that holds your heart is keeping your mind from remembering. Until you push your fear aside and allow yourself to believe my words, you will be able to save no one. If you love Bradyn, you must listen to me. You must try to remember. It is the only way the darkness will be vanquished."

"I don't understand what you are saying. Please, can't you just tell me what it is I need to know? Can't you explain to me the things that I cannot remember?" The wave of terror grew higher within her. If she could not remember, Bradyn may be killed. But what was she supposed to remember? Everything felt vaguely familiar, and yet none of it made sense or roused any specific memories from her past. A shallow sigh escaped her lips. "I want to remember, but I can't. I can't."

"Perhaps, you should wake the boy," the angel suggested mildly. "Perhaps you should have him remind you of today's date."

"Today's date…" her voice trailed off. Yes. She knew today *was* significant, but why? Why? She looked down at Kendall sleeping in her arms. A breeze of cool air pushed a thick lock of blond hair across his forehead. Studying his face and pondering the angel's words, she wondered at his revelation. *Was* Kendall her son? She shook her head. It was impossible! She had been with child once, yes, but her child had been killed at the hands of her brutal husband. Looking back at the angel hovering next to her, she felt anger ripple through her. "No, you are mistaken. Kendall is not my son. I remember Sadie, my sister-in-law, she…" Rian stopped because she could not finish the sentence. She did not remember the circumstances of Kendall's birth at all. Or did she?

As Rian studied Kendall's sleeping face, she realized that there was so much she did not remember about the months that passed between the time she had learned she was with child and the night she had murdered her husband. Much more than she wanted to admit. Squeezing her eyes tightly shut, she shuddered at his next words.

"Forget what you think you remember, Moriana. Forget what you have let yourself believe. Remember the truth of your past. Search your heart, the memories lie there."

The cool breeze stiffened into a light wind. As it touched her face, Rian felt her spirit spiraling upward. Her mind, furiously churning to recall her past, felt on the verge of exploding. Then light dawned upon her. A vivid memory of a dark night seven years past came into full focus. Today was Kendall's birthday! He had been born seven years ago this very night.

The picture of a tiny red infant screaming lustily in her arms, his lungs full of vibrant new life, surfaced in her mind. Her mother, Jackson, and Sadie were standing over her, all three of them crying. They were smiling down at her with expressions of pride mixed with grave worry. Words echoed back to her from a long forgotten dream. Rian heard her mother's voice. *"It's a boy, Rian. You have a beautiful baby boy."*

Tears welled in her eyes and slipped silently between her shut lids to the crowns of her cheeks. "Yes! I remember now," she said aloud. After she had believed her baby was lost, she had been so mind-sick for such a very long time. Her mother and brother had been there that night. The night that Rian had been certain her baby had died. She remembered lying in her bed as the labor pains wracked her body. It was all so hazy, but now she remembered watching Jackson as he'd wrapped the baby in a heavy blanket and left her room…

"Jackson! Where are you taking my baby?" she had called to him.

"Shhhh, rest now." He mother's voice was soft and soothing. *"Jackson is protecting your son. Your little boy is so very important. He must be hidden away. The Dark One must not be able to find him, Rian."*

She had cried and slept in delirium for days. A vast emptiness filled her heart and pushed all sanity and reality from her mind. She wanted her baby so badly! Her unconscious mind had been assaulted with horrible images. Vicious nightmares stalked her fevered sleep. When she had finally regained some of her strength, her mother had told her that the baby had died and Rian began to believe she had dreamed that Jackson had taken her son away. And, when she had finally shot her husband, Jackson and Sadie had saved her life by bringing her to the Territory. They had been so afraid for her. Looking over the past seven years, Rian realized the angel was right. She had forgotten so much!

Opening her eyes and gazing down at Kendall, she felt a sudden rush of overwhelming love. Her tears wetted his hair as she wept and fiercely hugged him to her chest.

Rocking him gently, there was one very big detail that bothered her. "How could I forget such as thing? How could I not know that my own son was alive?"

"Your memories were taken from you, my child. They were taken to keep you and your son safe." There was heavy sadness in the angel's voice. "It was not a pleasant thing to take such a blessed thing from you, but when you nearly lost the baby all those years ago, the side of Light set a Guard around your aura and obscured the events of your baby's birth in your memory."

"But Jackson told me that Kendall was his son! Why would he lie to me? He never lied to me…he always protected me!" The sob that had been threatening to burst from her chest did as she turned to look up at the angel's glowing face. "Why?"

"It was for your protection that he told you your baby had died. Your brother did what was right for you, Moriana.

He was called to guard both of you. Jackson was told of the dangers that would come when your son was born. Kendall's future is charted, his fate is sealed. He cannot, nay, he *must* not be found until the appointed time."

Rian shook her head again. "But why couldn't I remember it? How could I spend seven long years not knowing that Kendall is my son?" She kissed Kendall's cheek and buried her face in his hair. But she had known. A small part of her, buried deep inside, *had* known. It was the reason she loved him so dearly. He was the reason that she had wanted to live when all had been so dark and hopeless. Kendall had always been the light shining in a black sky, urging her forward, even when she wanted to give up.

"You must understand, Moriana. The bond between a mother and her child is very strong. Even with your memory altered, the power of your auras has been difficult for the Guard to hide. If it had not been for Jackson bringing you to this wilderness, you would have been discovered already. It was the only way to keep you safe, to keep the Destroyer from discovering where you and the child were. Had he been able to search out your auras, he would have come for Kendall and taken him away from you. For these seven years, the Destroyer's search for the child has been futile. But as the time for battle draws near, your auras will become visible to him again. Soon the Destroyer will be able to see you fully. And, after tonight, he will know that Kendall lives. In this life and the next, he will seek him out. He has terrible plans for your son."

"Why does he want Kendall? What has Kendall done to make the Destroyer fear him?"

"The Destroyer fears what he cannot control. He needs Kendall. Kendall is marked. His purpose is set, but as long as the Destroyer cannot find him, he cannot become what the Evil One wants him to become. Do you understand, Moriana?"

His question was ridiculous to her. *Of course I don't understand!* She wanted to scream at him. "What has Kendall been marked for? What purpose must he fulfill?" she demanded, a hand pulling Kendall to her chest in a frightened, possessive motion. The young boy squirmed in his sleep, but did not awaken.

"Kendall's fate, his future, has no place in your thoughts tonight, Moriana. He will be protected by Light until the appointed time, of this much I can assure you. But now there are more pressing circumstances at hand. So much hangs in the balance. Your life and Bradyn's are teetering on a precarious ledge. The fate of Kendall and the fate of your unborn child are all directly linked to the events that will take place this night. You must understand. You must remove all other thoughts from your mind and listen to my words."

Again Rian stared up at him in disbelief, but this time she did not question his words. "I am with child," she said. She placed a hand on her stomach and felt a flutter of protectiveness and excitement race through her veins. Another question tugged at her mind. "What else of my past have I forgotten? What else do I need to remember?"

"There are memories which you have forgotten, and more you must remember, but it will come in time. The path you walk tonight will open doors in your memory as you journey onward. But first the spirit that is in you must be brought to bear. You have to abolish this fear that holds you and go forward in faith. The side of Light will go with you."

"If you know that am I going to have a baby, and you knew that Kendall is my son, do you know what the outcome of Bradyn's fight with the Destroyer will be? Can you tell me what I can do to save his life?" The sure certainty that he would be able to help her was crushed by his answer.

"Together you will fight him, Moriana. Bradyn needs the spirit that is in you if he is to face and defeat the Destroyer. It has not been given to me to know if you will triumph in this fight." Slowly he lowered himself to the ground and the brightness of his light grew a bit dimmer. Rian could see the anguish in his eyes as he looked up at her. "Come down and walk with me for a while. There is more I need to tell you."

"What about Kendall?" she replied. Her fingers tightened about the boy's thigh and shoulder. "He is sleeping and I will not wake him." The defiance she heard in her voice startled her, though the angel's countenance remained unaffected.

"Very well," he answered. Stretching out his palm toward Kendall, a bolt of vibrant yellow electricity shot from his hand. It circled the sleeping boy and lifted him from Rian's arms in a gently glowing orb of light. Hovering above the ground, Kendall slept on completely oblivious to the angel's presence, or the tenuous predicament in which his newly self-discovered mother found herself. Rian sat staring in awe at the ball of quietly revolving light for a moment before dismounting.

The angel offered her his hand and she took it without hesitation. Together they walked along the rim of the plateau's steep drop. Both were silent for a long space of time. Rian's gaze was torn between the angel's face and the barely visible twinkle of Bradyn's aura. She waited impatiently for the angel to begin telling her what it was that he had come to her to say, but he remained silent.

They progressed along the plateau until they came to an impassable drop of rimrock that fell in excess of five hundred feet to the valley below. Standing at its edge and looking down the sheer cliff face gave Rian a sudden rush of vertigo. Here the angel turned and looked her fully in the face.

"I want you to close your eyes and look inward, Moriana. I want you to search your soul for the memory of the one whose spirit you hold inside you." He stepped off the edge of the precipice and grasped her other hand. "Close your eyes," he instructed when she failed to do as he told her.

Nervously, she obeyed him. At first she saw only blackness and swirling colors behind her closed eyelids. Then she felt her body moving and realized he was pulling her forward. She opened her eyes and looked at the cliff not two inches from her feet. Panic took hold of her. "No!" she shouted. She tried to look into his face, only to be blinded by luminous white light. "Please, don't pull me forward," she pleaded.

"Close your eyes and search your soul, Moriana." The sound of his words, deep and commanding, immediately compelled her to heed him. "Do not think of Bradyn, do not think of Kendall, and do not think of yourself. There is a spirit inside you. Can you see it?"

Her eyes tightly closed, Rian shook her head. "No. I see only darkness." She desperately tried to see what he wanted her to see, but it was no use. There was nothing but blackness. Then, little by little, she felt warmth in her finger tips. A circular heat began moving through her hands. It was soothing and, momentarily, her mind was empty save for the knowledge of how wonderful it felt as it radiated up her arms.

The warmth moved higher into her shoulders and neck. Then it permeated her chest and abdomen sending a prickle of gooseflesh across her skin as it did so. As it moved through her body, she inexplicably began to see a light. A tiny, almost imperceptible flicker, it did not emanate from outside of her body, but from deep within her heart. The breath caught in her throat as it grew into a brilliant glow. "I…I see something," she whispered. "A light."

"Look into the light, Moriana. You will see the truth." His voice was miles away, an echo that sounded across a fathomless white space.

The brightness was as blinding as looking directly into the sun, but it was a soul light and Rian could not merely shut her eyes to block it from view. As it grew and came in ever stronger waves, a tingling pain seized her head and radiated from the scars across her back. Memories whirled past her, but she was helpless to reach out and grasp a single one with her mind's eye.

Then she saw her. A woman came to her through the blinding whiteness of space. Dressed in pure white, a gruesome crimson stain ran the length of her torso. The instant Rian saw her, she knew her. It was the gypsy girl. The girl that the feudal lord had murdered. Immediately, she noticed the girl's eyes, a captivating, deep amethyst that could only be described as spell-binding. Black hair fell to her waist and when she smiled, Rian understood why one look at her had captured the young lord's heart. She was beautiful. Dark and lovely.

Her voice was the laughter of a brook when she spoke. "Hello, Moriana. I've been waiting here for a long time. It is good to finally meet you."

Chapter Fifteen

Hoof beats thundered through the night as Liam Briggs led his group of men toward Laramie. He laughed into the starless sky when he thought of how wonderful his revenge would be. He would show no mercy to Kyle or Tessa. They would beg for death, but he would make their ends slow and painful. Never again would that woman torture his existence. Never again would Kyle Bodeen double-cross him. Liam would make certain that his face was the last thing either of them saw before they died.

As the miles sped past, every rock and tree, every bush and scraggly sagebrush took on a skeletal, menacing shape. A tangible energy ran through his men. Liam could feel the blood-lust racing among them as he glanced over his shoulder and saw his own excitement reflected from their faces in the light of the full-moon. They could taste the death that was fast approaching. It was for this very purpose that they lived; to take the lives of men.

The riders crested the final hill that separated them from Laramie and looked down upon the city lying dark and encompassed by a thick black fog. Liam felt his blood run cold. The presence of menacing power was in the town tonight. Recognizing the shroud of evil as a foreshadowing of the vengeance he was about to have, Liam gave a loud shout and signaled his men onward.

The sound of pounding hooves falling in perfect unison poured over the hill and into the valley below. Liam felt the adrenaline rush through his body as the deafening charge drowned out the sound of his own heart beat. Drawing his revolver, he fired two shots into the air. His men followed suit; firing and whooping as they charged into the dark city.

They rode down the main street in rows of three, Liam riding out front. As he surveyed the empty street, he was reminded of earlier that afternoon when the earth had shook and the sky had gone flaming orange. He caught movement out of the corner of his eye and saw that the ravens were still there. By the hundreds, they lined the roof tops and littered the vacant street.

The picture of Kyle Bodeen jumped out in Liam's head. Trying to remember what Kyle had done that startled him earlier, Liam stifled a shudder. A memory of Kyle's face and the anger in his expression came to him. Kyle had been furious when he'd seen what Liam had done to Tessa. But that wasn't what had been so unsettling about him. Straining to recall what it was about Kyle that had disturbed him back in the hotel room, Liam suddenly wanted a drink. More aptly put, he *needed* a drink. He hadn't had a shot of bourbon in hours.

"Let's ride on up to the Silver Lady, boys!" he called to his men. "I need a drink and I'd bet the ranch that we'll find who we're looking for inside."

His men hooted and fired a few more rounds into the air. Liam smiled. There was nothing quite like coming into town with a little fanfare. His men were ready, he was ready. *Let's kill 'em now and have a drink or two to celebrate. Then we'll see about riding out to find Preston and finishin' his sorry ass.* He was eagerly looking forward to the task that lay at hand.

As they headed toward the Silver Lady, Liam glanced in the direction of the Cattleman Hotel as they passed by it, wondering for the first time since entering town where Cameron was. Probably in the saloon playing a round of Black Jack, Liam guessed. His brother had a pension for the game and this was Saturday night, the best night of the week to make a killing if a fella knew how to play his cards right. The place would be hopping with cowhands fresh off the range with pocketfuls of money to burn. Or so Liam thought, until he noticed that the street in front of the saloon was completely empty. No horses were tied to the hitching post. No wagons lined the sidewalk in front of the mercantile. *Strange,* Liam thought, puzzled. *Sure is quiet in town tonight.*

The lights of the saloon shone brightly enough, but as the riders neared the building, Liam couldn't see a single soul standing at the bar. There were no cowboys sitting at the tables, no chorus girls dancing on the stage.

Uneasiness crept over him. Something strange was going on in Laramie tonight. The ravens and the heavy darkness had unsettled him, but the empty saloon gave him the downright creeps. "Hey, Wes!" he shouted over his shoulder as he dismounted and tied his horse to the hitching post. "Why don't you and Billy go on up to the hotel and see if you can find Cameron?"

"Sure thing, Boss." Wes followed the order fast enough, but the uncertainty was very apparent in his voice.

All of the men were uneasy. Liam saw it in their faces as they followed his lead and got off their horses. As the men looked around the vacant street and stared inside at the empty saloon they all wore an expression of doubt. Their eyes all asked the same question that was running through Liam's mind; *"Where the hell is everybody?"*

"Sure is quiet," Liam heard one of them mutter in a low, edgy voice. "And look, the saloon is empty. Never seen it empty on a Saturday night." A murmur of agreement passed along the ranks.

"What's that you're saying, Jeremiah?" he asked.

The tone of his voice and the dead-pan glare he gave Jeremiah made all the men look at their boss. If any one of them had been getting the idea that Liam Briggs was unnerved by the silent town, his tone made them think otherwise. His eyes full of domineering defiance, Liam let them know that he was here to finish what he had come for and, whether they liked it or not, so were they.

"I reckon there's a good reason the town is dead tonight. Come on, let's go in and see if we can find out why," he ordered. "Jeremiah, you and Cass stay out here and wait for

Wes to get back. I'm going in to see if I can find Kyle and Tessa."

Starting up the stairs in front of the building, Liam wondered if he would find Kyle and Tessa upstairs in her bedroom. The sudden thought that the two of them had left town with his five thousand dollars caused him to frown. His hand came to rest on the swinging door and Liam relaxed a little. Elijah Claymore, the bartender, stood wiping tumblers behind the counter. Liam was about to call out to him and ask him if he knew anything about the strange goings on in town tonight, when he heard a shout from up the street.

"Hey, Briggs! We found Cameron. You better git up here, there's something wrong with him!"

Wondering what the hell had happened to his brother, Liam raced up the street in the direction of the Cattleman Hotel. *If Kyle Bodeen has so much as laid one finger on Cameron*...Liam swore under his breath and charged up the steps of the hotel. "Where's Cameron?" he demanded. "Where's my brother?"

"Up in yer room, Liam." The shifty, spooked look in Billy's eyes bothered Liam. Billy Baker was a lot of things, but a scare-easy, yellow coward wasn't one of them. Whatever had happened to Cameron, it wasn't a small thing.

Liam took the stairs two at a time, irrational anger at his brother brewing inside him. Why the hell did Cameron always need him around to think for his sorry ass? The dumb son of a bitch couldn't stay out of trouble for five minutes if Liam wasn't there to tell him what to do. Shaking his head, Liam wondered what could have possibly happened to his brother in a town that was completely empty tonight.

Smashing open the door, Liam stopped dead in his tracks. Wes stood beside a chair that pointed toward the west-facing window. An old man with a head full of disheveled white hair sat there, his posture was strikingly stiff. Liam couldn't see his face, because the old man's back was to him as he sat there staring out at the black night. Glancing around the room, Liam saw that no one else was present. Confused, he shouted, "Where the hell is Cameron?"

The horrified look on Wes's face was all the explanation Liam needed as the old man in the chair turned to face him. "I'm here, Liam," Cameron whispered. "But I won't be for long. Neither will you. We're all dead men."

Liam nearly choked on the scream that burst from his lips. His eyes went wide with terror as he saw the shell of a man that had once been his younger brother. His face was pale, his eyes were sunken and blood-shot, his lips were blue, and his hair…Liam couldn't take his eyes off his brother's hair. It was white. So horribly white. "Cameron! What happened to you?" he cried with mingled pity and disgust at his brother's loathsome appearance.

Cameron sat staring into space with a blank expression on his face. Slowly a dreadful smile parted his lips. He didn't answer. Instead, he started shaking and manic chuckling filled the room. It was hysterical and bone-chilling. Liam watched in horror, trying to hold the panic he felt rising in his blood at bay as he listened to his brother's chuckle grow into high-pitched, frenzied laughter. Fury took Liam for one brief moment of bravado and he was across the room in two paces, pulling his brother from the chair and slapping him soundly across the mouth.

"Stop it!" he snarled at Cameron. "Stop it right now, you filthy little bastard, and tell me what the hell is going on!"

Cameron's laughter died away, but the vacant smile remained. "*He* is here," he answered simply.

"Who is here?" Liam asked the question between tightly clenched teeth. When his brother just sat staring at him with the same eerie look on his face, Liam slapped him and asked again, louder this time, "Who the hell is here, Cameron? Tell me!"

"The One who owns your soul, Liam," Cameron answered. His tone was light and taunting, like that of a child chanting a nursery rhyme. "The One who owns my soul." Cameron's smile widened. "*He* is here."

Liam couldn't breathe for a moment, the sheer lunacy in his brother's words made him sick. He yanked Cameron up to face level hoping to scare the stupid chatter right out of him. "Enough of your foolish jabbering. Tell me what is going on in this town tonight. Where are Kyle and Tessa?"

At the mention of Kyle's name, Cameron started laughing again. Tears welled in his eyes and he held his sides from the wracking force of his laughter.

Frightened and furious at once, Liam tossed him to the floor in disgust. Turning to Wes, he ordered, "Tell the boys to split up in pairs and search this town. I want Kyle and Tessa found right now. When you find them, bring 'em to me!"

Liam did not like the look that Wes gave him. It was the look of a man who was contemplating cutting-out and saving his own carcass. "Did you hear me?" Liam asked. His voice was quiet. He glared at Wes, silently daring him to run.

Wes just nodded, but his eyes kept darting toward the door.

"Good." Liam replied. "Now get downstairs and give 'em my orders."

As Wes walked past him, Liam reached out and grabbed his arm. Spinning him to look directly into his eyes, Liam warned, "And don't you even *think* about leaving town, Wes, or I'll kill you."

Wes blinked. "What's wrong with Cameron, Liam? If you can tell me that, I won't leave town. If you can tell me that what he says ain't true, I'll stay and help ya kill Bodeen. But if you can't tell me, you'd better just shoot me now. 'Cause I have a feeling that if what Cameron said is even *half* the truth, a bullet through the head would be a far sight better than meeting whoever it is that showed up in Laramie tonight."

"What did Cameron say before I got here?" Liam's eyes narrowed as he studied Wes's face. "Did he tell you more than he told me?"

Wes shook his head. "He didn't say much. Just kept repeating, 'I saw the Devil. He is real. I saw the Devil. He is real.' over and over again." Pulling his handkerchief from his pocket and wiping it across his sweaty brow, Wes asked,

"What do you think happened to him, Briggs? If he went stark, ravin' mad, something drove him to it. I know Cameron has always been a weak link, but I didn't ever figure him for soft in the head."

Liam blew out a breath and ran his fingers through his hair. Cameron was still lying on the floor where Liam had tossed him, curled into a fetal position and mumbling inaudibly. "I think Kyle or Tessa drugged him," he said in a matter-of-fact tone. "Can't think of a better explanation. Maybe they thought it would be a good distraction so they could get out of town."

"Then how the hell do you explain his hair?" Wes's voice was dubious and his eyes were shifty with fear. "His hair is whiter than my great granddaddy's was at eighty!"

Stumped for an immediate answer, Liam drew his eyebrows together in a frown. He was about to tell Wes to shut up and get about his business when Cameron started making an awful noise in his throat. Once, Liam had come across a calf that couldn't find its mother. It had been dehydrated and exhausted. "Engaged in active dying," Liam liked to call it. The calf had been making a horrible gurgling noise as it laid waiting for its life to end. It was the same sound as Cameron was making now. Repulsed, and not a just little frightened, Liam turned to leave the room with Wes close on his heels.

He was about to slam the door when Cameron called out to him. "Liam! Come back! He's waiting for you! I saw him. He is here in Laramie with his demon bride. He has Tessa!"

When Cameron said her name, Liam paused. Walking back to where his brother lay writhing on the floor, he stooped down beside him. "Who has Tessa?" he asked. The quiet of the room closed in as he waited for his brother to answer him.

"The Devil!" Cameron screamed. "He has Tessa, only she isn't Tessa anymore. He turned her…somehow." Cameron's eyes grew glassy and unfocused. "I don't know how Kyle did it, but he turned her."

"What has Kyle got to do with it?" Liam demanded. Pulsating disgust riveted him at the mere mention of the man's name.

"Kyle is the Devil." Cameron answered. His voice was a wizened whisper. "And he's waiting for you, Liam. He's waiting for all of us."

Unfounded panic threatened to consume him. Shoving it aside, Liam shook his head. "Cameron, I don't know what those two did to you, but you have lost your head. I am going to find Kyle Bodeen and when I do, I am going to kill him. Then we'll see who the Devil really is."

"Leave town, Liam." Cameron's voice was weak as he clawed at Liam's shirt with the frantic desperation of a drowning man. "Leave town while you still can. If he finds you, you're a dead man. Please listen to me. I saw what he did to Preston. Leave now and don't look back. Forget about your revenge. Just be thankful to escape with your life."

"Preston? What the hell do you mean, you 'saw what he did to Preston'? Is Preston here in Laramie?" Liam grabbed his brother's shoulders and shook him fiercely. "Answer me, Cameron! Is Preston here in town?"

Cameron's glazed stare grew distant and despondent. Slowly, he nodded his head. "I saw him kill Preston outside the Silver Lady. In the alley beside the mercantile. He isn't human, Liam. He isn't human."

"Who killed Preston?" Liam asked trying to stay calm. "Did Bodeen kill Preston?"

"The Devil killed Preston." Cameron murmured in a trance-like voice. "I saw the Devil. He is real…" he voice grew quieter, "I saw the Devil…he is real." Liam didn't notice that his brother had pulled his gun from its holster as Cameron whispered; "I saw the Devil…he…is…real…"

The sudden blast of a gunshot knocked Liam off balance and he tumbled backward to the floor. As the smoke cleared, he pulled himself up into a sitting position and stared down at his brother in stunned horror. Putting a hand over his mouth to suppress a gag, he looked at his brother's face and felt the vomit come gurgling up his throat. Cameron had blown off half of his own head.

* * * *

Bradyn was aware of dimly lit surroundings when he first regained consciousness. As his head began to clear, the first thing he felt was a nasty cramping pain in his neck and shoulders. He was half-standing, half-hanging from his arms, which were suspended in the air above his head. He closed stiff, lethargic fingers over the constraints that bound his wrists and felt the intertwining links of cold metal chain. His chin was lying on his chest.

Not wanting to make any sudden movement, he opened his eyes and looked down. He saw the origin of the faint light which lit the room. A burning candle stood at his feet. Its eerie, flickering glow illuminated his naked torso and he saw that blood was dripping down his chest. At first, he thought he had been cut or even stabbed. But as he stared down at the blood, he realized first, that the blood was not his and second, that it formed a pattern. Blinking, he felt sickened when he realized what it was. An upside-down star painted inside a crude circle. A Pentagram. The sign of the Goat.

Lifting his head, he stifled a groan as the vertebrae in his neck protested with several wicked snaps. The candle gave off very little light, but he could see the rough hewn timbers that formed stalls to his right and left. Hay littered the dirt floor and the thick odor of manure attested to the fact that he was in a barn or stable. Searching the darkness that lay just outside the small circle of candlelight, Bradyn could see the yellow luminescence of two eyes, watching him.

"Hello, Bradyn." Tessa said as she stepped from the shadows and into the weakness of the candle's glow.

"Tessa." Bradyn murmured. "Where is Liam?" His eyes darted to the darkness beyond her shoulder, wondering if the eyes he felt were hers alone.

"Liam?" Tessa asked. The name sounded familiar, but forgotten somehow, in her tone. "Ah, yes. Liam Briggs." Her smile was chilling. She shrugged. "He is in Laramie…I suppose."

"Where am I?" Bradyn asked. His throat felt dry and scratchy. *How long has it been since I had a drink of water? How long have I been here?*

"You want to kill Liam, don't you, Bradyn." An evil glitter made her eyes gleam as she avoided answering his question. "I sense your desire to have his blood. I can smell it on you like the cheap perfume of a two-bit whore."

Bradyn's eyes narrowed as anger began to creep over him, replacing his fear. "Tell me where I am." His fingers tightened around the chains binding his wrists.

Her laughter, soft and jeering, echoed to the dusty rafters many feet above. Bradyn heard the flapping of wings and felt the air churn around him. "Patience, Bradyn. All in good time. You will know your purpose soon enough," she chided.

"I have no business with you, Contessa," he replied. "I came into town to settle the score I have with Briggs. If you're smart you'll let me go before I decide there is a score to be settled with you as well."

Again, she laughed. "You are so horribly dense, Bradyn." She stepped closer and bent to pick up the candle. Holding it near his face, she murmured under her breath, "Pity. Such a handsome face. Seems a waste really."

Bradyn glared at her but said nothing. She scared the living daylights out of him. The way she was looking at him, almost like she wanted to eat him alive. And her smile repulsed him. It was downright wicked. She was nothing like the fun-loving girl he had known a few weeks back. "What's happened to you, Tessa?" he asked.

Her smile deepened. "I've been set free, Bradyn. I'm free of Liam and free of having to entertain men like you," she answered. "I met someone who can give me everything I want."

A foggy half memory of the moment in the alley came to him. There had been someone else with Tessa. Someone who had grabbed him from behind. He wondered now if that was the person to whom Tessa was referring. "When are you going to let me go?" he questioned.

"You will be set free when you are no longer of use to us."

"And when do you suppose that will be? I have business I want to attend to with Briggs, I told you that already. I don't give a damn what you and yours are planning. I sure as hell don't want any part of it." Scalding anger climbed up his spine and settled at the base of his skull. If he weren't tied in chains, he would have been mighty tempted to slap that smug smile right off her face.

"The only business that you need to worry about is the business of the man who holds you captive, Bradyn Preston."

"Then I want to speak to this man," Bradyn demanded. "I suggest you go get him, Contessa."

Tessa stepped closer and ran a hand over his shoulder. Gone was the serpentine yellow in her eyes. She looked as she had the day he had first seen her. She offered a smile that was seductive and full of sensual promise as she leaned close and whispered against his ear, "He can give you your freedom, too, Bradyn. He will deliver Liam Briggs to you, but you must agree to help him." Tessa pulled back and tilted her head. Blue eyes gauged his reaction to her words and his reaction to her closeness.

"Help him do what?" The searing cramps in his shoulders and neck were making his breath come in short gasps. Sweat stood out in cold beads on his forehead as he wriggled his wrists and tried to loosen his shackles in vain.

"Quiet," Tessa whispered as she ran her hand up his cheek and placed a finger over his lips. Her face was so close to his, the blue of her eyes reflecting the yellow of candlelight. "Patience, remember? He will be here soon and he will tell you what you must do for him."

Furious, Bradyn lunged at her. The chains clattered against the beam to which he was bound with a resounding clang.

Tessa deftly stepped backward. "Ah, ah, ah," she chided in a sing-song voice, the yellow glitter returning to her eyes. "Mind your manners, Bradyn. You don't want to make me angry, I assure you."

She turned to leave with the candle lifted overhead. With her back to him, she said, "I am going to leave you to think for awhile. When I return, he will be with me. He will tell you what it is you must do. I hope you will think long and hard about accepting his offer, Bradyn. If you don't choose to obey him, it will go very badly for you, I'm afraid."

As she walked away, taking the light with her, the candle's glow passed over the narrow corridor and the stalls that lined each side. When she opened the heavy oak door at the end of the stable, Bradyn strained to see what lay beyond it. There was only darkness. The last shred of light disappeared as she shut the door behind her.

Bradyn was enveloped in thick blackness. He felt panic seeking to seize him. Shutting his mind against it, he fought to think. Rian's face came to him. He wondered if she was safe. He worried that perhaps he was being held while men approached the ranch to kill her and the kid. He wondered if Briggs was behind his capture.

Then Bradyn remembered seeing Tessa come out of the saloon on the arm of another man earlier that night. *Who is he? Is he the one that wants to strike a bargain with me?* Bradyn wondered what kind of deal anyone would want to make with him. *What could I possibly have to offer? What will he ask me to do?*

Tessa had implied that if he cooperated he would be given his meeting with Briggs. Bradyn recalled the way her eyes had turned yellow. He thought about the strange circumstances surrounding his arrival in Laramie. Somehow, he greatly doubted that any of it was a coincidence. He had a feeling that his coming meeting with this man Tessa had referred to would be no normal conversation between mortal men. Deep in his heart he felt a familiar churning and, in the blackness around him, the presence of pure Evil.

He blew out the breath that he had been holding and forced himself to remain calm. The darkness of the stable pressed in close. He felt its claustrophobic fingers twist around his heart. Trying to distract his mind from the heaviness of the black silence that encompassed him, his thoughts turned to Rian. For all his fear and unease, he could not help the smile that came with the memory of her face. He could see her eyes so clearly, the love in them when she'd looked at him, the happiness when he'd told her he loved her, the deep amber concern when she'd warned him not to go into Laramie. *"You'll be killed,"* she had said. And right now, Bradyn couldn't help but wonder if maybe she had been right.

* * * *

Tessa climbed the stairs that lead to the roof of the livery. She knew that hot candle wax dripped down her right hand and wrist, but she couldn't feel it. Opening the hatch to the rooftop, she climbed out of the stairway. At first she could not see Kyle, only the flocks of ravens that were scattered across the roof. Then she saw him. His back was to her as he faced to the east. Cigar smoke curled upward and disappeared into the thick fog above. The tails of his long black coat rippled in the cool night air.

"Is our guest awake?" he asked without turning.

"He is," Tessa answered as she stepped up beside him and looked down on the city lying desolate and dark at their feet.

"Has the spirit taken him yet?"

Tessa could not see his features under the brim of his hat, but the red of his eyes glowed from the blackness that was his face as he lifted his cigar to his mouth again. "Not yet," she replied. "He has no idea why he is being held."

"Did he *ask* you why he is here?" More swirling smoke drifted upward as Kyle turned and looked into her eyes.

"He did."

"And what did you tell him, my love?" The red in his eyes grew brighter with brimstone excitement.

"I told him to wait and all would be explained to him," Tessa answered. She smiled, her spirit reflecting his maniacal fervor.

"Excellent," Kyle whispered as he turned once again to the east.

"What are you looking at?" Tessa murmured. She tried to follow his gaze, but the heavy black fog that had settled in over the rooftops of Laramie blocked her vision.

"There is a woman following Preston," he answered. "Until she is revealed, we cannot use him. We cannot bend him to our will. His spirit is too strong. But she is the key. She is his weakness, and when he learns that her life is in danger, he will kill to protect her." The chuckle that sounded from his throat was deep and menacing. "But I will turn him against the one he loves by using his love against him. Then he will learn that the Shadow within him is stronger than the Light. I will bend him to my will and he will fall."

* * * *

Gunfire echoed through the stillness. Kyle and Tessa turned in the direction from which it came. They watched as black men passed by on horseback underneath them and proceeded up the street in the direction of the Silver Lady.

"Liam Briggs," Kyle smiled. "Right on time." He wrapped an arm around Tessa's shoulder and she felt the raw evil energy that ran through him as his smile gleamed white and lethal. "The pawns are gathering," he said with anticipation.

Turning his attention back to the night sky in the East, Kyle was a little bothered that he hadn't been able to see the woman's aura yet. *But it is of little consequence,* he thought as he slowly lifted his cigar to his lips. *When she shows up, it will be all too easy. The side of Light has already lost the battle. I have their king.* He exhaled a cloud of bluish-black smoke and dropped the spent cigar to the rooftop. Grinding it under his boot heel, he smiled again and said, "Check. Mate."

* * * *

Rian remained captured in the vastness of white light as the beautiful woman came toward her. Frightened by her sudden appearance, yet eager to know her name, Rian asked, "Who are you, my lady?"

Her amethyst eyes sparkled as she smiled. The warmth in her expression set Rian's racing heart at rest. "I was once called Aurelia, but that was many long years ago. Now, I am the spirit that lives in you, Moriana. The spirit of the Avenger."

Rian was filled with sudden awe. "But I thought that Bradyn is the Avenger...isn't he?" As if because of her doubt, the vision of the gypsy girl flickered and became almost transparent. Rian fought to thrust her fear from her heart and the form of the woman grew bold once again.

"Ah, yes. Bradyn. The man who holds your heart," Aurelia said. Rian sensed the quiet anguish in her words.

Aurelia came closer and took Rian's hand between her own two. "I feel your love for him, Moriana. It shines from your eyes the way my love once shone from mine." The sadness of her smile made Rian's heart break for her. It was the smile of tragic loss.

"I once loved and was loved as you are now. But a man I did not love took my love from me. I have been given the task of fighting the Destroyer each time he begins life anew. Until he is completely abolished from the earth in the final battle, I am bound to live on as a spirit in the heart of one who has virtue. You are that one this night, Moriana."

Rian remained quiet. She was afraid of offending the beautiful woman by telling her that it was ludicrous to think that she, Rian Keene, could possibly be the Avenger. But the doubt in her heart and the fear in her mind screamed out against it with every shallow breath she took.

Unmindful of her stunned silence, Aurelia continued, "The night the Evil One was brought to life and given the power to destroy, He who is Light gave my life back to me. I walked among the ashes of all those that I loved after the Destroyer had brutally taken their lives, but the man I loved could not be found." Her voice murmured deep, agonizing pain. "Then I saw him. The Destroyer had hung him upside-down on a tree and made him watch while his soldiers took the lives of all those we so dearly loved. After our people were dead, the Destroyer killed him. He died with a dagger plunged into his heart." A single tear slipped down her flawless cheek.

Sickened and saddened at the horrors Aurelia had witnessed so many years before, Rian still could not stop herself from replying, "I am truly sorry for your loss, Aurelia, but I think you are mistaken about me. I cannot be the Avenger."

Aurelia looked solemnly at her for a moment. When she spoke, her words puzzled Rian. "I lost him in life, but he has been called to his own purpose. His spirit fights for the side of Light even as mine does."

"I do not understand. The man you loved was also given life?" Rian asked.

"He was." The angel spoke as he moved to stand beside Aurelia inside the space of white light. "The night that the Devil raised his foul champion and sought to wage war on the children of men, the side of Light brought forth two spirits. One was the spirit of the Avenger the other was the spirit of the Protector. Each time the Destroyer is regenerated, the two spirits are marked in two human souls. The Protector has always been born of the same bloodline as the Avenger. He is the guardian sent to watch over the Avenger until her time of Awakening."

"Jackson," she breathed. The sudden realization was staggering. It made perfect sense to her. That was why he had brought her to safety in the wilderness of the Wyoming Territory. It was why he had told her Kendall was not her son, but his. It was the reason he had given her the dagger. The dagger that had hung forgotten on her thigh now grew warm as if sensing its purpose was on the verge of being discovered.

"Yes, your brother was your Protector for the time. But when he lost his life while fighting to keep you and Kendall from harm, another soul was marked to carry the spirit of the Protector."

"Bradyn." Rian felt her heart stop beating when she spoke his name. She knew it to be true as surely as she saw the angel and Aurelia standing there in the vast brightness. Bradyn had been chosen to be the Protector. *Her* Protector.

"Yes," Aurelia answered. "The one you love. Only once before has the spirit of the Protector rested on a man who was not the blood relation of the Avenger. When the spirit of the Avenger and the spirit of the Protector meet outside the confines of blood relation, the two will fall in love. Precautions were taken to ensure it never happened again after the first time the two were joined apart from a common blood bond. It is dangerous to both, for the love of the two spirits weakens them to the Destroyer. However, in order for the prophecy to be fulfilled, it must be so now."

"What prophecy?" Rian asked. It felt like a foolish question to her. For some absurd reason, she knew that it was something she must have once known but had somehow forgotten.

"The side of Light decreed that the Destroyer would be given reign to walk the earth for a season in each new generation, free to prey on mankind until he meets the Avenger in battle," the angel explained. "But in due course, one will be born who will have the power to abolish the Destroyer from the world forever. It is said that this One will be born of the love of Light and Shadow. Do you see, Moriana? You are one of Light and you have loved one who is of Shadow."

"The child I carry will be the Final Avenger?" She felt overwhelmed and a little unbelieving. It all seemed too vast to comprehend.

"The child you carry is of utmost importance, Moriana. Without your love for Bradyn, the one who must finally defeat the Destroyer will not come to power. The child inside you, Bradyn's child, must be brought into the world. The time of the Final Avenger is drawing near." Aurelia's eyes gleamed amethyst excitement. "When the Final Avenger conquers the Destroyer, I will be released from my task. The spirit of the Avenger, my spirit, will be set free."

Rian placed a hand on her stomach. The knowledge that the life inside her, still small and imperceptible, was so very important in this struggle between Light and Darkness frightened her to the core of her being. As a bolt of lightening splitting the sky, she instantly realized how everything had fallen so effortlessly into place.

Her whole life sped before her eyes. Every circumstance, no matter how trivial, had been set in motion for a higher purpose. From the moment she had fallen in love with her late husband to the day Jackson had been killed to Bradyn's sudden appearance on the homestead, none of it had been a coincidence. All of it had to be exactly as it was. Remembering her husband, she felt the scars across her back grow warm and doubt crept in once again. "I have blood on my hands, I have murdered a man. I do not think I am the one of virtue that must defeat the Destroyer."

"The sins of your past do not change your calling, Moriana," Aurelia assured her. "You have been chosen for this task and only you have the power to see it through. If you do nothing, the Destroyer will kill Bradyn. He will find Kendall and work his wicked plans with him. He will lie in wait to kill the baby that is now in your womb. If you do not face him this night, no one, not even Bradyn, will be able to stand against him."

The grave understanding of her mission left her speechless. Could it be true? Was she the one chosen to kill the loathsome demon? Terror at the thought of facing such a monster caused the light around her to dim and she felt herself slipping into darkness. She screamed, her eyes still shut, as she began plummeting into the black chasm below her. It was only momentary. Then the angel appeared at her side. Reaching out and taking her by the hand, he lifted her into the air. Rian felt the coolness of the breeze and saw the light flood around her once again.

Then the angel whispered words that comforted her heart and brought courage to her soul. "Do not fear the path that is Light, my child. Rejoice that you have been given this honor. Rejoice that your end will not be as the Destroyer's. For even if he knows victory this night, his destruction is sure. Darkness cannot win over Light in the end." The angel gripped her fingers tightly. "Will you go forward and fight for us, Moriana? Will you fight for the side of Light? "

Rian opened her eyes and she saw that she no longer stood on the precipice. Her feet were not on solid ground but firmly planted in the black swirling air above the deep drop of the cliff. The angel and Aurelia were standing beside her. As she looked out across the land to the place where evil spun its blackened web around the city and saw the blue of Bradyn's soul, a swift courage flooded her heart. Then the words were past her lips before she could even try to stop them.

"I will."

Chapter Sixteen

Bradyn could not say how long he was kept in the darkness, suspended by chains, every breath a torturing agony. He only knew that it was long enough for his entire life to pass before his eyes in a drawn out progression. From his childhood through the black memories of his youth to the years of his adulthood, he found no consolation in his past. There was only bleak hopelessness. A few times he roused himself from brief, tormented dozing. The nightmarish images of the men he had killed marching single-file in bloody procession, or the picture of Helena and the baby quietly accusing as they both lay in a spreading crimson pool, tortured his half-conscious mind.

In the blackness of his prison, he realized that he had walked through life wanting to die for many, many years. He had been unafraid of Death, always taunting it and daring it to take him. Never before had he feared for his life. Until now. A single bitter tear slid down his cheek when he thought of Rian.

Her face was a sweetly haunting memory that oppressed his mind to a greater degree than the memories of his violent past. She seemed unreal at times, only a dream, in the terrible darkness. Her love had given him a second chance and still he had stubbornly tempted Fate. Unwilling to leave his past behind and look to the future, a future with her, he had foolishly ridden into town to get his revenge on Liam Briggs. His bitter fool's errand weighted the musty air. Death sought to claim him because of his own reckless willfulness.

The sure, silent knowledge that tonight he would meet his end flooded him with desolate sadness. Bradyn's sadness was not for himself, but for her. He wondered what she was doing this very moment. He pictured her putting Kendall down to sleep and then climbing into her own bed while fear for the man she loved left her sleepless long hours into the night. He knew she would wait for him right up until the very last minute, hoping against hope that he would come back. Bradyn imagined her packing up their belongings and leaving her homestead to take Kendall to safety when he did not return, as she had promised him she would. Wordlessly, he prayed that she would be safe. He prayed that evil men would not find her and take her life. The sob that caught in his throat nearly choked him when he considered, once again, that her life would not be in danger if it had not been for him.

"Your heart is black. You've murdered again. There is no hope for you, Bradyn Preston. Your only future is blackness and utter pain…" He heard the accusing words of his nightmare over and over again. He recalled the dream, the image of Rian's bloody body lying broken at his feet. Terror gripped his soul when he realized that the words might assuredly prove true. He may not have plunged a knife into her heart, but by chasing after his revenge, he might as well have. In coming to Laramie, by venturing out to meet certain death, he had driven a dagger into their love.

He pondered Tessa's words: *"I hope you will think long and hard about accepting his offer, Bradyn. If you don't choose to obey him, it will go very badly for you..."*

He wondered, for the hundredth time since she'd left him in the darkness, what he would be asked to do. When it came right down to it, he knew the answer was simple. They would want him to do the only thing he had ever done. The only thing he had ever been good at, besides cheating at cards of course. Gun-fighting and death. Bradyn wondered what the conditions would be. He had been promised his meeting with Liam Briggs, but that was no longer such a savory notion to him.

Then, another thought occurred to him. What if he was asked to kill in order to keep Rian alive? It seemed a little foolish at first. After all, even if they knew that she was the one who had nursed him back to health, even if they had already found her, how could anyone possibly know he had strong enough feelings for her to care whether she lived or died? It seemed ridiculous to assume anyone could know he loved her. But, the more he thought about it, the more certain of it he was. It was inexplicable, perhaps it was the dream combined with all of the odd things he had witnessed tonight, but as the minutes slipped by he felt more and more strongly that Rian figured into this predicament somehow. And that singular thought terrified him.

The complete darkness was sweltering and heavy against his skin. He heard the intermittent flapping and scratching of the ravens. He felt one of them peck at his ankle in the blackness and Bradyn lashed out at it. He sent it flying away with a swift, angry kick. The others moved around him in a flurry of wings. None of them approached him, but all of them took up a deafening protest to his mistreatment of one of their own. "Just try to peck me again." Bradyn growled as their cawing echoed in the pitch-black room around him. "Just try it, you filthy, vermin infested bastards."

The furious flapping and squawking continued until the heavy door at the far end of the stable creaked open. Bright lantern light was at first only thin rays of broken beam. It spilled through the opening door until it completely illuminated the room. The wash of light sent the screaming ravens to perch high in the rafters overhead, where they grew silent.

Bradyn squinted as the light touched his face. For a moment he was unable to see the person who held the lantern. But, as the light moved closer, his eyes adjusted to the glare and he saw Tessa coming toward him. As promised, she was not alone this time. A man walked beside her. He was tall and sharply dressed, and, as he approached, an air of elegance emanated from his carriage.

Although Bradyn wasn't able to fully see his face, the man was instantly familiar to him for two very different reasons. Primarily, Bradyn's first thought was that he had met the man somewhere before, recently. Had it been in Denver? Or maybe it was in Dodge? He couldn't immediately place him. Straining to recall where he'd seen him before, Bradyn also felt a secondary familiarity. He felt he had known this man a very long time ago. It was the same strange sense of déjà vu that he had experienced when he'd looked at Rian the very first time he'd seen her and again the day they'd buried Cheyenne Joe. He felt a tight hitch in his gut. He knew that the presence of something unseen was trying to make itself known to him yet again. A faint recollection of a time long forgotten flashed across his mind and then was lost from memory as the man addressed him.

"Good evening, Bradyn."

He still could not quite see the man's face because he eclipsed Tessa, who stood behind him holding the lamp. But when he moved closer, his eyes were the first thing that captured Bradyn's attention. Two shining red orbs glowed from a face that appeared black and almost featureless against the light behind him. Then he saw white glistening fangs as the man came to a stop before him and smiled. The fear in Bradyn's heart tripled in that instant. It was not the face of a man that he was looking into, but the face of a demon.

"Who are you?" Bradyn asked. For all his mustered strength he could not keep the slight quiver from his voice.

Tessa moved around the man and stood beside him then. Bradyn felt a peculiar revulsion when he saw that the man's eyes were green, not red, and his cold smile was full of beautiful, flawless human teeth. Bradyn shook his head in disbelief and stared at the man before him. "Kyle Bodeen," he murmured as his memory clicked at last.

"I'm surprised you remember me, Preston." Kyle's smile widened. There was no friendliness or warmth in his expression. It was the look of a man who was forced to make nice because he needed something from someone he could barely tolerate.

"I remember you," Bradyn snarled. His chains rattled as

his hands formed tight fists around them. "You're the dumb son of a whore who tried to pin that missing ace of spades on me in Tulsa a few years ago. You got a man killed."

Kyle's throaty laughter set the ravens to flying around the stable in a flurry of black wings again. "*You* got a man killed, you mean. It wasn't my bullet that sent the poor bastard to his grave, Preston."

Bradyn winced, trying to push the memory of the foolish, young cowboy out of his head. The kid had challenged him to a gunfight after Bodeen had planted an ace on Bradyn during a game of poker. Bradyn had tried to convince the kid that he hadn't taken the card. But the boy, who had been a little too drunk and much too eager to prove his prowess with a gun, had not backed down. When the kid had drawn his revolver, Bradyn had reacted out of pure instinct. The boy had died half-way in, half-way out of the saloon. His eyes had been wide with glassy, stricken panic and his legs splayed in an unattractive fashion as he'd drowned in his own blood. "The kid didn't leave me much choice, Bodeen," Bradyn said between clenched teeth. "If you hadn't put that ace on me in the first place, he would still be alive."

"I doubt it," Kyle replied. "That boy was too impulsive and reckless. If it hadn't been you, he would have picked a fight with some other gunslinger and still would have gotten his idiot head blown off. His kind lives to die for foolish reasons."

Furious, Bradyn fought hard to restrain himself from the stampede of profanity that charged to the tip of his tongue. "What the hell do you want, Bodeen?" he asked. His jaw made a loud snapping sound as he ground his teeth together.

"Tsk, tsk." With the cold, menacing smile still on his handsome face, Kyle chided him. "You will know your purpose soon enough." He folded his hands behind his back and winked at Bradyn. "I came to see you because I wanted to know if you were expecting any company tonight."

Confused, Bradyn shook his head. "What the hell are you talking about?"

"Excuse me, Bradyn. I forgot to offer you a drink. Give

the man some water, Tessa." Kyle instructed, ignoring his question for the moment. "Our guest here has a long night ahead of him. There's no use in facing your demons with a dry mouth, is there, Bradyn Preston?"

Tessa brought a canteen and pushed it against his lips. He drank several swallows hungrily. The water tasted strange. It had an oddly sweet flavor to it. He jerked his head away, refusing to drink more though he wanted to, and glared at Kyle. "Now why don't you tell me why you would think that I am expecting company," he asked. He ignored the cold smile that crept over Tessa's mouth as she replaced the lid on the canteen and went back to her place with the lantern at Kyle's back.

"There is a certain young woman in town asking for you." The red sparkle seeped back into Kyle's eyes just the slightest bit.

Rian! Bradyn fought with all his might to remain nonchalant. He thought he did a fair job of it, considering the circumstances. "Can't say as I am," he answered. "Did she tell you her name?"

Kyle's laugh was wickedly playful and he wagged an elusive finger at him. "You always were a sharp stick, Bradyn. Trying to see if I really know who she is, is that it? Well, you know exactly who I'm talking about, and if you care about her life, you'll listen to every word I say. In fact, you will *hang* on my every word like both your lives depends on it. Is that clear?"

Bradyn glared at him, fury suppressing his fear for the moment. *You'd better not even so much as breathe in Rian's direction. If you do, I will kill you, ya dirty son of a whore.*

As if reading his thoughts, Kyle leaned in very close and looked him directly in the eyes. "I asked you if I made myself clear." His whisper was a deep grumble akin to a wolf's snarl.

Bradyn saw the white of his teeth again. Long white fangs that were sharp and canine lined his mouth. Black, red-flecked eyes looked into his. They held the sinister promise of Death. He knew it was real, not a figment of his imagination, this time. Kyle's face was the most frightening thing he had ever seen, and if it hadn't been for the fact that just now he was scared for Rian's safety, Bradyn was certain he would have gone stark-raving mad right then and there. "I understand," he answered. His voice shook with rage as he fought like mad to hang on to his anger and not give way to the terror he felt beginning to ooze through him.

"Good." Kyle straightened himself and, in the lamp's light, his eyes were green once again and his teeth were no longer fangs. "I have a proposition for you, but first, I need to see to another matter. When I return, I'll want to know if you're willing to cooperate with me. A while longer in the darkness with your past should prove advantageous to us both."

Kyle turned to leave with Tessa following silently behind. Just before he shut the door, Kyle looked at him. "Remember, Preston. Her life hangs in the balance. If you want her to live, you'll do as I say."

Kyle's white-fanged smile and glittering red eyes were the last things Bradyn saw before he was plunged into darkness once again.

* * * *

"Where are we going?" Tessa asked when he had shut the door. Excitement for what lay ahead had brought the yellow glitter to her eyes. They shone brightly in the dimness of the livery tack room.

"I'm going back to the roof," Kyle answered. "I must watch for awhile longer before I go tend to Briggs."

"But what are you going to do with him?" she asked, nodding at the room in which Bradyn was chained.

"I am going to leave him with his thoughts," he replied as he slowly mounted the creaky stairs that led to the rooftop. "He must reflect upon his past."

"His past?"

"Yes." He paused and turned to look at Tessa. "His past is the key to his undoing. Bradyn Preston has led a very black life. Tonight he will remember every minute of it. Every drop of blood he has shed and every evil deed he has done. The opium, the darkness, and the ravens will do an excellent job in reminding him of it."

"So you put opium in the canteen..." she smiled and nodded. "Clever," she murmured. Then she frowned. "But, why the ravens?" she asked. Tessa cocked her head in an inquisitive fashion as the deep golden glimmer of her eyes grew even brighter. She climbed the stairs as she looked up at him with a curious expression.

"Ah yes, the ravens. With the fluttering of their wings the whispers of his past will come to him. The human conscience is a terrible thing," he mused. "It must be torture to have a soul that remembers every wicked thought and every vile sin." He turned and started up the stairs again.

Though his back was to her, Kyle could feel the evil smile of understanding that spread across her mouth as he pushed the hatch to the roof open and climbed out into the night. "His conscience is like a cloth woven of a single thread," he explained. "Pull that thread and all of it begins to unravel. Bradyn Preston will become the Shadow that is within him. He will not be able to resist its power."

As if in agreement with his words, the ravens on the rooftop took flight and began their horrible cawing. Kyle's smile widened. The flavor of victory hung in the dense, lifeless air around him.

* * * *

Plunged into fathomless darkness once again, Bradyn listened with tense alertness to the ceaseless flying of the ravens. He tried to close his mind against the hypnotic beating of wings, but when he did, he only saw the two blood-red eyes and vicious smile of Kyle's face. The breath in his body came in ever harsher gasps as he hung suspended in the dark. Terror worked its steely fingers into his heart, pushing his mind to the brink of insanity. Bradyn had always been afraid of black, enclosed places. The darkness twisted and grew into unrecognizable demonic shapes.

I feel queasy, he thought blandly. *I wonder what was in*

that water…it's making my head spin… He was repeatedly forced to swallow the bile that crept up his throat as he strained to see the ravens that now seemed to fill the entire barn. They kept flying closer and closer. More than once he felt the brush of feathers as their circular flight tightened around him.

Bradyn tried to recall Rian's face. He tried to search his memory and bring her image back to his mind's eye. But it was fruitless. Every time he would begin to envision her, every time he would almost have her face and her smile in his mental grasp, he would see the red, gleaming eyes and the horrid, lethal fangs. Rian's picture would turn into Kyle. And when it changed, Kyle would begin laughing at him, mocking him. *"Think about your past, Bradyn,"* he taunted. *"It will prove advantageous to us both if you remember how evil you are…"*

As the minutes wore on, Bradyn found himself slipping into the semi-conscious state between waking and sleeping. It was the place where genuine memories and horrible nightmares meet to form a tragically, twisted parade. He saw the first man he had ever killed go racing across the darkness in a haunting flash. Bradyn tried to call out after him.

It had not been an intentional thing, murdering that man. Back then, Bradyn had been only fifteen. He had been homeless, penniless, and living on the streets of New Orleans. And he had been so hungry…

The bustling noise of the French Quarter came to him as clear as if he were standing there that very moment. The hectic, hurried daytime crowds of wealthy businessmen, snobbish ladies, delivery boys, Negro slaves, housewives, and children were fading into the flamboyant, uproarious citizens that clamored for the nightlife of the city.

Bradyn had spent all day grifting passersby on the corner of Royal and Saint Peter's streets. His take for the day had been fair enough. More than plenty to buy a decent meal and a room to sleep in if he hadn't owed Rupert McAdams nearly fifty dollars in gambling debts. That night, Rupert had come to Bradyn's table, which sat just outside one of the

Quarter's fancy galleried buildings, and collected his cut. McAdams's "cut" had been the whole fifteen dollars Bradyn had managed to accumulate that day.

Tired, hungry, and with absolutely no where to go, Bradyn had wandered aimlessly down Bourbon Street. The taverns and saloons beckoned with their bright, cheery lights and boisterous patrons, but Bradyn steered clear of them. He had a large tab at most of them, and the ones where he didn't owe drinking money, he had over-extended himself with gambling debts.

The sharp ache of hunger drove him into a deserted alley where he dug through half a dozen rubbish piles, looking for something even remotely palatable enough to eat. He had found precious little.

He'd started out of the alley, the taste of stale, mold-infested bread clinging to his mouth, when he'd heard a familiar voice. Though the voice was inebriated and singing "Dixie," he had immediately recognized it.

Bradyn stopped and slipped to the shadows as Rupert McAdams stumbled by. Thinking he could easily knock the drunken man out and take back some of the money McAdams had taken from him earlier, Bradyn picked up a piece of wood and stole up behind the weaving, unsuspecting man. But then, unexpectedly, McAdams had turned. Shocked to see Bradyn, he had fumbled for his gun. Bradyn had only intended to knock him out, but McAdams reaction was unexpected and Bradyn had struck him with far too much force.

As he had pulled the heavy leather wallet from Rupert McAdams's expensive velvet coat, Bradyn felt sickened by the dead lifeless stare on his victim's face. Blood was pooling rapidly around his head and at any moment someone might have come by and seen him. Yet Bradyn sat helplessly staring down at the dead man, unable to look away. Then panic and reality had seized him. He, Bradyn Preston, had just committed murder. The revelation frightened him so badly that he had run away. Lunatic disbelief gave flight to his feet. Down the alley and into the night he had fled. But the memory of those sightless accusing eyes followed him long into the night and for many, many years after.

"I've murdered a man," he breathed into the blackness of the stable. His voice was crazed and high-pitched. He was no longer mindful of the chains that bound him, but of the terrible vileness of his past. He had killed many men in self-defense, but that night in New Orleans he had murdered a man in cold blood.

And there was a viscous irony. He hadn't even taken the man's wallet. "I dropped it when I ran away!" Bradyn screamed. His voice teetered on the brink of frantic laughter. "I dropped it when I ran away. Oh, God..." Bitter sorrow consumed him and he wept at his own words. Then, as if to spite him, the ravens began to caw maliciously as they swirled in maddening circle around him.

"You are Shadow...your heart is black, Bradyn Preston..." The words were a whisper. In the dark, Bradyn didn't know if they were spoken aloud or if he only heard them in his head, but it didn't really matter anymore. The words were true. He was a murderer, and if it meant saving Rian, if it meant saving himself, he knew he would murder again.

In that moment, with that single, dark admission, Bradyn felt the Shadow enter him. It was as if the blackness of his surroundings had been waiting for him to speak those very words so that it could flood his soul. The ravens cackling laughter echoed through the pitch-black as his soul fought against falling into utter darkness. But this time the darkness was not that of his prison. It was the complete blackness of his past that reached up from Hell itself to pull him down into lightless eternity.

Chapter Seventeen

Liam exited the Cattlemen's Hotel in a daze. He didn't even bother to look at the handful of his men who had disobeyed direct orders to go out and search the town for Kyle and Tessa. They stood in a small, confused group around the front desk in the lobby.

An agitated, spooked look passed between them when Liam walked right by. His eyes were sightless and glazed. Wes had already come and gone, taking the bulk of the hired guns with him as per Briggs's orders. He hadn't told the men what had happened upstairs either. But between the gunshot that they had heard earlier, and the blood-spatters on Briggs's shirt and pants, the men could pretty much guess what had gone down in the hotel room. The vacant, angered expression on Liam's face had told them the rest. None of them wanted to venture upstairs and see what was left of Cameron Briggs.

At first, Liam was so shocked by his brother's suicide he wandered, without aim, up the street. The picture of Cameron's face, blown in half, and the blood and brains splattered on the wall, curtains, and floor, consumed his mind. He nearly vomited again when he thought of the blood that had soaked Cameron's hair, a horrific blood-curdling contrast of crimson and white. Liam hit himself in the thigh repeatedly to dislodge the picture from his brain. But hitting himself only made his stomach reel and lurch. He coughed and gagged, trying to push the bitter bile back into his stomach.

Then, slowly, the reality of his brother's death began to sink in, like a covered wagon trapped in quicksand. Liam felt his nausea dissipate as his earlier fury returned. Kyle Bodeen was somehow responsible for this and he was going to pay for that too. Just like he would pay for Tessa.

His footsteps brought him to the swinging doors of the Silver Lady. Elijah Claymore was still standing behind the counter and the rest of the place was still empty. The unease that this had affected in Liam before was not present now. The fevered anger that burned in his gut was far too strong to give place to any nervousness. Pushing past the doors, which creaked in protest, Liam walked to the bar. "Where's Tessa?" he demanded of the bartender.

Elijah's back was to him. He just kept wiping tumblers. Each brush of the rag was slow and methodical.

Liam was taken aback for a moment. There was no reason Elijah should ignore him. He and the bartender had always gotten on fine. "Elijah?" he asked again, quieter this time. "Where is Tessa?"

Again, Elijah ignored him. Enraged, Liam reached across the counter to grab the man by the shoulder. But, when his hand touched the place the bartender's shoulder should have been, he only felt air. It was cold and damp.

"Elijah!" he yelled. "Turn around!"

The bartender turned then. His smile was empty and, as he looked right through Liam, the expression on his face sent ice to the center of Liam's soul.

"'Ello, Liam," Elijah nodded, his fingers still reverently wiping the whiskey tumbler in his hand. "Been wondering when you would wander in. He told me you would be along shortly."

Liam frantically tried to touch the man again and was met with the same result, cold, wet air. "What's wrong with you, Elijah? What's wrong with this town tonight?" his voice trembled.

"Can't be talkin' to thin air, Briggs," Elijah answered. "The men'll think I'm crazy if they see me talkin' to nobody. I'll get you a drink and we can go into the back room. We'll talk there."

"What the hell are you talking about?! There ain't a man in the..." Liam's voice trailed off as he caught sight of the reflection in the gaudy mirror behind the bar. He blinked, unable to believe what his eyes were telling him they saw. The saloon was full of cowboys. He turned and nearly stumbled in his haste. There were cowboys sitting at the tables, cowboys standing at the bar. They were hooting mutely as the chorus girls silently whirled on the stage. The pianist was hammering away on the ivory keys, notes without sound.

Liam reached out and tried to touch the cowboy standing next to him. As the cowboy turned his back and walked away, Liam pulled back his hand. The cowboy was constructed of nothing but moist air. Just like Elijah. "What the hell..." he muttered as he looked at his hand in shock. "What the hell is going on, Elijah?"

The bartender poured two fingers of bourbon into a crystal tumbler. "The storage room in back, Liam," he said. "The storage room is a safe place to talk."

Liam pulled the bourbon bottle from Elijah's hand. Both surprised and relieved that it was tangible, he put the bottle to his lips and guzzled a mouthful of the potent liquor. The bourbon sank into his tongue like ash and brimstone. It was hot and revolting. He coughed violently and spit it out. Confused and beginning to feel his terror return, Liam wiped the back of his hand over his lips and looked around the saloon again. The gaiety of laughter did not reach his ears. He watched as a man at the back table got up and stuffed a wad of cash into his pocket. The cowboy left the poker game with a round of back swatting and merry protest, soundlessly a winner.

Liam turned around. Elijah was gone. He saw the bartender's back as he made his way to the storage room. Liam followed.

"Elijah," he said once they were out of sight of the saloon. "You have to tell me what's going on in town tonight. Why can't I touch you?" When his voice quivered, it made the bartender smile.

"You ain't in Laramie anymore, Liam," he answered

cryptically.

Liam grunted like someone had just punched him in the gut. "Huh? What the hell are you saying? Am I…am I dead?" It seemed the only logical explanation. Why else would he be incapable of hearing or touching anyone back in the saloon.

Elijah shook his head. "No. No," he said. "You ain't dead, Liam. Not yet…you just aren't in Laramie anymore. They moved it…somehow. Can't remember how it got moved exactly. The whole thing is a little confusing to me. I just was told that I am a link or some such thing. He told me that I needed to talk to you. To help you remember. I'm his messenger, ya might say."

"What?! I don't follow you," Liam rasped. "If I ain't dead, but I ain't in Laramie…then where the hell am I?"

Elijah sighed. "I told ya. *They* moved it. He told me that it's all on account of what's gotta happen tonight."

Liam rubbed his temples. He felt like a two-year old who'd been set at a desk with slate and chalk and told to figure a difficult sum correctly on penalty of death. None of it made any sense. "Who is *he*, Elijah?" he asked with forced patience.

"Cameron saw him. Didn't he tell you about it?" Elijah replied.

"Cameron's dead," Liam answered.

"But you spoke to him before he shot himself," Elijah pressed. "What did he tell you, Liam?"

He stared at the bartender, his mouth agape. "Now how did you know that?" he asked. "How do you know that I spoke to my brother before he died?"

"Because, I saw you come into town earlier. You were about to come in the saloon when one of your men yelled out to you that Cameron was at the hotel and that you'd better come quick." Elijah paused. "And I heard the gunshot, Liam."

Liam narrowed his eyes. "Yeah, okay…but how did you know *Cameron* shot himself? That gunshot could have been fired by anybody."

"I know because *I* saw what Cameron saw. I watched

Cameron's hair turn white as snow when he ran up the street stark-raving nuts…that's how I know. I know who is in this town tonight. And I know why he's here. Came right into the saloon and told me himself." The bartender's eyes bored into Liam's like two shiny coals. "You're the only one who hasn't figured it out yet. But, you will. Mark my words, you will. He'll be comin' for ya directly."

"I have heard 'he' all night!" Liam shouted. "Who the hell is *he*?" Fear yanked the breath from him, though he would be damned if he showed it. "Cameron said it's the Devil. Is that who *he* is? Are ya gonna sit here and tell me that the Devil, himself, showed up in Laramie tonight, Elijah? Are ya?!"

"Liam," the bartender said. "There is no one as blind as the man who just won't see."

"What?!" Liam screamed this time. "That didn't make a whore's decency worth of sense! You want to know what I think? I think everyone in this piss-sad excuse for a town has lost their shit-for-brains! I think that you're all stump-drunk nuts…That's what I think!"

"Well now, that could very well be," Elijah nodded slowly. "But then you got a little problem with your theory, Liam. If I'm the one who's crazy, then tell me, why can't you reach out and grab a hold of me?"

Liam paused. The fury in his gut stalled for a moment. Elijah had him there. *Why* can't *I touch him?* It was a fearsome puzzle. Liam blew out a loud breath and conceded; "Okay, Elijah. You win. So all of this is real…all of this is happening. Fine." He waved a hand of defeat. "Why don't you explain it to me? Why don't you just tell me in as few words as possible what the *hell* is going on?"

The bartender nodded. "He told me all about you, Liam."

Liam rolled his eyes and was about to interrupt Elijah and tell him, for the last time, to spit it out and tell him who this "he" was. But the bartender's next words chilled him to the bone and paralyzed him with fear.

"He told me to ask you about Andersonville. He wanted me to ask you if you remember the night a certain man came to the prison." The bartender's eyes gleamed ebony and a hint of mirth reflected from their black depths. "You were a Union soldier, weren't ya? William Beckford Briggs. Enrolled in the 21st Illinois Infantry. Which battle was it that you were captured in, Liam?"

Liam shut his eyes and did not answer. If Elijah knew this much about him, then the bastard already knew that Liam hadn't been captured in any battle. It had happened in December, the year of 1862. Liam couldn't remember the exact day, but he remembered he'd been barely nineteen years old at the Battle of Stone River. That skirmish had been the very first actual engagement that Liam was involved in. He'd turned out to be a spineless, yellow-gut deserter and he ran. Confederate soldiers had found him a few days later. They'd drug him to living Hell on earth. Andersonville Prison.

Liam remembered all too well the horror that he'd lived within those sixteen-foot stockade walls. *Lived,* he thought bitterly, *now* there's *something to call it.* The soldiers that were held in that wasteland of rotting flesh and human misery were little more than walking corpses. Skeletons that were left to bake beneath a relentless sun. Disease and famine, heat and vermin, those had been Death's hungry hounds. They'd feasted lavishly on the shells of men who had once been strapping, robust soldiers.

The prisoners were fed next to nothing and forced to drink from a swamp that was laced with the odor of human excrement and tainted by the foul decomposition of the dead bodies that littered the ground around it. The stench of the place still permeated his nose whenever he thought about it long enough, like now for instance. But the screaming…the screaming in that place had been far worse than the odor.

You can get used to stench, but the screams of human suffering live on long after the smell of death has gone away, Liam thought morosely. The howls of pain and misery, the agony of soldiers who'd long since died, echoed back from a part of his life that had been black and timeless.

"Liam?" the bartender broke in on his thoughts. "Tell me about him," he coaxed. "Tell me about the man that came to Andersonville that night."

Liam put a hand against the wall to brace himself and lowered his head. He closed his eyes again and thought back to that dark night so far in his past it was a dream. Or, more correctly, a nightmare.

The inky black sky that hung over Andersonville Prison that night, dotted by the distant cold glitter of stars, would have been peaceful and serene had it not been for the constant sights, odors, and sounds of Death around him. The stark white stockade walls glared down at the prisoners in the moonlight. Inside the stockade's ominous blank stare was "The Dead Line" -- a weak run of fence that couldn't have held a herd of cows. But men are easier to trap than cows. All that the prisoners needed to know was one simple rule; if you crossed the Dead Line, you either got shot, or hunted down by the plantation hounds. The dogs were trained to track and tear a runaway human to shreds. In the full six months that Liam was imprisoned in that living Hell, he'd only witnessed one prisoner try to escape. The half-crazed, skeleton of a man had made it over the Dead Line and kept running, even after a sentry had shot him five times. His gaunt frame had hit the stockade wall with a sickening smack. Liam had watched him fall to the ground and convulse like a fish pulled from a river as the life ran out of him in a syrupy, crimson stream.

"Liam?" Elijah's voice interrupted his recollections once again. "Are ya gonna tell me about him? Time's runnin' out, ya know. I gotta cross over with the rest of 'em." The bartender scrutinized Liam for a moment. "You *do* remember him, don't ya?"

Liam lifted his head and glared at the bartender. "For shit's sake, Elijah. Course I remember," he spat. I've just spent a whole lot a time trying to forget, he thought wearily.

His mind wandered over that night. The memory of it was vividly clear, even though he'd not allowed himself to dwell on it much in the past sixteen years. After the Union soldier had been shot and his lifeless, sorry excuse for a corpse had been dragged away, Liam had sat in terrified silence for hours. He had listened with sickening dread to the moans and crying around him. The Lord knew he had never heard so many men plead for deliverance in his life…

"God save us!" The words echoed through the camp in a manic disjointed chorus of screams, groans, and whispers. The prisoners' tormented cries to the heavens had given words to the desperate fear in Liam's heart. *It's hopeless. I'm never gonna get out of here alive,* he'd thought over and over again that night.

"You know it's all a lie, don't you?" Liam still remembered how the voice at his side had startled his starved and petrified mind. *"God isn't listening tonight. He isn't going to save these poor pitiful bastards. Their prayers are all in vain."*

Liam had expected to find another prisoner setting at his elbow. He had been startled by the man's sudden appearance, but the way the man looked had frightened the holy hell out of him. He was all dressed up like some damn city dandy. And he didn't look like he'd been without a square meal a day in his life. *"How the hell did you get in here?"* Liam had hissed at him. *"You ain't no soldier, Mister."*

The man had laughed then. It was a quiet, threatening type of laughter. *"Well, if you want to put a fine point on it, neither are you, William Briggs. I may be wrong, but I think being a deserter disqualifies you as a soldier. Tell me, how're they taking care of you in here? Are you getting enough to eat?"* The man had convulsed with more sick, twisted laughter.

"Are you in my head?" Liam had asked in child-like tone of fear. *"You can't be real…"*

"Of course I'm real." The man grinned. *"Have a little faith, Liam."*

Liam had gone wide-eyed and stared at him. His barely lucid mind had been perplexed that this man should know his name. *"What're you doing here?"* he asked in a quivering voice.

"I'm going to take you away from this place, Liam," had been the man's unequivocal answer.

Liam had laughed himself then, a hysterical gag that rattled in the back of his dry throat. *"Are you in your right mind? Did you see what just happened to the last guy who tried to escape?! He's dead! They shot him."*

"And he made a fine attempt at getting out, didn't he? I liked

his pluck. You can't fault a man for trying, now can you?" The man reached inside his fancy black dress coat then, and pulled out a bottle of bourbon. *"How about a drink, Liam?"* he'd asked as he poured a shot into a crystal glass that materialized out of nowhere.

"Sure," Liam answered, licking his dry, cracked lips and staring at the alcohol greedily. *"I could sure use a drink right now, Mister."*

"I bet you could," the man answered and handed the glass to Liam. But, as he reached for the drink, the man pulled it back and smiled. His eyes were cold and lifeless. *"Now wait just a minute, Liam. Before you can have a drink, I have a proposition for you. I want you to hear me out. Sound fair?"*

"Sure. Whatever you say, Mister. Just let me have a damn drink."

The man had watched him with dark, hungry humor as he gave the drink to Liam, who had drained the crystal glass in a single swallow. The bourbon had been better than any he had ever tasted before.

"I bet you miss your mamma, don't you? And that pretty little thing with the curly golden hair. What's her name? Elizabeth? I bet you miss her too, don't you, Liam?"

Liam had blinked. *"How do you know about her?"* His squeal came out an airless rasp.

*"I make it my business to know, Liam. I know everything about you. You are…*special *to me."*

"Me? Why? What's so damn special about me?"

*"Let's just say that I have had my eye on you for awhile now, boy. You have a particular…oh, what shall I call it…*spirit *about you. You're a black one, Liam, and I like that. In fact, I like it so much I'm going to get you out of this filthy pit. All you have to do is make me one simple little promise."*

"What promise?" Liam had been suspicious, and full of disbelief. It had sounded much too good to be true.

"There's a matter I'm going to need your help with someday, Liam. Don't worry," he'd added hastily, setting Liam at minimal ease, *"it won't be right away. I want you to go see your mamma and that pretty little Elizabeth first. You'll have some time to go out and live your life. Free as you please. If you make me this*

promise tonight, Liam, I will reward you well. I'll give you everything you want. You'll have money and power and all that goes with it. But, when the time comes, I want you to give me your word that you'll be ready to do what I ask of you. I want you to give me your word that I can count on you, Liam. Will you do that for me?"

"What is it you're gonna need me to do?"

"You'll be told when the time comes, Liam."

"When will that be?"

The dark man's expression darkened, as if Liam's questions were beginning to irritate him, but a twinkle touched his eyes when he answered; *"It may be in a few years, it may be in twenty years. I don't know the exact time and place, but I need your word. You need to promise me that as long as there is breath in your body, you will be waiting to serve me the moment I call you. You are mine, from now on…is that clear? I won't take you out of this hell hole until I have your word."*

Liam had looked around the wasteland of scattered, make-shift tents. He had listened to the sounds of Death as he walked through the prison collecting the souls of dying men. He had made up his mind quickly. *"Yeah. You have my word. Whatever you say, Mister. Just get me outta here before I die with the rest of them."*

When the man heard Liam's promise his eyes began to glow red. His teeth glittered pure white evil as he smiled at Liam triumphantly. *"Then it's settled. I help you now. You help me later. Close your eyes, Liam."* His order was a victorious snarl. *"This may hurt a little…"*

Liam didn't *see* so much as *feel* the blinding red pain as the breath was torn form his lungs. It felt as if his heart was pulled up through his throat and out of his mouth. He knew he'd started screaming as the agony of hellfire ran the entire length of his body. Then everything went cold and Liam had imagined that it was Death, come to pay him a visit. Heavy, wet, bitter, cold Death. The man hadn't come to set him free, he'd come to kill him!

"You're mine…" his voice had echoed through the spiraling blackness as Liam lost all consciousness. *"For all eternity…You are mine, William Briggs."*

When he came to, Liam had been lying on the dusty road in front of his own house. Unsure if he had awakened from a nightmare or in a dream, he'd run to the front door and pounded with all his might. He had been certain that he would wake up back in that putrid Hell on earth before he got to see his mother or Elizabeth.

Remembering, Liam felt dark memories carve a burning hole in his useless heart. He'd never seen his mother again. He made it just in time for the funeral. She'd died of consumption three days before Liam returned home. As for the pretty, golden-curled Elizabeth, well as Fate would have it, the baker's son had come calling one hot summer day and she'd been more than happy to court him. Elizabeth had been a happy little house wife for nearly a month when Liam came back from that hell.

"Liam!" Elijah was standing next to him, shaking his shoulder roughly. "Liam! Wake up, boy. This ain't time for daydreams. You still haven't told me what I want to hear. Tell me about your promise."

Liam shook his head. "I wasn't in my right head. Starved and practically dying the way I was…I'd have sold my soul to the Devil for a piece of bread. It was a vain promise. Men make vain promises to get themselves outta dying all the time. The good Lord must have a list a hundred miles long of all the men who've told Him they'd change their lives if He would just get them out of a tight spot."

"That's a funny way of putting it, Liam. But, you didn't make no *vain promise*, as you call it, to God. You made your deal with the Devil, and he ain't reasonable when it comes to the promises you make him." Elijah smiled and Liam was struck by harsh reality. "Your debt has come due, son. You're gonna pay it back whether you want to or not. He didn't give you your freedom based on any vain promise, of that one thing I can assure you."

"I didn't mean a word of it!" Liam said. His voice sounded like a pitiful, childish whine. "It was a desperate vow. I was about to *die* in that place! He didn't give me a damn thing he said he would. I didn't even get to see my mother again. All that talk of rewards was a lie. A God damned lie!"

Elijah's laughter went through Liam like a blade of steel. "And just tell me something, Liam. Where *did* you get everything you have? There's not a cent you've come by honestly. You've spent your whole life murdering, stealing, and lying to get what you want. You've been making good on his promise for nearly twenty years. Now he wants to collect what you owe him."

Liam felt ill. His head began throbbing and his stomach felt like it had been twisted in knots around a hot branding iron. He couldn't stop the trembling that started in his hands. "I'll make good on my promise, but I want to make another bargain with him. If I keep my word and help him with whatever it is he needs help with, he has to give me Kyle and Tessa. That's my offer."

Elijah just started laughing again. "Well, why don't you see if you can't make that bargain with him?"

As if in answer to the bartender's words, Liam heard the creaking of the saloon doors. Hollow footsteps fell in slow, clanging echo as someone entered the Silver Lady. Liam felt panicked claustrophobia take him when he realized he was trapped.

"Go on," Elijah instructed. He began to flicker and fade from Liam's sight. "Get it over with. He's waiting for you. I think I'm gonna start crossin' over."

Liam watched as Elijah disappeared from view with a sick pit in his gut. He felt stuck to the floor for a moment. Then suddenly, as if they had a mind of their own, his feet moved out of the storage room and into the hallway that lead to the saloon. He tried to turn back, but it was no use. A power greater than his own will propelled him forward. Once he was in the saloon, he came to a dead halt and stared in stunned silence at the Devil's man.

Kyle Bodeen stood in the middle of the saloon. "Good evening, Liam," he said as he placed an unlit cigar between his lips. Liam watched in horror as the cigar flamed to life of its own accord. Kyle's eyes glittered emerald as a chilling smile spread over his face. He exhaled a plume of swirling greenish-black smoke and winked at Liam. "I've come to collect that promise, old friend. You're going to help me kill Bradyn Preston."

Chapter Eighteen

"What?!" Liam roared. "There is no way in hell that I'm gonna help you, Bodeen. I hate you more than I hate Bradyn Preston. I'd sooner go to Hell than help you do *anything*!"

Kyle's laughter filled the saloon. "Do you really think you have a choice? You don't even own your soul, Liam Briggs. You're gonna do what I say, when I say it. And there will be no argument on the matter."

"And what are you gonna do to me if I don't?" Liam challenged. His fear was a distant memory for the time being.

"You will. You don't have any choice. You are a pathetic coward, Liam. You always have been." Kyle laughed again. "Do you know how you can tell a coward, Liam? A coward is the one who will give away his soul for eternal servitude just to drag out his sorry life a few years longer. That's how you can tell a coward, Liam."

Kyle's laughter mocked him. Enraged, Liam charged at him, his fists ready to strike.

The smile remained on Kyle's lips, but a deadly fury caused his eyes to burn red. He lifted his hand and an arch of green electricity exploded out of his palm. Liam was stopped dead in his tracks and jerked from the floor in blinding agony. His arms and legs convulsed with the electric shock. Every inch of his body writhed and twisted as Kyle spun his hand and jerked it upward. Liam thought that the meat was being peeled from his bones. A scream, high-pitched and inhuman, pierced his ears. Then Liam realized that *he* was the one screaming.

His eyes went wide with terror as he watched the curtains and walls of the saloon erupt in emerald flame. Kyle rolled his free hand into a tight fist and brought it up to his waist. A loud rumbling filled the room as a jagged crack began to split the floor. Liam screamed again as he saw the cliffs of red and orange brimstone that burned in the growing chasm. Black smoke hissed as it was belched up from the bottomless pit.

"No! Wait!" Liam screamed. "I'll do anything you say, Bodeen. Just don't put me down there! Please!"

Kyle pulled back his hand and the chasm closed. The emerald flames flickered out and Liam thudded to the floor with a moan. "You see?" Kyle smiled. "A coward. But well played, Liam."

The wind knocked from his lungs, he lay there in dazed confusion for awhile, trying to collect his thoughts. Then Kyle's face appeared over him. "Who are you?" Liam whispered.

"You've had people trying to tell you who I am all night, Liam. It might have been in your better interest to listen to them." Kyle smiled coldly. Liam shuddered at the long, sharp fangs in his mouth as he put his cigar between his lips. "You could've spared yourself that unpleasantness a minute ago," he said.

"You—you ain't the Devil," Liam stuttered. "You can't be. I've seen him before."

"Nope," Kyle's evil smile spread around his cigar. "But I do his work. You can just think of me as 'the Boss's son' if that'll make it easier for you to follow orders. Now get up off the floor," he ordered. "We got a long night ahead of us."

Liam stood and brushed himself off with shaking hands. His body felt numb. There was a sharp throbbing in his head. His mind was a jumble of ten-penny nails. "What is it that you want me to do?" he asked.

"I'll let you know when the time comes. For now, go get your men and meet me in front of the livery. And, Liam," Kyle added with another dead and vile grin, "don't even think about crossing me, or going to Hell will be the least of your worries."

* * * *

Together they stood, hovering near the precipice of rimrock, watching the blackness as it grew ever thicker over Laramie. Rian didn't know how long they'd been there. It could have been minutes, it could have been hours. Time had ceased to exist inside the circle of brilliant light. She had seen the auras of green and red meet with Bradyn's soul light. She had watched in horror as his cobalt aura had sent deep blue sparks of agony into the dark mists around him.

"How long must I wait?' she'd pleaded. "He's in pain. They are hurting him. Please let me go to him now."

"The time is drawing near, Moriana. You must be patient," was the angel's answer. "The Destroyer will bring forth his soldiers. The stage for battle must still be set. It would prove dangerous for you if you were to go before the appointed time. The Destroyer must believe all is in his favor, or else he will murder Bradyn."

"Why are they gathering here? Why Laramie, of all the places on earth?" she asked.

"They gather here, because the Destroyer is drawn to you, Moriana. Though he cannot yet see your aura, he has been lead here by the Shadow within him. His need to destroy you is so strong he can do nothing but submit to it. He has been searching for you for years, and now that the appointed time has come, he will find you at last."

His words made her stomach lurch. Trying to gain a hold over the fear and doubt that sought to take her from the sphere of light, Rian watched the auras move in the blackness below. Until now, she hadn't really thought about whom the other aura belonged to, or which was which. She had merely known that they meant Bradyn harm and she had been afraid for his safety. Now that the thought occurred to her, she asked, "I see the two lights with Bradyn. One is red and the other is green. Who are they?"

"The aura of crimson that you see is the Destroyer's chosen bride. Her spirit is as old as Time itself. It is the spirit of the Temptress, Lillith. She was marked in a young girl many years ago. So it has always happened since the Destroyer came to existence. Now she has been brought forth to fulfill her purpose. Through her, the Destroyer has the power to control the minds of men. She gives him strength and will fight at his side. Like the woman, the Destroyer's body was marked out as a child. His light is the green. It is the color of his birth flames."

Rian studied the auras for a moment with puzzled fascination. "So the Destroyer is human? After all your talk of demons, I thought he must be some loathsome beast."

"He is in his human form, for now. But rest assured, Moriana, he is a foul and terrifying abomination in his demon state. One look at him will drive a mere mortal man to insanity." The angel pointed to the left of the glowing red and emerald auras. "Do you see that dim light just there?"

At first, she could not see what he was pointing at. Then, as she squinted and put the rolling fog into perspective, she saw a faint grayish-yellow aura. "Yes," she answered. "I see it. What does it mean?"

"It is the light of one who has looked upon the Beast in his true form. The grey around his aura signifies that the man is dying. He was trapped in the city when it crossed over. Now he will die alone."

The angel's explanation drew her attention to a sudden detail that had escaped her until now. "Where are all the others?' she asked.

"The others?" the angel replied.

"The other people," she said. "I can see only Bradyn, and now these other three, but I know that there must be hundreds of other people in town tonight. Why can't I see their auras?"

"There are no mortals there tonight," he said. "The city of Laramie, as you see it now, is not the city of Laramie at all."

When Rian gave him a confused look, he explained. "The human race is much too fragile, too content with the comings and goings of their mundane lives, to witness what must take place tonight. I told you earlier that this war, though fought for over six hundred years, is largely unseen by the vast majority of humanity. Even though it is for their future and safety you fight, they will not be able to see it. For their protection, Laramie has been moved onto another plain, into another dimension of Time and Space. The auras you see in the city now, and the auras that you will soon see, are only those of them who are called to this battle."

Rian cast her gaze over the plain below her and then back to the faint blue of Bradyn's soul. "You still have not told me how I must defeat this Evil, my lord. You have not told me how I can save Bradyn…or the human race."

"It is not for that purpose that I've come to you tonight, Moriana. The path to victory, the steps you must take to win this fight are written on your soul and no one can tell them to you. They will only be revealed as you go to meet the Destroyer and face him in battle."

Gunshots echoed faintly in the night and she strained to see what was happening in the darkness below. Then she saw the parade of twisted orange auras as they came into town at last. When she saw noted they numbered over twenty strong, she shuddered and looked at the angel. "Are they the soldiers?" she asked. "The ones he has been waiting for?"

The angel nodded. "They are his pawns just as the woman he has called to be his bride. The Destroyer believes that power lies in numbers and strength in the might of men. He gathers them to fight, thinking that the side of Light is weak with only two souls to rise up against him. He believes he can turn Bradyn as well, certain that you will be unable to stand against him alone."

Rian turned to Aurelia. The spirit watched the movements in the city with a granite expression. "He calls them every time," Aurelia said. "He used them to kill my family. To kill the man I loved. The Destroyer's men are ruthless. They are black souls destined for Hell's eternal torment. They fight well for they have nothing to lose. Those demons will prove difficult for you to stop, if you do not first defeat the Destroyer."

Rian repressed another shiver as she watched the men moving in the blackness. "Their auras are such a horrible color. Why do they twist and weave together like that? It makes it hard to tell one from the other."

"They are as one," the angel explained. "The evil that controls them runs in a single thread through every man. For years they have lived to serve only evil. They have gained their livelihood from the death and suffering of the innocent. At this moment, they are oblivious to the nature of their calling tonight, but soon they will learn it. Their leader must be broken and bent to the Destroyer's will. It will not be hard. He is a man that values his own well-being above all else. The Destroyer will have little trouble convincing him to join with him."

Aurelia's sigh caused Rian to look at her again. The woman did not speak as she watched the orange auras. She saw her expression of sadness and knew that Aurelia must be remembering that night so many years before.

Rian turned and watched as the auras moved through the town and then came to a stop. There was a splitting of color as a few of them appeared to move off in one direction, while the rest remained in one spot. "What are they doing?" she asked as she watched one of the auras move quickly away from the larger group.

"They are searching for a man. The aura of yellow that you see is their leader's younger brother. He has blindly followed his older brother since he was young. His spirit is too weak for the Shadow to use him, so now his life is forfeit because of his weakness. His end will come swiftly."

The angel's words were proven true not many minutes later. Rian saw the sickly yellow aura starburst into a red and amber prism before flashing out of existence.

"It is done," the angel said. "Now the Destroyer will collect the soul that is due him. The leader of those men will know his purpose."

The orange auras began to scatter, though a ribbon of light connected them as they moved through the blackness.

"There are so many of them," Rian whispered as fear forged doubt in her heart. "I am afraid."

The angel took her hand. "It has been said of old: 'You will fear neither the Terror of the night, nor the Pestilence that stalks the darkness.'"

Rian trembled. She remembered the words from the long-forgotten days of her youth. Her mother had read them to her often.

"Put on the full armor of God, so that you can take your stand against the Devil. For your struggle is not against flesh and blood, but against the powers of this dark world and against the principalities of Evil. Put on this armor so that when the day of Evil comes, you may be able to stand your ground, and after you have done everything, to stand."

Rian felt a tremor rise within her when he had finished speaking. A powerful churning excitement riveted her heart. The time was drawing near.

Aurelia touched Rian's shoulder. "The night I was called and sent forth to be the Avenger, a terrible fear was in my heart also, Moriana. When I saw the path of death and destruction the Destroyer had left, when I saw the ones I loved who had been so brutally murdered, I was paralyzed with terror. But courage was given to me. A promise was sealed upon my soul. The words of the ancient covenant are yours tonight, dear Moriana.

"For, lo, Foul Darkness fills the Land,
And terror seeks to take thee,
Fear not the Devil's brutal hand,
His power will not break thee.

"Arise; take up the sword of Truth,
Do not give place to fright.
For long and hard the Battle is
That beckons you this night.

"The Destroyer celebrates already,
Assured that victory is in sight,
But all shall be just as it should
When comes the morning Light."

Tears stung Rian's eyes as a valiance she had never thought possible filled every fiber of her being. Aurelia's words made the dagger on her thigh blaze hot. The sudden sizzling heat made her yelp in startled pain. Then the blade went cool again. She looked down and saw that a purple-white light shone through the leather cloth of her riding skirt.

The angel's eyes turned a piercing blue. Rian felt the electric current that ran from them as he looked at the purple glow radiating from her thigh.

"I see that you have the dagger," he said.

"Yes." Her voice was a mere whisper. "What does it mean? Why is it shining like that?"

"Take it out," he ordered. "Hold it in your hand!"

His voice vibrated like waves crashing upon a rocky beach. The blue of his eyes shot out dazzling sparks of electric flame. Rian's eyes went wide with fear. *Have I done something wrong?* She wondered numbly.

Sensing her doubt, he said, "Do not be afraid, Moriana. It is Providence you have the dagger. By it the Avenger will be brought forth from you. Now take it out and hold it in your hand."

With shaking hands, she fumbled to lift her skirt. The blade was blinding as she pulled its silver hilt from the sheath around her thigh. A furious red mark shone against the golden skin of her leg where the dagger had been resting. "Here. Here it is," she said in a quivering voice as she held it out to the angel. "What shall I do with it?"

"Hold it up!" the angel shouted as the distant roaring of thunder broke the silence of the valley. "Hold it up and let its light shine bright. The side of Light has its Champion! Show him that you are here!"

Slowly, Rian lifted the dagger overhead. The rocks of the cliff began to rumble and quake. Boulders broke loose and rolled down the face of the precipice like lumbering giants that had been awoken from centuries of sleep.

"Hold it up! Higher!" the angel's voice tore the air. The sound of wind and water rushed across the plain. "Let the Demon see the Light of his destruction! Let him see it and fear!"

Rian closed her eyes and lifted the dagger higher.

Anticipation and awe sent violent tingles coursing down her body in electric waves. In that instant, a bolt of light exploded from the dagger in an upward spiraling vortex. White fire licked the air around them and sent an expanding orb of light outward in all directions, encompassing the three of them at its center. Fingers of purple lightning erupted from the flame. She cried out as she saw Aurelia disappear into the crackling amethyst fury. "Wait!" she screamed. "You can't go!" Her voice was drowned out by the quaking of the earth and the angel's echoing voice.

"Therefore rejoice you Heavens, and all who dwell in them, because the Devil has gone down to Earth! He is filled with fury for he knows that his time is short!"

Then, as suddenly as it had appeared, the light was gone. It was pulled into the dagger and she saw Aurelia no more. The angel's voice was quieted and the darkness of night wrapped its blanket around them once again. Even the space of whiteness was gone. Rian felt a deep sadness when she knew that Aurelia had left them. A tear slipped down her cheek.

"Do not cry, Moriana. She has not left you, for her spirit is *in* you." The angel looked at her with a reassuring smile. "She will go forward with you to face the Destroyer. Her power is bound to the dagger. Once her spirit has taken you, as long as you hold the dagger in your hand, you will be protected from the Beast. Do not let it go, for the moment you do, you will become weak to the Destroyer and the strength of the dagger will begin to fade. He fears the dagger. It is the only weapon that can strike his heart and bring an end to his power."

"He knows that I am here now, doesn't he?" she asked. "He knows that I am coming." The knowledge did not inspire fear. Instead, her whole body vibrated with intense excitement. Immeasurable courage flooded her.

"Yes. He has seen your soul light now and he will be waiting for you. The fire of Hell and all its fury will be at his command. He will surely do his worst, but you must stand against him, Moriana, and with the strength of Light, you will." He touched her arm and the kindness in his eyes swept her face. "Remember your love for Bradyn. Only you can save him…but first you must see the path clearly. When you have come to understand the memories of your past, the path you must take will unfold before you. You will know the choice you must make."

Rian nodded silently. The dagger gleamed in her hand. She held it up before her face. "Is it time?" She knew his answer before he spoke.

"It is time. Take only the dagger with you. Go into the city and find Bradyn. You will have to fight the Shadow for him. It is already working its blackness in his heart. But, you are the one he loves. He will fight to defend you, though he may not recognize your face. You must be the one who saves him.

"Be careful, things may not be as they appear. The Enemy can bend images and reality to his will. If you succeed in bringing Bradyn back, the Destroyer will be very angry. I have told you already that he is a fearsome beast. His only desire is to have your blood."

The angel's countenance dimmed. "He will be difficult to kill. You must strike his heart in order to triumph. When you see it coming, when you see what you must do, remember these words: 'As water reflects the face, so the man's heart reflects the man.' You will be given understanding when it is time.

"Remember, Moriana," the angel warned, "one of you might perish so the Light will triumph…But this, too, is as it should be. Light finds strength in death, but Shadow can only triumph if it has life on which to feed.

He lifted her face to look at him as his image began to dim. "Hear my words, my dear Moriana. When the darkness becomes so heavy that you cannot see the light of your own soul and you think that battle has been lost, take courage and lift your eyes to the heavens. Do not fear the Shadow, or he who walks in it, for the Light in you is greater than his darkness." The angel grew transparent and a fading halo of light illuminated him. "Go now," he ordered, "Go now and take your stand."

Rian felt the dagger burn to life again. The heat of it did not scorch her hand…but it filled her with beautiful agony. As its light spiraled up her arms and wrapped around her body, she closed her eyes and breathed in the strength of it. The purple shape of a woman rose in the darkness before her. The spirit of the Avenger. There was a soft rush of air as the spirit entered her. When Rian opened her eyes, she and the Avenger were one.

In an instant, she was no longer standing beside the cliffs, but shooting across the sky in a purple arch of light. The blackened plain flew by beneath her as she was hurled toward the city. Then, like a star falling from Heaven, she descended into the darkness waiting below.

Chapter Nineteen

"Bradyn?"

The whisper of his name jerked him from his half-conscious state. Had he imagined it? He winced at the knotting cramp that pinched his neck. His head was resting at an odd angle back against the rough beam to which he was bound. Slowly, he raised it. "Rian?" he whispered. He struggled to open his eyes. They felt sewn shut and weighted with sand.

Green light greeted him as he managed to lift a drowsy eyelid. He blinked and tried to focus his vision which was grainy and doubled. "Rian?" he mumbled again through thick, rubbery lips.

A soft chuckle met his ears. "You love her don't you, Bradyn?"

Two black shadows blended into one as he squinted to see who was speaking to him. "Who're you?" he asked of the shape holding a sphere of glowing green flame in its hand. Two red eyes glittered behind the flame as spiraling smoke gave way to the form of a man. "Kyle," he murmured. "What are you, ya son of a bitch? What do you want with me?"

"I want you to be happy, Bradyn." His voice was steeped with mocking concern.

Bradyn's chuckle was a grunt. "Hmmph. Sure you do." The light hurt his eyes. He closed them and swallowed the hot acid vomit that burned at the back of his throat. His head was spinning and throbbing at the same time. "You must think I'm one stupid bastard, Bodeen."

"Do you love her, Bradyn?" Kyle did not speak the words when he asked, but Bradyn heard them just the same.

"Where is she?" he demanded. "Tell me where she is."

"She is safe, for now," Kyle replied. "You haven't answered my question. Do you love her, Bradyn?"

"I love her," he answered. There was no use denying it. He loved Rian more than he loved his own life.

"Would you kill for her?" Kyle's question was a thick sneer. Bradyn opened his eyes and saw the cruel, challenging smile on his face. "Would you kill to save her life?"

"You know I would," he replied. "That's why you've got me here. You want me to kill someone for you and you're going to make me do it by dangling Rian's life in front of my nose." He paused when Kyle's face changed to something of a scrutinizing expression. "That's it, isn't it?" he asked, doubt tugging his mind.

Red sparks flickered in Kyle's eyes. "Love is sacrifice, Bradyn. What are you willing to sacrifice to make certain that she lives? Would you trade your life for hers? Would you trade…your soul?" Emerald fire leapt upward from his palm. It trickled to the floor in liquid flame and circled Kyle's feet as he studied Bradyn's face.

Bradyn watched the fire grow higher as it spread and crackled upward. He could feel no heat in it. Frigid light emanated from the lapping green flames. He shook violently and tried to wriggle his wrists free from his shackles. His mind felt cloaked by a fuzzy curtain. What was Kyle angling at? There was a piece of the puzzle missing, but what was it? "Just tell me why I'm here, Bodeen. Quit trying to confuse me with all your fancy talk. What, exactly, do you want?"

"Rian," he answered. "I want you to speak to her on my behalf."

Bradyn squinted and inwardly lamented the dizziness that whirred through his head. His throat felt like parched, cracked earth as he coughed to clear it. "What do you want me to talk to her about?" he asked.

"She has two things that I want. I need you to convince

her to give them to me. If you do that, she will live. And so will you. If you can't persuade her to give me what I want, then both of you will die." Kyle's smile hadn't left his face. He pulled back his lips and Bradyn saw the fangs that lined his mouth. The grin was full of sharp, painful promises. To cross his demonic will would be certain death, the wicked smile assured.

"What could she possibly have that you would want?" Bradyn asked. He felt as if his spirit was floating above his body. Everything was numb and disconnected. The air burned his lungs as he took a deep breath and stared at Kyle with disgust.

"She has two things that belong to me. A dagger and a small boy. She stole them from me some years ago and I want them back." For the first time, the smile faded from Kyle's eyes. In its place came suppressed, yet glittering fury. "I want them back tonight," he added.

Bradyn had no idea what Kyle was talking about when it came to the dagger, but he knew exactly who the small boy was. *Kendall!* Instant realization and anger rattled him. "What do you want with the kid?" he asked aloud. The foggy drowsiness that had been clouding his mind began to clear as fear and anger began to trickle into his gut.

"That is none of your concern, Bradyn. You just get him for me." His words were a threatening growl. The black Shadow that shrouded him grew thicker and the green flames climbed higher around him. His voice softened. "I mean the boy no harm. He will be safe, I assure you."

"Don't listen to him, Bradyn. He's lying to you!" Rian's voice echoed through his mind. *"He wants to hurt Kendall. Please don't do as he asks!"* Her voice was so real. It was almost as if she were standing right there beside him.

Bradyn shook his head. "I won't do it," he said. "You can kill me if ya want, but I won't help you get that kid. Now I want to see her. Bring Rian to me!"

At his refusal, the entire room burst into emerald flame. "What?!" Kyle roared as he writhed and spat with wrath. "You can't deny me what I want! I own you. You are evil, Bradyn Preston. You will bend to my will! You will serve me!" He reached out to take Bradyn by the throat with a hand that had grown long and talon-like.

Even though Bradyn had never been more scared in his life, Kyle's reaction brought relief. He laughed in spite of the fingers clawing at his jugular. "You don't have her do you? If you did, you wouldn't be in here trying to get me to help y--." Kyle's hand tightened on his throat and choked off the last of his sentence.

Bradyn felt the life being squeezed from him. The room blurred in and out of focus. Anger riveted him. He felt a hot energy pulsate through his veins. Suddenly, from nowhere, brilliant blue light shattered the emerald flames. There was a blinding sizzle as cobalt electricity met oozing green vapor. Kyle jumped back, holding his hand and screaming in pain. Bradyn felt the power circulating through his own body, hot and savage, before it began to die away. He had no idea what had just happened. Stunned by confusion, Kyle's words barely touched his awareness.

"This isn't over yet, Preston. As soon as I kill your precious little lover, I will have your blood!" Wind filled the stable and there was a churning of sooty mist. Then Kyle disappeared from the room, emerald flames and all.

* * * *

Contessa stood on the rooftop watching as Liam's men gathered in the livery yard below. The heavy night air was sluggish as it circulated around her. She looked back to the purple light in the east. Kyle had left her immediately after the brilliant blaze had first pierced the night sky and sent a spiraling beam heavenward. He had said that the time had come to speak with Bradyn again.

Now, as Liam gathered his gunmen, Tessa felt that same odd energy begin to work its way through her stomach and up her spine again. A warm metallic taste filled her mouth. The flavor of fresh blood. The purple light twinkled and began moving across the sky. She blinked. It was coming closer.

Just as she was about to go after Kyle, she felt his

presence on the rooftop next to her. Black smoke rolled upward in a thick, liquid vapor and gave appearance to his form. The smile was not on his face as it had been when he'd left. This bothered Tessa. "Is all well?" she asked.

"You are needed for this matter, Contessa. Bradyn's will is stronger than I supposed. He is already being taken by the Spirit's energy. It is warring with the darkness in him. You know what you must do," Kyle instructed. "Here. Take this with you." He held out his arm. The veins in his wrist and the tendons along his outstretched hand began to glow. A green sphere of light rose from his fingertips and levitated above his palm. It was marbled with red and yellow sparks of color.

"What is it?" Tessa asked. Her tone was fearful and curious at once.

"It is the power to persuade Bradyn to do my will. He bares the mark on his chest. I've already explained its purpose to you; I trust I will not have to again?"

"You will not."

Kyle nodded. "Take this into your hand," he instructed.

Obediently, Tessa raised her hand next to his. The ball of light jumped to her palm and began whirring faster. The streaks of crimson began to widen and envelop the green orb until it burned the color of blood. Unable to stop herself, she reached up and closed her fingers around it. The light sank into her hand and remained glowing on the surface of her skin. For a moment she stood transfixed, looking down at her palm as if in a trance.

"Go now," Kyle whispered. His gaze was fixed on the eastern horizon. "She is coming. We do not have time to waste."

* * * *

Liam felt the cold wind that picked up as the bright purple light still off in the distance pierced the swirling blackness around the city. His men looked on in wonder as what appeared to be a falling star drew closer in the darkness. Not a sound could be heard in their ranks, only quickened, heavy breathing.

Suddenly a scream pierced the night and Liam and his men raised their eyes in the direction it came from. A black dragon-like form shot up from the roof of the livery and disappeared into the blackness swirling above the town. The ravens winged to life and circled in crazed flapping above the street. A hand of paralyzing awe grasped Liam. His men backed away and each searched the street for a line of retreat. "Stand your ground, men!" he ordered.

The beast cut back down through the mist and, before anyone could clearly make out its features, it was enveloped in thick black smoke. There was a splintering of earth as the cloud of darkness hit the street with a violent crash. Liam and his men watched with frightened captivation as Kyle stepped from the smoke and walked toward them along a widening, jagged crack in the ground.

The men all exchanged looks of utter terror. Laughter and fire shattered the darkness as flames ran in a rapid circle around the group of men with Kyle at their center. Trapped within the green fire, the men went stone still. There was nowhere to run. The ravens, which had not stopped their infernal circling, took up a horrible cawing and started flying faster.

In response to their loud cawing, Kyle looked up to the heavens and his eyes burned a furious red. He smiled as he watched the approach of the vibrant purple light.

Liam watched the light in fascinated silence. *What is it?* He wondered as the light pierced the ever faster encompassing darkness. The fog seemed to grow heavier. As if sensing the approach of light, it fought to suppress it from reaching the city streets below.

Kyle turned his gaze on the twenty men standing in a circle around him. Each of the men's chests glowed with a grayish orange aura that was connected by a writhing ribbon to the man next to him. The evil that held their hearts and wound in a single stream between them, binding them together, was becoming stronger.

Kyle raised his hand and walked toward Liam, the wicked smile on his face freezing the blood in Liam's veins.

When he reached Liam's side, he placed his outstretched hand on his chosen man's shoulder. His voice ricocheted up the street and drew the ravens lower in their flight. The fear that shot through the ranks of the men was quickly bent into subservience as Kyle spoke with a thunderous voice.

"Tonight the man whose heart is black and whose soul is darkness will bend his knee to my will. You will fight beside me to annihilate the One who comes to us. You have been bound to this and Death and Hell's eternal torment await those who fail me! Eternal life and everything your hearts desire await you if you succeed."

He turned and cast a lingering gaze on each man in succession. His expression was ice. It challenged any one of them to defy him. The crack along the ground continued to rumble and widen. Mountains of fire and the putrid smoke of eternal damnation reflected red from the faces of the terrified men.

"The man who is not willing to do my bidding will step forward now and collect his just due. The chasm waits to claim you."

Liam looked at the petrified faces of his men and knew their thoughts. They would do anything to stay the captivity of Hell. As much as he hated Kyle Bodeen, he had been willing to do anything to avoid being banished to the eternal flames. His men would give their souls in service of the Devil, just as he had.

Satisfied when no one stepped forward, Kyle lifted his hands. The chasm to Hell grew smaller and sealed itself shut. Then he gave a second call. "All those who willingly give their souls in servitude will stand now and swear this oath: Our lives for you. Our bodies to serve you until death."

The color of green and orange entwined and grew bold as the men stepped forward one by one and exclaimed in unison; "Our lives for you! Our bodies to serve you until death!"

An earsplitting clap of thunder echoed across the sky. In a single, uniform action the men all turned their gazes upward and watched as the purple light exploded through the blackness and began plummeting toward them.

Rian felt ice and fire engulf her as she was plunged into the black swirling fog. The rooftops of the city passed beneath with startling speed as she descended through the mists. Glimpses of clustered orange auras surrounding a green light greeted her through the thinning blackness. The scream of ravens reached her ears over the whirring of wind.

She was moving so rapidly, Rian was certain her descent would end in a harsh collision with the earth below. She closed her eyes and took a deep breath to steady her nerves. The bleak emptiness of evil encompassed her as she plummeted with maddening speed. Her heart jumped into her throat and the breath was ripped from her body as she fell to the street. She raised her arms to shield herself from the inevitable impact.

But the impact never came. Instead, she felt herself begin to float as dandelion dander on a gentle summer's breeze. Opening her eyes, she discovered that her body was levitating only a few feet above the ground. Turning her gaze, she saw that the orange circle of auras was only a few yards away.

Her eyes adjusted to the darkness and she watched as gradually the twisted, sickly auras rose like smoke, leaving behind the shapes of men. The blackness of the city made it difficult for her to see each face, but the awe and the hatred that was mingled in their expressions was as clear to her as the screaming of the ravens. However, it was not the group of men that fully arrested her attention, but the man that stood in their midst.

The scars across her back sizzled. The blurry memory of a monster, not man but not entirely inhuman, surfaced in her mind. She was tied to a banister and he was clawing at the purple sphere of light that surrounded her. The light had saved her life, but he had still managed to rip his talons across her back leaving horrible, permanent scars...

"Kyle?" she gasped as a loathsome, black fear captured her heart.

Kyle Bodeen came toward her, a smile parting his lips; a horrid twinkle in his green eyes. He raised his arm and the ravens stopped their cawing. They settled along the street and on rooftops, as if waiting to see what would happen next.

"Hello, wife," he whispered as reached her. "Seven long years spent searching and I find you at last."

Chapter Twenty

Her eyes were deceiving her! He was dead. She had blown a hole the size of a china dinner plate through his chest. He couldn't have survived that shot…could he?

"You're not real!" Rian shouted at him, putting up a hand as he approached. "I killed you."

His wicked chuckle sent razor chills through her. "You did not succeed, my dear Moriana. I cannot be destroyed with a bullet made by human hands. That would be far too easy."

Rian fought to keep terror from gaining a foothold. "Where is Bradyn?" she demanded.

"Ah, yes. The one you love." He chuckled again. "Tell me, wife, how is it you have come to love a man with a heart as black as mine? You haven't changed in these seven years. You've learned nothing from your past." His voice mocked her.

Rian ignored his insults and asked again, "Where is he?"

"Where is my son?" he returned. "Give him to me and you shall have your precious lover."

The spirit in her waxed hot. The smile that touched her mouth was cold and humorless. "You will never live to see your son, Kyle Bodeen. He is safe and far from here."

Crimson anger glowed in his eyes, but the smile never left his face. "I see the aura that binds the two of you. He is not as far away as you would have me believe. In any event, it is a small matter. First, I will kill you and your beloved Bradyn. Finding my son will prove quite simple after you are both dead."

"He is protected by Light," she answered, her voice defiant. "You cannot touch him."

Laughter shook the street and the windows of the nearby buildings began to rattle with the reverberation. "How long do you honestly suppose he can be protected? He is only safe as long as night is upon us. When morning light comes, and the world returns to its normal state, the angel guarding your son will have to cross over and leave him on the mortal plain. I will have him, Moriana. The side of Light cannot deny me what is mine."

Her body went numb with fear at his words, but the presence of the Avenger made fury from her terror. "I have come to ensure you do not find Kendall." Her voice shook with rage. "He is my son and I would kill to protect him. I would *die* to protect him," she added in a quieter tone that was no less determined.

Kyle's evil smile widened further. "And Bradyn? Would you die to protect him as well?"

"I would," she answered.

"Valliant words, my dear. You would truly *die* to protect a man who has cheated, robbed, and murdered his whole life? He is Shadow, Moriana. You know this." Kyle cocked his head and regarded her as a father would a small daughter trying to convince him to let her adopt a flea-bitten mongrel.

Rian's eyes narrowed at the needling smirk on Kyle's face. "He is not an evil man. He has made amends for his past wrongs. The evil that rules over you does not hold his heart."

"Would you stake your life on that?" he challenged.

"I would."

"Then we may be able to come to some sort of agreement after all," he said. The red in his eyes waned a bit and he rubbed his hands together like a starving man about to get a square meal. "Something of a trade, if you will."

"I'm listening," she returned.

"Bradyn may be of no use to you now. He has crossed over into Shadow and I know he is not the man of virtue you so vehemently claim. I hold his life in my hand even now. With one word I can destroy him." Kyle closed his fist and a loud scream tore the air.

Rian turned in the direction of the scream and saw red and blue light glowing through the walls of the livery stable. Deep navy sparks of agony radiated through Bradyn's cobalt aura. As the screaming went on, the color began to fade and grow transparent. His pain gripped her heart and she felt terror for his life consume her. "Leave him alone! Your fight is not with him, but with me!" she screamed.

"His soul light is dying, Moriana. *He* is dying. Give me what I want, and I will stay my hand. I will let him live."

Rian swallowed and turned to Kyle. "Stop this and I will give you anything. Anything but Kendall," she qualified.

"Do I have your word? I can have anything I want with the exception of Kendall?" Victorious green flames leapt into his eyes.

"Yes. You have my word," she conceded. "What is it that you would have?' she asked quietly.

"The dagger," he answered. "Give it to me."

"It is yours, but first you must let me speak to Bradyn."

"You will have your meeting with him. But you will give me what I want first." He held out his hand. "Give me the dagger now. Then we will strike a bargain."

* * * *

Red fire filled his senses. He was blinded by its burning. The screams of pain that were ripped from his lips made the blue light inside him blur and dim. When he thought he could bear the torturous flames no more, when he thought that surely he would cross over to eternal darkness, the pain stopped.

Bradyn felt a small hand on his torso. He looked down through eyes that could hardly open. The pentagram on his chest glowed bright for a moment. Again horrible pain and whirling disorientation made his vision flare red. Every inch of his skin burned with the fire that had consumed him only minutes before. Then it was gone.

"Bradyn?"

When he opened his eyes, he blinked. He had been expecting to see Kyle standing there once again. His eyes were surely deceiving him. "Rian?" he gasped. "What are you doing here? How did you find me?"

"I saw your aura," she answered. "They've hurt you! You're bleeding." The worry and fear in her voice were welcome and terrible at once.

"Rian, you have to leave! He wants Kendall. You have to go before he finds you! If you don't give him Kendall, he is going to kill you."

"I know what he wants, but I am not leaving without you, Bradyn," she insisted.

Bradyn watched her strain to reach the chains that bound him. He felt her fumble with the shackles. There was a click as a key rasped and turned in the lock. His arms fell free and he tumbled to the floor.

"Hurry! We have to go," Rian whispered. She rose and ran to the door at the far side of the stable.

"Wait!" Bradyn called after her as she disappeared into the night beyond. He fought to gain his balance and stand upright. "Rian, wait!" he shouted. But it was too late, she was gone.

Rubbing his wrists, he stumbled after her. The door was very heavy and he was light-headed. He had to struggle to open it wide enough to fit himself through. With a final tug, the door groaned inward and he escaped into the darkness outside.

The cool night air washed his face and chest as he stepped out onto the street. A devastating scene met his eyes. A group of twenty or more men stood in a circle around the livery yard. In their center, Kyle held Liam Briggs with a knife to his throat. Bradyn's eyes fell to the ground at Liam's feet.

"Rian!" he screamed. She was lying on her back. Blood smattered her face and ran to the ground in a pool from a large gash across the length of her chest. Her eyes, glassy and sightless, stared up at the heavens. "No!" he cried as he ran and knelt in the dust beside her.

"She's dead, Bradyn." Kyle's voice was full of triumph. "It appears I don't need you after all. Liam was more than happy to take her life to save his own in turn. I'll get what I want now that she is gone. You are free of your service to me."

Anger riddled him. Tears bit his eyelids. He rose slowly and clenched his fists as he turned on Liam and Kyle. "What have you done?!" he shouted.

"Since I've gotten what I want, I'll make good on my promise to you, Preston. You can kill Liam and have your revenge. Everybody leaves happy." Kyle's tone was cold and ridiculing. "Or at least *I* leave happy at any rate," he chuckled.

"It wasn't me, Bradyn." Liam protested. "He's lying, don't let him deceive y--." His voice was choked off as Kyle wrapped his hand around Liam's neck and squeezed, the knife still pressed against the base of his throat.

"You want revenge, don't you, Bradyn? To spill blood for the blood that was shed, for the love that you lost tonight? Here," Kyle lifted the silver dagger from Liam's neck and gestured to Bradyn. "Take this and have your just retribution."

When Bradyn hesitated, Kyle reminded him, "He killed your brother's wife and baby daughter. Even now your brother's blood cries out from the ground not five miles from here, where Liam left his body to be eaten by the birds. And now he has murdered the woman you love. Surely retribution is due you and no one would blame you for getting your revenge."

In the dim light, Bradyn's eyes fell on the dagger in Kyle's outstretched hand. Slowly, he reached for it.

"No, Bradyn! You are making a mistake," Liam pleaded. "Don't do this!"

Cold anger tore through Bradyn and he grasped the dagger. Raising it over his head, he brought it down in a swift motion. Liam's hand came up and grabbed his arm. A flash of blinding purple light slashed through Bradyn. He knew it was wrong to take his revenge this way, but he didn't care. Liam's eyes were clouded with terrified surrender.

"Revenge is the path of Shadow, Bradyn. You have crossed over. Only death will free you from your blindness," Liam said. "Do what you must."

"You've killed everyone that I've ever loved!" Bradyn yelled as he jerked his hand free. "You have tortured my existence and taken my soul from me. I could have walked away from that, but you killed Rian. For that, you will die."

Bradyn brought the dagger down in a gleaming arch and buried it deep in Liam's chest. With a scream of pain, he opened his eyes and looked at Bradyn. In that instant, Bradyn realized that he had made a terrible mistake. The person before him was not Liam Briggs at all. Deep sadness etched its way across Rian's beautiful face as she looked up at him.

"You see, Moriana?" Kyle turned her face so that he could speak into her ear, his triumphant smile holding Bradyn's eyes. "He isn't the man you thought he was. You lost our little wager and now you will pay with your life. I will have my son back."

With sick recognition, Bradyn watched as Kyle released her body and she fell with a soft thud to the dusty street.

"It is done!" Kyle shouted into the black swirling fog. The ravens began flying in a wide circle around the street. His deep, demonic laughter rumbled through the town, filling it with the thunder of evil victory. It shattered windows and shook the buildings to their foundations. Even the pebbles on the street vibrated and bounced as he laughed.

With terrified, wide-eyed confusion, Bradyn watched as Liam Briggs stepped out from behind Kyle where he had been shielded from view the entire time. Stricken, Bradyn turned to the place he had seen Rian lying when he'd first come out of the stable. Contessa rose and dusted herself off with a jagged smile. She winked at him as she went to stand beside Kyle. They had all tricked him!

The world whirred to a screeching halt. He was numb to the thick air and the ravens whipping around him as he looked at Rian lying at his feet. Kyle's quaking laughter and the screaming of the birds became hollow echoes from somewhere miles away. "Rian!" Bradyn cried and fell to his knees beside her. The dagger was still embedded in her chest. She struggled to breathe. "Rian!' he sobbed. "What have I done?!"

She opened her eyes and looked up at him. A sphere of purple light exploded outward and surrounded them as Bradyn lifted her in his arms. Bolts of amethyst electricity shot through the glowing circle of luminescence.

Kyle's laughter grew silent and the group of men stood watching the rotating ball of blinding light, their faces full of violent triumph.

"Bradyn," Rian whispered. "It must be so. The angel told me…to see the way clearly, and I did. I…I am the one sent to save *you,* not to defeat the Destroyer." Her breathing was ragged and labored. "You were deceived…to fulfill the purpose of Light. He thinks he has tricked you with shadows and mirages and that the victory is his… but he is the one who is deceived. He will not win this fight…he must not…win."

He wiped a strand of hair from her face. "I know now that I was wrong. My anger…I never should have done it. I should have known! I should have known it was you," he whispered against her hair as his tears wet the top of her head. "I'm so sorry, Rian. I am so sorry," he cried as he rocked her.

"No." She choked for a moment.

Bradyn turned her face up to look at him. Crystalline tears seeped from the corners of her beautiful amber eyes.

"No…it is as it must be…you have to listen to me, I'm dying." She fought to draw another tortured breath. "You have to take the dagger…it will give you…power…Do not let it leave your hand…it is the only thing that can destroy him. He told me…" She coughed and blood trickled from the corner of her lips. "The angel told me…to remember…"

"To remember what, Rian?" Bradyn urged.

"He told me to remember that as…as water reflects the face, so the man's heart reflects…the man." She tugged at his shirt and her eyes fluttered for a moment. "The beast will be hard to destroy…you have to find his heart and…strike there. You have to stay strong, Bradyn. He cannot be allowed to take Kendall. You must…stand."

"Don't leave me, Rian. I need you…I love you." Bradyn sobbed.

"The angel told me…that…Light finds strength in death, but…evil can only triumph if it has life on which to feed. This fight is yours tonight, Bradyn. You are strong…and good...the side of Light will protect you." She opened her eyes and looked up at him. "They are here," she whispered. A soft smile touched her bloodstained lips.

Bradyn followed her gaze over his shoulder through the rolling orb of purple light. White wings gave flight to angels that hovered over the city. The sight of them sent chills of wonder through him. Beautiful light cut through the black fog and illuminated the streets below.

"They've come for me…In the darkness…help comes," Rian whispered. She reached up and touched his face. "I love you, Bradyn…forever." Determination gave the softness in her expression a hard cast. "Now take the dagger…and destroy him." The brilliant sphere of light faded as her eyes closed for the final time.

Bradyn kissed her as tears streamed down his cheeks. He closed his eyes and hung his head. Rian was gone. He laid her on the dusty street and stared down at the dagger sticking in her lifeless chest as the town started rumbling with laughter again. The image of an angel, molded into the handle of the knife, gleamed up at him. Bradyn reached down and closed his fingers around it. Before pulling it from her chest, he glared up at the man who'd tricked him.

Kyle's face was black and ruthless as he stood in the center of the street, mocking Bradyn. "You fool! You have killed the Avenger. So strong was your desire for revenge you could not see that she was the woman you loved. The side of Light will never learn. They have called an evil man to do the task of a righteous one. They should have known it would end this way."

His riotous laughter was joined by the incessant cawing of the ravens. They circled and swooped around Bradyn, brushing him with their wings. "Kill him and drink their blood! Feast on their warm flesh and you will gain strength and long life!" Kyle shouted to his men.

Hearing that command, blue rage consumed Bradyn. He pulled the dagger from Rian's chest and rose to face the approaching men. He would die before he would let them touch her.

As they moved toward him, a bright orange glow wended its way around each man, changing them into hideous dog-like creatures that were gnarled and deformed. Grotesque faces with long snouts snarled at him. Matted manes hung from their necks and hair covered their bodies. They smiled, hungrily licking their lips.

The uncertainty that gnawed at Bradyn's heart vanished as a spellbinding heat began to shine from the dagger in his hand. A circular vortex of purple and blue erupted from its blade. Bradyn raised the weapon and stared at it as his whole body was devoured by light. He looked down and saw veins of sapphire and amethyst winding up his arms and over his chest. There was pain in the heat, and as it burned the blood pentagram from his chest, Bradyn yelled out. But after the bloody mark was gone, the pain melted away and he felt only fathomless power. The dagger's blade turned to flame, and Bradyn saw the history of its existence.

He saw the evil lord, the beautiful woman, and the man whom she had loved. He saw the women who had been called to be the Avenger in every generation. He saw the men who had been elected to protect them. He saw the origin of the beast and all his chosen brides. In an instant, Bradyn understood his purpose. All the questions that had assaulted him tonight were answered. He knew why Rian had been familiar to him since the first day he had seen her. The spirit lying dormant in her had been beckoning to the spirit lying dormant in him. He felt the power of the Avenger and the Protector surge into alliance and run through his blood as one. The dagger's sapphire and amethyst flame blended into alabaster light.

Kyle had gone silent as the transformation took Bradyn. "It can't be!" he roared. "You are not worthy of the task of the Avenger!" His wrath rose from his nostrils in tendrils of smoke. Then his chest began to quake with laughter. "It is a small matter," he shouted as his body began to grow and change. "I will make short work of you and *then* we will feast!"

Bradyn watched as the Destroyer took shape. His face became the face of a dragon. Black oily scales spread from his head, covering his neck, chest, and back. Four twisted horns grew from his brow into a hideous crown. Feathered dragon's wings of pure black rose into the air above his head as a tail like that of a lion whipped angrily behind him. Long muscled arms were soon coated with the glistening scales and his hands became huge grasping talons. The beast's legs were hairy, like those of a bull, and his feet were silver cloven hooves. The Destroyer roared. Green flame and smoke boiled from a mouth that was lined with long, dagger length fangs.

But fear was as distant to Bradyn as righteousness was to the Destroyer. The flaming blade of the dagger burned brighter and grew longer until it was a sword. Bradyn felt a strange binding between his shoulders. Silvery white feathers stretched upward and opened. Awed, he wondered at what point the wings had grown from his back. He lowered them and fixed his gaze on the closing circle of ravens and demons. Moving with agile speed, he lifted himself from the ground and came down between the approaching evil shapes that had once been men and Rian's lifeless body. The sword raised, he took his stand. Ready to fight them as the beast rose into the air with another deafening roar and the city erupted in emerald flame.

Chapter Twenty-one

The demon dogmen closed in, snarling, salivating, and gnashing their teeth like a pack of starving wolves. There was a growl as the first two lunged. Bradyn swung his sword. The blade sliced them both in half with a blaze of light and a hiss. Howls of pain and anger followed as they fell and dissipated into orange flame.

Two more crouched back on their haunches, ready to charge. Bradyn raised his weapon as a hand touched his shoulder.

"Your fight is with the Destroyer. Go. We will let no harm come to her."

The angels stood to his right and left, two on either side. Each carried a sword of gold.

"Go!" the angel shouted. "Destroy the beast!"

Bradyn hesitated for only a moment. Spreading his wings, he took flight and rose above the snarling pack. When he looked down, the angels had closed around Rian. The angel who had spoken lifted his sword as the demons charged. Two more angels moved forward into battle. Screams cut the air as limbs were severed and flung to the ground.

The blackness above the city was heavy and blinding. The ravens' cries were silenced, but they still flew through the burning streets. Bradyn dove and spun though them as he searched for the Destroyer. The dagger lighted his way through the thick fog, but he could not find the beast.

Bradyn passed beyond the edge of town and his eyes

came to rest on the church steeple. The beast was perched atop it. The Destroyer roared and the church burst into green flame as Bradyn approached. When the beast flew into the night sky, the hollow sound of beating wings reached Bradyn's ears. The Destroyer soared into the roof of black mist and Bradyn followed.

The fog was not only heavy, but deep. It swallowed him whole as he ascended. Just as he was about to break through the blackness, a blast of green fire erupted in his face. Taken off guard, Bradyn fought to keep his balance. The Destroyer slammed his fist into Bradyn's face and he catapulted to the street below.

As he toppled through the air, he heard the Destroyer scream and spiral after him. In the instant before Bradyn hit the ground, the Destroyer grabbed him and hurled him across the street. Wood and glass exploded around him. Green flame burst upward in a fountain of cold embers when Bradyn's body slammed into the church. The bell in the steeple began clanging upon his impact. Pealing gongs echoed through the town. He did not know pain, but only blinding white fury, as he picked himself up and flew at the Destroyer.

There was rupturing of trunk and earth as he slammed the Destroyer into an ancient oak tree. Fire and smoke poured from the beast's mouth as Bradyn darted into the air above him. Spreading his black wings, the Destroyer shot up from the ground and Bradyn flew at him again.

The impact of their collision hurled them higher into the sky. Bradyn grabbed one of the Destroyer's horns. The beast roared and tried to knock him away. With inhuman strength, Bradyn held on as the Destroyer rolled into a tailspin. He slashed the flaming dagger against the beast's chest again and again. Sparks, like a blacksmith's hammer on hot steel, exploded from the clashing of blade against scale.

"You can't kill me with that!" the Destroyer howled into the wind whirring past them. "You are a fool to believe you can defeat me! I have fought you a hundred times before. One slip and your power will weaken."

The Destroyer landed a powerful kick into his thigh. He broke free of Bradyn's grasp and flew higher. Bradyn followed fast behind him. Like bullets, they pierced the canopy of fog and were plunged into the light of a crimson full moon. Again, Bradyn reached out and took hold of the beast. As if in a dance they rolled across the starless sky.

"I will see your end tonight!" Bradyn shouted. "I swear it on my life!"

The Destroyer slammed his fist into Bradyn's chest. His vision blurred and he released his hold on the beast for a moment. Another crushing blow followed and Bradyn dropped lower in the night sky.

Determination and fury propelled him upward again. As the Destroyer shot toward him, Bradyn raised his sword and slashed it through a black wing. A scream split his ears as the Destroyer bellowed fire and smoke. The beast's eyes glowed red with rage. He grabbed Bradyn by the neck and shook him. Bradyn lifted his sword to strike again, but the beast was too fast this time. His mouth opened to meet the blow and Bradyn felt fangs sink into his wrist. In the flash of pain, Bradyn dropped the dagger. He watched it plummet through the mists back into the city below.

Tearing his arm free of the Destroyer's teeth, Bradyn dove after the dagger. As he fell from the sky and broke through the rolling mist, the choking fog clouded his vision. He squinted and tried to find the dagger's light. Breeching the blackness, he saw that it had landed at the feet of one of the angels. Dropping to the street, Bradyn took in the scene at a glance.

Fire still lapped at the buildings, though it did not devour the wood. The ravens flew in ceaseless pattern, their loud squawking now blending with the crackle of green flame.

The demon dogmen stood in a close circle around only two remaining angels. Twelve demons remained. Tessa stood in front of them. Her long hair fell in loose curls down a body that glittered with copper scales. She held a golden sword in one of her hands and the head of one of the angels in her other.

Several of the demons lunged at once and the two angels stepped forward to meet the onrush. Howls of pain filled his ears as Bradyn broke through the line of demons and ran to the place where the dagger had fallen. Its light was only a faint glow.

The dagger was almost in his grasp, when light exploded around him. The force of it knocked him backward as he saw the blade of Tessa's sword cut through one of angel's throat. The angel's body shattered into a thousand twinkling shards before it was snuffed out of existence.

"No!" Bradyn shouted as he watched the angel's fair head fall to the street.

The dagger was lying in the dirt at Tessa's feet now. Bradyn dove to grab it, gravel and dust spraying in all directions, scraping his chest and stomach. A blade drenched in blood touched his throat as he struggled to reach his weapon. In a swift movement, Tessa kicked the dagger away. Another powerful kick met his jaw and he was hurled backward again.

Wiping the blood from his mouth, he glared up at Tessa as she ran her tongue along the edge of her sword. "Hello, Bradyn." She smiled. Her eyes glittered yellow, like the eyes of a cat. Bradyn saw with disgust that her mouth was red and blood dripped from her serpentine fangs.

He moved into a crouch as the snarling demons gathered closer. Roaring filled the street and the Destroyer appeared over them. His landing shook the earth.

"Well done, my love," he praised Tessa. "Now, bring the dagger to me!"

The biggest of the demon dogmen ran to fetch the silver dagger lying a few yards away. Bradyn knew it was Liam as he offered the weapon to his master. A hideous grin of victory parted the Destroyer's mouth when he grasped the dagger in his hand. His red eyes fell on Bradyn. "Rise!" he shouted at him.

"Get up!" Tessa ordered. She landed a stout kick to his stomach this time.

Anger and pain caused his vision to blur. Slowly, Bradyn stood as the Destroyer walked toward him. In a swift motion the beast picked him up off the ground by the neck and held him in front of his face.

Without the dagger, Bradyn felt his strength ebbing. He struggled to loosen the beast's hold on his throat. It was fruitless. The Destroyer tossed him up. Deep gashes tore across his chest as a massive clawed hand batted him across the street. His body slammed into a building, nearly knocking him senseless. He slumped to the ground with a thud several yards from where the Destroyer stood.

The world tilted and began to whir. Dizzy, Bradyn heard muffled voices echoing around him. He could not breathe. Everything was numb and disconnected.

"He is weak." He heard Tessa murmur. "I think he is dying. Look, the soul light is leaving him."

Deep chuckling met Bradyn's ears. "He dropped the dagger. He is no longer indestructible. Let us finish him now, my love," the Destroyer replied. "Drink his blood while he is still living, you will become immortal. Your heart will grow strong and give me great power.

"Finish the angel and take the woman's body!" He heard the Destroyer shout to his demons. "Quickly! Midnight is nearly upon us."

Dazed, Bradyn sat up and shook his head. The final angel stood over Rian's body, ready to fight or succumb to death in order to protect her against the blood-thirsty demons. Three of the Destroyer's dogs charged. Splintering orange light shattered the darkness as the angel's sword sliced through them in an arch of electric blue.

Seeing the angel's unfaltering valiance, Bradyn felt a renewed surge of power. He pulled himself to his feet and stood with unsteady balance as the Destroyer and Tessa approached him.

Fury gave way to strength. He opened his wings and dove at the Destroyer. The beast roared with laughter and darted backward. But Bradyn was fast enough. He slammed into the Destroyer's arm with a harsh impact. The dagger flew out of the beast's hand.

As the dagger was hurled down the street, Bradyn darted after it, the Destroyer and Tessa fast on his heels. There was a splash as the dagger fell into a horse trough. Bradyn reached the trough first, the sounds of the chase right behind him.

He plunged his hand into the water and grabbed the weapon. For a split second, his attention was captured by the water. It did not move. He blinked as he saw his reflection. Vague memory assailed him as he pulled the dagger from the trough. *Rian said something about the water's reflection…What was it?*

Then the Destroyer and Tessa were upon him. There was a flash of gold as Tessa raised her sword and brought it down. As if in a trance, Bradyn moved to the side. The dagger in his hand burned to life, once again a sword of flame. He fought with his body as the two moved around him. But all the while his mind was reeling, trying to recall what Rian had told him not to forget.

Fireworks of crimson and white rained down onto the street as Tessa's blade clashed with his. The Destroyer jumped behind him. Before Bradyn could stop him, the beast lifted him over his head and hurled him down the street. This time Bradyn held onto the dagger and he opened his wings to stop his fall. Giving the nagging memory a chance to come to him, he took his stand on the street and waited as they came at him.

Past them, he saw that the snarling demons were closing on the angel. Out of the corner of his eye, Bradyn watched as the angel felled two more of them. Prisms of orange and blue burst outward as the demons met with the angel's blade.

"As water reflects…" he whispered, trying to remember her words.

The Destroyer was the first to reach him. Bradyn wasted no time. He lunged at the beast and drove the sword into its chest. Laughter echoed through the air. Tessa's mocking laughter joined with it.

"I've already told you that you can't kill me with that, Bradyn." The Destroyer bellowed.

Tessa pounced and her sword caught Bradyn's arm. He spun and stopped her next blow with the blade of his sword.

Purple-white light filled his vision as a wave of power streamed through him. A bolt of lightning shot from his sword and slammed into her chest.

Tessa could not stand against the force of the impact. Her body was hurtled backward across the street. She landed in a crouching position. As he watched her get up and sprint toward him, Rian's words came flooding back. *"As water reflects the face, so the man's heart reflects the man. Light finds strength in death, evil can only triumph if it has life on which to feed."*

A curtain of revelation was pulled back and the light struck him. In that instant, he knew what Rian's words had meant.

The discovery distracted him, and before he knew what was happening, the Destroyer had thrown him to the ground. The dagger clattered to the dust once again. Stunned, Bradyn barely had time to move to the side as the beast raised his hand to strike. Silver talons rent the air in a lethal flash. Red agony flooded Bradyn as he felt the claws rip across his abdomen. Fighting the pain, he grasped at the dagger lying only a few feet away. His fingers closed over it as the beast hit him again and sent him rolling down the street.

He came to a stop in a cloud of dust. Above him, their faces blurred in and out of his view as he struggled to pull himself to his feet. Blood poured from his wounds. Each breath was torture. The pain that wracked his body was blinding, but he knew he had only one chance to strike a fatal blow.

Tessa and the Destroyer circled him with taunting expressions. "I have been patient long enough," the beast snarled as they both moved in for the kill. "Now you are going to die."

"No," Bradyn growled through clenched teeth. "You are."

He lifted the sword overhead one last time and aimed it at the impudent Destroyer. In an agile flash of movement he swung and turned, slicing the blade through Tessa's heart just as she raised her sword to attack.

Tessa's surprised scream was mixed with the roaring of the Destroyer as she fell.

"She is your heart!" Bradyn shouted at the beast as he struck her again. "Without her you have no power!"

Red light splintered through the gash in Tessa's chest and enveloped her. She was obliterated in a starburst of crimson. In seconds there was nothing left of her except a thin red wisp of smoke.

Bradyn looked at the Destroyer. The beast began to writhe and howl as it changed form in a haze of green vapor. Without Tessa, it seemed, he could no longer assume his demonic form. Casting a quick glance up the street, Bradyn saw that the three remaining demon dogmen were changing too. They became the shapes of men once again as the Destroyer's power over them became worthless. The angel still stood over Rian. Bradyn felt relief to see he had lasted the fight. Rian's body had remained untouched.

When he looked back at the Destroyer, Kyle was standing where the beast had been. In his hand he held Tessa's sword.

"Let's finish this!" he shouted at Bradyn.

Bradyn tightened his fingers over the handle of the dagger as it became a sword of light one final time. *Please, God. I don't need much strength,* he prayed silently, *just enough to kill this bastard and avenge Rian's death.*

The two moved toward each other, wrath twisting both men's faces with deadly determination. The need to spill the other's blood coursed through each man's body. The first clash of metal on metal resounded in the night. Kyle was unwounded and quick, but Bradyn still had a small measure of the Avenger's power running through him.

The fight waged on as angry shouts echoed in the night. Kyle moved to the left and brought his sword down. Bradyn whirled to the right and brought his sword upward.

Sparks of red, purple, green, and blue sizzled as the blades smashed together. Kyle jabbed at Bradyn, who dodged and in a lightning flash, brought his sword over his head and down. It connected with Kyle's left arm, serving it just below the shoulder. The blow knocked Kyle to the ground. In another swift movement, before Kyle could gain his foothold, Bradyn slammed the sword down on Kyle's other arm, slicing through his wrist. Kyle was rendered helpless as his hand, fingers still clasped around the sword, fell to the street.

The flames of the blade became dim. Bradyn watched as the sword in his hand became the dagger once again. Ready to finish the fight, he stepped to the place where Kyle had fallen.

Kyle did not get up as Bradyn stood over him with the dagger raised to strike. Instead, he looked up at Bradyn and smiled.

"This isn't over yet," he whispered. "I will be back. You can't stop me. My son is alive and I *will* get him back. You can't keep him from me forever." Menacing chuckling shook Kyle's body, his were eyes full of cold humor. "I will win in the end."

"Go to hell," Bradyn grunted as he plunged the dagger into Kyle's heart.

A blast of green electricity imploded and then exploded outward in a shockwave as a beam of light shot heavenward from Kyle's body. The force knocked Bradyn to his knees. Thunder filled the city and the earth rumbled and shifted beneath him.

The buildings, still engulfed by emerald fire, began to fall one by one like a row of dominoes, the splintering of wood and shattering of glass deafening. The ravens flew in frenzied haste trying to escape the city. As they passed by him, Bradyn smiled wearily. He looked heavenward as he felt a gentle breeze touch him. The black fog rolled back and the night sky was visible again. Thousands of stars, dimmed only by the bright light of the full moon, glittered in an ink black sky.

He pulled himself to his feet and trudged up the street. The agony of his injuries made movement nearly intolerable. Twice, he went to his knees, but the need to reach Rian pushed him on. Kyle's other men had disappeared. So had the angel. Bradyn wondered where they had gone, but his mind, clouded by pain, was too drained to try to make sense of it just now. When he was only a short distance from her, and he could go no further on his feet, he sank to the ground and dragged himself to her side.

Rian's face was ashen and her body cold, but even in death she was beautiful. Exhausted and sobbing, Bradyn pulled her against him. His tears wetted her waxen cheeks as sweet, painless unconsciousness took him.

Chapter Twenty-two

He opened his eyes to the scent of flowers and the touch of a gentle breeze. The grass whispered around his legs as the sunlight warmed his senses. Bubbling laughter carried across a field alive with wildflowers. He turned and saw two children, dressed in white, playing among the blossoms. He immediately recognized the boy.

Kendall held the hand of a dark, curly-haired toddler. She giggled and wrapped her chubby arms around his waist as he put a wreath of flowers on her head. They tumbled through the grass, laughing with delight.

Happiness like none he had ever known filled his heart. The urge to pick the little one up and hold her in his arms brought tears to his eyes, though he did not know why. He watched as Kendall ran through the tall grass and dropped from sight. *"Come and find me!"* he called to the little girl.

"He is Moriana's son, and the son of the man that you fought last night." A deep voice at his side startled him.

Confusion tore his eyes from the little girl as she searched the tall grass for Kendall. He was surprised to see the angel standing there. The same angel who had spoken to him and stood against the Destroyer's demons the night before.

"Kendall is Rian's son?" he asked.

"He is. Moriana learned it just last night. It was hidden from her for these seven years to protect her life and the boy's. He has been hunted by the Evil One since the day of his birth. By defeating the Destroyer, you have stayed the hand of Kendall's fate. Now we must wait to see what the future holds for him. He has been called to dark paths."

The little girl squealed with joy as Kendall jumped from his hiding place.

"The child pleases you, does she not?" the angel asked.

He nodded, speechless, as he watched them play. At length he asked, "Who is she?"

"What you see is a foreshadowing, a glimpse, of what may be. This child is important. But her existence and future will be decided by your choices, Bradyn."

His gaze sought the angel's face as he frowned. "I have never made good choices, sir," he admitted. "In fact my whole life has been shaped by a majority of bad ones."

"Your past no longer controls the man who you have become, Bradyn. Your sins have been forgiven you. You no longer need to walk in the Shadow of what you have done, as you once did. Your future will be formed only by the choices you make from this day forward. Death cannot take you until your task is done, but the choices you make will affect the lives of others."

"What is my task?" he asked.

"You have a choice before you. The path of Light is not always as easy to follow as you would think. That which would appear right and just, may not always be so. And that which would appear evil, may in fact be good. You are called to know the difference." The angel turned to leave, his image growing transparent.

"Wait!" Bradyn called as the light of the sun dimmed and the field of flowers started to fade from view. "Wait! Tell me what happened to Rian! Where is she?"

The angel turned to look at him and his eyes were solemn. "Rian has fulfilled her purpose, Bradyn, but you have not yet fulfilled yours. Ask no more questions, my son. With the morning light you have yet another obstacle to face. The time has come for you to awake from your slumber." And then, the angel was gone.

He caught one final glimpse of the little girl as consciousness beckoned him. Her arms were laden with flowers and, just before she darkened from view, she caught his eye and smiled…

Bradyn woke up. He was lying on the street, staring up into the cool grey light of dawn. Slowly he rose and winced. Running his fingers over his side, he felt the deep cuts had already begun to heal. He looked down at them in wonder. They were healing even as he stared at them. Soon, they were only scars, warm and tingling to his touch.

He stood and dusted the dirt off his pants. The barrel of a revolver glistened at his feet. Rian's revolver. He bent and picked it up. It felt cold and real in his hand.

The street was normal. There was no trace of the destruction that was wrought the night before. Horses were tied to the hitching posts, and even at this early hour birds were chirping. The townspeople were still silent. Bradyn guessed that whatever enchantment had been over the city, it hadn't fully worn off yet. The angel had said there was one more task that Bradyn must face. No doubt, the sleeping citizens were not meant to be witness to that either.

The creaking of a door drew his attention. In the chilly light of daybreak, Liam stepped onto the porch of the Cattlemen Hotel. They locked stares across the street and Liam's eyes went wide with surprised terror.

Bradyn had little time to react as Liam bolted toward his horse. In three steps, Bradyn was next to him, pulling him from the saddle and throwing him back onto the steps of the hotel. His hand wrapped around Liam's neck, he pressed the muzzle of the revolver under the frightened man's chin. Anger clouded his vision as he clicked the hammer into place.

Liam's eyes were pleading. "Please, Preston! Don't shoot me!" he begged. His fingers pulled at Bradyn's shirt, his words frantically bargaining. "I'll do anything you want me to…just let me live! I can't let him get me! I can't die yet!"

Bradyn tightened his finger on the trigger. "You killed my brother…you killed his wife and kid, and you've killed countless others," he whispered. "Most important, you stood with the Devil last night. You don't deserve mercy, Briggs."

Memory flashed across his mind in a throbbing strobe. Rian's face haunted him. Bradyn remembered the fear in her eyes, even though she had looked like Liam, when she had pleaded with him to spare her life. Fury that Liam had helped to trick him into murdering Rian flared inside him. It would be so easy to kill him now. To take revenge for the hurt and the pain Liam had inflicted on him, but Bradyn couldn't rid himself of the look that had been on Rian's face.

"You have a choice before you." He heard the angel's words again. *"Your future will be formed only by the choices you make from this day forward."*

Seconds passed as he looked into Liam's ashen face. He wanted to shoot him, to blow his brains all over the steps of the hotel. He wanted to put to death the memories of his past. But in a sudden moment of clarity, Bradyn realized that he wanted to kill Liam Briggs for all the wrong reasons. He wanted to kill Liam to kill his own pain, to wash away his own sins. The desire to rid himself of his own past had driven him for seven long years. Now Bradyn realized that he had always acted out of instinct and anger. The choices he had made were his and no one else's. Liam Briggs was evil, but he had not made Bradyn into the man he that he was today.

"Your past no longer controls the man who you have become, Bradyn. Your sins have been forgiven you. You no longer need to walk in the Shadow of what you have done."

Stricken, Bradyn dropped the gun. It fell to the steps with a clatter.

Liam struggled to sit up. Bradyn tightened his grip around his neck and shoved him back down.

"You may think that you are getting away, Liam, but you're not," he promised. "You have lived the life of a coward and you will die one, reliving every life that you have taken and every drop of innocent blood that you have shed. The demons of your past will haunt you right up until you draw your dying breath," he vowed.

Bradyn let go of him and stood, surprised at the relief he felt in his soul. He had made a right choice after all. "Now get out of here and never come back. I will let you live today, but if I ever see your sorry hide again, I *will* kill you. I swear it."

Shaking, Liam gained his feet. His eyes kept darting to the gun lying on the stairs as he edged toward his horse. Bradyn watched him ride into the darkness of the west just as the sun was breaching the horizon in the east.

"Well done, my son." He felt the angel's hand on his shoulder. "Your choice has saved your life and the life of the woman you love."

Awestruck, Bradyn turned to the angel. "Rian?" he asked, his voice cracking with emotion. "She is alive?"

The angel smiled and moved to the side. "Look and see for yourself, Bradyn."

Over the angel's shoulder, against a pink and red sky splintered by the sun erupting in white light, Bradyn saw two silhouettes standing at the edge of town. Warm tears spilled from his eyes and trickled down his cheeks as he raced to her.

"Rian!" he shouted.

Her laughter echoed through the stillness of morning as she ran to meet him. "Bradyn!" she cried as she collapsed in his embrace. "Bradyn," she whispered against his fierce hug. "I knew you were the one. I knew you could defeat him."

"And I knew you would come back to me," Bradyn answered.

As they kissed, a kaleidoscope of light and passion made the world tilt and spin around them. Neither could have put their happiness or relief into words, but each felt it in the other's kiss. They had both faced their pasts, they had both fought their demons, and they had won. Absorbed in Rian's embrace, Bradyn felt a tug at his pant's leg.

"Did ya beat the bad guy, Mr. Bradyn?" Kendall asked, his eyes alight with flushed excitement.

"I sure did, kid," Bradyn answered. His voice was husky. "But Rian is the real hero. Her love gave me strength. I couldn't have done it without her."

"I'm so happy you're alive," Kendall whispered.

Bradyn exchanged knowing glances with Rian as Kendall hugged his leg. He nodded at her. They would have to tell him that she was his mother. Stooping, he lifted the little boy into his arms.

"Kendall," she began, "there's something I need to tell you. Something very important."

"I already know," Kendall said, startling them both. "You're my mama. Is that what you wanted to tell me?"

Wide-eyed, Rian stammered. "Yes…it is actually. How did you know, honey?" She looked at Bradyn and he shook his head, just as confused as she was.

"He told me." Kendall pointed to the angel, who had been standing, forgotten until now, in the place Bradyn had left him.

Rian and Bradyn both looked at the angel as he came toward them.

"Well, Kendall, it appears that you will have your wish," the angel said. "Your mother lives and Bradyn does too." The angel put his hand on Kendall's shoulder. "Remember, what we spoke about. If ever you are afraid, if ever you are in darkness, remember what I told you. Light will always be waiting to save you. You need only to ask."

Kendall nodded solemnly. "I will remember, sir," he answered quietly. "I'll remember everything ya told me. I promise."

The angel smiled at him. "I know you will, Kendall." He patted his shoulder again. "I know you will."

Bradyn and Rian exchanged a questioning glance, but neither spoke.

"Bradyn, Moriana," the angel addressed them. "Victory is yours this day. The sacrifices and the blood you spent will not be forgotten. Remember my words. The choices you make from this moment forward will shape your lives and the lives of those to come. Choose your steps rightly and, though you may stumble, you will never fall from the path of Light. Go now in peace. The Light of Grace be with you, my brother and my sister."

They watched as the angel was wrapped in brilliant white. Blinded by his light and the backdrop of the rising sun, Bradyn shielded his eyes and tried to catch one last glimpse of him as he disappeared from sight. Rian put her hand on his arm and he smiled down at her.

"I thought I'd never see you again," he said. Tears stung

his eyes, but this time he did not shed them.

Rian returned his smile. "I was afraid of that myself," she admitted. "But I knew you would make the right choice in the end. About Liam Briggs, I mean."

Bradyn frowned. "How could you have known?" he asked. "I didn't even know that I was gonna have to face him."

She smiled. "The angel told me. It was a test. He knew that you would not kill him, but he said that you needed to prove it to yourself. You are not one of Shadow any longer, Bradyn Preston. It seems everyone here knew it but you." She searched his face for a moment. "I love you," she whispered, her voice breaking as tears of joy glided down her cheeks. "I love you so much, Bradyn."

He pulled her against him and kissed her mouth. "I love you too, Moriana Keene." Her amber eyes were warm with affection and he frowned again.

"What is it?" she asked. Her voice was full of concern.

"I was just thinking. We need to do something about that last name. I like the sound of 'Preston' a lot better." He winked at her.

A huge smile of relief and joy spread across her face, making her eyes dance playfully. "Why, that sounds like a proposal, Bradyn Preston." She sobered. "Are you sure that's what you want."

Bradyn nodded. "I haven't been more sure of anything in my life," he replied.

"Bradyn?" Kendall asked.

"What is it, Kendall?" he asked, breaking his gaze with Rian long enough to smile down at the boy.

"If you marry Rian, that'll make you my dad, right?" The little boy studied him thoughtfully.

"Sure does, kid," he answered. "That is, if you'll have me for your dad," he added.

"'Course I will!" Kendall exclaimed. "Gosh, a mama and a dad all in one day! Guess I'm pretty lucky, right, Auntie Rian? I mean, Mama," he quickly qualified.

Rian laughed. "I guess we are all very lucky, Kendall," she said, smiling at Bradyn and the little boy. "But I wouldn't say luck has much to do with it. We're all three pretty darn blessed."

"Come on," Bradyn said as he hoisted Kendall to his shoulders. "Let's head back to the ranch."

"The horses are tied just past the church," she said as she fell into step beside him.

"Hey, Bradyn?" Kendall asked as they walked toward the church.

"Yeah, kid?" Bradyn answered.

"If you are gonna be my dad, does that mean you'll help me out with the chores?"

"You bet your life I will." Bradyn chuckled as he pulled Kendall from his shoulders and set him on the horse with Rian. "You and your mama have been doing way too much man's work for the past year. We're gonna see about changing that first thing after we get back."

"Golly, this is the best day of my life!" Kendall shouted. "I bet there ain't a boy in the whole world as happy as me!"

Bradyn locked eyes with Rian as he climbed onto his bay. Their happy laughter mixed and carried on the morning breeze as they set off in the rising sun toward home.

Chapter Twenty-three

Autumn had come quietly. The heat of August and September had stepped aside to usher in October's last gentle warmth and the whispers of frost to come. Rian sat in the porch swing that Bradyn had built for her, watching the setting sun's light flicker through the branches of the willow tree. Kendall played with his wooden horse at her feet. The silver badge pinned on his shirt caught the glare of the sun and glinted up at her. It was no longer an accusing reminder of her past, only another token of relief. Her heart was filled with contented joy as she ran her hand over her stomach. The baby was not yet perceptible, just a tiny swell below her navel, but already she could feel its stirrings inside her.

She told Bradyn that she was expecting on the long ride home that fateful morning. He had simply smiled and nodded his head. His reaction had led her to think that she hadn't been the only one the angel had told of the child's coming. The pride in Bradyn's eyes had been unmistakable as he'd sidled his horse along hers and kissed her tenderly. "As soon as we've washed the stench of death off of us and had some rest, we're going back into town to fetch the preacher," he said.

She and Bradyn had been married for almost four months now. Their wedding was a quiet, hallowed affair, performed by the town preacher on the plateau where she had sat looking down on Laramie that night so far in her past it felt like a distant dream. She sighed, causing Kendall to look up from his playing.

"Do you feel well, mama?" he asked. His little face was solemn with worry. "Do you need a drink of water?"

Rian smiled at him. "No, honey. I'm just happy," she whispered. "I don't think I've ever been so happy in my life. I have you and Bradyn."

"And the baby?" Kendall asked. His eyes were bright.

Rian laughed softly. "And the baby," she murmured.

"Did I hear someone mention my name?" Bradyn asked as he came out onto the porch with a mug of coffee in one hand and his other behind his back. He handed her the cup and kissed the top of her head.

"We were just talking about how happy we are," Kendall announced. "Weren't we, mama?"

"That's right," she said. "Life is full of wonderful things to be thankful for."

"And full of surprises," Bradyn added, pulling a bulky package wrapped in brown paper from behind his back. "I thought maybe you'd appreciate this," he said as he handed it to her. His blue eyes danced with anticipation and boyish excitement. "Go on…open it," he urged when she looked up at him inquisitively.

Rian pulled the string from the brown paper. "What is it?' she asked him.

"See for yourself," he answered, a smile three miles wide on his face.

She tore back the paper and gasped. It was her quilt. A bright baby blue square of new cloth was hand-sewn with crooked, but painstaking and tiny stitches over the place the old blood-stained patch had been.

"You fixed it," she whispered as tears stung her eyes. It was both endearing and sad to her. She had grown accustomed to the blood stain and the singed holes. They were reminders of Bradyn's entrance into her life.

Rian turned the quilt over as a tear slid down her cheek. The yellow patch had been replaced too. The red-checkered square of material was familiar. It was a piece of the shirt that she had been going to alter to fit Bradyn. Jackson's old shirt. She laughed then. "It's beautiful, Bradyn. Thank you," she murmured and kissed the hand he rested on her shoulder. "Thank you."

"I hoped you would like it," Bradyn pushed his hands into his pockets, returning her adoring smile with a crooked grin of pleasure. "My stitches leave a lot to be desired and I was almost certain that I would have to replace the blue patch a second time after I poked about a hundred holes in my finger trying to sew that one on." He chuckled. "Almost made a mess of it, but then I got a little better at stitching."

"Darling," she teased, "that's what a thimble is for." They laughed together.

"Well, I nearly asked you for help a couple times, but then it would have ruined the surprise," Bradyn admitted. He took the quilt from her and unfolded it. "Might as well try 'er out," he said as he wrapped it around her shoulders and took a seat next to her on the swing.

Rian took a sip of the warm coffee as Bradyn put his arm around her shoulder and squeezed her. "I'm glad you're happy." His voice was husky and when Rian met his gaze, she saw the love and happiness in his beautiful eyes. She nodded wordlessly as he kissed her.

"Who's that comin'?" Kendall stood and pointed in the direction of the bluff overlooking the house. In the sun's setting light, a man came galloping down the hill and across the field.

For a split second, Rian felt frightened déjà vu, remembering the day she had first seen Bradyn crest that same hill. Bradyn stood and walked to the yard as the stranger pulled his horse to a halt and dismounted.

"Howdy, Bradyn." The visitor's voice carried to where she and Kendall stood on the porch, looking on curiously. He looked to be a man in his early forties. His weathered face cracked into a smile as he reached for Bradyn's hand.

"Hello, Pete." Bradyn clapped the man on the back and shook his outstretched hand. "I never would have expected to see you here. What brings you out this way?"

"Got some news for you, Bradyn."

"Well, come on up to the house and have a bite," Bradyn said. "I'm sure Rian has some chicken and whatnot leftover from dinner."

The two men came toward the porch and Rian gave Bradyn a questioning look.

"Rian, this here is Pete Andrews. I used to know Pete when he was Jace's deputy marshal." Bradyn introduced him and Pete tipped his hat to her. "Pete, this is my wife, Moriana."

"A pleasure to meet ya, ma'am." His grey eyes twinkled. "I always figured Bradyn would land himself a pretty woman when he got the notion to settle down. Looks like he did just that." He winked at her.

Rian blushed and Bradyn said, "That little cowpoke there is Kendall, Rian's son."

"Hello, son." Pete said and shook the hand that Kendall politely offered.

"Nice to meet ya, Mr. Pete." Kendall smiled. "Are you a lawman?"

"Sure am, son. I've just been made Marshal of the whole Wyoming Territory," Pete answered. His eyes glowed with pride as he patted the boy on the head.

"Gosh!" Kendall's eyes went wide with wonder. He stood studying the marshal with wordless admiration.

"Well, you've had quite a ride, Pete," Bradyn said. "Why don't you come on in and let us fix you up some grub and get you a drink. Kendall, why don't you see to Pete's horse?"

"Yes, sir," Kendall said. "I'll take good care of him for ya, Marshal!" he called over his shoulder as he headed for the animal.

"I don't want to be a bother," Pete hesitated, looking at Rian. "I just have some news to give you and then I'll be on my way."

Rian smiled kindly. "Don't even think twice about it, Mr. Andrews. It's no bother at all, and I've heard that news is always better served on a full stomach. Besides, you've come a long way. There's no sense in riding out again at this late hour. Did you come all the way from Cheyenne to find us?"

"No, ma'am. I came up from Laramie. I got wind that you were still around here, Bradyn. Had to do some asking around, but I finally came across someone who'd seen you. The preacher there gave me directions to your place, but it seems he is better at memorizing the Holy Scriptures. They were the worst directions I've ever had the displeasure to come across. I was about to give up finding your ranch for a lost cause and head back to town when I came up over that bluff," he explained as he followed them into the house.

Bradyn chuckled and pulled a chair from the table to offer their guest. "Well you found the right place, Pete. So tell me, what was important enough to call you away from your duties as marshal to visit us?"

"Couple of things, actually," Pete answered as he rummaged through his vest pocket. "The first is this letter I got from the sheriff down in Denver a few weeks back. You'll want to read that yourself. It seems that Liam Briggs was found dead about six weeks ago. Shot himself in some seedy whorehouse down there. He left a letter. In it, he admitted to killing your brother outside Laramie late this last spring."

Bradyn's eyes found hers. She bit her lip as Bradyn took the letter from Pete. He read the note with a frown on his face.

"Sorry for your loss, Bradyn," Pete said in a quiet voice. "Jared was a dear friend and a great man. We'll all be worse off for having lost him."

Bradyn cleared his throat and nodded. "When I came through Cheyenne in June and found out he hadn't been back to town in over a month, I figured the worst had happened, Pete," he said. "Can't say as I'm surprised at the news. I had a hunch Liam was responsible." He cast Rian a quick glance and she nodded with understanding. There was no sense in bringing up the fact that they'd already known.

"The other bit of news came to me unexpected," Pete continued, digging through his other pocket. "When I was in Laramie, the postmaster got wind that I was looking for you. Asked me to deliver this letter to Moriana, since I was coming out your way."

Rian's hands shook as she took the envelope from his hand. It was addressed: *"Mr. Edmund Lachlan, New Orleans."* Until that moment, she had almost forgotten about the letter that she had posted to her uncle the day after she and Bradyn were wed. Excitement welled in her as she hurriedly opened the letter. It had been a long time since she had received any correspondence from home.

The letter read:

"My dearest Moriana,

The receipt of your letter left our home in an uproar of joy and sorrow, I can assure you. Your Aunt Melinda has gone on about nothing else for these past two days. There is so much to tell you and so much we desire to know about how you fare, I hardly know where to start.

The news of Jackson's death was a terrible blow. He has been our only insight into your lives since you left New Orleans. When his letters ceased coming, I feared the worst. I am happy to learn that you were present with him in his final hours and that he had the love of family as he was taken in death. He was a good man, and I am certain you miss him dearly.

As you are probably aware, your mother passed not much more than a year after you and Jackson left. Jackson conducted written intercourse with her lawyer and, as you may or may not know, he arranged that the whole of your father's estate be left to you. Jackson not only made provisions to bequeath his birthright to you, but he also left to you the entire holdings of his own personal estate as well should he succumb to an untimely passing. He wanted to be certain that you and Kendall were looked after and comfortable should anything happen to him. I would have had Jackson's lawyer send the paperwork to you straight away when I received your letter, but I was not certain if that course of action was the best. Instead, I am enclosing the lawyer's address and you can direct a letter of inquiry to him when you wish.

Learning that Kendall is your son shocked us, as you can imagine. The news that he is well and already seven years old was astonishing and happy for your aunt and I. As was the news of your marriage and the upcoming arrival of your second child. We send all of our best wishes and hope that in time, as soon as the infant is old enough for travel, you would come to visit us. Your aunt, I might add, insists that you come and stay with us as soon as you are able. Melinda says that it will give you the chance to attend to your late mother's estate, as well as the affairs of your blessed brother, and give us the joy of seeing you once again. I heartily second her sentiments. Your aunt and I have missed you and your brother greatly these past years. She thinks that Kendall and our son, Gavin, would hit it off smashingly. Do you remember that your aunt and I were incapable of having children? At any rate, we adopted Gavin nearly five years ago. He is just now turned six, and he is a charming boy. We cannot imagine our lives without his presence.

Forgive me, dear Moriana. This old man does tend to scribble on. I shall close with sending my deepest condolences for the loss of your brother and my sincerest congratulatory well wishes for you and your new husband. Give Bradyn our best, and kiss Kendall for us. And, Moriana, please do not hesitate to write us. We are eager to know of your life and health, and if ever there should be anything you lack, you only need ask.

With all my love;

Your Uncle Edmund"

"Rian?" Bradyn's voice broke in on her silent reading. "Is something wrong?"

Ripped from memory, Rian shook her head, uncertain if the tears would stay at bay. "No. It's a letter from my uncle, Edmund." She smiled at Bradyn's worried frown. "I just haven't heard from him in a long time," she explained. *A very long time.* The look Bradyn gave her was warm with understanding. She folded the letter and tucked it into her skirt pocket, wiping the stray tear that had managed to escape. Her heart alive with joy, she began to put together a meal for their guest.

* * * *

They sat and visited long hours into the night. Rian laughed as Bradyn and Pete took turns relating stories about their adventures while working for Jared as deputy marshals. She had let her son stay up to visit, since Pete was the first welcome guest they had received to their home in seven long years. She watched as Kendall's eyes danced with excitement. For nearly three hours, he fought sleep, hanging on every word that came out of Bradyn or Pete's mouth.

As the night wore on, his tired body won out. He curled contentedly against her shoulder as he let himself be captured by sleep's beckoning embrace. His small snoring interrupted the conversation.

"Looks like we put half of our audience to sleep, Bradyn," Pete chuckled quietly.

"I'll go put him to bed," Rian whispered.

Bradyn pulled out her chair and helped her to her feet. He assessed her for a moment. "Why don't you let me carry him up the stairs?' he asked. "You look pretty tired yourself."

Rian shook her head. "I want to do it," she answered. "He's getting so big, I won't be able to carry him much longer." She gave Bradyn a pleading expression and he smiled with resignation. "Why don't you show our guest to the guestroom while I get Kendall tucked in. There are extra blankets in the chest at the foot of our bed. It may be chilly tonight."

Pete rose and nodded at her. "I'm much obliged, Rian. Thank you for dinner."

"You're welcome, Mr. Andrews," she replied. "Your visit was a wonderful surprise. You are welcome in our home anytime."

Bradyn walked with her to the foot of the stairs. Before she started up, he kissed her cheek and gave her a searching look. "I'll take care of Pete. Once you get Kendall settled, go to bed," he whispered. "You look worn out, Rian."

She nodded and carried Kendall to his room. Wearily, she dressed the sleeping boy for bed and kissed him goodnight as she tucked the blankets around him. As tired as she was, the same feeling of loving awe came over her as she watched him sleep. He was her son.

* * * *

They lay in bed that night after Rian had seen Kendall tucked in and Bradyn had shown Pete to the guestroom, now her old bedroom on the second floor. Bradyn thoughtfully rubbed her fingers, wrapped tightly around his, as he stared up at the dark ceiling. Rian sighed and snuggled closer to him.

"Is that a happy sigh…or a worried one?" he asked her softly as he kissed her brow.

"Maybe a little of both…but mostly happy," she answered. Her voice sounded sleepy.

Bradyn smiled in the darkness and wondered again how miserable his life would be right now if he hadn't been blessed to find her, blessed to know her love. "Do you want to go to New Orleans when the baby is big enough?" he asked.

Rian turned against him. He felt her stare in the dark. "I don't know if I want to go back there just," she whispered finally. "I'm not sure I want to face the memories."

He was quiet for awhile. He understood her uncertainty all too well. He wasn't exactly fond of the idea of going back to his home stomping grounds either. The memories of a Bradyn he no longer knew lived there. He rested his cheek against her head and whispered, "We don't need to think of that now, Rian. There will be plenty of time to worry over it later. I'm sure the inheritance and your family can wait a few months for us to make up our minds."

"You're right," she murmured against his neck. "We can think about it later. Right now, I am still getting used to just being here with you."

"You make it sound like you're not sure if you made the right choice," he teased, rubbing his hand along the soft skin of her shoulder.

"Don't misconstrue my words, husband," she giggled. "I said no such thing. You are the most wonderful part of my life. I still can't believe you're real sometimes." She rubbed her nose against his neck. "I love you so much, Bradyn Preston," she whispered.

Bradyn pulled her face up to his and in the darkness his lips found hers. She sighed as he ran his fingers over her thigh. "I love you more than life itself, Moriana," he murmured as he rolled her to her back, kissing her again. His love for her sparked to life a burning passion. The need for her consumed him. And, though tired as he was, Bradyn decided sleep could wait…

* * * *

He was in the field again. The sunshine in a cloudless, azure sky warmed him as the deep grass, littered with beautiful flowers, whispered around his legs. Beside him, the little girl was holding his hand as they walked. Her bright blue eyes twinkled with delight as he picked a soft white blossom and gave it to her. The smile on her face filled him with joy. Oh, how he loved her!

Suddenly, she pulled her hand from his and giggled. "Come and find me," she called as she darted through the thick grass.

"No!" he shouted, unfounded fear filling him. "Come back! Come back!" He watched as her head disappeared below the rolling waves of green. The urge to run and find her spurred his legs into motion, but his feet grew too heavy to lift. He could not reach her.

The sky grew dark. Black clouds, rimmed by dark red, blotted the sun from view. Terror gripped him as he searched the field for her. *Where has she gone?*

"Come find me…" He heard her whisper. "Come and find me…"

"Where are you?!" he screamed, his voice a taunting rasp. "Come back! Come back! Don't you know he is coming? It's not safe for you to leave me!"

Thunder pierced the air. A dark figure stood at the edge of the darkened field. His eyes were red. "I see the evil in your heart," he called to him. "You and I are the same. Do not try to deny me what is mine!" The dark man smiled. His mouth was full of sharp fangs.

"Where is she?" he shouted at the dark man. Anger made his voice shake. "Give her to me!" Then he saw her.

The dark man held her in his arms. Her face was full of fear. "You're too late," he laughed. "I found her first. She is mine."

He watched as the figure bared its long white teeth and sank them into the little girl's neck. The little girl's scream was drowned out by the sound of his own…

Kendall sat up in bed, his heart pounding, his body drenched with sweat. It was the nightmare again. The one he had almost every night now. He wanted to call out for Bradyn, or his mama, but he didn't. Being scared was for babies, and he wasn't a baby anymore.

"It was only a dream," he whispered to himself as he lay down and pulled the covers up around his chin. "Dream's aren't real…they aren't real. Mama says so." But the words did little to soothe him. As he stared out his bedroom window at the moon, hanging nearly full in the cool autumn sky, he couldn't help but wonder if his dreams were very real indeed.

With time, his heartbeat stilled and his breathing returned to normal. Sleep once again wove its warm spell over him. As he drifted off, the voice of the angel from that night so many days behind him, echoed through his tired mind.

"Rest now, Kendall. For the days of childhood are fleeting, soon they will be past. Then, in a moment, you will be taken by your future. You have been marked to walk a dark path. But remember, my son, there is always light in the darkness. All you need to do is ask."

The words comforted him, and when Kendall slept, he knew only deep, dreamless peace.

Epilogue

From the diary of Moriana Keene
June 28, 1879

How long it has been since I last opened your pages, old friend! Exactly one year. As I read my last entry, my heart is filled with joy and sad remembrance. The shell of a woman that I was is now a stranger to me. Those horrible memories no longer have sway over my soul. I have faced the shadow of my past, and in the end, victory was given to me. The knowledge of my crime is no longer a fear that holds me prisoner. I have been set free by the truth.

The blessings in my life are too numerous to count. The day after my last entry in this dairy, a man came to us. He was hurt and standing in Death's very grasp. Just the memory of how close I came to never knowing his love takes the breath from me. The day Bradyn called me his wife is the greatest joy I have ever known, seconded only by the knowledge that Kendall is my own son and the birth of our baby girl. Rowyn Victoria Preston.

She is beautiful, a miracle in her own right. She is the image of her father. When I first saw her, I thought surely my heart would break, for there seemed not enough room in it to hold all my love and happiness. Bradyn loves her dearly. I see it in his eyes when he holds her in his arms. He is so very proud.

Kendall adores his baby sister. He has a fierce protectiveness for her that astounds me. Already, they share a connection. Her very first smile was for him.

My memories of the night that the angel told me of her coming grow weak; as a dream that is slowly forgotten over time. Bradyn does not speak of it, but I know he was told, as I was, that our children are called to great tasks. My only prayer is that Bradyn and I are given the grace to prepare them for what lies ahead. I know not what the future holds for my dear Kendall, or our precious Rowyn…

About the Author

Born and raised in Southwestern Montana, Monika Weigand (writing as Caitlynn J. Gabriel) has always held a love in her heart for great books. Inspired by the Old West, Stephen King, and the Clint Eastwood Western, she decided to write her own take on the paranormal romance and horror genres, thus "To Stand with Angels" (along with the sequel "At the Devil's Right Hand", a work still in progress) was born.

When not writing, Monika spends her time enjoying her two beautiful children, her wonderful husband, and taking advantage of the beautiful Montana outdoors.

Available now from Eternal Press

Soul Market

by Sonnet O'Dell

Every parent hopes their little girl is going to be special, but Cassandra's mother always hoped her little girl wouldn't be.

When her mother died, she revealed the terrible truth, that when sunset came, she would be drawn into another world. A nightmare world, where monsters really did lurk in the dark shadows.

Three years later, Cassandra is still learning to control her magic, while doing the odd magical job for cash. She never dreamed something as big as finding several missing people would fall into her lap.

Despite the police telling her to leave the case be, she can't, because the law is fuzzy about the rights of the Preternatural groups involved. The police department may not care, but Cassandra does.

Something is out there in the dark and she is determined to do something about it.

I'd walked for a while when my feet began to sound louder than normal, like they were giant feet. I stopped but the loud sound didn't. It wasn't the sound of my feet that had been drowned out, by something or someone coming along the tunnel behind me. I looked behind me now my eyes had grown a little used to the dark, but I still couldn't see anyone. I kept walking, faster until I was power walking.

Then I was jogging until finally I broke into a run, trying to lose whatever was behind me. My pulse beat fast in my neck. I couldn't see any turnings or openings so I kept going straight ahead, until I ran out of places to run. I came to a wall and knew it was a dead end.

Available now from Eternal Press

Day 94

by D.M. Slate

The aftermath of a meteor impact visits havoc and horror on a young family.

In the wake of a large meteor collision, a ghastly epidemic is unleashed upon rural Colorado. Joslin, Grant and their two young children barricade themselves in their home in the quarantined city. Their fight for survival begins; battling airborne disease, lack of electricity and running water, starvation, brutal Colorado winter and worst of all, the morphs. The violent morphs, both victims and carriers of the disease, soon become more numerous and aggressive. Joslin and Grant risk all to protect their children.

Shards of broken glass littered the floor of our bedroom. The wooden door was sturdy, but it had a large glass window in the top-half of the door. He'd shattered the window, and the dresser in front of the door shook with every swing of the ax. I pulled the home-made gas mask over my mouth and nose, and cautiously approached the door. The ax became embedded in the wood; he had a difficult time pulling it free. I was done trying to rationalize with this monster.

I crept along the bedroom wall with my back pressed flat, hiding my presence. He was still struggling to get the ax free. I never thought that he'd come back with an actual weapon. In every scenario I'd imagined, we were on equal fighting grounds. This changed my entire plan. As he wrenched the ax back and forth, I jumped up in front of the dresser and introduced my can of mace. Fluid shot out of the can thru the broken window, landing squarely on his face. I heard the liquid sizzle as it came in contact with his skin.

He stopped, stunned, before unleashing a grueling scream. Tears threatened to escape my eyes, but I refused to feel guilty. He forgot about the ax and backed away from the door, tearing at his eyes with both hands. With a surge of determination I stood tall, and shouted as loudly as I could, "Go Away. I swear to God, I'll kill you if you try coming back in."

Wrong thing to say. His head jerked up and he looked the door, as if welcoming the challenge. That instant I knew one of us would die before this ended. He came at the door with new-found strength, and tore the ax away in one savage movement. I backed away, but didn't retreat out of the bedroom. The weight of the wall against my back was the only thing keeping me standing. My knees shook and knocked together, but I refused back down. At this point, it's him or me - and if it's me, he'll get the kids, too.

Breinigsville, PA USA
31 May 2010
238911BV00001B/1/P

9 781615 720941